❧Winner of the MAGGIE AWARD of Excellence❧
❧Winner of the GOLDEN LEAF❧
❧Winner of the PASSIONATE PLUME❧
❧BOOKSELLERS' BEST AWARD Finalist❧
❧NATIONAL READER'S CHOICE AWARD Finalist❧
❧CAROLYN READER'S CHOICE AWARD Finalist❧

"You get all the feels in all the right places when reading a Grace Callaway book....The love affair between Wick and Bea is beautiful (and scorching). I loved this story and all of its intricacies of how beauty is perceived." - Angela, *Goodreads*

"Wick and Bea bring out the best in each other and I love how their relationship progressed in an organic way. Their love story is both incredibly steamy and heartfelt (the best of both worlds!)...I really enjoyed the mystery arc, which actually took a surprising turn that I didn't see coming. Unlike most historical romances that I read this year, Callaway crafts an interesting and engaging mystery that actually holds my interest." -*Romance Library*

"The writing (as always) was absolutely wonderful and held me captivated from beginning to end. The emotion flowed off the pages and it felt like I was right there with the characters. Absolutely mesmerizing. Beatrice and Wick were perfect for each other and had sizzling hot chemistry and I couldn't get enough of it!" -Candace, *Goodreads*

"I absolutely adored Wickham and Beatrice's story!! The connection they had was there from the start even though they were adversaries. I loved watching them work through all their obstacles and how they helped each other overcome their past." -*Historical Romance Lover* Blog

"Brilliant addictive reading." -Maggie, *Goodreads*

"THE DUKE REDEMPTION is well written, engaging, romantic, and very, very steamy. I totally enjoyed seeing the passion turn to love. Bea and Wick each brought something the other needed – he felt his worth and honor again, and she felt beautiful and desirable. They treated each other as equals, and I believe their future will continue to be filled with joy and passion." -*Roses Are Blue*

"This newest story by Grace Callaway is near the top of my list of wonderful reads...I loved how Beatrice, despite suffering several tragic events in a short period of time, still retains her backbone to persevere in life and (deep down) stay open to finding true love and happiness. Wickham is an appealing blend of caring and sensitivity while being protective and commanding with those around him. There are plenty of heated and very sensual moments between this couple, balanced with tender, loving and spirited interactions. I greatly enjoyed discovering the HEA of two deeply decent and good people who deserve each other!" -Allison, *Goodreads*

## ADDITIONAL PRAISE FOR GRACE'S BOOKS

"Readers looking for a good historical mystery/romance or a historical with a little more kink will enjoy *The Duke Who Knew Too Much*." -*Smart Bitches, Trashy Books*

"You know when a book is so good that you are still reading it at 2 am....This book had it all: drama, laughter and a few tears as well. The chemistry between Harry and Tessa just sizzled off the pages....If I could I would give this book ten stars, but I'm only allowed to give 5/5 stars." -*Boonies123 Book Review* on *The Duke Identity*

"Grace Callaway is a remarkable writer." -*Love Romance Passion*

"I'm still ugly crying AF!! I am so in love with Adam and Gabby. This was the perfect blend of romance, steamy sex, and intrigue...My heart hurt for all the things Adam went through...and I cheered for Gabby as she emerged from her safe shell." -*Estela Reads Romance* on *Regarding the Duke*

ALSO BY GRACE CALLAWAY

## GAME OF DUKES

The Duke Identity

Enter the Duke

Regarding the Duke

The Duke Redemption

The Return of the Duke

## HEART OF ENQUIRY

The Widow Vanishes (Prequel Novella)

The Duke Who Knew Too Much

M is for Marquess

The Lady Who Came in from the Cold

The Viscount Always Knocks Twice

Never Say Never to an Earl

The Gentleman Who Loved Me

## MAYHEM IN MAYFAIR

Her Husband's Harlot

Her Wanton Wager

Her Protector's Pleasure

Her Prodigal Passion

## LADY CHARLOTTE'S SOCIETY OF ANGELS

Olivia and the Masked Duke

Pippa and the Prince of Secrets

**Cover Design**: © Erin Dameron-Hill/ EDH Graphics

**Cover Image**: © Period Images

# The Duke Redemption

## Game of Dukes

Book 4

# Grace Callaway

*The beauty that addresses itself to the eyes is only the spell of the moment; the eye of the body is not always that of the soul.* -George Sand

Here's to the beauty of the soul.

# PROLOGUE

## HYDE PARK, LONDON, 1833

"HOW ARE MATTERS PROGRESSING, MY DEAR BEATRICE?" THE
Duchess of Hadleigh leaned over the side of the open carriage,
the plume of her bonnet bobbing over her honey-gold curls. "Has
Croydon spoken of his intentions?"

Perched on a bay mare next to the carriage, seventeen-year-old
Lady Beatrice Wodehouse saw the excitement that lit her mama's
violet eyes. Considered an Incomparable in her youth, Mama
remained a stunning beauty, and Bea thought of herself as a pale
imitation: her own locks were a lighter shade of gold and her eyes
clear lavender. Papa liked to say that Mama and Bea looked like
sisters, which always made the former blush and the latter hide a
grin.

It was common knowledge that the Duke of Hadleigh doted
upon his beautiful wife. Although Bea's younger brother Benedict
was wont to roll his eyes whenever Their Graces expressed affection, Bea was inspired by her parents' happiness. It fueled her
dreams of finding everlasting love...dreams that might be coming
true this very day.

Bea peeked over at Peter Mansfield, the Duke of Croydon. He sat astride a white stallion a few yards away. The Season's premier catch, he had been detained by admirers the moment they arrived at Rotten Row. Her pulse quickened when he turned his dark head in her direction, his mouth curving in a heart-stopping smile.

Warmth rushed into Bea's cheeks...and other unmentionable parts of her person. Last week, Croydon had stolen a kiss in the garden, awakening a strange need inside her. She couldn't stop thinking about the warm brush of his lips against her own. At night, she tossed restlessly in bed, dreaming of the mysteries of the marital bower...

"Well, Beatrice? Has His Grace confessed the reason for today's ride?"

"*Confess*, Mama?" Pushing aside her wanton curiosity, Bea managed a teasing tone. "You make him sound like a criminal."

"Your future is no joking matter," Mama chided. "Do remember to curb that wit of yours: no man wants a bold, overly clever wife. And fix your skirts, dear. You must display your assets to their fullest advantage."

Used to her mama's lectures, Bea bit her tongue; she knew better than to argue. She smoothed her plum velvet riding habit and adjusted the small hat perched atop her pale ringlets.

"All the marriageable misses have set their caps for Croydon, and who can blame them?" her mama went on. "A handsome duke worth twenty thousand a year is rarer than a unicorn, I daresay, and he's singled *you* out for his attentions."

A fact that never ceased to amaze Bea. Although she was a duke's daughter, she'd grown up in the country. Mama was not fond of Town life, and Papa had taken trips to London alone. For Bea's debut, however, the duke had brought the entire family to the nation's capital, leasing a grand townhouse for the Season. Bea had to admit that she still felt like a fish out of water in the sophisticated, glittering world of the *ton*.

"When His Grace asked permission to ride with you today, he mentioned he had a *specific* matter he wished to discuss." Mama looked at her expectantly. "Are you prepared to give him a reply?"

*Would 'Yes, yes, yes!' qualify?*

She opted for a demure response. "Yes, Mama. With your and Papa's permission, of course."

"You have it. Oh, how happy you'll be! As a duchess, the world will be your oyster, and I know Croydon will cherish you as you deserve." Mama's face was wreathed in smiles. "Now when His Grace returns, be sure to suggest a ride away from this brouhaha. The section by the Serpentine will be perfect for a *tête-à-tête*. I'll follow at a discreet distance to give the two of you privacy..."

A tinkling, bell-like voice cut Mama off. "Lady Beatrice, fancy meeting you here!"

Bea glimpsed Miss Arabella Millbank weaving through the crowded path, shaded by a lacy parasol. The pretty, raven-haired heiress had debuted with Bea, and the two had become fast friends. Since Arabella had grown up in London, she was well versed in the ways of Town. She'd saved Bea a seat at every function, advised her on the latest fashions, and shared the juiciest tidbits of gossip. Bea was grateful for the other's kindness.

"Good afternoon, Your Grace." The flounces on Arabella's skirts fluttered as she curtsied.

Mama arched her brows. "Have you lost your chaperone, Miss Millbank?"

Bea cringed at the frosty tone of the question. Mama did not conceal her dislike of Bea's friend. Arabella had addressed the topic in her matter-of-fact way: *It's to be expected, dear Bea. Her Grace doesn't favor me because my family's fortune comes from import-export.*

Bea didn't like to think that her own mother would hold such pretensions. Gathering up her courage, she'd asked Mama about it point-blank.

*Any prejudice I have against Miss Millbank is due to her character,* Mama had retorted. *Your trusting nature will be your downfall, Beat-*

*rice...but I suppose I am to blame. I kept you sheltered too long in the coun-*
*try. Heed my words: things are different in London.*

Bea saw no reason to distrust Arabella, who had been nothing but kind.

"My chaperone is back there somewhere," Arabella now said brightly. "When I saw Lady Beatrice standing here, I simply had to rush over to say hello."

"What perfect timing you have," Mama replied.

As Bea was puzzling over her mother's dry tone, the Duke of Croydon rejoined them.

"Good afternoon, Your Grace." Arabella's green eyes sparkled as she twirled her parasol. "What a magnificent mount you have."

"Thank you, Miss Millbank." Croydon patted the Arabian's neck before turning to Bea. "I apologize for the delay, my lady. I had not seen the Yardleys for some time, and there was much to catch up on."

"I hope you had a nice visit," Bea said sincerely.

"Quite. Although I missed the present charming company," Croydon murmured. "Are you ready to continue our ride?"

"Indeed we are," Mama cut in. "Why don't you escort my daughter along the quieter path by the Serpentine, Your Grace? I'll follow behind after I return Miss Millbank to her chaperone."

Bea rode to the leafy, shadowed path with Croydon. Here, the walk was sparsely populated, the chatter of crowds replaced by birdsong and buzzing insects. As promised, Mama was following discreetly behind—so discreetly, in fact, that Bea did not even see her.

Bea slid a sidelong glance at her companion, wondering if he would take the opportunity to steal another kiss. *Not that he'd have to steal what I would willingly give.* The brazen thought warmed her cheeks even more than the sunshine.

The duke's stallion, Attila, seemed to take a liking to Bea's mare, Midnight Star; when Attila came too close, Star lurched away with a nervous whinny, jostling Bea in the sidesaddle.

"She's a bit skittish," Bea apologized, tightening her grip on the reins.

"I don't blame her for being shy. Attila, stop being a brute," Croydon ordered.

Seeing the stallion's chastised expression, Bea couldn't help but giggle.

"May I compliment you on your laugh, Lady Beatrice? It is so unaffected and carefree. Qualities that, I daresay, are as rare and admirable as your beauty."

Bea's heart raced at the duke's intent expression, the vivid blue of his eyes.

"Thank you, Your Grace," she said breathlessly.

"As it is just the two of us, could I tempt you to call me by my given name?"

"That...that would be forward, wouldn't it?"

"Such informality would be improper," he said gravely. "Unless we had a more intimate connection, that is. I have a question to ask you, my dear. I will, of course, speak to your father, but I wanted to know where your wishes lay first."

She felt faint with expectation. "Yes, Your Grace?"

"Lady Beatrice...would you like to be my wife?"

"Yes," she breathed. "I would like that very much—"

"That'll teach you to steal from your betters, you filthy guttersnipe!"

The shouting shattered the magical moment. Startled, Bea swung her gaze in the direction of the voices. Two figures were just up ahead on the path. A man on horseback was dragging a boy up by the scruff, lifting the child's kicking feet clear off the ground. As Bea watched in horror, he raised his other hand, which held a gleaming black horsewhip.

"What the devil?" Croydon muttered.

Instinct propelled Bea into action.

She galloped forward. "Desist, sir! You're hurting the boy!"

As she pulled to a stop, the man's gaze roved with slow insolence over her. He had thick jowls and square, pugnacious features. His clothing was costly and ostentatious, gold buttons and fobs scattered over his expansive torso.

"Who are you to interfere in my business?" he demanded.

"I am Lady Beatrice Wodehouse, daughter of the Duke of Hadleigh." Bea saw with anxiety that the child still suspended from the man's beefy fist had a swollen eye and bleeding lip. "Let the boy go, sir. Can't you see that you're hurting him?"

"Bloody pickpocket deserves a thrashing." Scowling, the man shook the boy again, the force sending the child's tattered cap to the ground. "He filched my coin purse and thought he could get away with it!"

Croydon drew up beside Bea. "I am the Duke of Croydon, the lady's escort. And you are?"

"T. Edgar Grigg, industrialist." The man smirked. "You may have heard of me."

Bea did indeed recognize the name. Grigg was a coal merchant whose showy advertisements were seen everywhere in Town. The papers credited him with advancements in the delivery of the resource to London, which had an insatiable need for coal-driven power. His warehouses lined the banks of Regent's Canal, and some mockingly referred to the miasma of smoke that hung over the city as "Grigg's Gold."

"'Elp me, milady!" The boy's pleading gaze latched onto Bea. He couldn't be more than eight years old, with a mop of brown hair and missing front teeth. "I ain't done nufing, I swear!"

"You must put the boy down, Mr. Grigg," Bea said as calmly as she could over her thundering heart. "I'm sure this is all a misunderstanding."

"There's no misunderstanding," Grigg snarled. "This thief picked the wrong pigeon to pluck."

"I swear on me ma's grave that I didn't steal nufing. Me pockets are empty, see?" The boy turned out the pockets of his threadbare trousers and jacket. "A wrong against me you'll regret, but a favor to me I'll ne'er forget. 'Elp me milady, please. Don't let the cove 'urt me!"

*The poor child...he's babbling in pain. I have to do something!*

"The child doesn't have your purse," Bea said. "I must insist that you let him go."

"Are you calling me a liar?" Grigg raised his whip in a menacing manner.

Star let out a whinny, backing away. Bea steadied her mount.

"Kindly refrain from speaking to a lady in that tone," Croydon said sharply.

"Gladly, Your Grace," Grigg said with a sneer. "If her *ladyship* will refrain from intruding in my business."

After an exchange of stares with Grigg, Croydon turned to her.

"Let us continue on," he said in a low tone. "It is not our affair, after all."

Bea stared at him in shock. "We cannot abandon this child."

"While your kindness is admirable, the boy is a street urchin," Croydon said curtly. "You haven't been in Town long enough to know what that sort is capable of—"

"Bloody hell!" Grigg roared in pain. "The filthy cur *bit* my hand!"

Bea's breath held as the boy, freed from the industrialist's grip, made a run for it. He darted away, quick as a minnow. Grigg recovered with equal speed.

Shaking his whip, he shouted, "You're going to pay for this, you li'l bugger!"

He urged his mount forward; on instinct, Bea did the same. She was faster, cutting him off as he neared his prey with his whip raised. Barricading his path, she met Grigg's gaze: whatever she meant to say evaporated at the rage blazing in his eyes. He paused with his whip held mid-air...then brought his arm down viciously, his lash slicing through the air.

With a terrified neigh, Star reared.

The mare's sudden bucking jerked Bea's grip from the reins. She flew from the sidesaddle, arcing backward, landing with a bone-jolting thud. Stars streaked across her vision, shouts exploding in her ears. She blinked up through a haze of pain, saw a shadow hovering over her face—a hoof, its edge glinting like a scythe.

A scream burst in her throat as it descended.

STAFFORDSHIRE, SEVEN YEARS LATER

Wɪᴄᴋʜᴀᴍ Mᴜʀʀᴀʏ ᴇɴᴛᴇʀᴇᴅ ᴛʜᴇ ʙᴀʟʟʀᴏᴏᴍ ᴏғ ᴛʜᴇ ᴄᴏᴜɴᴛʀʏ house wearing a domino over his evening clothes and a black demi-mask. Similarly disguised guests were twirling around the dance floor. The females—a mix of sophisticates and ladies of the night—were garbed in a variety of costumes, their jewels ranging from priceless diamonds to artfully cut pieces of glass.

Wick had selected the masquerade for his night's diversion because of the anonymity it offered. He was, at the moment, travelling incognito. As the public face of one of the country's most successful railway companies, Great London National Railway (also known as GLNR), he did not wish to be recognized on this trip to Staffordshire.

He was on a discreet and vital mission to obtain a tract of land that was the difference between success and failure for his company. Through great expense, GLNR had obtained the necessary Act of Parliament to run a route from London to Manchester. The ambitious venture had gained instant popularity with the investing public, who couldn't get enough of the company's shares, driving up the value.

The project had been poised to become GLNR's greatest triumph...until the mistake had been uncovered.

While GLNR had been purchasing the necessary territory for the railway for months, a portion of the planned route through Staffordshire had somehow been overlooked. Obtaining that tract of land was turning out to be a surprisingly Herculean challenge. Since Wick handled GLNR's negotiations—his partner, Adam Garrity, managed the company's financial concerns while his other partner, Harry Kent, was the scientist in charge of research and development—it was up to Wick to get this last, but critical piece of the puzzle in place.

Wick prided himself on his ability to negotiate outcomes that satisfied both parties. Yet the owner of the land, a prickly and reclusive spinster named Beatrice Brown, was proving to be the most obstinate adversary he'd ever dealt with. He'd sent her multiple generous offers; she'd turned them all down flat. When he'd invited her to London to discuss the matter in person, she'd refused that too and in a decidedly unfriendly manner.

Wick was not one to give up, however. If the mountain would not come to Muhammed...

"'Ello, luv." A purring voice distracted him from his thoughts. "Looking for company this eve?"

The woman was dressed as a canary, her voluptuous form barely contained by her skimpy frock dripping with yellow feathers. Her smile was about as genuine as her diamonds and thus left Wick cold. There'd been a time in his past when he hadn't thought twice about paying for his pleasures. Back then, he'd engaged in other vices too, drinking and gambling, spending money as if it flowed as freely as the Thames. His recklessness had led to his disgrace.

To the failures that, even now, caused his chest to tighten in remembered shame.

It had taken him a decade to redeem his honor. He'd gotten out of debt, stopped his bad habits, and dedicated himself to his work. Now, at three-and-thirty, he'd achieved financial success beyond his dreams. From time to time, however, he wanted a respite from his driving ambition. From a life that was busy and rewarding yet also...solitary.

Thus, when the innkeeper of the establishment where he was staying had mentioned this infamous masquerade, hosted by a local libertine couple, he'd decided to see it for himself. He'd hoped to find some diversion, even if it was just for the evening. Someone who might temporarily fill that restless void inside him.

The trouble was that nothing seemed to assuage that strange emptiness. Maybe there was no cure...or maybe he would only know it when he found it. Whatever the case, the canary didn't fit the bill.

He made his refusal polite. "Alas, I've just arrived and yet to gain my bearings."

"Suit yourself." She moved on, shedding feathers along the way.

Wick continued his trek around the ballroom, which replicated the ambiance of a Venetian carnival. Canvas *trompe d'oeil* murals hung on the walls, creating an illusion of colorful buildings, canals, and bridges. Beneath the crisscrossing strings of lanterns, jugglers, sword-eaters, and fire breathers drew *oohs* and *aahs* from the guests. Footmen dressed as gondoliers darted through the crowd bearing trays of refreshment.

Yet beneath the gilded novelty lurked a dreary familiarity. The same cloying mix of perfume, sweat, and spirits. The same hungry lust in the eyes behind the masks. The same glittering, meaningless pursuit of pleasure. Even Wick's own reaction was predictable: surrounded by a throng of people, he had a heightened awareness of being alone.

A practical man, he'd considered solutions to the plaguing restlessness. Since he was rich and blue-blooded, the younger son of a viscount, he'd been hounded by marriage-minded misses for years. The marital union, he'd observed, could lead to happiness: both his business partners were blissfully leg-shackled and his older brother Richard, now Viscount Carlisle, had also made a love match.

Yet no lady had sustained Wick's interest long enough for him to consider making a proposal. Perhaps he wasn't built for marriage...or even a long-term affair. Out of habit, he rubbed his thumb against his signet ring. It was a reminder of the woman he'd failed, of the responsibility that came with even casual liaisons.

Wick shut out the past, reminding himself that he wasn't looking for a relationship. He just wanted to distract himself for an evening. To discharge some of his tension so that he would have his full powers of concentration on the morrow, when he would deal with the stubborn Miss Brown. He departed the ballroom, passing through the atrium to a series of candlelit public rooms. Here, he began to appreciate how the masquerade had come to earn its notorious reputation.

Dressing screens had been set up to create intimate nooks for rendezvous. If the undulating shadows behind the silk panels were any indication, the guests were taking full advantage of the quasi-privacy. There was the unmistakable rustling of clothes being shed, accompanied by assorted moans and grunts.

As Wick passed an opening between screens, his gaze met with that of a lady reposing upon an oversized chaise longue. She was striking, her powdered wig and crimson gown capturing the sumptuousness of a bygone era. The tiered diamond necklace dripping over her bosom could have paid for a small London townhouse.

"Well, hello there." Her husky voice matched her looks, her painted mouth curving with genuine lust beneath her black demi-mask. "Looking for someone?"

*Not any longer,* he could have said with an easy smile. Or he might have simply sauntered over and run a finger along her bare shoulder in answer. After all, the lady was attractive and available...exactly what he should be looking for. Yet confronted by what he'd thought he wanted, he felt the void deepen inside him.

"I'm previously engaged, I'm afraid," he heard himself say.

*What the bloody hell is the matter with me?*

"The more the merrier, darling." She toyed with her necklace, the glittering web trailing over the generous mounds of her breasts. "Bring your friend. There's plenty of room here for three...or more."

He ought to have been tempted. For some reason, he wasn't.

What he was...was bored.

"As much as I appreciate the offer, my engagement is private," he said courteously.

If the woman took insult, she did not show it. "If you change your mind, you are welcome to return. Variety is the spice of life, after all."

"Quite," he murmured.

With a bow, he continued on. The level of debauchery increased with each passing chamber. In the billiards room, the privacy screens had been pushed aside, the masked guests forming a train of writhing bodies so depraved that even Wick's brows went up.

That was the only part of his anatomy to do so, however. As provocative as the scene was, he felt no desire to join in. If naught enticed him in that array of licentiousness, he acknowledged ruefully, it was time to call it a night. He went back to the corridor, intending to head out...when raised voices grabbed his attention. They came from an open door at the end of the hallway.

"That is enough, sir!" a woman's voice commanded.

"You've been a dreadful tease, pet," a male voice said. "Time to pay the piper."

*"Let go of me!"*

Wick sprinted to the room, pushed open the door. The study

was small, dominated by a desk and book-lined walls, with a small sofa by the fire. A man dressed like a pirate had a woman pressed up against one of the bookshelves, his arms caging her as she struggled.

*The despicable bastard.* With smoldering fury, Wick stalked over.

"Pick on someone your own size," he growled.

As he grabbed the cad by the scruff, the man let out a startled shout, stumbling backward into Wick. With an oath, Wick caught his balance...and found himself staring at the barrel of a pistol.

His gaze travelled beyond the weapon to the lady holding it. A white satin mask covered her face, leaving only her eyes and mouth revealed. Brassy red curls cascaded over her shoulders and back. Her tall, willowy figure was clad in a gown of unrelieved black, her arms encased in matching black satin gloves.

The gloved hands holding the small, pearl-handled pistol were notably steady. As was the gaze the lady aimed at the bastard who'd been accosting her.

"Get out," she said in cultured tones.

The man, whose face was pale beneath his piratical eye patch, needed no further encouragement, running off like a cur with its tail between its legs. Wick resisted the impulse to go after the bounder and pummel an apology out of him.

Instead, he turned to the woman. "Are you all right, miss?"

Her gaze shifted to him. Her eyes took on the color of the candlelight, mysterious and flickering. A strange awareness stirred his nape.

"I had the situation well in hand." Her voice was calm, with a pleasing musical lilt.

"That I do not doubt." Wick offered her a wry smile. "Would you mind lowering the pistol? I give you my word I mean no harm."

She blinked, as if she'd forgotten she still held the gun. After a moment's hesitation, she slipped it into the folds of her skirts. The way another lady might tuck away a handkerchief.

"My thanks, sir." She moved to stand behind the desk, putting it between them. "For intervening in that unpleasant situation."

As she spoke, his gaze was drawn to her mouth. Framed by the edge of her mask, her lips were rosy and plump. He suspected the rest of her face would be equally enticing. The satin mask molded to her delicate bone structure, and if her neck and shoulders were any indication, her skin was as smooth and flawless as porcelain. It was too dim for him to see the color of her eyes—some shade of blue, he reckoned—but they were large and almond-shaped, fringed by the longest lashes he'd ever seen.

She'd opted for a costume not in the current style. The classical column suited her figure which, while slender, was also rounded in his favorite places. Her gown's scooped neckline revealed the lovely rounded tops of her breasts, medium sized and with a firm jiggle that made his palms itch to test their heft. Her straight skirts flowed over her lush hips, the kind that would cradle a man as he plowed her...

Wick frowned. What was the matter with him? He had no business lusting over the lady, even if she was the first to arouse his senses in longer than he cared to admit. Having just escaped a mauling, the last thing she needed was more male attention.

He cleared his throat. "My intervention, as it were, was quite superfluous. Shall I return you to your friends?"

"I came alone as that would better serve my purpose."

"Ah." It was all he could think to say to her frank reply.

There was only one reason a female like her would come alone to a place like this. She was here to partake in wild, anonymous, no-strings-attached tupping.

The lust he'd suppressed licked hot and low in his belly. Yet his honor refused to let him yield to temptation. She was clearly a lady and vulnerable...she could be in some sort of shock.

"Then allow me to escort you to your carriage," he said. "Or to summon one for you."

Her gaze fixed on her skirts, the way she smoothed them out a veritable art form.

"I'm not ready to leave," she said crisply.

"It's too dangerous for you to be here alone—"

"I am not alone, am I?" She raised her compelling eyes to his again. "I came for a specific reason tonight, and I gather you did as well."

Her directness affected him like a blow to the chest. His breath shortened, his blood pounding in his veins. What *was* it about this female that he found so intriguing? Was it her mysterious beauty? The contrast between her physical delicacy and uncommon backbone?

*Maybe it's just her maddeningly delectable tits.*

"I would not take advantage," he said candidly.

"No, I believe you would not."

She was studying him, one arm beneath her peerless bosom, the other hand propping up her chin. With her head tilted and lips pursed, she looked like an innocent bluestocking...*perish the thought*. For despite Wick's worldly attitude about sexual matters, his honor would never permit him to seduce a virgin.

Luckily, neither he nor his honor had grounds for concern this eve. Encountering a maiden at this masquerade was as likely as finding one in a Covent Garden nunnery. This lady, who he guessed to be in her mid-twenties, was probably a widow or married lady out for some fun.

He found he didn't like the idea of her being married. Not that it was any of his business.

"May I ask you a question, sir?"

"I am at your disposal." *More than I ought to be.*

"What do you think I'm dressed as?"

He cocked his head. "Don't you know your own costume?"

"I do," she said seriously. "Tonight I am looking for a man who can guess the nature of my disguise. I do not intend to leave until I find him."

The idea of her rifling through the males in attendance caused an odd tightening in his gut. Jealousy? Surely not. He hadn't felt possessive over any woman before.

Bemused by his reaction, he lifted his brows. "What do you intend to do when you find this paragon of discernment?"

She looked him in the eye. "I intend to have relations with him, of course."

## 2

*I DID IT. I JUST PROPOSITIONED A MAN.*

Heart pounding, Bea was grateful for her mask. Not only did it hide her defect, it concealed her furious blush. As she waited with affected insouciance for the stranger's reaction to her scandalous offer, she took the opportunity to study him further.

Tall and broad-shouldered, he had the lean build of an athlete. His cloak framed his trim torso, narrow hips, and long, muscular legs. His black half-mask underscored his high cheekbones, straight nose, and strong jaw, all of which could have graced a sculpture. Above his noble forehead, his golden-brown hair had a thick, enticing wave. Her hands curled with the instinctive desire to feel that glinting richness between her fingers.

In her entire life, she'd never done anything this forward. This *brazen.* Clearly, she was no longer the innocent and naïve debutante she'd once been.

Seven years had changed her. Changed everything.

*You want this,* a voice inside her said. *A taste of passion. Not to go to your grave a virgin.*

The memory of her only kiss stirred up dregs of longing and pain. She pushed aside the feelings; it was easy to do, for she'd had years of practice. Time enough to rage, mourn, and come to peace with the vagaries of fate.

*While I cannot change the past, the present is mine to decide.* Resolve swelled inside her. *And I've made up my mind to experience, just once, a lover's touch.*

Tomorrow, she'd return to her normal life of safety and seclusion. To the life she'd carved out for herself—one that had purpose and meaning, yes, but which always left her alone when darkness fell. For this one night, days shy of her twenty-fifth birthday, she wanted...more.

Taking a lover would be her birthday present to herself.

Excitement shivered through her as she met the gaze of her potential bedpartner on the other side of the desk. She had only three requirements for her lover, the first one concerning physical attraction. Obviously, she wanted to find him desirable...but she hadn't expected a man to have the effect *this* fellow had on her. Her heart raced, and her insides felt as quivery as an aspic. She felt like the heroine of a sensation novel rather than the sensible spinster she knew herself to be.

When it came to appearance, the man was faultless, and she was quite certain he met her second requirement as well. She wanted a lover who knew how to please a woman, and this stranger, with his easy charm and gentlemanly comportment, was clearly comfortable with the opposite sex. He exuded a natural, virile confidence that she hoped extended to the bedchamber.

Bea had one final requirement, one that was rather self-indulgent. Yet even disfigured old maids had standards, and she wanted her first, and perhaps only, time to be with someone with a modicum of intelligence: a man with the ability to see beneath the surface. Not of her mask, of course—which she would never remove for she knew that would only open the door to pain and rejection—but to the heart of her.

The living, breathing woman who lived behind the beastly scar.

To that end, she'd devised a simple test.

She didn't think the challenge was difficult, yet not a single man thus far had succeeded in guessing what she was dressed as. The bastard she'd dispatched with the pistol, for instance, had thought that she was a black cat. Had his eye patch prevented him from noticing her lack of a tail, pointy ears, and whiskers? Sadly, his deduction was better than the other guesses she'd received, which had included a raven (one that was wingless and featherless?), a black sheep (without wool?), and a leopard (don't even get her started).

In a fit of desperation, she'd ignored her instincts, coming with the piratical cad to the study. When he'd started pawing at her, telling her that he couldn't wait to drop his "anchor" in her "wet harbor," she'd known she couldn't go through with her plan. Not with him.

She was desperate not deranged.

He hadn't liked being told no. Luckily, she'd come equipped with another deterrent. Not one for self-delusion, she was fully aware that her behavior tonight was risky: she would not add lack of preparation to her sins.

The Adonis before her let out a slow breath...an exhalation that suggested that he'd come to an internal decision. Was it her fanciful imagination, or was that interest flickering in his heavy-lidded eyes? The wobbly feeling spread from her center to her limbs.

"Pardon me if I seem slow-witted," he said. "Are you implying that if I correctly guess your costume, you wish to...go to bed with me?"

"I'm not implying it, sir." She frowned, some of her giddiness fading. Had she overestimated his intelligence? "I am stating it quite clearly."

"But I do not even know your name."

"Anonymity is no barrier to bed sport. Indeed, it enhances discretion."

"Indeed." His brows inched upward. "Done this before, have you?"

She hadn't, not even close. Yet to achieve her goal for the eve, she had to play the part of a woman of experience. One who knew what she was about and what she wanted from a lover, which Bea did...in theory, at least.

Intellectually, she understood the difference between love and sexual pleasure. The scar had done her a favor by tearing away the curtain of modesty that shielded maidens and, frankly, set them up for disappointment. She saw the truth of things: love was an ephemeral emotion, one that could not be trusted. To yield one's heart and happiness to another was an act of ultimate folly. The pain of losing Croydon had taught her that lesson, as had watching her parents' blissful union crumble before her eyes.

Sexual pleasure, on the other hand, was more akin to an appetite. Like hunger or thirst. If Bea was honest—and she made it a habit not to lie to herself—she'd had cravings of a carnal nature for years, since her first kiss. While her dreams of love had turned to ashes, her needs still remained.

Tonight would allow her to finally satisfy her curiosity. As long as she was clear in her mind that this rendezvous was a physical thing only, with no expectation of anything more, no harm would come of it. All she needed to do was stay in control of the situation and her emotions, two things she'd learned to do very well.

She ran her finger along the edge of the desk, making the movement casual. "I prefer to be direct in all matters, sir. I am not looking for entanglements, merely an evening of pleasure. If that offends you—"

"Only a madman would be offended to be approached by a beautiful lady. Last time I checked, I'm not a candidate for Bedlam." His smile managed to be both boyish and sensual. "Although, come to think of it, that is probably what a Bedlamite *would* say."

"You seem in full possession of your faculties."

"Now that I've lured you into complacency," he said with a wink, "may I take a closer look at your costume?"

*Here's your chance. Take it.*

Screwing her courage to the sticking place, she left the safety of the desk and went to the door, locking it with a decisive click. If this was going where she hoped it would, she wanted no interruptions. She rejoined the stranger, who was now regarding her with a bemused expression. Waving a hand at her gown, she indicated that he should look his fill.

He circled her without haste. His scrutiny was masculine and courteous. His gaze had a startling effect on her: it felt like a physical touch, a caress that caused her blood to rush in her veins, goose pimples prickling her skin.

When he reached the back of her, she twisted her head to see his reaction. The few men who'd bothered to look at the back of her dress hadn't spent much time doing so, seeing naught of interest in the folds of plain black silk. Would this stranger be different?

She held her breath as he raised a large hand, stretching it toward her right shoulder blade. Anticipation danced along her spine. His fingers paused a hair's breadth away from her.

"May I?" he asked.

That he'd asked permission caused something warm to tumble inside her.

"Please do," she said softly.

Even as she strove to sound self-assured, her lungs pulled for air, fighting against the constriction of her stays as his fingertips grazed her bare shoulder. It was the briefest of touches, yet it conveyed many things about the man. The gentleness of his strength. His knowledge of a woman's pleasure... and his enjoyment of it.

His fingers trailed lower, her pulse beating a rapid cadence as he unerringly sought out the line of camouflaged fasteners. His touch was as expert as her maid Lisette's, freeing the tiny ebony buttons from their black silk loops.

He pulled out the hidden panel of silk. In the candlelight, the orange and white-spotted pattern had an otherworldly sheen, deepening her sense that something magical was unfolding.

"A butterfly," he said in husky tones. "Red Admiral, I believe?"

"You know butterflies, sir?" she asked in disbelief.

"I know beauty." He released the panel on the other side. Finding the silken loops at the tip of each wing, he attached them to the buttons located beneath the pleats at her shoulders. The rasp of his fingertips sent shivers over her as he spread her wings...literally.

"And the metamorphosis is complete," he murmured.

*He sees what no one else does.* Her heart bumped against her ribs. *He's the most handsome man you're likely to meet, and he'll undoubtedly be a fine lover. Don't turn lily-livered now.*

Spinning to face him, she blurted, "Would you care to have relations with me?"

His smile faded, his gaze turning intent. "You are certain this is what you want?"

"I wouldn't ask otherwise. If you are not interested, however, then just say so." Hearing the defensive edge to her reply, she cringed inwardly.

After all these years, the memories of rejection still haunted her. How her so-called friends had turned their backs on her. How the veneer of acceptance had worn off, revealing society's malicious core. The fake sympathy had been the worst of all.

*It's such a shame that Lady Beatrice has turned into Lady Beastly.*

She shut out the mocking voices. Reminded herself that the man she was dealing with hadn't seen her scar. If he rejected her offer, it wasn't because he found her revolting.

Besides, he had every right to decide with whom he chose to spend the evening. His behavior had shown him to be a gentleman; perhaps he was only here with her now because he felt honor-bound to stay after she'd nearly been assaulted by the ruffian.

Her insides knotted at the thought. The last seven years had taken much from her, but she still had her pride. Sometimes it felt like the only thing she had left.

She leveled her shoulders. "Sir, you are under no obligation—"

Her next words were lost in the breath that whooshed from her lips. Shocked, she registered that he'd swept her into his arms and was carrying her to the desk. Setting her on the hard surface, he ran his arm over the blotter, sending its contents thumping onto the rug with thrilling imperiousness.

He moved to stand between her legs. Trembling at the feel of his hard thighs edging hers apart, she stared up at him. At his lazy, sensual, devastating smile.

"You could never be an obligation." His thumb traced her bottom lip, causing the tips of her breasts to tighten beneath her bodice. "You fall under a different category completely."

"What category is that?" she managed.

"You, angel, are a fantasy."

He bent his head. At the first touch of his lips, firm and velvety soft, a swoony feeling swept over her. His kiss was like the rest of him: male and masterful, designed to please a woman.

He was better than a fantasy. Better than anything she could have imagined. And he was hers for the night.

## 3

*SHE TASTES LIKE HEAVEN AND SIN.*

The lady's lips melted against Wick's with a curious innocence. At the same time, she returned his kisses with a bold, feminine desire that heated his blood. By God, she was a delightfully
greedy wench. Equally delightful was her lack of coyness: she
made no effort to hide that she was as hungry for him as he was
for her.

Wick tilted her head back and deepened the kiss. He plun-
dered her sweetness, her needy moan burning through him like a
fever. He licked into her silky cavern, courting her tongue. She
followed his lead to perfection, their flesh gliding and twining in a
slick, hot dance that made his trousers grow tight.

He was hard...from a damned kiss.

*Down, boy. No need to rush things.*

Releasing her lips, he nuzzled her ear. Her subtle, flowery
scent was as fresh as she was.

"Take off your mask, sweet," he murmured. "I want to see
you."

She went stiff in his arms. "My mask stays on."

He lifted his head to look at her. This woman, who hadn't

seemed discomfited holding a man at gunpoint, now had a thread of panic in her voice. Because she feared revealing her identity?

"You may rely upon my discretion," he assured her.

"I keep my mask on. That is non-negotiable."

Ordinarily, telling Wick that something was non-negotiable was like waving a red flag in front of a bull. He loved a challenge, and if there was anything that he was good at, it was bargaining. Part of that skill involved being able to read others: to know when to advance and when to retreat. Seeing the unmistakable anxiety in his lover's eyes, he knew now was not the time to push.

Instead, he untied his mask and domino, tossed them aside. Her gaze roved over his face, her jaw slackening. Before he could decide if that was a compliment, she lifted her chin.

"I'm still not taking mine off," she informed him.

Why did he find her streak of obstinacy so damned enticing?

"As you wish, angel. What about the rest?" He hooked a finger into the top of her sleeve, giving it a teasing tug downward.

She gnawed on her lip. "Everything else...you may remove."

If only all negotiations were this easy. He had a foot in the door; he would work to gain more of her trust. For now, he wasn't complaining.

He kissed her thoroughly while making short work of the buttons at the back of her gown. His erection tested the limits of his tailoring when he discovered that she'd come dressed to fuck: her only undergarments were short stays that ended beneath her bust, a chemise, and stockings. Not only did that mean fewer impediments on the path to pleasure, it also meant that her glorious shape owed little to padding or lacing.

He stripped her of everything save her white silk stockings. A man who'd seen his fair share of naked women, he felt his breath hitch at her splendor. Her arms crossed in reflexive modesty.

"No, don't cover yourself. Let me look," he ordered huskily.

He imagined her cheeks were flushed beneath her mask. Slowly, she let her arms fall. The small act of obedience burgeoned his already stiff cock; when it came to bed sport, there was nothing he enjoyed more than a woman's lovely surrender... especially when the woman was strong and independent, as this one clearly was.

Trust was a gift. One that he avoided in relationships but welcomed in bed. When it came to tupping, he knew exactly how to use sweet feminine submission for his partner's pleasure and his own.

Her hands balled as she let him look his fill. And look he did, feasting his gaze on charms so abundant that his eyeballs twitched in their sockets, trying to take in all that she had to offer. Her surging breasts, ripe and full, tipped with the palest pink nipples. The sensual dip of her waist, absurdly tiny compared to her tits and the lush flare of her hips. Then there were her long, shapely legs and between them...hell.

He registered three things at once.

First, she had the prettiest little cunny he'd ever seen. Second, she was as hot-blooded as he'd hoped, her shy patch of curls visibly damp with dew. Third, she was not a true redhead.

"Christ, you're perfection," he said thickly.

She made a sound, and he swooped down to swallow it as he pressed her back onto the desk's hard surface. He ravished her mouth thoroughly before continuing his tour of her delights. He trailed his tongue along her downy neck, the graceful slant of her collarbone, the deep crevice between her tits. She gasped when he cupped the mounds, enjoying their firm heft.

"Such pretty nipples." He teased one taut peak with his breath, enjoying her shiver of response. "Do you like to have them licked?"

Her long lashes lifted, her eyes wide. "Y-yes?"

"You don't sound certain." He blew softly upon one nipple, then the other, and her shiver became a full body tremor. "Why is that?"

"Because I...um, I suppose it depends." She wetted her lips.

"My enjoyment would be based upon how well the activity is carried out, would it not?"

*Oh ho.* Another challenge?

"Angel," he said, amused, "you do know how to throw down the gauntlet, don't you?"

Before she could reply, he set his mouth upon her.

*Heavens.* What he was doing was...indescribable.

A moan broke from Bea's lips as her lover licked her nipples, going back and forth between her breasts. Prior to this, she'd thought that the sole function of that part of her anatomy was to suckle babes; now she realized there were other benefits. As he swirled his tongue, humid pleasure bloomed at her core.

"Oh," she gasped.

"Was that a good *oh*?" He lifted his head. The wave of hair that had fallen over his brow enhanced his boyish yet sensual appeal. "Or do I need to do better?"

Earlier, she hadn't meant to challenge his expertise; she'd only been trying to cover up her lack of experience. But if this was the result of her inadvertent words, then she had no regrets.

"You can do better?" she blurted.

He gave her a lazy smile. Then he did something with his tongue that made her arch against the desk, panting.

"You're sensitive, angel. Have you ever come from having your tits sucked?"

She didn't know if it was his wicked language or his question that caused the spasm between her legs. She surmised that by "come" he was referring to the clandestine relief she'd discovered in the privacy of her bed. If what had transpired thus far was any indication, her self-induced releases were nothing compared to the pleasure this stranger could give her.

Staring up at his handsome face in wonder, she rocked her head against the desk. "No."

He flashed a grin. "There's a first time for everything."

He set his mouth upon her again, this time applying suction. The hot, deep pull tautened some invisible web of sensation inside her. As he suckled, pleasure blazed from her nipple to the apex of her thighs, molten pressure mounting at her core. He left to tend to her other breast, his fingers continuing to play with the nipple he'd abandoned. She whimpered as he rolled and tugged on the stiff bud while his tongue lavished attention upon its twin.

Desire built and built. Her legs moved restlessly, the place between them throbbing with desperate need. He gripped her hips, yanking her down toward him, and she gasped when his thigh hit her exactly where she needed it. Her hips moved of their own accord, rubbing her sex against the rigid column of his leg. The friction opened her floodgates, and she moaned as bliss inundated her.

When she had the strength to lift her eyelids, she met his intent gaze.

"Was it good?" His crinkled eyes and knowing smile told her that he knew it was.

"It was splendid," she admitted.

"You're splendid." His lips skimmed the surging curves of her breasts. "I can't wait to see if you taste this sweet everywhere."

"E-everywhere?" she stammered.

He was kissing his way between her ribs, over the rapid rise and fall of her belly. Before she could regain her wits enough to stop him, he pushed her thighs apart, his big hands holding her splayed as he put his mouth...*there*.

"*Heavens.*"

She didn't mean to shriek, but the hot swipe of his tongue on her most intimate place was definitely shriek-worthy. Strangled sounds tore from her throat as he pleasured her in ways she hadn't imagined, not even in her most carnal fantasies.

"Devil and damn, you're sweet." The growly edge to his voice made her tremble against the desk. "As ripe and juicy as a peach. Eating your pussy just makes me want more of it."

His gaze holding hers, he dragged his tongue up her quivering seam. She shuddered at the sensation and at his deliciously lewd language, which was enriching her vocabulary by leaps and bounds. When he licked his lips, shameless arousal poured through her. He was enjoying this as much as she was...well, perhaps not *quite* as much. Her head fell back onto the blotter as his mouth swirled fire over her senses.

He found her secret spot. Flicked that hidden peak of sensation with his tongue. Her hips bucked, a garbled plea leaving her lips.

"That's it, angel. Rub your pretty pearl against my tongue," he said in guttural tones. "Show me how much you like my mouth."

Whimpering, she obeyed. She rode the slippery friction, faster and faster. Then he captured her pearl between his lips, sucking and lashing it at the same time...and she soared on a crest of pleasure once more.

He lifted his head, his eyes smoldering. He slid a finger inside her spasming sheath, and she jolted—not from pain, but from the startling sensation of having something enter where nothing had gone before. Her intimate muscles squeezed around his thick digit.

"Such a sweet girl, coming in my mouth," he rasped. "I can't wait to screw deep inside you, feel this tight, wet little pussy holding every inch of my cock..."

His words stirred as deeply as his finger, releasing a torrent of yearning. Years of suppressed need broke over her. At the same time, she clung to her last vestiges of sense: now that they'd arrived at this juncture, she needed to bring up a critical matter.

"There's, um, something..."

She didn't usually fumble with words, but this was an awkward topic, one that no amount of practice had quite prepared her for.

As she tried to recall her rehearsed phrasing, he stripped off his waistcoat and shirt...and her mouth went dry at his virility.

His shoulders and arms were corded with ropey sinew, and delineated blocks of muscle paved his torso. Light brown furring covered his chest, the hair narrowing into a line over his abdomen, the trail leading into the waistband of his trousers. Her gaze dipped lower, her heart pounding at the sizeable bulge of his manhood.

That part of him would soon be inside her...and could lead to irrevocable consequences if she didn't use precautions. Specifically, the French letter tucked alongside the pistol in her skirt pocket.

He reached for his discarded waistcoat; the sight of the sheath he withdrew filled her with relief, along with an absurd urge to laugh. Not only was he prepared, he was nonchalant about it. The fact that he took responsibility for the consequences of his pleasure spoke volumes about his character.

He cocked a brow at her. "What were you saying?"

"Never mind. I think you've got the matter, um, covered."

His lazy smile reached his eyes. "I don't know what arouses me more, your peerless charms or your discretion."

As he undid the fall of his trousers, she leaned up on her elbows to watch. Her eyes widened as his erect member sprung free from its confines.

*Goodness...he's huge. How will he fit?*

The rosy-brown pole was long and thick, ridged with prominent veins. When he gripped it in his big hand, his fingers barely reached around the girth. Her pulse fluttered with trepidation; simultaneously, a burst of dew moistened her core. She noted with fascination that he was getting wet too.

Moisture leaked from a slit in the tip of his instrument, dribbling into his gliding fist. He brought himself to her. Rubbed the blunt, velvety crown of his cock up and down her slick folds until she writhed against the desk in hapless delight.

"Ready for me, sweet?" he rasped.

Was she ready? To experience whatever adventure lay ahead?

*Yes, yes, yes.*

"Come inside me," she whispered.

Wordlessly, he donned the sheath, securing the strings, and then...*oh then*...

Her breath became a moan, one that his big, hard cock pushed out of her. There was no dramatic tearing like she'd feared. After momentary discomfort, her muscles softened and stretched, accommodating his slow, inexorable incursion. The sensation of having a man inside her, of being joined in this most elemental of ways, filled her with wonderment.

"Christ, you're tight. The way you're gripping me..." Although his jaw was ruddy with pleasure, his brows drew together. "Are you all right, angel?"

"I'm fine." She touched his jaw, feeling the taut leap. "It's just, um, been awhile."

*Forever...I've been waiting for you forever.*

"Has it, sweet?" His eyes went heavy-lidded. "Then I'll go slowly. Until you beg me not to."

As she considered that puzzling statement, he kissed her. The hot mating of their tongues incinerated her thoughts. He took her mouth the way his cock was taking her pussy: gently, firmly, a possession of thoroughness rather than force. Patience rather than aggression. And it made her want more.

More of his tongue, his cock...*him.*

"Please," she breathed against his lips. "I want...I want..."

"This?" He bucked his hips, jolting her with bliss. "Harder like this, angel?"

"Yes," she cried.

"What about deeper?" He pushed her knees back, and before she could fully register the new position, he drove inside her at an angle that made her see stars. "Do you want my prick all the way inside your snug cunny?"

She moaned her answer as he took her deeper, harder, to a place beyond her wildest imaginings. The erotic slaps of their mating flesh filled the room. When he began suckling her breasts, in time to the rhythmic thrusts of his cock, she slid her fingers into his hair, holding on as yet another release crashed over her.

"I can feel you coming." His blazing eyes seared into her. "The way you're milking my cock, everything about you, goddamned *perfection*..."

He surged into her once, twice, burying his face in her neck. His harsh groans heated her ear as his big body shuddered over hers. Afterward, he scooped her up, carrying her to the sofa by the fire, settling her atop him.

Overwhelmed, she snuggled against him and drifted into blissful oblivion.

~

When Bea opened her eyes, her lover was asleep.

Gently, so as not to awaken him, she disentangled herself from his arms, which held her securely even in slumber. She rose, and her breath held when he mumbled something, his long limbs shifting against the sofa. She waited until he stilled, then she tiptoed about, getting dressed and gathering her things.

At the door, she paused to take one last, memorizing look at the man sprawled on the sofa.

His face was even handsomer with the shadow of a night beard. His muscular chest rose and fell in peaceful splendor. He was a magnificent fantasy, and he'd been hers...for one night.

*Thank you*, she whispered in her heart. *I'll never forget the beauty I found in your arms.*

Opening the door, she walked out.

## 4

"SPARE NO DETAILS, BEA," FANCY SHERIDAN SAID. "I WANT TO 'ear *everything* about the masquerade!"

The next afternoon, Bea was having tea with her bosom chum in the gazebo. All around the sprawling gardens of Camden Manor, butterflies floated, dipping to visit the plants she'd put there to entice them. Ducks splashed on the ornamental pond, scattering diamonds over the water's surface. Sunshine burnished the tall stone wall that protected the garden and manor house from prying eyes.

It was a normal summer day in Bea's sanctuary, yet she had a heightened awareness of everything. It was as if last night's adventures had removed some invisible veil between her and the world. Everything seemed more vibrant, more alive, her senses drinking in the world around her. The warm breeze caressing her skin. The scent of clipped hedges, lavender, and verbena. The pleasant soreness of muscles never before used...

Seeing the curiosity shining in Fancy's doe-brown eyes, Bea wanted to share her discoveries with her dearest friend. When Bea had purchased Camden Manor five years ago, she'd arrived broken in spirit, afraid to trust in anyone or anything. All she'd wanted was privacy, the safety of seclusion.

Then the Sheridan family had come along.

Fancy's papa, Milton Sheridan, was a travelling tinker, and he and his family had come to Bea's estate looking for work. Since Camden Manor had been left in shambles by the previous owner, Bea had cautiously hired them on. Not only had the Sheridans proved to be indispensable in the tasks of restoring the estate, they'd shown Bea true kindness and what she, the privileged daughter of a duke, had never had: acceptance for who she was.

The Sheridans had helped her regain confidence in herself and find new purpose. They were a wandering family, but they made Bea's estate a permanent stop on their route, staying the summer until after the harvest in a cottage she kept reserved for them. All year, Bea looked forward to their arrival. While in her new life she was known as Miss Beatrice Brown, a wealthy spinster, she trusted the Sheridans with the truth of her past.

Fancy, in particular, had become Bea's closest confidante.

At two-and-twenty, Fancy was two years younger than Bea, although her plaited hair, large brown eyes, and petite figure in its patched dress made her appear even more youthful. She had not been born a Sheridan—her papa had found her as a babe abandoned in a field—but her family treated her as one of their own. Life as a travelling tinker's daughter had given her a wisdom beyond her years. By nature, Fancy was shy and rather timid...until one got to know her.

Unlike Bea's so-called "friends" in London, further acquaintance with Fancy revealed her true beauty, inside and out. Only a girl as loyal and sweet as Fancy could have taught Bea to believe in friendship again. Fancy was the type of friend who would go along with anything, stick with one through thick and thin. Indeed, she'd created Bea's butterfly costume, sewing being one of her many assorted skills.

She'd even wanted to accompany Bea to the masquerade...but

Bea had drawn the line at that. It was one thing for her to take a risk, another to endanger her friend. She would not repay the kindness of the Sheridans by causing Fancy harm.

Bea could, however, share the experience vicariously with her chum. Taking a fortifying sip of tea, she gave an abridged version of last night's events. She described the handsome stranger, how he'd been the only man who had guessed her costume.

"And I, um, spent the evening with him," she concluded, her cheeks hot.

"Was it nice? Did it 'urt when 'e...*you know*..." Eyes wide, Fancy made a circle with thumb and index finger on one hand, poking her other index finger through the hole.

Bea sputtered on her tea. "Heavens, wherever did you learn that horrid gesture? You're better off just saying it, dearest."

Fancy cast a nervous glance around the garden despite the fact that there was no one to eavesdrop...except perhaps Bea's dog Zeus. Bea had found the brindle bull terrier bleeding at the side of the road; some bastard had left the animal to die from injuries sustained from dogfighting. She'd rescued the dog, naming him after the God of Thunder for the lightning bolt-shaped scar on his forehead. At present, Zeus lay sprawled on the gazebo floor, his snores conveying his degree of interest in the conversation.

"What was it like to 'ave...relations?" Fancy's face turned the color of beets.

*How do I describe the visceral, all-consuming pleasure?*

Waking up this morning, Bea had felt somehow...changed. Filled with energy despite her lack of sleep. Last night hadn't been about losing her virginity; it had been about discovering *herself*. The myriad, wondrous sensations she could feel. The headiness of sharing pleasure with another. The joy of feeling, on the most primal level, that one was desirable.

"It exceeded all my expectations." *An understatement, if ever there was one.*

"In what way?"

Knowing what Fancy was asking, Bea said frankly, "I didn't know that there were so many aspects to lovemaking. Besides kissing and the actual act, I mean. And to answer your earlier question: no, it didn't hurt, exactly. It wasn't entirely comfortable at first, but after a period of adjustment, it felt quite...natural."

*Such a sweet girl, coming in my mouth.* Her lover's deep voice played in her head, giving her a delicious shiver. *I can't wait to screw deep inside you, feel this tight, wet little pussy holding every inch of my cock...*

Given his size—which had been *a lot* more than a few inches—she still didn't comprehend how he'd fit. But he had, her body accommodating to his. Her intimate muscles fluttered, their slight soreness a reminder of how well and thoroughly they'd been used.

Fancy's eyes widened. "What is there besides kissing and the actual act?"

"Well, there's touching. And the kissing..." Bea cleared her throat. "Suffice it to say, it isn't limited to the mouth."

She feared that the skin might burn off her cheeks completely if the conversation continued. At the same time, she wanted Fancy to have the facts that she, herself, had been lacking. Her own mama had only alluded to the sexual act with confusing euphemisms... The thought of her departed mother brought the usual pangs of sadness and guilt, and she shut out the bittersweet memories.

"Sweet Jaysus." Fancy blinked at her. "And you liked it?"

"I did," she replied with candor. "And I didn't even have to use the, ahem, device you obtained for me. He had one with him."

Bea had learned about the sheaths from her maid Lisette who, being French, was armed with much practical knowledge. The question had been how to secure one of the contraptions; Bea couldn't risk the scandal that such inquiries in the village would cause.

Fancy had again come to her aid. As a tinker's daughter, she had ways of obtaining whatever was needed. She'd snuck into her brother Liam's supply of "Gentleman's Goods" and, sure enough, had located the item. She and Bea had giggled helplessly as they'd examined the long tube made of sheep's gut.

"'E sounds like a true gent," Fancy mused.

"He was a gentleman in every sense of the word," Bea said.

Except, perhaps, for his wicked turn of speech during their lovemaking. Given that Bea had found his earthy vocabulary titillating—and that she'd propositioned a complete stranger—she supposed she wasn't much of a lady.

*Oh well.*

"Then I'm 'appy for you," Fancy said simply. "Will you be seeing 'im again?"

She suppressed the pang of yearning. "Heavens, no. I don't know his name, nor he mine, and that is the way it ought to be. It was a one-time affair."

"But if 'e was 'andsome and kind, wouldn't you *like* to see 'im again?"

Fancy's question highlighted one of the key differences between her and Bea. Despite having a dazzling array of practical skills—the legacy of her tinkering family—Fancy possessed the heart of a dreamer. She believed in love, the triumph of good over evil, and faerie tale endings. An eternal optimist, she had no wish to be cured. If life presented her with a crate of lemons, she'd happily make lemonade for the entire village.

Bea, on the other hand, was a realist. She'd paid the price for being too trusting. She now understood that beauty and love were not the keys to happiness: true contentment lay in controlling one's own destiny. If anyone threw lemons in her direction, she'd scoop them up and toss them right back. Or she'd slam the gate and let the lemons splat where they would.

"And have him run for the hills when he sees my face?" Her smile was sardonic, the taut pull of her damaged right cheek a reminder of what she'd become in the world's eyes. "Last night only happened because I wore a mask. Because he could not see who I truly am."

"Maybe 'e *did* see who you are." Fancy leaned her elbows on the table, her heart-shaped face stubborn with hope. "The cove guessed that you were a butterfly, didn't 'e? Maybe 'e wouldn't care about the scar, which ain't 'alf as bad as you make it out to be. You're beautiful, and the right man would see it. And your beauty ain't just on the outside. You're generous, caring, and—"

"Rich. Don't forget my best feature," Bea said.

Fancy gave her an exasperated look. "Your money ain't your best feature."

"It is to me. It's the source of my independence, the reason I can live life on my own terms." Terms that would *not* include a handsome and masterful lover, she told herself, no matter how wonderful the experience had been. "Last night was a fantasy, nothing more. I'm glad to have satisfied my curiosity. But now I'll move on and tend to the things that truly matter."

"What's more important than love?" Fancy said philosophically.

"This was lust, not love." The important distinction had to be made and, Bea thought, *never* forgotten. "And you're one to talk: you turned down two proposals this year."

Fancy snorted. "Those 'ad naught to do with love. Those 'ad to do with fellows wanting a housekeeper, cook, and nanny for their children. I already do all that for me own family, why would I be wanting more o' the same?"

Despite Fancy's optimistic nature, she could also be startlingly astute. While Bea didn't believe in love for herself, she supported her friend's dreams. Fancy had always wanted a husband to love and who loved her in return...and Fancy deserved to have what she wanted.

"One day you'll find what you're looking for." Reaching over, Bea patted her friend's small but capable hand. "No one deserves love more than you."

"You deserve it too," Fancy said doggedly.

Bea smiled, ready to change the topic from love. In truth, she did have something rather troubling to discuss. She removed a folded piece of paper from the pocket of her skirts, placing it on the table.

"Enough of faerie tales," she said. "I received a letter this morning."

"Another one?" Fancy scowled. "From that blighted railway fellow who won't let you be?"

For the last two months, Bea had been engaged in a contentious exchange of letters with an obnoxious industrialist by the name of Wickham Murray. Murray wanted to build his railway through her estate and had sent repeated offers to buy her land. Despite Bea's refusals, the letters kept coming. He wouldn't take no for an answer, proposing that they should meet in person in London—the last place on earth she wanted to be.

His behavior fit with the stories she'd read about him in the papers. According to the articles, he'd been dubbed "The Iron Duke" for a number of reasons. The obvious one was his success: the company he ran with two partners, Great London National Railway, was the premier business of its kind, earning him an exalted status. Murray's moniker also referenced his will when it came to getting what he wanted: his charm and negotiation skills were legendary.

And, if the scandal sheets were to be believed, his prowess extended into his personal affairs.

Blessed with "godly" looks and wealth, he was said to cause a female frenzy wherever he went. Even if women succeeded in attracting his notice, they didn't hold it for long: his affairs were short-lived and too numerous to count. One of the more lurid scandal rags even claimed to have interviewed his past lovers; according to these "anonymous sources," his stamina and male equipment were the true reasons he was called The Iron Duke.

There was a final connotation to his moniker. The term "duke" was evidently used to refer to the men who ruled London's under-class, and Murray, despite his aristocratic roots, had cut his teeth with this cunning, ruthless group. Before he'd become a railway industrialist, he'd made his fortune working for a moneylender; how the younger son of a viscount had ended up in that world remained a mystery.

Bea could sum up what she knew of Murray in three words: charming, arrogant, and shady. As she contemplated the new missive, however, she didn't think he had written it.

"This letter seems different from Murray's other ones," she said. "He typically uses expensive stationary with his company crest, not this thin stuff. His penmanship is bolder than this hand, and he's always signed his name whereas this note is anonymous. Not to mention, the tone is decidedly less polite."

"What does it say?"

She pushed the letter toward her friend. "Why don't you give it a go?"

Despite Fancy's many talents, there were a few skills she hadn't mastered. Reading and writing weren't considered impor-tant to the tinkering life, especially for the womenfolk. Lately, however, she'd expressed an interest in learning her letters, and Bea had taken it upon herself to teach her friend. She thought it a fair exchange for Fancy, being a proud sort, refused to take any more than a seamstress's wages for the clothing she sewed for Bea, no matter how hard Bea tried to give her more.

Fancy bent over the letter, her index finger following the words as she read them aloud. "Con... con..."

"Try sounding it out, dear," Bea encouraged.

"Con-si-der...you—no *yourself*...warn...warned. Leave your es... estate. Or you will re...regret it."

"Well done."

Fancy raised wide eyes. "Sweet Mary, Mother o' God. *You will regret it?* What does that mean?"

"One cannot be certain, but it does sound rather like a threat, doesn't it?" Bea said baldly.

"If Murray didn't send this, then who did?"

Unfortunately, the industrialist was but one of Bea's problems. For years after her accident, she'd wondered what it was about her that drew bullies and gossips. Now, she no longer cared. She answered to herself and her conscience and didn't give a damn what others thought or said about her.

"You know how popular I am," she said sardonically. "How some feel about me...and my tenants."

Having been a social outcast herself, Bea did not turn away others in a similar predicament. It had begun innocently enough, when she'd given shelter to Sarah Johnson—now Mrs. George Haller—a former prostitute who couldn't find any place that would accept her and her bastard babe. Word had spread that Bea would take in anyone who worked hard and wanted to better themselves, and people who'd been shunned by society flocked to her estate.

Since Bea had land that needed farming and these good folk needed work, she thought it was a match made in Heaven. Others disagreed...or they had different bones to pick with her. Her most vociferous detractors were Squire Crombie, who owned the neighboring estate, and Reverend Wright, the rector of the nearby village. Thomas McGillivray, who headed a coalition of pottery manufactory owners in the northern part of the county, was also a foe. Then there was Randall Perkins, a troublemaking former tenant whom Bea had ejected from her property one month prior.

All the men had their reasons for wanting Bea gone. Would any of them stoop to sending a threatening note?

Fancy gnawed on her lower lip. "We need to do something 'bout this."

"Yes, but what?" Bea drummed her fingers against the table. "Ordinarily, one could enlist the help of the magistrate but..."

"Squire Crombie *is* the magistrate."

"Precisely. And you know what kind of assistance he'd like to provide me."

Fancy snorted. "A boot to the backside, perhaps?"

"He's never forgiven me for outbidding him on Camden Manor," Bea acknowledged with a wry grin. "It is possible, however, that I'm making a mountain out of a molehill. The note could be harmless. Someone's idea of a practical joke."

"It don't sound like no laughing matter to me." Fancy hesitated. "'Ave you thought about contacting your brother? 'E's a duke, ain't 'e? Surely 'e could do something."

Bea's throat constricted as she thought of the last time she'd seen Benedict, now the Duke of Hadleigh. Over five years ago, standing at their parents' graves. They'd fought, both saying things that couldn't be taken back. And the wounds they'd inflicted hadn't just been done with words. Benedict's obsession with revenge had caused untold suffering...

She didn't know how to heal the breach with him. Didn't know if she wanted to. Too much had happened: she and her brother were not the same people they once were.

Benedict continued to send her letters now and again. Since they all had the same message, she didn't bother replying. He couldn't convince her that she was still Lady Beatrice Wode-house...any more than she could change the path he'd chosen.

Or whom he'd chosen to take it with.

"Involving my brother is more trouble than it's worth," she said starkly.

Fancy knew her too well to argue. "You being alone in that manor gives me a worry."

"I'm not alone. I have Zeus...and Gentleman Henderson." What her butler lacked in the conventional skills expected of a servant, such as politeness, he more than made up for with his talents as a former prizefighter. "If anyone dares to trespass, he'll dispatch them forthwith."

"Even so, I'll ask me da and the boys to make sure all the locks are in working order—"

Zeus shot up, startling both women. The hairs stood upon his neck as he let out a low growl.

"What is it, boy?" Bea said tersely.

The bull terrier let out two fierce barks, dashing out of the gazebo and toward the far wall of the garden. It was then she noticed the waving of the tall brush on the other side...as if something—or *someone*—was disturbing it.

"Sweet heavens." Her heart punched against her chest. "There's an intruder!"

## 5

As Wick battled through tall, prickly brush to assess the stone wall that surrounded Miss Brown's rustic fortress, he was not in the best of moods. Last night, he'd experienced the most profound pleasure of his life. Pleasure that hadn't just been about sinking his cock in an available cunny (albeit the tightest, wettest, most addictive cunny he'd ever had).

He'd experienced a...connection. One deeper than lust. One that had felt rare, so undeniably *real* that he'd thought his masked lady felt the same way.

Damnit, she'd *cuddled* with him while he fell into a deep post-coital slumber. Before that, she'd come at least three times that he'd counted and possibly more than that, given the way her sheath kept squeezing him so tightly (hence, the most addictive cunny).

Despite all that, he'd awakened in the study alone.

*She didn't even bother to leave a note goodbye.* He glared at the unsympathetic, and rather high, wall. Had he been nothing more to her than a convenient cock? A way to scratch an itch?

Devil take it, he felt...used.

Cursing himself for an idiot, he found a foothold and began his ascent. They'd made each other no promises: she hadn't even given him her name, for God's sake. She was a one-night diversion like so many before her. If he felt disappointed, then it was his own bloody fault.

Shaking off his displeasure at waking up alone, he'd made the journey to Miss Brown's; the front gate of her estate had been locked. With no one there to open it, he'd had to pick the lock—a trick he'd learned not in the underworld but at Eton (who said boarding school didn't impart useful skills?). Then he'd ridden up the graceful drive.

He had to admit that the recalcitrant Miss Brown knew what she was doing when it came to land management. He'd passed thriving farms on the way over to the manor, cattle dotting the lush grazing lands and farmers at work scything the hayfields. The lawns around the drive were well-tended, with natural clumps of trees here and there and smooth sweeping grass leading up to the ivy-covered mansion.

The large, three-story house had an elegant, balanced design, with sparkling arched windows that promised excellent light and two wings flanking the main structure. It was the sort of house Wick could imagine himself living in if he ever settled down. Ready to do business, he'd knocked on the door and been greeted by her mountain of a butler, whose missing teeth and scarred fists better suited a prizefighter than a man in service. And Wick was using the term "greeted" loosely.

"No invitation, no entry," the giant had boomed.

He'd slammed the door in Wick's face.

Despite Wick's persistent ringing of the bell, the impertinent bastard would not open it again. Wick had thought about giving up...for approximately half a minute. Backing down was simply not in his nature. He'd gone to look for another way in and found *another* wall surrounding the garden behind the house.

Which led to his present precarious position half-way up said wall that, he now suspected, was designed *not* to be scaled. The sole of his boot slipped on the smooth rock, and he gritted his teeth, holding on by his fingertips until he could get a secure foothold again.

To motivate himself, he recalled the latest correspondence that he and Miss Brown had exchanged. He'd sent her a courteous missive containing a princely offer.

Her reply?

*Perhaps a certain thickness of the skull affects your comprehension, sir, so I shall repeat myself once more: my land is not for sale. Accept that fact or don't, but the result will be the same. Kindly refrain from wasting my time. Any further contact from you will be construed as harassment.*

Harassment? When all he'd done was offer her *twice* as much money as her bloody estate was worth? Nonetheless, he'd maintained a polite tone in his next note, inviting her to London at the expense of GLNR.

Her response had been succinct:

*I'd rather meet with the devil himself.*

*Sincerely,*
  *Beatrice Brown*

She was sincere all right...a sincere pain in his arse.

As determined as she was, he was *more* so. Inch by inch, he climbed her wall. At one point, he made the mistake of looking down; his hat slipped off, tumbling into the brush before hitting the ground with a thud. Clenching his jaw, he trained his gaze upward again, grasping onto stone and mortar until his hand closed around the iron railing at the top. Avoiding the spiked metal tips, he swung himself over to the other side.

"Hold it right there!" a female voice demanded.

Startled, he lost his grip. He cursed as he fell through the air. Muscles braced for impact, he grunted when his back hit bushes. He tried to catch his breath whilst disentangling himself from leaves and branches. Rolling inelegantly to the ground, he stumbled to his feet...and found himself staring at the barrel of a pistol.

His gaze travelled past the firm grip of the slender fingers. Past the billowing blue sleeves. Up to the face of the blonde staring at him.

~

*Dear heavens, it's the stranger...from the masquerade.*

Astonished, Bea lowered her pistol, waving down Zeus who was growling, ready to attack. She gawked at the man who'd scaled her wall. What in God's name was he doing here?

Shock and some strange, giddy emotion coalesced, fueling the mad thumping of her heart.

He was even more magnificent in the sunlight. The dimness of the study had hidden the richness of his chestnut hair, the sunkissed gilt threaded through its thick waves. His impossibly handsome face looked as if it had been chiseled by a master hand, and his eyes...they weren't brown, but an extraordinary shade of hazel. A bronze starburst surrounded his pupils, melding into irises of a deep forest green.

His beauty was...mesmerizing.

Then his gaze strayed from hers, shifting to her right cheek —*to her scar*. His heavy eyelids lifted, his pupils darkening, his expression turning into one of shock.

The spell shattered, shards of anguish lodging inside her.

*How could I have forgotten...?*

Her pain and humiliation deepened as she saw the lines that creased his perfect face. Disgust, no doubt. Her fingers twitched to pull her ringlets over her cheek. But she refused to give into the instinct to cover herself. To give into shame. It was too late, anyway. What was seen could not be unseen, and the light of day revealed everything. Now he knew what lay behind the mask—

Then the realization struck her. *He might not know who I am.*

The mask she'd worn had concealed her face. And the bold, loose red curls of her wig had been nothing like her own white-gold hair, at present secured in a top knot, with dangling ringlets in the front. Last night, she'd worn a loose black gown designed to facilitate amorous activities; it bore no resemblance to her current blue frock, with its fitted bodice, full Bishop's sleeves, and skirts that draped over several layers of petticoats.

She was not the same woman she'd been last night. She clung to that thought like a drowning person to a piece of driftwood. To the fervent hope that her lover would not recognize that he'd slept with her. With Lady Beastly.

She drew up her shoulders. "Who are you, sir, and what are you doing here?"

She was proud of how detached and imperious she sounded. Exactly as one would sound when encountering a stranger tres-passing upon one's land. And not the way a woman would address the man who'd taken her virginity during a steamy night of pleasure.

His gaze met hers. "I might ask the same of you."

She prayed that the candlelight had hidden the color of her eyes as it had his.

"This is my estate. I live here," she said.

"*You* are Miss Beatrice Brown?"

Surprise lanced through her. *How does he know my name?* There was a sudden edge to his tone that she didn't like.

Fancy didn't like it either, apparently. She stepped forward, a determined look on her heart-shaped face. Despite her natural shyness in social situations, the tinker's daughter knew how to deal with troublemakers, having encountered her fair share on her travels.

"It's no business o' yours who she is." Fancy pulled herself up to her full height...which, unfortunately, was a full foot shorter than the gentleman's. "You be trespassing on private property. Best you climb back o'er that wall afore we 'ave Gentleman Henderson throw you out!"

The stranger didn't look intimidated. Instead, he quirked a brow. "Would Gentleman Henderson be the giant who slammed the manor door in my face?"

"He's the butler," Bea informed him. "He was doing his job."

"From the looks of him, his job is pounding men to a fare-thee-well in the ring."

"We don't judge by appearances here," she said curtly.

"How commendable."

She studied the stranger through narrowed eyes. He'd schooled his features, his bland expression hiding his reaction as well as any mask. She didn't know if he recognized her...didn't know what his motivations were in coming here. Yet all her instincts were telling her that this man, with his too-good looks and smooth-as-cream manners, was as dangerous as any cutthroat.

"State your name and your business, sir." Her tone made it clear that this was not a request.

For some reason, his lips twitched. Then he swept her an elegant bow.

"Wickham Murray, at your service," he said.

Oh, dash it *all*.

"You're Mr. Murray of the Great London National Railway company?" she asked sharply.

He flashed a dazzling white smile. "In the flesh."

Dear God, she'd seen far, *far* too much of his flesh. Why, oh why, had she ended up sleeping with the blasted enemy?

At the same time, recognizing the folly of what she'd done helped to stem her pain. She didn't miss the way his gaze flitted to her scar, knew that a man with his beauty must find her imperfection disgusting. Resentment surged that her night of ecstasy—what was supposed to be the memory of a lifetime—was now ruined.

*When will you learn? Happiness never lasts. In this instance, not even for a few hours.*

Keeping her frustration and anger in check, she said, "You've wasted your time coming to Staffordshire, sir. As I wrote you repeatedly, I have no intention of selling my property and nothing you can say or do will change my mind."

*Not even taking me to bed—or upon a desk, rather—and making me come.*

*Thrice,* an irksome voice in her head reminded her. As if she needed reminding.

She folded her arms over her bosom and gave Murray a get-thee-gone look.

"As I wrote *you* repeatedly, Miss Brown, my job is changing minds." Before she could reply to that arrogant statement, he turned to Fancy and smiled. "Beg pardon for my rudeness, miss. I don't believe we've been introduced?"

Fancy blinked, looking confused. She was no doubt torn between what she knew about Murray and what now faced her: a swoon-worthy Adonis who was returning her outburst with uncommon courtesy. As the daughter of a travelling tinker, Fancy wasn't used to being treated with respect. Yet Murray addressed her the same way he might a duchess in a drawing room.

"I'm Fancy Sheridan," she said uncertainly. "Miss Beatrice's friend."

"How fortunate Miss Brown is to have such a devoted companion." Murray bowed to Fancy, whose cheeks turned rosy. "Or, I should say, *two* loyal companions."

He crouched and crooked his fingers at Zeus. With a stab of annoyance, Bea watched as her dog trotted over. After sniffing Murray's hand, the brindle bull terrier licked it.

Murray gave Zeus a few pats before rising.

"I do apologize for dropping in, Miss Brown," he said. "Trust me, I was as startled as you were by the precipitousness of my arrival."

Good-natured humor lit his eyes, which irritated Bea further. Rare was the man who was confident enough to laugh at himself; her papa, brother, even Croydon, had never mastered the art of not taking oneself too seriously.

That Murray looked the way he did *and* possessed a charming personality was simply unfair.

"As long as your departure is equally precipitous, I'll have no complaints," Bea snapped.

Oh, perfect. Juxtaposed against his charm, she came off like an ill-tempered fishwife.

He seemed unperturbed. "May I ask a more convenient time to return?"

"When hell freezes over would be suitable."

He looked at her. His mouth did that odd twitching thing again.

"Tomorrow then. Noon?" he asked.

"I won't be at home."

"Generally...or just to me?"

She gave him a look that would have made a lesser man run for the hills.

Murray just looked...amused. "All right, have it your way. But we have business to settle, Miss Brown, and it will happen, if not tomorrow, then sometime soon. Until then."

"There's nothing to settle," she began.

He'd already turned and headed back to the wall. To her astonishment, he started to scale the barrier again, a display of male athleticism that she told herself was *not* responsible for her racing pulse. Reaching the top, he vaulted over the iron spikes, pausing to look back.

"Adieu, ladies," he called.

Did the blasted man just *wink* at her? Before she could aim a squinty glare in his direction, he disappeared down the other side.

"Why didn't 'e just ask if 'e could leave through the manor?" Fancy asked in perplexed tones.

"Because he's an arrogant bastard who enjoys showing off, that's why," Bea muttered.

## ❧  6  ❧

USUALLY WHEN BEA VISITED HER TENANTS, SHE SPENT TIME taking in the fertile farms and robust livestock. She took great pride in her flourishing estate and the accomplishments of her farmers. As she rode past the farms today, however, she was lost in her thoughts.

*Does Murray know that I'm the masked lady? Has he given up and returned to London?*

She hadn't seen him since yesterday, yet his absence felt like the calm before the storm. Her intuition and what she'd read about him indicated that he was not a man who would give up easily—if at all. Beneath his easy charm lay predatory instincts. He reminded her of the lion she'd once seen at the Zoological Gardens in Regent's Park. Tawny and sleek, the beast had been taking a lazy stroll, seemingly unaware of the rabbits released into its cage.

The next instant, it had pounced on its supper.

She did not plan on becoming fodder for any man. No matter how attractive, charming, or skilled in bed he was. Yet her position was precarious, and she'd slept poorly, plagued by the possibilities. If he figured out that she'd been his lover at the masquerade, what would he do with the information?

Would he hold it over her? Use it like a bargaining chip? Would he threaten to ruin her reputation if she didn't sell him her land?

Her hands knotted on the reins. *What's done is done. You can't take back that night.*

The dashed thing of it was, even with the looming threat...she wasn't sure she wanted to.

Her first experience of lovemaking had been magical, and she wouldn't let anyone—not even her lover—take that away from her. And what could Murray do to her, really? As she'd told Fancy when they'd discussed the matter, in the eyes of Society, she was *already* ruined because of her scar. Who cared if her damaged reputation suffered a few more dings? Certainly not her.

*I'm not going to fret over the unknown,* she resolved. *I shall simply cross the bridge with Murray if and when I get there.*

She dismounted at the Ellerby residence, one of the two dozen cottages on her property. When she'd first purchased the estate, the abodes had been in shambles due to the previous landlord, who cared more for profit than the comfort of his tenants. One of Bea's first projects had been to modernize the bungalows, replacing the thatched roofs and antiquated heating systems. She'd had new wells dug so that fresh water was minutes rather than miles away. New windows, floorboards, and fresh coats of paint had completed the renovations.

The tenants did their part, keeping the properties in shipshape. Tying up her horse, Bea took her basket and walked up the path to the Ellerbys' cottage, admiring the trimmed rosebushes and the sparkle of the spotless windows. She knocked on the cheerful yellow door, which promptly swung open.

Bea lowered her gaze to meet the farmwife's twinkling blue eyes.

Standing a shade over three feet tall, Ellen Ellerby had once earned her living as a curiosity in a travelling circus. Then she'd met her husband Jim, and the two had started a new life on Bea's estate...literally. Balanced on Mrs. Ellerby's hip was her babe Janey, and the shouts of her four-year-old son, Johnny, could be heard from within the house.

"'Ello, Miss Brown." The good lady ushered her inside. The cottage was neat as a pin, a curtain separating the main room from the sleeping quarters. "I was 'oping you'd arrive soon. I've got me oatcakes ready to throw on the backstone."

"You needn't have gone to the trouble, Mrs. Ellerby. How's Janey today?"

"She's a cranky li'l mite." Sandy-colored strands slipped from Mrs. Ellerby's cap as she shook her head. "She's teethin' and noisier than 'er older brother..."

At that instant, Johnny ran toward Bea, shouting, "Miss Brown, you're 'ere!"

"...if that can be believed," his mama finished dryly.

"Hello, Johnny." Bea smiled at the adorable boy, enjoying his unaffected welcome. Because she'd known Johnny all his young life, he was used to her scar and thought nothing of it.

Indeed, none of Bea's tenants looked twice at her mutilated cheek, and her estate was the one place where she didn't bother to wear a veil. In truth, the farmers' reception of her was warmer than that of her own family after the accident. Memories flooded her: her papa's frustration, the countless quacks he'd consulted and "cures" he'd pressed upon her. Her mama's weeping despair. And her brother—Benedict hadn't been able to look at her without being consumed by rage...

Out of habit, she shut the images out.

Here, in the new life she'd built for herself, she had a different kind of family. One not of blood but of truer kinship. Bea and her tenants had the shared pain of being outcasts, their bonds deepened by the gift they could give one another.

Acceptance.

The thing Murray—and others who'd tried to buy her land—didn't understand was that Camden Manor was more than an estate: it was a safe place to land. One that had saved Bea in her darkest hour and now offered refuge to others as well.

One that she would not sell, for any sum.

"Did you bring me somefin', Miss Brown?"

Johnny's eager question returned Bea to the moment.

"Lord Almighty, where are your manners?" his mama exclaimed. "You don't ask a guest for presents!"

"It's quite all right." Bea gave Johnny a conspiratorial smile. "As it happens, I do have something for you in my basket. Would you like to see it?"

"Yes," Johnny said instantly.

"Yes, what?" Mrs. Ellerby prompted.

Johnny's brow wrinkled. "Yes...I want to see what she brung me?"

"Yes, *miss*." His mama's gaze aimed heavenward. "Lord above, 'ave all my teachings fallen on deaf ears?"

Since this was a common refrain, Bea hid a grin and brought her basket over to the trestle table that served multiple purposes. One end had been set for tea, while the end closest to the stove had a bowl of batter for Mrs. Ellerby's oatcakes. Finding an empty place, Bea set down her hamper and took out a package of sweets.

Johnny immediately made a grab for it.

"Now what did your mama teach you to say?" she asked.

The boy flashed an angelic smile. "Thank you, Miss Brown."

"You're welcome." She handed him the treats, and he took off with a joyous whoop, declaring that he was going to go show his friends.

"Mind you share those sweets," Mrs. Ellerby shouted after him. Bouncing her babe against her hip, she turned to Bea. "You spoil 'im, miss."

"I've brought a few other things as well." Bea unpacked the

spices and tea that had come in her monthly shipment from London.

"You're too generous," her hostess protested.

"It's nothing, really. May I hold Janey?"

Mrs. Ellerby transferred the babe into Bea's waiting arms, and Bea laughed when Janey immediately made a grab for her bonnet strings. Settling into one of the chairs, she untied the plum-colored ribbons, dangling them for the babe, who wrapped her tiny fist around one with a happy coo.

"Pay mind, miss, or she'll ruin your fine hat," Mrs. Ellerby warned.

Ever efficient, the farmwife had already set to work on the oatcakes. Her adoring husband had built the kitchen to suit her smaller size, with lower surfaces that she could easily reach. She ladled the batter onto a heated griddle, forming perfect circles.

"'Tis just a ribbon. Poor little angel," Bea murmured to the babe. "You need it more than I do, don't you, with your sore gums? Growing teeth is hard work."

In apparent agreement, Janey stuffed a ribbon into her mouth. Bea cuddled her closer, struck by her usual longing. She would never hold her own child in her arms.

"Speaking o' work, my Jim says the hay 'as cured nicely and will be ready for collecting on the morrow." Mrs. Ellerby flipped the cakes with an expert flick of her wrist. "The farmers and lads 'ired from the village will be out in the fields at dawn."

"Excellent," Bea approved. "I've made arrangements for the refreshments during the harvest. And everything is set for the ball as well."

To celebrate the closing of the harvest, Bea held a party for her tenants at the manor every year.

"I can't wait to kick up my 'eels." Mrs. Ellerby brought over a plate of steaming cakes, her eyes sparkling. "No one leads like my Jim."

Bea smiled for the Ellerbys were accomplished dancers. "These cakes look delectable."

"They're best when hot. Set Janey down, miss, and fix yourself up an oatcake."

Bea carefully placed the dozing babe into the nearby bassinet. She helped herself to one of the cakes, spreading on a layer of butter and blackberry jam before folding it in half. Cutting a piece, she took a bite. The sweetness of the fruit and richness of the butter melded perfectly with the warm, nutty cake.

"I've yet to have an oatcake to match yours, Mrs. Ellerby," she said sincerely.

Her hostess flushed with pride. "I expect it's the splash o' milk I add. Or the pinch o' nutmeg."

"The result is delicious." Bea sampled some more before asking, "How have things been?"

Sociable and well-liked amongst her peers, Mrs. Ellerby was an excellent source of all the goings-on. Bea was listening to and making mental note of the lady's observations: Mrs. Haller's possible pregnancy which she'd yet to announce, Mrs. Denton's row with Mrs. Kenny over some missing chickens. Not surprisingly, the subject of the railway also came up.

Gossip had been swirling for months that a railway would be built through the Midlands...specifically through Camden Manor. Bea's property had the geographic advantage—or to her mind, *dis*advantage—of being situated in a valley that not only offered the easiest terrain for laying track but provided the shortest distance between stations. Understandably, Bea's tenants were worried that their homes and livelihoods could be taken from them, despite her constant reassurances.

"We know you don't want to sell Camden Manor, miss, but in the village they're saying the factory owners won't be satisfied until they get their railway," Mrs. Ellerby said fretfully. "And you know 'ow powerful those men are."

Bea did indeed know. The northern part of the county was

dominated by thriving pottery manufactories, the wealthy owners wielding significant clout. A railway would make the transport of their goods cheaper and more efficient, and they'd made no secret of their support of Great London National Railway's plan. Indeed, the head of their coalition, a patronizing prat by the name of Thomas McGillivray, had paid Bea a visit; their meeting and subsequent communications had been none too friendly.

Bea wondered if the factory owners knew about Murray's visit —or if he was in cahoots with them. The idea that he might have an alliance with that noxious bunch tightened her throat. At least the gossip hadn't yet picked up his presence. Heaven help her should anyone discover that she'd lain with the enemy...

A knock on the door awakened Janey, who let out a squall of displeasure.

"Who'd that be, I wonder?" Mrs. Ellerby frowned, getting to her feet.

"I'll see to Janey while you find out," Bea volunteered.

She'd just picked up the fussing babe when she heard smooth, masculine, and damnably familiar tones coming from the doorway. The hairs on her nape tingled, and she turned, Janey in her arms, to see a pink-cheeked Mrs. Ellerby returning...with Wickham Murray.

Even knowing the threat he posed, she couldn't help but gawk at him.

He'd removed his hat, the rich waves of his hair glinting as he ducked his head to avoid a low-hanging beam. His tobacco-brown frock coat clung to his wide shoulders, his bronze cravat a perfect match for the subtle striping in his waistcoat. His muscular legs were encased in biscuit-colored trousers that tucked into gleaming black boots.

As his heavy-lidded hazel gaze glided over her, she had to resist the urge to turn away her damaged cheek. Her pride would not allow her to shrink away from his judgement, whatever it may be. His eyes didn't linger on her face, however, moving instead to the babe in her arms.

His mouth softened, the flare of gold in his eyes eliciting a traitorous flutter in her breast.

Dash the man, why did he always have to look as if he'd climbed out of bed? And not the way a normal person would look, with mussed-up hair and sleep lines upon their cheek, perhaps a dried-up trail of spittle or two. No, *he* radiated a lazy, magnetic sensuality.

Mrs. Ellerby was staring at Murray as if he'd descended from the mythical Olympus. "Miss Brown, you 'ave a visitor...beg your pardon, sir, I didn't catch your name?"

Alarm shot through Bea, dispelling her daze. If Murray revealed his identity, he would be throwing kindle on the rumors about the railway...

"How shoddy of me. John Smith, at your service, madam." Murray bowed. "I am an acquaintance of Miss Brown's looking into acquiring some land in this area. I was hoping she might be persuaded to give me a tour of the neighborhood, to help me make a more informed choice."

Bea's first reaction to his discreet alias was relief. Then resentment welled: *acquiring some land, indeed...over my dead body.* Studying his expression, she couldn't tell if he'd figured out that they'd been lovers. God, if she'd known who he was, she would never have slept with him...

*Liar,* a voice whispered in her head. *Even now, you don't regret it.*

"Mr. Smith being a friend o' yours," Mrs. Ellerby said, beaming, "I invited 'im to join us for a spot o' tea."

"I hope I'm not interrupting, but Mrs. Ellerby mentioned oatcakes." Murray smiled at the farmwife. "It was an offer I could not refuse."

Mrs. Ellerby giggled like a debutante.

Grudgingly, Bea had to admit that Murray didn't seem to hold the typical prejudices against people who didn't fit society's mold.

He was as charming to Mrs. Ellerby as he'd been to Fancy. At the same time, she recalled all the stories in the papers about his prowess: she did not doubt that his ability to appear kind and genuine was part of his arsenal as a negotiator. There was a reason why this man got his way in boardrooms and bedchambers across the land. A reason why he was confident that he could convince her into selling Camden Manor.

Bea's jaw tightened. He could take himself and his bloody charm off to perdition.

Janey, tired of being ignored, let out a screech. Bea rocked her, making soothing sounds to no avail. Mrs. Ellerby moved to take the infant, but Murray beat her to it.

"Why don't I have a go?" he asked.

Before Bea could react, he took the wailing babe from her. The instant Janey felt new arms around her, she looked up. Her face, which had been scrunched up in mid-wail, smoothed. She blinked at Murray, letting out a gurgle as he cradled her against his broad chest.

"Janey ne'er quiets so quickly." Mrs. Ellerby looked as astonished as Bea felt. "You've a way with babes. 'Ave you children o' your own, sir?"

"No, ma'am, but I have three nephews and spend time in the company of my friends' progeny. Children tend to like me," Murray said.

The claim might have sounded immodest had Janey not been cooing and fluttering her eyelashes at him. Bea caught Mrs. Ellerby's eyes, which were wide with a message that anyone could read: *a man who looks like 'im and is good with babes? Land 'im quick before someone else does!*

"Are those the oatcakes, ma'am?" Murray peered over at the table with polite interest as Janey yawned, snuggling against him. "They're quite different from what I grew up with in Scotland."

"'Ere in Staffordshire, we're famous for our oatcakes," Mrs. Ellerby said proudly. "I'll make you up a fresh batch."

"You needn't go to the trouble."

"It's no trouble at all, especially since you've got Janey asleep again. Why don't you give 'er to me, and then you and Miss Brown can 'ave a nice chat in the garden while I finish up in 'ere."

As much as Bea dreaded being alone with Murray, she knew this was a confrontation that could not be put off. She had to glean his intentions...and make her own position clear.

"The garden is this way," she said in cool tones. "Follow me, sir."

Mrs. Ellerby's garden contained thriving vegetable patches and a cluster of fruit trees near the back fence. As Wick followed Miss Brown's rigid, velvet-clad figure to the little orchard, he was acutely reminded of the masquerade. Two nights ago, she'd possessed the same determined posture as she'd gone to lock the study door before propositioning him.

He doubted that he was to be treated to the same kind of enticing offer now.

*Shame, that.*

He had no doubt that Miss Beatrice Brown was his mysterious lady butterfly. He'd known it the instant he'd "dropped" into her garden yesterday. She might have worn a mask and wig at the masquerade, but he'd recognize her musical voice, bee-stung lips, and glorious form anywhere. Of course, he couldn't bring up their rendezvous in the presence of her friend; he was a gentleman, after all, and would never damage her reputation that way.

Seeing her *had* been a shock...but not because of her scar—the reason, he gathered, that she'd worn such a concealing mask. He wondered about the origin of that thin pink ridge, which started at the top of Beatrice's right cheekbone and curved down her cheek, like half a heart. That she felt she had to hide her unusual beauty caused an odd tightening in his chest. Initially, the mark had surprised him, the way a smudge of paint on the Mona Lisa's cheek would be distracting.

The *true* surprise had come from the fact that Beatrice Brown —whom he'd pictured as a prune-faced spinster, cackling as she penned her savage missives—was the most stunning female he'd ever met. No scar could dim a beauty as rare as hers.

She had bone structure that would make a sculptor weep and eyes…God, her *eyes*. They weren't blue, as he'd initially guessed, but a remarkable shade of lavender. The color was as unique as she was. Paired with her lustrous white-gold hair, she looked exactly like the angel he'd called her. And the other parts of her, encased in a severe plum velvet riding habit…well, he knew from experience that they could indeed transport a man to heaven.

Just thinking about their lovemaking brought a rush of heat to his groin…and an uneasy twinge to his conscience. He'd had difficulty falling asleep the night before. Staring up at the crack in the inn's ceiling, he'd mentally reviewed the cues he'd picked up on. How her kiss, while passionate, had held the flavor of innocence. How surprised she'd seemed by her own responses.

How incredibly snug her pussy had been.

At the memory of that lush, exquisite constriction, he swallowed. What was her degree of experience exactly? Surely no maiden would have gone to a masquerade and offered up her virginity to a stranger. And yet…

He could not ignore the uneasy feeling in his gut. He had to know whether or not she'd been an innocent. For years, he'd striven to redeem himself for his early mistakes—to earn back the honor he'd lost during his days as a selfish, reckless rake. The notion that he might have regressed to his old ways was appalling and not something he could condone.

If he had indeed compromised a chaste female, he would do the right thing. His code of honor demanded that he make an offer of marriage. Whether she—or he—wanted it was irrelevant. When you took a lady's virginity, you owed her the protection of your name: that was how a gentleman conducted himself.

Reaching the back fence, the farthest point from the cottage, Miss Brown turned abruptly. Sunshine filtered through the bowers of the apple trees, dappling her lovely features.

"Mr. Murray, you and I have business to discuss," she declared.

Was it perverse of him to be aroused by her directness? In a society that valued demure females, he'd always admired women who knew their own mind and went after what they wanted. Even at the masquerade, he'd been drawn to her lack of coyness, her determination to take the bull by the horns...or, more precisely, him by his cock.

*Stop thinking about her and your cock in the same sentence,* he chided himself.

"Indeed, we do." He decided to return the favor of her directness. "I know that you and I met two nights ago, Miss Brown. At the masquerade."

Beneath the brim of her bonnet, she paled. She did not lose her composure, however. She clasped her hands in front of her, her gaze steady. "I see."

"I did not know your identity at the time. But given our negotiations concerning your property, this rendezvous of ours obviously complicates matters."

Her glorious eyes narrowed. "In what way?"

"I do not, as a rule, mix personal and business matters. Bad form and all that." He cleared his throat, trying to think of the most courteous way to ask the question that no gentleman ought to ask of a lady...and that, as a gentleman, he *had* to ask. "Given that we have, ahem, blurred the lines between work and play, we must face the consequences. To wit, there is something I must say to you. Something that concerns both of our futures."

"I know what you want."

"Do you?" he asked with relief. He was not a tongue-tied sort, but devil and blast if he wasn't making a hash of this.

She gave a tight nod. "What you ought to know is that I will not concede to your blackmail."

He frowned, not comprehending. "My...blackmail?"

"The fact that we slept together gives you no leverage when it comes to my land," she said bluntly. "Nothing has changed since we last corresponded. I will *not* sell this estate, and there's naught you can do about it. Threaten to ruin my reputation if you must, but Camden Manor still won't be for sale. I don't give a farthing what anyone says—"

"Hold up." He stared at her incredulously. "Are you implying that I would use the fact that we were intimate to *extort* you into selling your land?"

"Your reputation as a negotiator precedes you," she said with chilling incivility. "You're known as a man who attains his desired ends—no matter the cost."

An unfamiliar roar sounded in his ears. It took him a moment to recognize it as...rage.

*How bloody* dare *she?*

"I am not a damned extortionist," he said through clenched teeth, "and your accusation is nothing short of slander. If you were a man, I would call you out for the insult to my honor."

She reacted by lifting her brows. "If you weren't intending to blackmail me, then what *consequences* did you wish to discuss? What were you going to say to me?"

"I was *going* to ask if I'd taken your virginity," he bit out. "Was I your first lover?"

❧

She was prepared for blackmail, not a query about her sexual experience. He caught her off-guard, and it cost her. She couldn't form a coherent response, words dashing against her skull like maddened butterflies. At the same time, telltale heat throbbed in her cheeks.

"Bloody hell." He looked staggered. "You *were* a virgin?"

Bea realized her ongoing silence was incriminating, but she felt paralyzed. She didn't want to lie outright; she didn't want to tell him the truth. He was looking at her, with his jaw taut and brows drawn, as if she were a creature he'd never beheld before.

*He went to bed with a butterfly*, the voice in her head whispered. *And woke up to a beast.*

That painful realization jolted her into action. She would *not* hang her head. Would not suffer the humiliation of being this man's regret.

She lifted her chin. "I find your question impolitic, sir."

"That's rich, considering you seduced me under false pretenses."

"I beg your pardon?" Outrage replaced mortification. "I never lied to you!"

"You led me to believe that you were a woman of experience." His jaw could have been carved from granite, save for the ominous ticking of the muscle there. "You acted like you'd played that particular game before. You never, not once, mentioned the fact that you were a damned virgin."

Was he upset that he'd bedded a virgin...or a disfigured woman?

*What does it matter?* she thought bitterly. *He regrets lying with you.*

"The state of my virginity is no business of yours," she said stiffly.

"The hell it isn't. I am not the sort of man who goes around deflowering innocents."

His eyes flared, hinting at the predatory instincts behind his sensual charm. A wise woman would not poke the sleeping beast.

"Oh, please, you deflowered no one." Wisdom had never been

one of her finer qualities. She gave a dismissive wave. "I was an equal and willing participant."

"Be that as it may, my cock was inside your theretofore untouched cunny. That, I believe, is the very definition of deflowering."

"Your *language*, sir."

Her remonstration didn't sound as indignant as she planned. This was due to her sudden breathlessness, in turn due to the memories steaming up her brain. The body part he referenced suffered an indelicate spasm.

"You didn't seem to mind my vocabulary during our interlude." He raked a hand through his hair, pinning her with a baleful stare. "I would never have spoken to you in that fashion had I known that you were untouched. Hell, I never would have *touched* you."

Which was exactly why she'd disguised her lack of experience. Hearing that he regretted their encounter, no matter that he had good reason, cinched her throat. In the light of day, her fantasy was unmasked for the delusional and desperate ploy that it was. The truth was there, staring at her every time she looked in a mirror: she would never have a real lover.

No man would want to wake by her side and make love to her in the sunlight. No man could accept her imperfection. No man would bring her happiness...for that, she had to rely on herself.

Feeling the terrifying prick of heat behind her eyes, she took a breath and regained control. Yes, she'd acted like a fool. She, of all people, ought to have known that there were always consequences for the choices one made: the taut pull of her scar served as a constant reminder. The important thing was not to compound her stupidity. She had to manage the situation with Murray and get on with her life.

She drew her shoulders back. "If I misled you, then I apologize. I would point out, however, that we are both adults who consented to spend an evening together. One evening. I believe I made it clear that there would be no messy entanglements, and you agreed."

"That was before I was in full possession of the facts." He'd started pacing before her, the latticed sunshine picking out the bronze in his hair as he muttered, "How could I have known that you were a virgin? How many maids would infiltrate a blasted orgy? Only one...and I had the luck to find her. Of course."

His obsession with her prior maidenly state was beginning to annoy her. As was the fact that he seemed to be talking as if she were not there.

"I may have been a virgin, Mr. Murray," she said crisply, "but I was never a lunatic. I was—and am—fully capable of making my own decisions."

"There's no other choice." He came to an abrupt halt, his gaze locking on hers. "I must make you an offer."

Surely, he couldn't mean...

"An offer for what?" she asked warily.

"For marriage." His brows slammed together. "What else would I be referring to?"

Pressure built at her temples. *Breathe in, breathe out...stay in control.*

"Seeing as you're also trying to buy my estate," she said acidly, "there could be a variety of offers on the table. None of which I'll be accepting."

"Your estate. Right." He exhaled. "That is a complicating factor we'll have to deal with."

"No, we won't. Because I'm not going to marry you."

"You don't have a choice, Miss Brown. Your honor and mine are at stake." His tone gentled, as if he were explaining things to a slow-witted child. "I took your innocence, and I must do the right thing."

*If he mentions my innocence one more time...*

The tension in her head burgeoned, but she managed to hold onto her temper.

"No one knows what we did," she pointed out. "Ergo, no harm done."

"You know, and I know. As a gentleman, I must abide by my conscience. And my honor dictates that, since I divested you of your virginity, I must offer you my name."

"Will you please stop talking about my dashed virginity?"

He raised an eyebrow. "I didn't realize the subject offended you."

Her head felt like a corked champagne bottle that had been thoroughly shaken. "You made me an offer, and I don't accept. Let us leave it at that. Your obligation is fulfilled."

"The circumstances are regrettable. But as I said at the masquerade, you could never be an obligation, angel." He cocked his head. "Why won't you consider my proposal?"

Good God, where would she begin?

"Clearly, we,"—she flicked her fingers at him, then herself —"are not a match."

He regarded her steadily. "Why?"

He wanted to make her spell it out? Her cork popped. *So be it.*

"You're an Adonis. In the eyes of society, I'm hideously scarred." She was proud of how matter-of-fact she sounded; the truth couldn't hurt her if she didn't let it. "We're as mismatched as two people could ever be."

A crease deepened between his brows. "You cannot be serious."

"I see things as they are, sir. Of course, I'm serious."

"Then you're also deluded," he said brusquely.

She bristled. "I beg your pardon?"

"When I first saw your scar, I was surprised." His tone was as no-nonsense as hers. "But it's just a scar. It doesn't change the fact that you're a singularly beautiful woman."

*Just a scar?* she thought incredulously. *He has to be lying.*

The memory flashed. Six months after her injury, her parents had forced her to attend an intimate soiree hosted by her then-fiancé the Duke of Croydon. She'd been looking for Croydon in the garden when she overheard him and Arabella, whom she'd believed to be her friend, having a whispered conversation on the other side of the hedge.

"She used to be so beautiful. Perfect." Croydon's voice had been hoarse, ravaged. "To look at her now…"

"You cannot blame yourself," Arabella's silvery tones had replied. "It's difficult to see what Lady Beatrice has become. You've been very honorable to stand by her side when everyone has been calling her Lady Beastly."

*Lady Beastly.* The name no longer felt like a javelin to the heart but the twinge of an old injury. The last thing Bea needed was to re-open the wound.

She faced Murray. "You strike me as a man of the world. As such, you ought to understand that society judges a woman's worth by her beauty. When her looks are damaged, she has as much value as a cracked vase or a torn painting and might as well be relegated to the rubbish heap."

"Surely you are not classifying yourself as *garbage?*" He sounded incredulous.

"Of course I'm not. That is society's belief, not mine." She gave him a scathing look. "Being rich, I have the privilege of deciding my own destiny, and I have no intention of accepting proposals motivated by pity."

"I don't pity you," he said with a hint of impatience.

"Please." She didn't fight the urge to roll her eyes. "A man like you would be interested in a woman like me?"

"Well…yes."

His voice deepened, causing a ruffling up her spine. Seeing the flare in his hazel eyes, she acted on instinct, retreating as he followed her step for step. Her spine collided with something—the fence. He didn't touch her, his spice-tinged nearness setting off thrills of panic.

"I proved my interest during our night together. Several times," he said in a dangerous growl.

Her bosom rose and fell in rapid surges, mere inches away from his chest. What he was suggesting...she knew it was not possible. Maybe once upon a time, but not now. A man like him could have any woman; why would he choose one who would forever be shunned by society? Who would make him a laughingstock?

"Because I was wearing the mask," she retorted. "You didn't see who I truly am."

"If you'd stayed, you might have discovered what it would have been like with nothing—not even your mask—between us."

"Right." She meant to scoff, but she only sounded breathless.

"Do you think I'm that shallow of a man? That I can't see beyond a mere blemish?"

*My scar is so much more than a blemish!* she wanted to shout. *It is how the world judges the entirety of my worth.*

She looked into his handsome, intent face...and saw Croydon. The relief that he hadn't been able to hide when she'd released him from their engagement. When he realized that he wouldn't have to marry Lady Beastly.

"I think you're a man." She forced herself to shrug, feeling the rough scrape of the fence through her riding habit. "Nothing more, nothing less."

"Then why did you pick me at the masquerade?"

*Make it impersonal. Get rid of him. This has gone too far.*

"Because you were the best looking of the lot that night," she replied emotionlessly. "And because you seemed like the kind of man who knew how to please a woman and to do so with discretion."

"Right," Murray muttered.

She wouldn't let herself contemplate why he looked oddly disappointed.

"Now that matters are settled, please move aside," she said in cutting tones.

"Matters between us are far from settled."

She glared at him. "Pardon?"

"We've settled nothing," he said. "There's still the matter of my honor to deal with. Not to mention the negotiations for the railway."

The railway. *That* must be why he was pretending to have a personal interest in her.

The recognition hurt, but it also came as a relief. Now that she understood what his true motivations were, she could guard herself against him. She was no longer the same trusting twit who'd once been so easily deceived by others.

"If you think to secure my property through matrimonial means, think again," she advised him.

He stared at her. "Are you implying that I'd *marry* you for your land?"

"I'm not implying it."

"Damnation, woman."

He planted his hands on the fence next to her shoulders. The leashed power radiating from his strapping frame ought to have intimidated her...but all she felt was a deep, tingling awareness. Surrounded by his heat, his addictive scent, she pulsed with yearning.

"First, you accuse me of blackmail, then of being no better than a fortune hunter. One might think,"—he dipped his head closer, his breath heating her ear—"that you're deliberately trying to get rid of me, lass."

Heavens, was that the faint lilt of a Scottish accent? She felt woozy, every fiber of her being responding to this charismatic man. A man who wanted to marry her...

*Because he feels duty-bound. Because he wants your land. Don't be a ninny—don't lose control and let yourself be hurt again.*

"Only an arrogant cad would think otherwise." To emphasize her point, she placed her palms on his chest and pushed.

He didn't budge, his eyes glinting with amusement. "Is that the best you've got, angel?"

"You don't want to try me," she warned.

"But I have tried you, my dear. And from what I recall, you were..."—the new husky timbre of his voice quivered through her insides—"very, very sweet."

His eyes were aimed at her mouth, and she couldn't quell her physical response. Her nipples throbbed, her pussy dampening. His hypnotic gaze sucked her back into the night of passion, the joy of her own surrender...

"The oatcakes are ready!"

Mrs. Ellerby's voice slapped Bea back to her senses.

"Move back, you oaf." She shoved at him.

This time, he stepped back. "It would be rude to make our hostess wait." His eyes gleaming, he swept her an elegant bow. "We'll continue our negotiations at a later time, angel."

"We're not continuing anything," she said in a furious whisper. "*Stay away from me.*"

She marched off, praying he didn't see her shaken state.

## ✣ 8 ✣

When Bea arrived at the fields the next morning, the farmers were at work collecting the sun-cured hay. The sky was a bright blue canopy as she rode her mare, Zeus loping along by her side. It was a day that exemplified the proverb, "Make hay while the sun shines."

Bea had always enjoyed taking part in the communal harvest, and today, more than ever, she needed a distraction. Needed to get her mind off that blasted Wickham Murray.

*It's just a scar. It doesn't change the fact that you're a singularly beautiful woman.*

She told herself that he couldn't have meant those words. He was glib, a man who knew how to charm and get what he wanted. At the same time, she'd come to the grudging conclusion that his proposal hadn't been prompted by mercenary reasons.

His affront had been genuine when she'd accused him of wanting to marry her for her land. Moreover, a confirmed bachelor like Murray would probably sell his soul rather than give up his freedom. With his negotiation skills, he had to believe that there were easier, and less permanent, ways of achieving his goals.

That left his honor as the motivating factor for his offer.

As much as it pained her to admit it, her interactions with him thus far supported that he was, indeed, a gentleman. He'd intervened at the masquerade when she'd been accosted. His manners toward her and her friends had been annoyingly faultless: Fancy, Mrs. Ellerby, and even little Janey had seemed to fall under his spell. In contrast to his amicability, Beatrice felt like an ill-tempered shrew.

How else was she to behave? Her grip tightened on the reins. She couldn't let his compliments or her dashed attraction to him distort reality. And the reality was this: she'd lost Croydon because of the scar. Her parents and her brother soon thereafter. Her entire life as she knew it had disappeared the instant her horse had sliced open her face.

She'd learned her lesson: if beauty was a broken promise, then love was an outright lie.

Now she had a new life, one she'd built for herself that had purpose and meaning. She wouldn't let any man—no matter how courteous, handsome, and attractive he was—take it away from her. She wouldn't open herself up again to pain.

With proficiency borne of practice, she shut out the troubling thoughts, returning her attention to the surrounding fields. Haymaking was a laborious task. Earlier this week, the men had cut the grasses, spreading them out to dry and raking once more to ensure even curing. Now they were collecting the hay, using pitchforks to pile the stuff onto horse-drawn carts. It would take two full days of work to stack and store the fodder in the barn, ensuring the livestock had feed for the winter months.

Arriving at the refreshment tent her servants had set up earlier, Bea dismounted, leaving her mare to graze. Zeus followed her to the tent. Beneath the striped awning that provided shade from the sun, Mrs. Ellerby and her fellow farmwives were organizing the food and drink.

"Good morning to you, Miss Brown." Mrs. Ellerby bobbed a curtsy, as did the other women.

"Hello, ladies." Eyeing the trays of sandwiches, Bea asked worriedly, "Do you think there's enough? Shall I send for more?"

"There's plenty, miss," Mrs. Haller said, smiling. "Enough to feed an army, I'm sure."

When Sarah Haller had first come to Camden Manor, she'd been starved and desperate, a former prostitute with no means of feeding herself or her bastard child. Now her blonde curls were shining, her blue eyes bright, and she had the wholesome prettiness of a doll. She also had one hand resting on her aproned belly, and Mrs. Ellerby was right: it *was* difficult to tell whether the Hallers might be expecting a new bundle of joy.

Mrs. Ellerby snorted, setting out a platter of cheese and cold mutton. "You best beware feeding the men too much o' this fine food, miss. After a meal like this, they'll be wanting a nap."

"One couldn't blame them." Looking out into the fields, Bea saw the groups of men, the powerful and tireless arcs of their pitchforks sending hay soaring into the carts. "It must be hard toiling in the sun."

"Toiling, my arse. They're amusing 'emselves with a game."

This came from Mrs. Gable, another of the wives. Beneath her cap, her ginger curls poked out haphazardly, curls that she'd given to her son Billy who was pouring lemonade into tin cups under her watch. He did so with meticulous care, filling each cup with the precise amount, his attention fixed on the task.

At twelve, Billy had yet to speak a word and avoided looking people in the eyes. Bea had the sense that he lived in his own world, marching to the beat of his own unique drum. Mrs. Gable had confided that, in the prior village they'd lived in, the boy had been mercilessly bullied for being different. To her and her husband's relief, the residents of Camden Manor were far more accepting of Billy's oddities, and she'd been bringing him more and more to public functions.

Bea thought this was good for the lad. Today he did not reply to her soft greeting, but he did cast her a quick, side-long glance.

Knowing what an improvement that acknowledgement was, she gave him a warm smile of encouragement.

To his mama, Bea said curiously, "What sort of game?"

"Can't bring a group o' males together without 'em wagering on something." Mrs. Gable lifted her chin toward the group pitching hay into a cart some twenty-five yards away. "They've a bet on who can clear their patch the quickest."

Amused, Bea observed the men at work. Straw hats shaded their faces so she couldn't make out who they were, but their pitchforks whipped through the air, the cart piling rapidly. This might be a game, but the competition was getting the work done.

The tallest of the group, in particular, showed impressive strength. He moved with athletic grace, wielding his tool with potent efficiency. She wasn't surprised when he finished first, whoops erupting from the other men. He tossed off his hat, and her heart shot into her throat as the sun hit those rich brown waves, picking out the glints of bronze.

He turned suddenly; even from the distance, she felt the heat of his gaze burning through her.

*Dash it...what is Murray doing here?*

In truth, she ought to have expected him. His amicability hid a tenaciousness that rivaled Zeus's when he got hold of a bone. She steeled herself as Murray prowled toward her.

"Mr. Smith's quite the sight for sore eyes, ain't 'e?" Mrs. Ellerby murmured beside her.

If Bea wanted confirmation of Murray's effect on women, then she needed to look no further. Mrs. Ellerby wasn't the only one reacting to him: Mrs. Gable was fussing with her cap, Mrs. Haller smoothing her apron. Mrs. Sears licked her lips the way Bea had seen her do at tea, when there was a particularly good cake to be had. Mrs. Sears's reaction was particularly telling since she'd just celebrated half a century and the birth of her fifth grandchild.

Apparently, Murray's animal magnetism affected all women, regardless of age.

Clearing her throat, Bea asked, "How long has he been here?"

"Since the crack o' dawn when me and Jim arrived," Mrs. Ellerby replied. "The wind could've knocked me o'er, miss, when 'e said 'e wanted to 'elp with the harvest. When I asked 'im why, 'e says if 'e's to buy an estate, 'e wants a taste o' real country living... as if that would amount to anything more than the 'unt and 'ouse parties for a toff like 'im."

Bea shared the other's amazement. Why would Murray offer to help with the harvest?

*What is the blighter up to?*

"Whate'er Mr. Smith's true reason might be," the farmwife went on, giving Bea a knowing look, "Jim weren't about to turn down an extra pair o' 'ands during 'arvest. Hay don't collect itself, as 'e likes to say."

"Indeed," Bea said faintly.

"Now these eyes o' mine ain't no stranger to the world, Miss Brown, and I don't mind telling you what you already know: Mr. Smith is a looker. But there are fine-lookin' gents and then there are fine-lookin' gents who can make 'emselves useful. Mr. Smith is keeping up with the best o' the lads...and adding to the scenery while 'e does it."

It annoyed Bea that the other was right. And she couldn't strip Murray of his halo: revealing his true motive for being here would only cause more problems. Saying he was a railway man would be like throwing a lit match to kindling. She would have to deal with an inferno of worry from her tenants, especially since everyone now believed him to be her personal acquaintance.

She held onto her irritation like a shield, hoping that it would protect her from Murray's mesmeric charm. But as he neared in that long, loose-limbed stride, she felt a quiver in some deep, primal part of her. Lord knew he was dashingly handsome in his tailored attire, but in this sweaty, fresh-from-the-fields state he was pure temptation.

His shirt was untucked, the fine linen clinging to his broad shoulders. He'd rolled up his sleeves, revealing sinewy, veined fore-arms (who knew that *forearms* could be so carnal?). He'd aban-doned his cravat, the open collar of his shirt revealing a glimpse of the curling hair on his chest, and her fingertips tingled with the memory of stroking that light furring and the hard planes beneath. Her gaze followed the corded length of his throat, sheened with honest male sweat, upward to his defined jaw, beau-tiful mouth, and his eyes...

The bronze around his pupils lit up the green of his irises like the sun shining through leaves. His eyes crinkled at the corners as he smiled at her. A slow, sensual smile that made her heart pitter-patter as if she were a miss fresh from the schoolroom rather than a spinster on the cusp of her twenty-fifth birthday.

He swept her a bow. "Good morning, Miss Brown."

Zeus, the traitorous creature, bounded over to him. The bull terrier wagged his tail as Murray murmured, "Hello, boy," and patted his head.

"Mr. Smith." Aware of their audience, which included not only the wives but the men who'd followed Murray in from the field, Bea said pointedly, "What a surprise to see you here."

"When you told me about the harvest, I was curious to experi-ence it for myself," he said easily. "I've found nothing substitutes for hands-on experience...don't you agree?"

Sensing the subtext, Bea narrowed her eyes. If he thought he could gain the upper hand by bringing up their dalliance, then he was bound for disappointment.

"Perhaps some things ought to be tried *once*," she said with cool emphasis.

His lips twitched. "Only once?"

She shrugged. "Repetition can be tedious."

"On the other hand, there's that old adage: practice makes perfect."

Flustered by the wicked gleam in his eyes, Bea tried to think of some clever repartee.

Luckily, Jim Ellerby cut in. "Now me, I don't mind repeating things, but I really don't mind 'aving an extra pair o' 'ands when I'm doing it." The brawny farmer clapped Murray on the shoulder as if they were long-lost cronies. "Smith, I 'ad my doubts 'bout you, on account o' you being a toff, but you're a fine worker. Ne'er seen a fellow pitch hay as quick as you did back there."

"Maybe you 'ave the makings o' a farmer after all," Mr. Gable said with a guffaw.

This was no small compliment from Mr. Gable, who was burly and strong as an ox. Grunts of agreement rose from the other men as well. A few of them buffeted Murray on the arm, and he returned the masculine gestures with good-natured punches of his own.

Bea watched on in amazement. By all rights, as a wealthy gent amongst the laboring class, Murray ought to stick out like a sore thumb. Instead, he was like a dashed chameleon, able to fit in wherever he happened to be.

"The winner o' the contest deserves a drink," Mr. Ellerby declared.

Mrs. Gable handed her son a tray of cups and nudged him forward. "Go on, Billy, and bring the gent some lemonade."

Billy shuffled a few steps over to Murray, his gaze averted. Silently and abruptly, he shoved the tray in Murray's direction, almost hitting the other in the midsection. The action would seem rude to anyone who didn't know the boy; Bea saw the worried looks exchanged between Billy's parents.

Before she could intervene, Murray took one of the tin cups.

"Thank you...Billy, is it?" When no reply came, he smiled and sampled his beverage. "Nothing like lemonade on a hot day. I'm sure the others would like one of those drinks too, lad."

Without looking up or replying, Billy made the rounds to the others.

Mrs. Gable hurried over to Murray. "I'm sorry, sir. Billy's just learning—"

"He's a good lad," Murray said. "A helpful one, too."

"He tries." Mrs. Gable bit her lip. "He's just different, see, from the others—"

"Every flower blooms in its own time, ma'am, and in its own way."

Murray's gentle words struck a chord in Bea, surprise and some deeper feeling reverberating through her. He was the most *confounding* man. How could a tenacious industrialist and reputed rake be...caring? For there was no doubting his sincerity, nor its effect on Mrs. Gable who looked as if he'd given her a gift.

Which he had, by not treating Billy like a pariah. For seeing beyond the boy's oddities to his positive qualities. *For being a man who can see beneath the surface.*

With a desperate shiver, Bea shut out the thought.

"You're very wise, sir," Mrs. Gable said.

"I can't take credit for the saying. I stole it from my sister-in-law. She uses it to console my nephew."

"Console him, sir?"

"He has the double misfortune of being the youngest of three boys *and* my namesake."

As his rueful words drew laughter from the others, Bea told herself that she was *not* interested in Murray's family and background. At all. Yet she couldn't stop the image from forming: of him playing with his nephews, who, if they had the Murray blood, must be altogether too charming.

*Family, children...* Her throat cinched. *Things that can never be mine.*

In a flash, she saw the worst of the dangers Murray posed: he resurrected her old dreams.

She *had* to talk to him. Seeing him with Billy and her other friends convinced her that he wasn't entirely a bad sort, surely not the cold-hearted railway tycoon the papers made him out to be. She would give him a final refusal of both his offers—for her hand and her property—and hopefully, that would be that.

"The hay won't collect itself, lads," Mr. Ellerby declared. "We best get back while the sun is still a-shining."

"The sooner we finish, the sooner we can celebrate," another of the men added.

Mr. Gable sauntered over, a half-eaten sandwich in hand, and thumped Murray on the back.

"Think you'll be up to another wager, Smith?" he asked between large bites.

"Why not?" Murray set his cup down on the refreshment table. "I'll take a sandwich with me."

"That's the spirit. Get the man a sandwich, will you, luv?" Mr. Gable asked his wife. "And another one for me while you're at it?"

Her gaze aiming upward at her cap, Mrs. Gable went to fetch the food. The others were busy eating and palavering. Bea saw her opening.

"Mr. Smith," she said in an urgent undertone, "before you go, I should like to—"

"Now, Miss Brown, you heard Ellerby. Hay doesn't collect itself." Murray's eyes gleamed with humor. "I'm sure there will be plenty of time to chat tomorrow night at the ball."

"The *ball*?" Her voice rose sharply. "Surely you aren't going—"

"Who's not going to the ball?" Mr. Ellerby ambled over.

"Don't look at me." Mr. Gable hitched his thick shoulders. "You know *I* wouldn't miss the finest celebration in the county. But seems like Smith 'ere might not be going."

"*Not going?*" Ellerby's rugged features pulled taut, as if the notion of not attending Bea's party was tantamount to sacrilege. "Smith, Miss Brown's harvest ball ain't to be missed. There'll be food, drink, and dancing...and I'll be bringing some o' Ellen's cider. Finest you'll e'er taste."

"Is Mrs. Ellerby's cider as good as her oatcakes?" Murray inquired.

"It's *better*."

"Then I wouldn't miss it for the world."

"Good man," Ellerby said approvingly. "Best be getting back to the fields, then. The hay—"

"Won't collect itself," Murray and Gable said simultaneously.

The two men chuckled. They slapped each other on the back, like two schoolboys congratulating each other on a trick well played and headed back toward the fields.

Mystified, Bea watched after them.

*I'll talk to him at the ball*, she told herself. *Then I'll settle everything once and for all.*

THE EVENING OF THE HARVEST BALL, WICK WAS GETTING ready at his suite at the inn. He'd just stepped into the copper tub when he heard a knock. Assuming it was his valet Barton, he called out, "Come in" as he sank into the hot sudsy water.

Christ, that felt good. He was a fit man, one who excelled at boxing and other gentlemanly sports. But two days of farm work had nearly killed him.

The footsteps on the other side of the dressing screen didn't sound like Barton's. Wick saw why when a female stepped around the wooden panel...the maid who'd brought up the water for his bath. She was buxom and seemed to be missing the fichu she'd been wearing earlier. Her breasts were nearly spilling from her neckline.

"May I, er, help you?" he asked.

She held up a tin jug. "Wanted to see if you needed more 'ot water, sir. And if you be wanting me,"—her eyes wandered boldly over his wet chest, lingering at the point where the suds just covered his groin—"to 'elp with your bath?"

The Pig & Whistle had advertised that their lodgings came with "all the conveniences," but Wick hadn't expected this particular one. Nor had he any interest in it. He refused the maid's services, assuaging her pout by telling her to collect a coin from his valet on her way out. When the door closed behind her, he lay his head back against the tub's edge, his well-used muscles relaxing in the silky water.

There'd been a time in his life when he would have taken the maid up on her offer without thought. In his early twenties, he'd been a shallow, arrogant bastard, one who thought only of himself and his own pleasures. His behavior had been the height of irresponsibility...and he and others had paid the price.

His signet ring gleamed wetly on his right hand, a reminder of what his excesses had cost. Of the woman whom he hadn't loved but whose heart he'd recklessly broken. Monique had died a decade ago, and while he hadn't killed her, he bore responsibility for her death.

As always, when he thought of that ignominious period of his life, he thought of the people he'd hurt. Back then, he'd blamed everyone else for the consequences of his feckless behavior...especially his older brother Richard. He still didn't know how Richard could forgive him for being a selfish cad—and for causing waves in Richard's courtship of Violet. Luckily, everything had turned out happily for the pair, but Wick knew he didn't deserve the love and support the couple gave him so unconditionally.

He expelled a breath and reached for the bar of soap, specially blended for him by an apothecary on St. James's Street. There was no changing the past. In the intervening years, he tried to make up for it by getting his financial affairs in order and making amends where he could. He'd adhered to a strict code of behavior...until the masquerade. As he ran the soap over his chest, he thought wryly that it was just like him to find a virgin at a bloody orgy.

And not just any virgin but Beatrice Brown.

The most entrancing and exasperating lady he'd ever met.

There was a certain irony to the fact that he, considered one of London's most eligible bachelors, didn't seem to warrant the slightest consideration from her. She'd thrown his offer back like it was a too-small fish when many a marriage-minded miss would have given their eyeteeth to land him. Admittedly, Beatrice's refusal didn't put him off in the slightest. It wasn't just the challenge of her that he enjoyed—although he did adore their banter —but the complex sum of who she was.

A sultry masked lover. A vulnerable innocent. A caring and capable mistress of the estate.

He had a feeling that he was just scratching the surface of Beatrice. That she would take a lifetime to know...and she would never bore him. While his honor had obliged him to make her an offer, he'd been surprised to discover that he was far from unwilling to make her his bride. In the past, whenever the topic of marriage had come up, he'd heard the slamming of a cell door. Or, worse, the tense, inescapable silence that had characterized the state of affairs between his own parents.

The notion of marriage to Beatrice, however, brought a strange sense of calm. In her presence, the void inside him seemed to lessen. Curiosity had once prompted him to ask Richard how the other had known that Violet was "the one."

*Just knew.* Richard had shrugged in that stoic way of his that had always reminded Wick of their dead papa. But then his brother's eyes had lit with humor. *My lass has a way of making an impression, no?*

Since Violet had pushed Richard into a fountain on their first meeting, Wick couldn't disagree. He had a particular fondness for his sister-in-law and saw resemblances between her and Beatrice. Both were unconventional ladies. Spirited and strong, they were fiercely loyal to those they cared about.

Working alongside Beatrice's farmers, who gossiped more than housewives, had given Wick the opportunity to learn more about his future bride. According to the men, Beatrice was generous and kind, giving everyone a fair shot, even those who were shunned by society. She was good to her word and expected others to be too. No one knew anything about her past or the family she'd been born into, but she treated the Sheridans—Miss Fancy and the rest of the travelling clan—as if they were her kin.

At the same time, she suffered no fools. Ellerby had told him that she'd ejected some bastard named Randall Perkins from her property after he'd been caught harassing her lady's maid. Perkins, apparently, had been none too happy about losing his cottage, yet Beatrice had stood firm.

Her strength of will didn't surprise Will one bit; hell, he admired her for it.

*Miss Brown is an independent female, make no mistake about it.* Ellerby had given Wick a man-to-man look. *But that big, empty manor 'ouse must get lonely. My Ellen reckons a strong woman like Miss Brown needs an even stronger man to make 'er happy.*

Was Wick the man for the job? As he lathered his hair, he felt self-doubt creep over him. He'd come a long way since his younger days, but even now he felt wary of being trusted with another's happiness. Most women wanted him for his looks or money, not his character, a fact that had suited him just fine...until Beatrice.

For some reason, her comment that she'd only been drawn to his physical qualities and perceived abilities in bed had stung. Her assumption that he would try to *blackmail* her was even worse. What kind of a man did she think he was? Moreover, what had happened in her past to give her such a cynical view of human nature?

Nonetheless, he thought as he rinsed, physical attraction and sexual compatibility gave them common ground to start. Both were ineffable yet necessary qualities that he was looking for in a mate—ones that, for him, were either there or not.

Luckily for him, both were present in spades with Beatrice.

Memories of the masquerade washed over him. Christ, she'd been hot, as hungry for him as he'd been for her. Those breathless pants she'd made, the way she'd rubbed her drenched virgin cunny against his tongue and then his cock, begging to be taken. The way she'd surrendered completely to him, her pussy milking him of his seed...

Laying his head back against the tub's edge, he fisted his rod, the flesh already turgid and pulsing. He frigged himself idly, not with the intent to climax but just to enjoy the sensations of arousal. Of desire brought on by thinking about Beatrice.

His lust was amplified by possessiveness. He had never taken anyone's virginity before, had never wanted to. Yet knowing that Beatrice had lain only with him, that he alone had known her sweet and generous passion, made him want to be not only her first lover but her last.

The more he thought upon it, the more compatible they seemed. Sexually, obviously, but also in their personalities. He found her resilience not only admirable but reassuring. While she might surrender delightfully in bed, in life she was an independent woman. Sensible and self-possessed, she wouldn't have unrealistic expectations of marriage. He would do his utmost to be an excellent companion to her, but she wouldn't depend on him for her happiness—which meant he could not disappoint her.

He rose from the bath, water sluicing over his hard frame. As he toweled himself off and rang for his valet, he knew that courting Beatrice Brown would not be easy. Then again, negotiation was his specialty, wasn't it? The biggest obstacle seemed to be her stubborn refusal to see her own beauty; he decided he would work on that at the ball tonight. There was, of course, the looming complication of his railway and her land...

He donned his robe and told himself, *One disaster at a time.*

"OH, FANCY," BEA BREATHED. "IT'S *BEAUTIFUL*."

"Do you like it, truly?" her friend asked eagerly.

That evening, while the harvest ball was in progress, the two women had snuck away for a private celebration of Beatrice's twenty-fifth birthday. They'd gone to one of Bea's favorite spots, a massive oak tree situated on the far side of the pond. According to her gardener, the tree was over a century old: it had giant, heavy branches that hung low to the ground, creating a cozy, leafy cocoon hidden from the outside world.

Darkness had fallen, and Bea and Fancy had hung their lanterns upon the overhead branches, bathing the space in a golden glow. They sat upon a natural indentation in the sprawling base of the tree that made a perfect bench. From the other side of the pond came the sounds of the ball: a lively reel, stomping steps, and laughter drifted over on the balmy breeze.

Earlier, Bea hadn't seen Murray at the party...not that she'd been looking for him. Or, if she had, it had been so that she could talk to him and tell him to leave her be. Then Fancy had pulled her away from the celebration. As Bea didn't like a lot of fuss, no one knew that it was her birthday except her dearest friend. Fancy, being Fancy, had brought her a gift.

Nestled in an old candy box, the organdy cap was trimmed with two rows of good quality lace and tiny rosettes made of ribbon. The cap had trailing ribbons embellished with more rosettes. The stitching was neat, the craftsmanship impeccable.

"I adore it." Bea held up the cap, admiring her friend's handiwork. "It would fetch a pretty penny at any Bond Street millinery. How did you come up with the pattern?"

"A lady in the village was wearing one like it. I asked her where she got it, and she looked down 'er nose at me." Fancy mimicked an affected aristocratic accent. *"You couldn't afford it, gel. It came direct from London and is the crème de la crème of fashion."* She paused, rolling her eyes. "I may not know what *crème* means, but I know 'ow to sew a few pieces o' fabric and lace together, I do."

Such was Fancy's talent that she could merely look at an item of clothing and reproduce it. Not only that, but she could take a few scraps—a bit of lace here, some ribbon there—and turn it into a masterpiece.

"The woman sounds horrid. I wish I'd been there to give her a piece of my mind." Although Fancy always took such incidents in stride, Bea was indignant on her friend's behalf. "I shall cherish your present all the more..."

She trailed off, turning her head at the sound of rustling leaves. An instant later, the branches parted, and Murray stepped through, ducking his head to avoid low-hanging bowers.

She sprang up from the bench, Fancy following suit.

"Good evening, ladies. What a charming hideaway." He bowed, then said with a smile, "Pardon my interruption. I just arrived and was told Miss Brown might be by the pond...and I believe I just heard mention of a present. Is it a special occasion?"

Bea hesitated, gripping her cap. But when she'd stood, the box that had held the gift and the accompanying note had slid to the ground, and now Murray bent to pick it up. There was no way he could miss the large, painstakingly formed letters.

"*Happy Birthday, Beatrice. From Your Friend, Fancy.*" He tilted his head at Bea. "Today is your birthday?"

Seeing no reason to lie, she gave a terse nod.

"Happy returns," he murmured. "I'm afraid I didn't bring you a gift."

*You were my gift.* She felt the warmth of his regard, his eyes taking on the flickering gold of the nearby lantern, and she couldn't suppress a shiver of longing. *That night with you was my one indulgence...and perhaps my greatest mistake.*

"Why would you?" She collected herself. "You didn't know. And even if you did, there'd be no reason for you to go to the trouble."

His brows drew together, and he looked as if he might say something.

She decided it was time to take the bull by the horns. "Fancy, would you mind giving Mr. Murray and me some privacy?"

"Are you certain that's a good idea?" Fancy said, her brow puckered.

"Go on and enjoy the party, dear." Beatrice kept her expression composed. "I need to talk to Mr. Murray alone, and it might as well be now."

With clear reluctance, Fancy left, sending Murray a look of warning on her way out.

"This is quite the lavish abode," Murray commented.

He was looking around, his handsomeness gilded by the lantern light. His outfit struck the perfect chord for the occasion, the blue cutaway and smoke grey waistcoat and trousers elegant yet not too formal, his silver cravat tied in a casual knot. It said a lot about him that he'd chosen not to lord over the other guests with excessive finery.

It reinforced her conclusion that he wasn't a bad sort. She knew she'd reacted rather defensively thus far and had decided to try a different tact. Surely he could be reasoned with; surely if she laid out the reasons why she must turn down his proposals for her hand and her land, he would understand. He would go away...and so would the foolish, painful yearnings he stirred up.

She took a breath. "I'd like to offer you an apology, sir."

His gaze met hers. "What are you apologizing for, exactly?"

"I have been churlish," she admitted. "Our meeting at the masquerade was supposed to be an anonymous, one-night affair. Seeing you afterward was a surprise. A discomfiting one. Nonetheless, that does not excuse my rude behavior and for that I am sorry."

He regarded her with some surprise. His dawning approval caused her toes to curl in her slippers, for what reason she could not fathom.

"I accept your apology," he murmured, "although it is quite unnecessary. I'm the one at fault with my precipitous appearances."

"Are you saying that you're sorry for dropping by uninvited?"

"I didn't say I was sorry. Just that the fault was mine."

At his unrepentant grin, she felt her lips quiver. "Regardless, we have not been going about this like reasonable adults, have we?"

"Not unless your definition of reasonable includes pitching hay for two days." He gave her a rueful look. "It nearly killed me, and my back may never recover."

His honesty startled a laugh from her. "Why did you volunteer in the first place?"

"Because I wanted to impress you with my manly skills," he said mournfully.

It was fun to banter with him, to be playful. She nearly retorted that she and his manhood were quite well acquainted, but she caught herself. Heavens, the man's flirtatious charm was subtle yet irresistible, making it all too easy for a woman to lose her head...and her purpose.

She straightened her shoulders. "Now that we have that out of the way, I see no reason why we cannot address our mutual concerns with respect and civility."

"I agree."

Encouraged, she went on, "There are, obviously, two issues before us. I'll begin with my estate. I will not sell it to you, sir, for any sum."

He didn't counter her statement. Instead he asked in neutral tones, "Why not?"

"Camden Manor is more than a piece of property to me. It is my sanctuary."

"Not only yours." His gaze was shrewd. "Your estate provides a refuge for your tenants as well."

His insight caught her off-guard. Shifting uncomfortably, she said, "My motives aren't altruistic. I need tenants to farm the land. But I'll not discriminate on any basis other than honesty and effort, a willingness to work hard."

"Your farmers hold you in high esteem, Miss Brown. As do I."

His gentle sincerity made her heart somersault.

She cleared her throat. "Then you understand why I will not sell you my land."

"I do. But that doesn't take a compromise off the table."

She frowned. "What sort of compromise?"

"Before we get to that, I want to hear your reply to my proposal of marriage. That, I take, is the second issue before us?"

A part of her wanted to press him on the railway because there was no compromise possible that she could see. At the same time, anxious butterflies swarmed her at the mention of his other offer, and she wanted to get it over with.

"As flattered as I am by your proposal, I cannot accept," she stated.

"Well, you're nothing if not consistent." He quirked a brow, not seeming the least bit offended. "Would you mind telling me why?"

"As I said before, we are not a match physically."

He gave her a lazy, heated look. "That was not the case at the masquerade."

"I had a *mask* on," she said in exasperation. Was the man being purposefully obtuse?

"And it wouldn't have mattered if you didn't." All sensual indolence fled him as he stalked up to her, took her chin in his big hand, making her meet his eyes. "Do you really think a scar could diminish your beauty? Could change a man's attraction to you?"

*Yes.* A fist pounded painfully in her chest. *Because it has before. Because before...it changed everything.*

"What happened, angel?" His voice gentled, as if he could somehow read her mind. "Did someone hurt you?"

Her throat closed. He was a light that threatened to expose her darkest corners. The part of herself that she kept locked away because the pain was too much to bear. She held onto her composure, the shield that had helped her to survive fortune's slings and arrows. She drew the shutters over her heart. Shoved the memories back where they belonged.

She met his gaze evenly. "Neither my scar nor my past is subject to discussion."

He studied her. "You're right. Discussion isn't getting us anywhere, is it?"

Surprised but relieved at his capitulation, she nodded. "It would be more productive if you simply accepted—" Her words ended in a gasp as he moved, quick as lightning, sweeping her feet off the ground.

"What in heavens are you doing?" she demanded breathlessly.

"Being more productive," he told her.

～

Wick's initial strategy for the evening had involved a lot of talking and bargaining, an exploration of alternatives. He'd planned to find common ground with Beatrice and work from there to stake his claim. Certainly, it hadn't included making love to her at her ball. But with an opponent like her, a man had to think on his feet, throw her off balance. The moment he kissed her, quieting the nonsense she was spouting, he knew it was the right plan of action.

With a whimper, she slid her fingers into his hair, pulling him closer, telling him the truth obscured by her words. She wanted him. Nearly as much as he wanted her.

Still kissing her, he carried her to the bench formed at the base of the tree. He settled her in his lap, tilting her head back for deeper access. He delved into her honeyed mouth, his hand fisting in her hair when her tongue boldly sparred with his. She was so full of passion, of life. How could she think, for even a moment, that she ought to spend the rest of her days locked away on this bloody estate?

"By God, you're sweet," he murmured. "I've dreamt of kissing you again."

Her neck arched as his lips found her ear. He tongued the sensitive lobe before giving it a gentle nip. She squirmed against the taut ridge of his erection.

"Murray?" she whispered urgently.

A man could drown in the luminous pools of her eyes. "Call me Wick, angel."

"Wick," she said hesitantly. "If we make love tonight, it changes nothing."

There was no *if* about it. He was going to plow her so hard they might not remember their own names, let alone the conflicts between them.

"Just be with me, Beatrice. Right here, right now." He hooked a finger into the bodice of her ivory, off-the-shoulder gown. He found her nipple, strumming and rolling the straining bud until she began to pant.

Still, she argued, "This is just a meaningless tup. I'm making you no promises. And you can't say you compromised me... Are you listening? What are you...oh, *heavens*..."

As a man capable of managing multiple tasks, he had, in fact, been listening to her while he'd tossed up her skirts. What he'd found made his stones burgeon. Lord Almighty, she was *drenched* for him. As he petted her through the slit in her drawers, her nectar coated his fingers.

"This isn't meaningless," he said thickly. "Passion like this is special—*you* are special. Whatever it takes to convince you that you're the most beautiful woman I've laid eyes on, I will make it happen. In the meantime, I know you have made me no promises. Tonight is just about pleasure—yours and mine. Can you let the rest go, just for now? Can you give yourself over to me, to the pleasure of the moment?"

To convince her, he ran a finger up her dewy cleft, finding the peak of her sensation. He diddled her, circling and pressing her slick bud while watching her expressive face. Passion glazed her eyes, her cheeks flushed with need.

She wetted her kiss-swollen lips. "I can't think..."

"Don't think. Feel, Beatrice. Just let go."

He felt the instant she surrendered, her body relaxing against his. Triumph surging through him, he frigged her harder, faster. He captured her mouth again, plunging his tongue inside, an erotic reminder of the pleasures yet to come. Her thighs stiffened around his hand, wetness gushing into his palm as he swallowed her cries of release.

Once her trembling subsided, he brought her to her feet. He was so hard that he feared ripping through his trousers. He tugged her over to a nearby branch; it was thick, about waist height off the ground. Turning her away from him, he pressed his hand against her spine.

"Bend over for me, angel," he said.

～

In some distant part of her mind, Bea knew this was not a good idea. But the goal was to be in the moment, wasn't it? And it was her birthday after all...

Her body seemed to have a mind of its own, obeying Wick's wicked order. The wide branch supported her torso, but it was a bit high, her toes just touching the ground. Her hands clutched the rough wood as she heard the rustle of her skirts and petticoats being pushed up, felt the balmy night air on her stockinged legs. She twisted her head to look at him, and reality suspended at the dark male hunger on his face.

"I wish you could see yourself," he said in a low, heated voice. "Your lovely bottom arching for my touch, your long legs so pretty in those white silk stockings. Then there's that sweet, shy pussy of yours playing peekaboo through your drawers. All that beauty...the sight of you would make any man hard."

She trembled, arousal reawakening her spent nerves.

"Not that I would allow any man to see what's mine," he added.

Although his deep, possessive tone ruffled her senses, she countered, "I'm not yours."

"In this moment, you're mine to pleasure as I wish. And there are so many things I want to do to this lovely body of yours."

He reached for her drawers, and she heard a widening rip. Before she could protest, he bent his head, his tongue swiping boldly up her exposed cleft. Licking her in this position was so *debauched*.

It made her feel wild, her head falling forward as he skillfully and methodically destroyed her capacity for reason. There was a delicious relief to surrendering her thoughts and worries, to simply letting go. Soon there was only his heated possession, his laving strokes and clever swirls making her pant and grind against his mouth with helpless need.

"Christ, I love eating your pussy." His voice was velvet, dark and seductive, blocking out the rest of the world. There was only him and her and pure, carnal pleasure. "You love being eaten, don't you, angel?"

"Yes." The admission left her as a moan.

"You want to give me more of your sweet pussy?"

"Whatever you want," she gasped.

"That's my lass."

She felt his fingers push inside her, heard his low purr of approval when her muscles clutched on the fullness. He stretched her, driving into her passage, building the pressure.

"You've got two of my fingers, sweeting. Can you take another one?"

He stirred inside her, and she sighed, "Yes."

He added to the fullness. It was too much, not enough.

She arched into his stroke. "Please, I need..."

"Say my name."

"Wick," she breathed.

"You're so bloody beautiful, my Beatrice."

He withdrew, and she was about to protest when she felt him spreading her, his fingers replaced by his *tongue*. She moaned as he licked into her clenching passage, stabbing into her with heated strokes as he manipulated her pearl. She catapulted into bliss, heard his reverent oath as she gushed against his mouth.

"Devil and damn, you undo me," he growled.

Panting, she turned her head to see him rising, unbuttoning the bulging placket of his trousers. His cock was hugely erect, the head weeping seed as he gripped the fleshy shaft. His gaze was trained on her bared sex, and lust sharpened his features, his nostrils flaring as he jerked his fist.

"Stick up that bottom for me," he said in gritty tones. "Show me that pretty pink slit of yours."

His command sizzled through her. What he was doing—pleasuring himself whilst he looked his fill of her pussy—was shamefully titillating. And, at the same time, empowering. The knowledge that he found the mere sight of her arousing made her intimate muscles clench.

"Christ, that's nice." His gaze locked with hers. "Angel, do you want me to come for you?"

"Yes." Her reply was throaty. "Please come for me."

His jaw tautened as he pumped fiercely. With a rumbling groan, he began to spend. His seed blasted from him in milky streams, lashing her bottom and thighs with heat. She inhaled the musk of his pleasure with feminine satisfaction. His gaze hooded, he trailed his fingers through his spend, and she quivered as he rubbed his slick essence into her skin, marking her even more deeply.

"Angel," he said hoarsely, "that was—"

"Bea, are you there? You have to hurry!"

Bea froze at the sound of Fancy's voice. Luckily, Murray was a man of action. He yanked down her skirts and hauled her upright. Fastening his trousers, he put himself at a respectable distance just as her friend burst through the leaves.

Fancy's panicked expression chilled Bea to the core.

"What's the matter?" she asked tersely.

"Fire," the tinker's daughter gasped. "The barn's on fire!"

FINGERPRINTS OF SMOKE SMUDGED THE MORNING SKY. AS BEA stared numbly at the smoldering remains of the barn, she was still unable to comprehend all that had happened in the last few hours. Around her, her tenants were going through the smoking rubble, seeing what could be salvaged, which she didn't think would be much. She counted her blessings, however.

Hay and a barn could be replaced. Lives could not.

Gratitude welled as she saw Wickham approaching her in his long-limbed stride. He was sweaty, smoke-stained, and, in her eyes, he'd never been more handsome. During the crisis, while she'd been occupied with the task of getting water to the barn, he'd taken command of the scene. His natural authority had bolstered the others. He'd organized lines so that the arriving water could be passed in buckets man to man. He'd put others to work beating the flames with blankets.

He, himself, had taken an even greater risk. He'd led a team of men, wet handkerchiefs tied over their faces, into the burning structure to haul out what hay they could. Thanks to their efforts, half the fodder had been saved. His courage and strength had been a beacon in those dark hours.

He arrived at her side, his hazel gaze trained on her face. "You ought to get some rest, angel. You've been up all night. I'll keep an eye on things."

"I'm not leaving. And you've been up all night too." She took out a handkerchief and, reaching up, wiped a streak of ash from his jaw. She didn't miss the surprised warmth in his eyes. "I can't believe what was supposed to be an evening of celebration ended like this. But I suppose we ought to be grateful that the accident didn't cause more damage."

"I don't think this was an accident."

Wick's words jolted her, spreading icy prickles over her skin.

"Why do you say that?" she asked.

He cast a glance around, making sure no one was within earshot, before answering her.

"When I was hauling out the hay, I saw a smashed lamp in the barn," he said in a low voice. "The barn itself reeked of linseed oil."

Linseed oil...an extremely flammable substance. One that had no business being in the barn.

The recognition chilled her. "You think someone did this deliberately?"

He gave a grim nod. "I found something else too—"

"Miss Beatrice, there you be!"

Milton Sheridan's spry figure was headed their way. She and Wick exchanged a look, and she saw in his nod the tacit agreement to continue their troubling discussion later. As she tamped down her rising worries, she saw the tinker had a stranger following behind him, Fancy bringing up the rear. Fancy was regarding the newcomer with an expression akin to awe.

Bea couldn't blame her friend: the dark-haired gentleman had an air of exceptional refinement. His clothes were precisely tailored to his large build and made from fabrics that had the sheen of highest quality. He was handsome in an austere sort of way. Beneath his elegant hat, his grey eyes were assessing Bea with an intensity that might have discomfited another lady.

Bea, however, was used to being stared at. She wasn't wearing a veil, so her scar was in full view. Lifting her chin, she returned his stare and was surprised when his lips tipped up at the corners. It softened his severity and made him look more approachable.

"Miss Beatrice, this gent be looking for you," Milton Sheridan said. The tinker had a long grey beard and bright blue eyes and, as a testament to his profession, everything he wore was either patched or mismatched.

To Bea's surprise, Wick stepped forward. "Devil and damn…is that you, Knight?"

"Murray?" The stranger—Mr. Knight, apparently—looked equally taken aback. But he took Wick's extended hand, the two exchanging a firm handshake. "I haven't seen you since the Garritys' ball."

"Indeed." Wick gave him a measuring look. "What brings you to Staffordshire?"

"I was about to ask the same of you."

Bea blinked when two pairs of male eyes shifted to her. In the next instant, the men were staring at each other again, gazes locked like two bucks who'd just spotted the other on his territory.

Wick crossed his arms over his chest. "What business do you have with Miss Brown?"

"It is not Miss Brown I seek." Knight's quietly menacing tone matched his. "I am here for Lady Beatrice Wodehouse; her brother, the Duke of Hadleigh, gave me this address."

Shock percolated through her. *Benedict? After all this time, what does he want?*

"You've got the wrong lady," Wick said.

With a feeling of foreboding, Beatrice cleared her throat. "I'm afraid he doesn't."

That evening, Bea sat down to supper with her guests. Managing the crisis of the barn had taken most of the day, and she'd only had a quick nap before Wick, Fancy, Mr. Sheridan, and Severin Knight had arrived at eight o'clock. Her lady's maid Lisette had helped her to quickly don a blue taffeta gown, arranging her hair in its usual style, with ringlets over her cheeks. Due to the presence of visitors, Bea had summoned her companion, Lady Tottenham.

Known as Tottie to intimates, the lady had applied to Camden Manor for a position two years ago. While Bea had not been looking for a companion, she'd felt sorry for the elderly woman, who didn't have friends or family to take her in. Thus, Bea had given Tottie a place to stay...and quickly discovered how the lady had earned her name. Tottie had a fondness for her "medicine," which she carried with her in a filigreed flask, and it could make her a bit wobbly on her feet.

Nonetheless, Tottie was a harmless dear who spent most days happily napping in the sun. And she could prove useful on occasions like this evening, when a chaperone was required. Bea noticed, however, that her companion's chair next to Mr. Sheridan was presently empty.

Where had Tottie gone?

The soup course was served. It was Bea's favorite spicy mulligatawny, yet she found she had no appetite. An ominous feeling occupied her stomach.

Who had set fire to her barn? Possible suspects rattled about in her head, her nerves on edge. She'd told the Sheridans about the linseed oil, asking them to be discreet, and she wished she could bring up the topic now. Yet she couldn't discuss the subject in front of Severin Knight; he was a stranger with a nebulous connection to the past she'd left behind. She'd invited him tonight so that she could discover his, and her brother's, intentions.

At present, Knight sat to the right of her, Wick to her left. Sandwiched between the two, Bea couldn't miss the waves of hostile energy that passed between them, and it added to her unease. On the surface, the two were as different as night and day. Mr. Knight was the epitome of restraint and precision, his dark hair cut ruthlessly short, his grey cravat—the exact shade of his eyes—tied in a crisp knot. He was perfectly buttoned up, his broad shoulders rigid beneath his jacket of spotless charcoal superfine.

Wick, on the other hand, looked like some pagan god of sensuality. His thick, wavy mane had that artful, just-risen disarray. The casual folds of his cravat had probably taken his valet hours to perfect. His stark evening wear fit him like a second skin, adding to his sleek, predatory air.

He was making chitchat with Fancy, who was seated on his other side. Fancy had traded her usual plaits for a topknot, and her pretty pink frock was one of her own creations. She blushed at something he said. Then Wick shifted his gaze to Bea, his eyes flaring with possessive gold. Remembering their tempestuous lovemaking beneath the tree, the heat of his virility upon her skin, Bea felt a flutter at her core, accompanied by an inexplicable sense...of panic.

Last night seemed magical and faraway, as if it had taken place in a different world. In the darkness, it had felt safe to surrender, to abandon herself to desire. To experience the pleasure and happiness of those precious moments in Wick's arms.

Yet, as always, reality brought an end to dreams.

While she'd been cavorting with Wick, some bastard had committed arson on her property. It was only luck that no one had been harmed. And now her past had caught up with her in the form of Severin Knight, sent by her brother, whom she hadn't seen in five years. The sequence of events—delight followed by disaster—felt uncannily familiar.

With her accident, she'd been caught unprepared. She'd put

her faith in others, thought that they would help her out of the mire of despair. Instead, they'd abandoned her, each for their own reasons.

Papa...because he couldn't stand to look at her when she was no longer his pretty princess, Croydon for much the same reason. Benedict because the sight of her rankled his pride, filled him with the need to avenge her honor, even when she'd begged him to leave things alone. Arabella and her so-called friends had deserted her because, well, they'd never really liked her anyway. And even her poor mama had left her: the duchess's heart hadn't been able to bear the aftermath of Bea's accident.

Yes, Bea knew what happened when one depended upon others.

As seductive as her games with Wick had been, it was one thing to relinquish control during lovemaking and another to do so in real life. Feeling the longing his possessiveness stirred in her, she knew this game was too dangerous to play. She couldn't trust herself to keep her emotions separate from their sexual encounters. During the fire, she'd started to lean on his strength, to believe that he would stand by her side...to trust him.

Even though she *knew* that he wanted to build a railway across her land. That he was beautiful, and society saw her as a beast. That there could be no happy ending for them.

*I need to regain control—over myself and the situation.* After supper, she would have a clear accounting with Wick...but first she would discover what her brother's emissary wanted.

"Tell me, Mr. Knight," she said with a resolute smile. "How do you know my brother?"

Knight waited until his soup bowl was cleared and replaced by a dish of poached mackerel garnished with fennel and mint.

"His Grace and I have had some business dealings, my lady," he said. "I own silk factories in Spitalfields as well as other manufactories in London and beyond."

That explained his finery. His blue waistcoat had the gleam of first-rate silk.

"Is that how you two gentlemen know one another as well?" She looked from Knight to Wick. "Through business?"

"We've had a few interests in common." Wick's tone was noncommittal. "What is the purpose of your visit here, Knight?"

Even though Bea wanted to know the same thing, she didn't appreciate Wick taking the reins from her. This was her home and her guest. She'd made it quite clear that lovemaking changed nothing between them; why did he think he could speak for her?

*Just one more reason to end things with him,* she thought grimly.

"Whatever the reason," she said, giving him a quelling look, "friends of my brother are always welcome."

"That is kind of you, my lady. I do, indeed, have a particular purpose for this visit, and it is perhaps better explained by this." Removing a note from his coat, Knight presented it to her. "A letter of introduction from His Grace."

Beatrice ran her thumb over her brother's seal, her chest tightening with trepidation...and a pang of nostalgia. Inhaling, she broke the wax and scanned the lines written in Benedict's scrawl:

*Beatrice,*

*I hope enough time has passed for both of us to forgive, if not forget, the words we exchanged at our last meeting. Whatever our differences, we remaining Wodehouses must stick together.*

*As a gesture of my good will, I send you a gift. Although I can think of few men who are worthy of you, Severin Knight has my full endorsement. Not only because of his wealth and influence, both of which are vast, but because he is a decent fellow, and each of you has something the other needs.*

*Hear him out, my dear sister. For the sake of your own happiness and the future of our line.*

*Your brother,*
  *Benedict*


Beatrice raised her eyes to Knight's grey gaze.

"Benedict says I am to hear you out," she said slowly. "What is this about?"

"Perhaps, after supper, I might have a word with you alone..."

"Over my dead body will you be alone with her," Wick said flatly.

Knight raised his brows. A look that clearly said, *That could be arranged.*

"Whatever you have to say," she said, "you may say it here."

"As you wish." Knight adjusted his cufflinks before speaking. "I have recently come into an inheritance. An unexpected one that comes with certain obligations. Obligations that I am not in a position to fulfill on my own. Thus, I am in search of a partner."

Bea frowned. "What sort of a partner?"

"A wife—a duchess, to be precise." Knight's smile had a taut edge. "It turns out my inheritance included a collection of titles. The fifth Duke of Knighton, Marquess of Wroxley, Earl Wroxley, and so forth."

In the time it took Bea to blink, Wick shoved back his chair, rising. Bea had never seen him look so foreboding, his jaw clenched and hazel eyes blazing.

"A word outside, Knight," he said in clipped tones. "*Now.*"

WICK STALKED INTO THE MOONLIT GARDEN. HE DIDN'T BOTHER
to look behind him, knowing that Knight wouldn't back down from
a challenge. He and Knight had crossed paths plenty of times in the
London underworld where they'd both made their fortunes. From
past experience, he knew the other was a worthy competitor
whether it came to business, women, or a game of cards.

Wick respected the bastard, sometimes even liked him.

This was not one of those times.

Knight appeared, Beatrice not far behind him.

"What in heaven's name are you doing, Mr. Murray?" she said,
her brow furrowed.

"Go back to supper," he said evenly. "This is between Knight
and me."

Her lovely eyes flashed. "And this is *my* home. Mr. Knight is
my guest."

She wedged herself in between him and Knight, who remained
impassive.

Wick knew the cunning nature behind that bland mask.
Knight belonged to the elite group of men known as "dukes" of

the underworld—and now it appeared the bastard was a bona fide duke as well. Knight's moniker, the Duke of Silk, alluded to the fact that he controlled the territory of Spitalfields, a center of silk weaving and clothing manufactory.

There was another reason Knight had earned that name: the cull's manner was smoother than the expensive fabric his weavers produced. He was well known for his exploits with the fair sex. Wick didn't want him anywhere near Bea.

Much less *proposing* to her.

"Not for long," Wick said grimly. "His Grace will be leaving."

Knight arched a dark brow. "Will I?"

"Find yourself another duchess," Wick bit out. "Beatrice is spoken for."

"Since when?" Beatrice said.

"Since..."

Too late, Wick realized that while she was spoken for in his head, she hadn't yet agreed in reality. But, devil take it, the writing was on the wall. He'd taken her virginity, and she was a genteel lady—the sister of a *duke*, apparently. They'd shared pleasure not once, but twice, their lovemaking teaching him, a seasoned rake, new things about desire.

Marriage wasn't a possibility: it was a forgone *conclusion*.

He was aware of Knight watching on with an unreadable expression. As much as Wick wanted to spell out to the bastard precisely why Beatrice belonged to him, he could not. He would never dishonor her in that fashion.

"Precisely. No man has any claim on me," Beatrice stated.

He couldn't let that stand. "Perhaps our negotiations haven't been completed, but I thought last night's discussion was rather *productive*, wasn't it?"

*Three orgasms* productive for her. And marking her lovely arse with his seed had been one of the most intensely erotic experiences of his life. Just the thought seared his groin with heat.

Her cheeks turned rosy, but she did not back down. "No promises were made. I refuse to be an obligation."

Bloody hell, this again? "Why the *devil* do you persist—"

"Ahem."

They both swung their glances to Knight, who'd cleared his throat rather pointedly.

"Perhaps I should leave the two of you to iron out certain details?"

"Leaving would be an excellent idea," Wick growled.

"I shall take myself back to the inn." Knight bowed. "May I look forward to the pleasure of a future audience, my lady?"

"I should like that," Beatrice said determinedly. "In point of fact, as you are a friend of the family, you must stay at the manor."

"Now wait just one minute—" Wick thundered.

"You'll be far more comfortable here than at the Pig & Whistle," Bea cut him off. "With Lady Tottenham in residence, everything will be quite circumspect."

*Circumspect my arse*, Wick fumed. Her bloody chaperone had *literally* drunk herself under the table. He was certain Lady Tottie was still there, dozing peacefully on the Aubusson.

"Indeed." Knight's brows lifted. "Thank you for the invitation, my lady. If you'll excuse me, I'll bid you adieu for now and return tomorrow morning with my things."

"Good night, Your Grace," Bea said.

Knight bowed, casting a smug look at Wick as he strode off.

Holding onto his temper by his fingernails, Wick bit out, "What the devil are you doing?"

She faced him. "Being hospitable to my brother's friend."

"Are you trying to make me jealous?" *Because it's bloody working.*

"I'm not trying to make you anything," she said flatly. "I was going to have this conversation with you later, but since we are here, we might as well have it now."

If her tone wasn't enough to penetrate his rage, then her expression would have been. Gone was the Beatrice of last night, whose face had glowed with the joy of feminine surrender. Gone was the Beatrice of this morning, who'd let him help her, who'd wiped ash off his jaw with what had felt like *wifely* tenderness. Gone even was the Beatrice who verbally sparred with him, their bantering exchanges full of promise and heat.

Masked in cold silver moonlight, the woman before him might have been a stranger. The recognition was enough to take the edge off his haze of anger. Anger, he realized now, that had prevented him from thinking clearly.

He was no longer a hot-headed rake. He was a businessman known for his ability to identify his opponent's motivations and weaknesses, to adjust his strategy to attain winning results. Why, then, was he charging like a maddened bull at Beatrice when that only made her dig her heels in deeper? He'd already discovered better ways of negotiating with her.

In the past few days, he'd seen that she was a fair and practical woman. When he'd gone about things in a way that respected her terms, the results had been rewarding. She'd let him make love to her last night, seemed appreciative when he'd helped her to fight the fire. He *could* win her trust...but he had to go about it the right way.

With her, it was about give and take. Knowing when to push and when to pull back.

Not only was Wick up to the challenge, he *craved* it.

"Just because we made love does not give you the right to make decisions for me," she continued in cold, remote tones. "Tonight just proves an affair is not possible between us. I will not give up my independence. I will not let another man control my future or my happiness ever again. Marriage is out of the question, and whatever we had...it ends now."

Another man might have heard that Siberian speech and high-tailed out of there for fear of catching frostbite. Yet now that Wick had tamed his jealousy, his brain was working in full force.

What most people didn't understand was that the key to negotiating wasn't talking.

It was listening.

And what he heard from Beatrice...was pain.

"What other man?" he asked quietly.

She blinked. "Pardon?"

"You said you wouldn't let *another* man control you again. Who did it before?"

Her throat worked. "I don't...it's none of your—"

"Last night, you were hotter than fire in my arms. Now you're cold as ice. I didn't take you for a woman who played games," he said deliberately.

He knew his strategy to appeal to her sense of fairness succeeded when her shoulders stiffened in their frame of blue taffeta.

"I'm not playing games. It's just that I've had a chance to think about us—"

"And you're comparing me to some man in your past. Allow me the courtesy of knowing who my rival is."

"He's *not* your rival." Her gaze darted; she had a hunted look.

Instinct told him not to back down. "Who is he?"

"If you must know, I was once engaged. After my accident,"— her voice wavered, but she kept her chin up—"the engagement ended."

And Wick remembered last night when he'd asked her if she really believed a scar could change a man's attraction to her. She *did* believe it...because of some bloody fool.

"Who ended it?" he asked.

"I did. But only after..." She bit her lip. "After I overheard him and my best friend at the time. The two of them were talking in the garden about how I'd become...Lady Beastly."

~

Bea had told one person about the scene with Croydon and Arabella. Her brother's reaction had guaranteed that she would never repeat that mistake. She hadn't even confided in Fancy about what had happened: it was too humiliating.

But Wickham had a way of seeing through her masks. Of tearing them away.

Seeing the harsh set of his features in the moonlight, she felt the raw pain of a scab being ripped off. Did he finally see her as others did? Was he realizing that he, Prince Charming, had no business being with Lady Beastly?

She braced herself for his response.

"Are you in love with him?" he bit out.

It took her a moment to comprehend what he was asking. *That* was why he looked angry? Because he thought she might be carrying the torch for Croydon?

"No," she blurted. "That is, I fancied myself in love with him at one time. But hearing what he and Ara—my friend said in the garden cured me of that foolishness."

"Good," Wick said gruffly. "The spineless cad doesn't deserve your love. I would call him out—if you wanted me to."

*He would call Croydon out for me? More importantly, he would give me the choice?*

Warmth flooded her chest, thawing the icy dread.

"But perhaps your papa already had his satisfaction?" he asked.

"No." Seeing his scowl she said hastily, "I led Papa to believe that breaking off the engagement was my choice. I didn't tell anyone at the time...it was too mortifying."

She *had* told Benedict about it, but that had been years later. Too late to change anything, to do anything except stir up bitterness and anger. To cause the chasm that separated them to this day.

"*You* have naught to be embarrassed about. Your ex-fiancé and so-called friend are the ones who deserve to be shamed for their despicable behavior." Wick curled a finger beneath her chin, making her look into his steady gaze. "I wish you hadn't felt like you had to keep their ugly secret, but I am honored that you told me."

Her throat thickened. No one had seen her so clearly before. No man had ever just listened, without trying to fix or change her. She didn't know how to react to the novel feeling: of being exposed yet protected at the same time.

Then his hand moved from her chin to her right cheek. When his thumb brushed the top of her scar, she froze. A part of her wanted to pull away, to dissolve into the darkness of the garden. Another part of her waited, suspended in viscous longing.

"How did this happen?" he asked softly.

His thumb traced the path of her scar. His touch was so casual and gentle that heat pressed behind her eyes. And the past, long buried, surfaced.

"I was riding...in Hyde Park," she said haltingly. "There was a man. He was beating a boy, a street urchin whom he said had stolen his purse. The boy ran, and the man went after him with a whip. I tried to stop him. But he frightened Star, my mare, and I was thrown. Star reared again, and her hoof came down..."

Her throat clenched, that moment swamping her, that moment she'd thought would be her last.

"The physician said I was lucky. I could have been trampled to death," she finished hollowly.

In the months that followed, she'd questioned if she *had* been lucky. If the alternative wouldn't have been better than the slow death of having her life, her family, and herself fall apart in small, brittle pieces.

"My brave angel, look at me." He waited until her eyes returned to his. "You *were* lucky."

"Lucky to be Lady Beastly?" She couldn't keep the bitterness from her tone.

"Lucky to be alive. To survive and become the woman you are today." The warmth in his eyes was as mesmerizing as his touch, tracing upward now along her knitted flesh. "This scar is a part of you. Because of that, it is beautiful. Because beautiful, Lady Beatrice, is all you could ever be."

Tears spilled. She could no longer hold them back. When he took out a handkerchief, blotting away the dampness on her cheeks, hope broke free, its wings beating inside her heart.

"I acted like a troglodyte earlier," he commented. "I'm not going to apologize for it."

"Why not?" she asked with a sniffle.

"Because you ought to know the man who's courting you." He folded the square of linen, returning it to his pocket. "I'm a gentleman when it comes to most things, but I will not tolerate another man trying to poach what's mine."

His possessiveness ought to have annoyed her. She tried to summon up some sort of indignation but gave up when she realized the truth: what she truly felt was...wanted.

"You're courting me?" she blurted.

"Since you won't accept my offer of marriage, that seems like the next best option," he said pragmatically. "Perhaps it is for the best. This way, we can get to know one another better, and you can reach the inevitable conclusion in your own time."

She drew her brows together. "What inevitable conclusion?"

"That we, angel, are meant to be together."

She couldn't look away from the mesmerizing conviction in his eyes. When a man looked at a woman like that, it could turn her brain to mush. But she was made of sterner stuff.

"What about your railway and my land?"

"We'll come to a compromise."

"What if we can't?"

"We will," he said firmly. "With your permission, I'd like to send for my surveyor, Mr. Norton. He'll evaluate your land and figure out a way to run the railway without disturbing the farms."

"And if he cannot find a way?" she persisted.

"Then you'll keep your land and I'll figure out another plan."

He toyed with a ringlet at her temple, his tone earnest. "There are legal protections you can take to prevent your land from becoming mine when we marry. I'm willing to sign whatever you want. I will not take your estate from you, Beatrice. If you decide to participate in the railway venture, it will be your choice."

He brushed his lips against hers, softly, sweetly. A kiss of tender persuasion.

"Will you give me the honor of courting you, my lady?" he asked with husky formality.

How could she deny him...or the longing in her heart? He was offering her the impossible: her old dreams rebuilt into a new reality. One based on passion, possibility, and choice. Besides, agreeing to be courted wasn't the same thing as agreeing to marriage. If she and Wick discovered that they were not compatible, or if circumstances changed, then they could call things off.

The promise of Wick—of what he was offering—was too tempting to resist.

"Yes," she whispered.

"Good." He brushed his lips across her forehead. "Then invite me to stay with you."

She blinked. "You want to stay here, at the manor?"

"There's no way in hell Knight is staying under your roof when I'm not," he said flatly. "You have a chaperone. One who literally drinks herself under the table, but a chaperone nonetheless."

*So that's where Tottie went,* she mused.

"More importantly, there's danger afoot, and I want to stay close to you."

The reminder of the barn fire made her swallow. "You really believe it was arson?"

His nod was stark. "I didn't get to show this to you earlier, but in addition to the broken lamp and linseed oil, I found this."

He withdrew something from his jacket pocket, handing it to her.

"A pocket watch?" she said, her brows knitting.

The timepiece was made of gold and heavy in her palm. The cover had beaded edges and an ornate pattern featuring swirls that looked like flames. At the center of the cover was a crest, inscribed with the letters *H. C.*

"Those could be initials. Anyone you know?" Wick asked.

"Good heavens." Her eyes widened. "The squire who owns the neighboring land—his name is Horace Crombie."

She continued examining the instrument. Opening the cover, she examined the dial face, the hands arrested at a quarter to twelve. The time the watch had been dropped? The face didn't bear the usual inscription with the watchmaker's name and address; it said only "London, England." To the left of "London" was a tiny symbol that resembled two *U*'s, one nestled inside the other. Turning the piece over, she found the back cover contained the same design as the front, with no stamps or maker's marks to indicate the object's origin.

"Does this Crombie have an axe to grind with you?" Wick said bluntly.

"Aye, the old bastard does," Mr. Sheridan's voice cut in. "And 'e's not the only one."

The tinker ventured into the garden, accompanied by Fancy.

"I 'ope we're not, um, interrupting," Fancy said tentatively. "Mr. Knight left, and we wanted to check on things."

"Everything is fine," Bea assured her. "Mr. Murray and I are discussing the barn fire. He found a clue that might lead us to the arsonist."

Frowning, Wick turned to Mr. Sheridan. "Who else would want to wish Lady Beatrice harm?"

"As to that, sir,"—the tinker lifted his brows—"where be you wantin' to start?"

## 13

THE NEXT AFTERNOON, WICK ESCORTED BEATRICE TO SQUIRE Crombie's estate.

"Let me take the lead today, angel," he said.

"Horace Crombie is my problem," she replied from the other side of the carriage. "I have my ways of dealing with men like him."

"That's precisely my concern."

He was sure she intended to look business-like in her navy carriage dress, the belted pelisse and flaring skirts trimmed with military-style gold braiding. Her bonnet had strings of blue ribbon, its dark veil currently pinned up. Her pale blonde hair was parted in the middle, ringlets dangling over her cheeks, and her accessories were simple pearls at her ears and gloves of cream kid.

Knowing Bea, she had no idea that the severity of her ensemble highlighted her svelte femininity, the delicacy of her strength. When a man looked at her, he wouldn't be thinking about sitting across a desk from her; he'd be fantasizing about bending her over said desk and discovering the fire beneath that tantalizingly cool composure...

Her eyebrows winged. "You don't think I can manage the squire?"

"Manage? Yes. With diplomacy...?" He gave her a significant look.

Over dessert last evening, Beatrice had shown him the anonymous threatening note she'd received and, with the help of the Sheridans, she'd compiled a list of suspects for the arson. As the list had grown, so had the knot in Wick's gut.

Christ Almighty, the lady was a magnet for trouble.

She'd had a series of squabbles with Crombie, who apparently held a grudge against her for outbidding him on Camden Manor, which he'd wanted to annex to his own estate. Their most recent skirmish had occurred last month. According to Bea, a fence had come down between their properties, and when she'd gone to fix it, she'd found that the squire had gotten there first. His workers, she'd claimed indignantly, had been planting the poles an extra six feet past her property line. When the workers had refused to desist, she'd waited until nighttime to send her own men out.

In the morning, Squire Crombie had found a pile of fencing on his doorstep. She'd had her own fence put in; nailed upon it was a map of her property lines. Her butler, Gentleman Henderson, had been posted there as well, shotgun in hand, to dissuade the squire from retaliation.

Crombie was not Bea's only enemy. The Reverend Mr. Henry Wright, the village rector, held a prejudice against the tenants to whom Bea offered safe harbor and preached fire and brimstone about her at his weekly sermons, which she'd ceased to attend. Randall Perkins, the former tenant who'd been caught assaulting her maid Lisette, was also a possible culprit. Perkins had been laying low since then, although there'd been sightings of him in the nearby villages. Apparently, he had a birthmark, the port-wine stain on the left side of his face making him rather conspicuous.

*Then* there were the factory owners up north.

When Wick had heard that the Potteries Coalition had

harassed Beatrice, he'd felt a surge of fury. The leader, Thomas McGillivray, and the other bastards were key investors in GLNR's current scheme...and a large part of the reason Wick had come to Staffordshire incognito. The Coalition had grown impatient with the delay in laying track, and Wick hadn't wanted them breathing down his neck while he did his job.

He would not, however, tolerate the damned bastards ganging up against Beatrice. Despite her protest, he'd told her that he would take care of the factory owners since he had a business relationship with them. This morning, he'd sent a note off to McGillivray, whose offices were in Stoke-Upon-Trent, to set up a meeting.

As if on cue, Beatrice reminded him, "I'm letting you take the lead with the factory owners."

He wondered if she'd read his mind. Then again, she'd probably been saving that argument to use as leverage. In her shoes, he would have done the same thing.

Devil and damn, if he didn't enjoy the way she kept him on his toes. He admired her tenacity: the strength of her will, her desire to do the right thing. Discovering that she'd received her scar while rescuing a boy from abuse made her all the more beautiful in his eyes. The fact that she'd trusted him with the painful memory felt like a gift. It was a sign that they were making progress.

That didn't mean he'd back down, however. Nor did he think that she wished him to. Their verbal sparring was their own special way of flirting.

"As I caused that particular problem," he said mildly, "it's only fair that I deal with it."

"Since Crombie despises me for buying the estate he wanted, this is my problem to contend with," she countered. "Give and take, Murray. This is how this relationship is going to work."

She looked so adorably pleased with herself that he couldn't resist. Twitching the curtains together, he snatched her from her seat and onto his lap, quelling her squeal of protest with his kiss. He couldn't afford to let things get too heated—the journey to Crombie's wasn't long—but this being Beatrice and him, tongues got involved. Before he knew it, he had his hand up her skirts, and she was moaning against his lips.

"Damn, lass," he said hoarsely. "You're wet for me already."

"I can't help it." Her cheeks flushed, she squirmed as he fingered her dewy petals. "Especially when you do that. And even more so if you were to go a bit higher..."

Her brazen demand made him grin. And his cock strain against his trousers.

"I'd like nothing more than to diddle your pearl until you come for me," he murmured. "But we're nearly there."

"Why did you start this if we couldn't finish?"

It was the closest to a pout that he'd seen from her, and he loved it.

He chucked her beneath her chin before settling her back on her side. "Because I couldn't resist you, Madam Practical. And also because I wanted you to have a preview of what I'll be giving you tonight."

"Tonight?" In one of her quicksilver changes, she transformed from the confident lady of the manor to an endearingly novice lover. Her eyes soft and voice even softer, she asked, "Are you planning to visit me in...my bedchamber?"

He knew a rendezvous wasn't proper. Yet she was going to be his wife sooner or later, he rationalized. Making love to her might actually speed up the courtship, and he wasn't above using pleasure to seal this particular deal.

The choice, however, would be up to her.

"If you'd rather observe proprieties," he began.

"There's a servants' passageway that connects our chambers. Use that instead of the main hallway so you won't be seen."

*Well, that's that.* His lips twitched.

"An excellent plan." Being granted entrée into his lady's most intimate realm wasn't helping matters down south, however; he had to get himself under control or he'd bust a seam before they reached the squire's house. To distract himself, he said, "Speaking of plans, what are yours for Crombie?"

"My approach will be simple." The softness left her eyes, her features honed with determination. "I'm going to make him admit that he's a sniveling, vindictive snake-in-the grass."

"Ah," Wick said. "This is going to go well."

Deciding to use surprise to their advantage, Beatrice hadn't sent word ahead of their visit. She'd timed their arrival to coincide with the end of luncheon. The squire's belly would be full, his mind soft and drifting toward midday sleepiness...the perfect time to corner him.

Her and Wick's plan was to visit the suspects one by one—with the exception of Randall Perkins, whom they would have to find first—and interrogate them. She'd conceded the Potteries Coalition to Wick since she suspected he would, indeed, have more leverage with them. The fact that he was willing to help her against his own interests amazed her. Yet it wasn't in her nature to depend upon others, and she was determined to do her part with the remaining suspects.

She hadn't expected to find the squire with company. Or to kill two birds with one stone. For as she and Wick were led into Crombie's study, the pale-haired man who rose along with the squire was none other than Reverend Henry Wright.

The thought leapt like a flame. *What nefariousness are the two cooking up together?*

The two men were opposites in appearance, the squire being corpulent and balding whereas the rector was tall, with long, thin limbs that reminded Bea of a spider. The latter had a full head of snowy hair that, in combination with his sharp features and icy blue eyes, gave him a chilling air. His gaze skimmed over Bea's scarred cheek, his lips curling with disdain. She kept her composure, even as embers of anger and humiliation burned beneath her breastbone.

*He hates me, but would that be enough for him to set fire to my property?*

Suddenly, Wright's expression smoothed, and she realized that Wick had come to stand at her back. The charming Adonis was gone; in his place was a fierce Scotsman whose lethal stare and bunching muscles signaled that the enemy had better beware.

As much as she valued her independence, she couldn't deny that she liked Wick's protective streak. She'd never had a man who'd stood by her before. Never known how special that could make a woman feel, even if she was fully capable of taking care of herself.

Crombie waddled forward, his lips spreading in an unctuous smile that didn't hide the calculating look in his eyes. "What a surprise to see you, Miss Brown. And your guest...Mr. Murray, was it?"

Earlier, she and Wick had decided that there was no longer any point in hiding his true identity. Once he met with the factory owners, gossip was bound to spread like wildfire about the railway. It was better to try to control the information that was disseminated: Bea planned to tell her tenants that Wick was a representative of GLNR who was here to explore the possibility of coexistence between a railway and the farms. She would reassure them of her intent to prioritize the farms over all other concerns.

For now, she introduced the squire and the reverend to Wick.

"Your reputation precedes you, sir," Crombie said. "Partner in that railway company, aren't you? The one in all the papers, wot, that has the public rioting to get shares?"

"Great London National Railway has enjoyed some success," Wick said easily.

"What brings you to Staffordshire?" the squire demanded. "Business?"

"In part." Wick did not elaborate.

Crombie grunted, waving them toward his desk. "Why don't you have a seat and tell me what brings you here."

They all went toward the chairs, with the exception of Reverend Wright.

"As my expertise is in spiritual matters and not the material," he said with frigid hauteur, "my presence will add nothing to the discussion. I shall see myself out. Good day."

He left, blanketing the study in awkward silence.

"I didn't realize you and the rector were friends," Beatrice said as she and Wick seated themselves across from the squire.

"Wouldn't say we're friends. The reverend had some business he wanted to consult me on. Given my magisterial role."

Crombie mopped his face with a handkerchief. If she didn't know the man, she might have taken his sweatiness as a sign of nerves, but the truth was he was usually red-faced and perspiring, looking on the verge of an apoplectic fit.

"What sort of business?" she asked.

"It was, ahem, confidential. None of your business, wot."

The squire wetted his thick lips, his gaze shifting between her and Wick. Wick was being good to his word and letting her take the lead. Leaning back in his chair, a boot propped over one knee, he was observing the unfolding events with a faint curve to his lips.

Crombie started up again. "Now what was it you wanted to see me about, Miss Brown? If it's about that fence—"

"Actually, it's about my barn." She didn't have time for shilly-shallying. "It caught fire the night before last."

"Ah, yes. I did hear about that." Was she imagining the smugness in Crombie's tone? "Unfortunate business, I'm sure, but accidents do happen. I fail to see why you've come to me about it."

"Because it wasn't an accident."

His veiny jowls reddened. "If you're accusing me, sirrah——"

"I make no accusations, merely observations." Opening her reticule, she withdrew the pocket watch and placed it on his blotter.

Crombie's brow furrowed. "Why are you showing me a pocket watch?"

His bafflement seemed genuine. *Dash it.*

"It isn't yours?" she prodded. "It bears your initials on the cover."

He squinted at the front cover, then picked up the watch. "Demme, if it don't. But it isn't mine. Although if you know where to find a fine timepiece like this, I wouldn't mind commissioning one of my own. The one the old squire gave me has seen better days."

Fishing around in his waistcoat, he retrieved a pocket watch. Scratched and dented, it was indeed a poor relation to the one Wick had found.

"I'm afraid I do not know the watchmaker," Bea said tightly.

"Too bad. The workmanship is top-notch, wot." Crombie was still examining the watch, a covetous gleam in his eyes.

Bea held out her hand. "I'll have it back, if you please."

"Still don't see what the watch has to do with anything." Reaching across the desk, he slapped it into her palm. "Now back to your slanderous remark——"

"Pardon, Crombie. Did you injure your arm recently?"

The query came from Wick. He was looking at Crombie's wrist. When the squire had reached forward, his jacket sleeve had caught, revealing the cuff of his shirt...and the bandage poking out beneath.

*An injury.* Suspicion bled through Bea. *From setting the fire?*

Hastily, the squire tugged the sleeve of his jacket back in place.

"It's a scratch. Cut myself in the kennels when I was checking up on the hounds." He rose, wheezing at the sudden movement. "Now if there's nothing else, I'm a busy man."

Since Bea had no proof of his wrongdoing and no further questions, she got to her feet as well.

She inclined her head. "I appreciate your time, squire."

"Then next time," Crombie said with a harrumph, "don't waste it."

## 14

"SHALL I STYLE YOUR HAIR AS USUAL, MY LADY?" LISETTE asked.

It was later that evening. After returning from Crombie's, Bea had wanted to strategize the next steps for finding the arsonist, but Wick had insisted that she go up for a nap first. When she'd protested that she wasn't tired, he'd chucked her on the chin and said that *he* was.

They'd gone to their separate chambers and, apparently, the events of the past two days had affected Bea more than she realized. She'd slept so soundly that Lisette had had to rouse her to dress for the supper that she was hosting for her two guests and the Sheridans, who would be arriving shortly.

Now she was seated at her rosewood dressing table. Typically, she would have told her lady's maid to do the usual topknot with side ringlets partially covering her cheeks. Yet tonight she had the urge to see if she might try something...different. For obvious reasons, she did not have mirrors mounted on her walls; why torment herself, after all?

"Lisette, do you have a hand-held looking glass?" she asked.

The other's blue eyes widened in surprise. "*Mais oui.*"

"Fetch it, please."

When the dark-haired maid returned, she handed Bea the requested object. Inhaling deeply, Bea held up the oval mirror and looked at herself. She hadn't done so for a long time. After her injury, her papa had been determined to "fix" the damage. He wouldn't let her hide in the country, insisting that she stay in London to be treated by the best physicians. As part of the quacks' "treatments"—she shuddered, thinking of the caustic creams and ointments, poultices made of everything from duck fat to sand to ground-up parts of exotic beasts—she'd been forced to assess herself in the mirror daily and report any changes to the angry red mark.

She'd known, far before her father had, that her scar was here to stay. She'd resented having to put herself through disappointment again and again. Even worse was the guilt of knowing that her ugliness had ultimately destroyed her parents' marriage. After months of futilely trying to fix his broken daughter, Papa had given up. He'd stayed away from the house more and more; around a year after her accident, he'd been found dead...in his mistress's bed.

Mama hadn't survived much longer, the pain of her broken heart too much to bear. Among her last words, she'd whispered to Bea, *Don't be foolish like me, my daughter. Don't entrust your happiness to another.*

After the loss of her parents, Bea had used a portion of her inheritance to purchase Camden Manor. She'd wanted nothing more to do with her old life—or her scarred face that had wrecked so many lives. She'd focused on what mattered: what she could accomplish, what she could control.

Now, as she looked at the reflection she typically avoided, she tried to see herself impartially, the way a stranger might. It wasn't difficult: she *was* somewhat alien to herself after all this time. As she perused her own image, she felt a curious sensation in her chest. It felt like that first ray at dawn, breaking through the darkness, illuminating a thought that became a revelation.

*I'm not...beastly?*

The scar was there. A ridge of knitted flesh that started at the top of her right cheekbone, curving up before going downward, stopping a few inches shy of her mouth. It was visible, would draw attention, and yet...it was also somehow *less* than the scar of her memory.

Less red. Less raised. Less glaring.

The mark had flattened, she saw objectively, time weaving it into the fabric of her skin. Her cheek would never be perfect again. But maybe beauty wasn't just about perfection?

Wick's life-altering words washed through her. *Your scar is a part of you. Because of that, it is beautiful. Because beautiful, Lady Beatrice, is all you could ever be.*

Through his eyes, she saw herself as desired and special...and *that* was true beauty.

The scar had defined her, but it had never been all that she was. She'd always known that; Wick had helped her to *feel* it. And she wanted her outside to match what she was feeling on the inside. Now that she was being courted by the most attractive man she'd ever met, was it wrong to want to look her best?

She realized that Lisette was standing by, awaiting her instruction. When the maid had applied for a position several months ago, Bea had hired her on the spot, no questions asked. Not only because she'd liked the way Lisette had arranged her hair, but because of the fresh bruise on the maid's cheek and the fear etched on the other's delicate features. As the weeks passed, Lisette's confidence had seemed to blossom—until that bastard Randall Perkins had tried to assault her.

Bea thanked God that Gentleman Henderson had found the two in the stables. A weeping Lisette had told Bea that the butler had arrived and dispatched Perkins before anything had happened. Bea was grateful that the maid hadn't been harmed and that the incident hadn't caused Lisette to retreat into her former shell.

Courage took many forms, one of them being the ability to carry on despite one's past. To not allow old fears to become a prison...and to remain open to new possibilities.

Bea exhaled. "Perhaps we could try something different? A coiffure that is more *au courant*, that might accentuate my favorable features?"

"*Oui*, my lady," Lisette said. "I know a style that has been made fashionable by the Queen herself, if you'd care to try it."

Bea smiled. "Let's give it a go, shall we?"

～

Supper went off without a hitch.

Bea had been worried about Wick and Severin Knight—the Duke of Knighton rather—but the two had been on their best behavior. Both had their own brand of charm, and she could scarcely credit that, after years of avoiding society, she had not one, but two such charismatic gentlemen at her table. They made easy conversation with Mr. Sheridan and Fancy, asking questions about the tinkering life.

Having heard Mr. Sheridan's colorful tales before, Bea sipped her wine and enjoyed the camaraderie. She noticed that Fancy seemed to be enjoying the evening as well. The latter had overcome her natural shyness enough to carry on a conversation with Knighton.

After supper, Bea decided to forgo the formality of separating the sexes, announcing that the gentlemen could have their cigars and brandy in the drawing room. Mr. Sheridan took out his fiddle, and Fancy accompanied him on the piano, the two giving a rousing performance that ranged from country dances to a stirring Irish ballad.

Afterward, Knighton invited Bea to take a turn with him

around the drawing room. Since she wanted an opportunity to speak privately with her guest, she agreed.

"May I compliment you on your looks, Lady Beatrice?" the duke asked.

She smiled. "Thank you, Your Grace. I thought I'd try a new style."

Lisette had arranged her hair so that it no longer covered her face. Parted in the middle, the front of her hair was braided, then looped over her ears. The rest was arranged in a coronet and augmented with fresh flowers from the garden. Bea had donned a lilac gown that Fancy had made for her, but that she'd never had occasion to wear. The dress bared her shoulders, nipping in at her waist before cascading in frothy skirts trimmed with blond lace.

Bea was rather pleased with the results, a feeling deepened by Wick's smoldering look of appreciation when she'd descended the stairs.

"You are irresistible, angel," he'd murmured. "Prepare to be ravished later on tonight."

She wished she could be alone with him right now. Although he was seated beside Fancy playing a duet, he was keeping a close watch on her and Knighton, his gaze unmistakably proprietary. In the interest of peace, she'd better complete her business with His Grace posthaste.

She'd had her reason for inviting Knighton to stay, and it wasn't, as Wick had suggested, to make her lover jealous. Or, rather, that hadn't been the sole reason. She wanted to learn more about the duke's connection to Benedict. Knowing her brother, she had a bad feeling that trouble was brewing.

"I hope you are finding your stay comfortable, Your Grace," she said.

"Indeed. You are all that is hospitable, my lady."

"Any friend of my brother's is a friend of mine. Tell me, how do you know him?"

"As I mentioned, Hadleigh and I had some business together."

"Does the business involve you owing my brother money?" she asked bluntly.

Knighton frowned. "No. Why would you think that?"

"Because I wouldn't put it past Hadleigh to buy me a husband."

Her brother had always been wild. Her accident and their papa's early death had given him power and wealth before he was ready for such responsibility. Benedict's marriage soon thereafter had exacerbated the worst of his qualities, fanning the flames of his arrogance and pride. He'd been hell-bent on avenging Beatrice's honor...even when she'd begged him not to.

When she'd tried to stop him, they'd fought so badly that now, five years later, she was getting information about her brother from a virtual stranger.

"That is an insult to him and to me." Knighton's eyes turned the chilly grey of London fog.

"Then what is the nature of your association with Benedict?" she persisted.

"I did him a favor once. In return, I asked him for an introduction," he said in even tones. "No other promises were made."

They rounded a corner, and she asked, "Why would you want to meet me, Your Grace? Surely you could find yourself a suitable duchess in London? One without my unusual history?"

"Yours is not the only unusual history, my lady."

"Oh?"

"My recent inheritance of this duchy came as a surprise to me and the rest of Society. Although I am the legitimate issue of the prior duke, my mama, for reasons of her own, kept that a secret from me. I never knew that I was the heir of a duke until my father summoned me to his deathbed." Ghosts flitted through Knighton's eyes. "The title is now mine, and it comes with certain responsibilities that I am ill-equipped to handle."

As he didn't strike her as a man who'd be ill-equipped for anything, she canted her head. "Those being?"

"I have four younger half-siblings, all of them bastards."

Her eyes widened at his concise reply. "I see."

"While my father provided for them materially, he did not instruct them in the proper way of living. They are...unruly," Knighton said tonelessly. "Be that as it may, they are now my responsibility, and I plan to launch them into the *ton*. For that, I need help."

What he needed was a miracle. "Why do you think *I* could help you?"

"You are a duke's daughter with an impeccable pedigree. You are mature, seasoned, and you've survived the worst of Society." He reviewed her qualities the way one might when selecting a broodmare. "Meeting you in person confirms my assessment of you."

"What is your assessment, precisely?"

"You have the strength and spirit that I am looking for in my duchess, Lady Beatrice. To be frank, I believe you will not wilt in the heat of Society's disapproval of my half-siblings, nor will you back down from the challenge of keeping them in check. Moreover, you possess the maturity to understand the sort of marriage I'm proposing."

She raised her brows.

"A partnership," Knighton clarified. "One unclouded by sentiment, based rather on respect and shared goals."

It was strange how, not long ago, such an arrangement might have appealed to her. But not now. Not after Wick.

He was, she noted, no longer at the piano with Fancy. He stood with an arm resting on the mantel, a glass of whisky in hand. His casual posture belied his brooding expression. She couldn't blame him; she'd feel the same way if he was having an intimate *tête-à-tête* with a female who had intentions for him.

To Knighton, she said, "You do me an honor with your offer, Your Grace, but I cannot accept."

"May I ask why?"

*Because the only man I'd consider marrying is Wick.*

"When it comes to marriage, I am looking for more than mutual respect," she said.

Knighton surprised her by taking her hand. "It is not only respect I offer, my lady. I am open to other delights of marriage,"—he brushed his lips over the back of her hand with startling warmth—"which, I assure you, can be thoroughly enjoyed without complicating emotions."

Wasn't it strange that this precise idea—that tupping could be enjoyed without sentiment—had led her to the masquerade? And that fate had seen fit to pair her with Wick, the one man who could make her realize the truth?

Emotionless coupling could indeed be pleasurable. But *intimate* coupling was far better.

"Lady Beatrice, I believe it is my turn to escort you around the room?"

Wick's low, lethal tones broke her reverie. He'd approached, looking none too pleased.

She pulled her hand from Knighton's grasp.

"Yes, of course," she said, flustered. "If you'll excuse me, Your Grace."

Knighton inclined his head, a flicker of amusement in his grey eyes. "I look forward to continuing our conversation at a later time, my lady."

## ❧ 15 ❧

NEARING MIDNIGHT, WICK OPENED THE PANEL FROM THE servants' hallway and entered Beatrice's bedchamber. He saw that his lover's private domain was as well-appointed as the rest of her home. Airy and high-ceilinged, the room had celestial blue walls and white moldings, which suited the angelic beauty of its occupant...who, as it turned out, had a devilish streak.

Beatrice was waiting for him in her bed, a canopied white confection that made him think of clouds. Ordinarily, the sight of her with her white-gold hair loose and shining, dressed in a simple white nightgown, would have made him instantly randy.

Come to think of it, he *was* randy. But he was angry too.

He stalked over to her side. "What the devil does Knighton want from you?"

She peered up at him with those rare lavender eyes. Eyes that had been focused on the bloody duke all night. Eyes that ought to have been turned toward Wick, her lover and husband-to-be. It had taken all of Wick's willpower not to call Knight—Knighton, damn the duke's eyes—out.

He hadn't wanted to look like a jealous fool, although he'd felt like one. Which irked him further. How did Beatrice manage to tie him up in knots when no lady ever had before?

She set aside the book she'd been reading. "Hello to you, too."

"You didn't want to talk about it in the drawing room, said we would do so later." Crossing his arms, he informed her, "This is later."

She sighed. "The gist of it is, along with his title, Knighton inherited four illegitimate half-siblings. He wants a duchess who has the pedigree and wherewithal to launch them into Society."

Wick narrowed his eyes. "And he asked you to fulfill this role?"

She toyed with the coverlet. "I do meet the requirements."

"I'm going to kill him."

"There's no need." She gave him a smile that was probably meant to be pacifying. "I declined the offer. Told him that I wanted more than a marriage based on mutual goals and respect."

"And he let it go?"

"Actually, he said he could offer more than that," she hedged.

"What exactly did he offer?"

She bit her lip.

"Spit it out, Beatrice."

"The, um, delights of marriage," she muttered. "Minus emotional complications."

His hands balled at his sides. "Knighton's a *dead man*."

"Wick, I turned him down."

"I don't give a damn," Wick ground out, pacing alongside the bed. "The bastard knows you're mine, and he's going after you anyway. I'm going to wring his bloody neck."

"Will you always be this much of a troglodyte?" She sounded exasperated.

"Will you always attract this much male attention?" He shot her a glance—then nearly groaned at her puzzled expression. "Devil take it, you have no idea, do you?"

"No idea of what?"

"Of how goddamned beautiful you are."

From her furrowed brow to the way she sunk her teeth into her plump bottom lip, he knew that she didn't. It was precisely that vulnerability mixed with her physical charms and passionate spirit that made her a magnet for male attention. And she had no clue about the extent of her desirability and probably never would.

He'd have to spend a lifetime convincing her.

"You make me *feel* beautiful," she ventured softly.

"You should feel that way because you *are*." His irritation was no match for the luminous wonder in her eyes. Going to her, he tipped up her chin. "Inside and out, Lady Beatrice Wodehouse, you are the most irresistible woman I've ever met."

"I feel the same way about you," she breathed.

"That I'm an irresistible woman?"

She blinked, then rolled her eyes. "No, you idiot. Just the irresistible part."

"An irresistible idiot, am I?" Smiling, he tucked a silky tress behind her ear. "Have a care love, or all that flattery will go to my head."

"I think it has already." She directed her gaze to the bulge in the front of his robe.

"Minx," he said with a grin. "You'll be taking care of that soon enough. Now be a love and move over."

She made room for him, and he settled into the pillows, gathering her in his arms. With her head tucked against his chest, the fresh, flowery scent of her hair in his nostrils, he felt oddly content...even though he was as hard as a rock.

"Wick?"

"Hmm?"

"There's something I have to tell you...that I meant to tell you when you first came in."

At her hesitant tone, his sense of peace fled. "If Knighton said anything else to you, I swear I'll—"

"It's not about him. It's about us, and our, um, plans for tonight."

Feeling her tense up, he rolled them over. He lay atop her, his weight braced on his arms, and looked into her face, which was as red as an apple. "What is it, love?"

"I can't make love tonight," she blurted.

He frowned, not because of what she was saying but because of her obvious distress.

"That's fine, of course," he said gently. "I want you to tell me when you don't feel like making love."

"It's not that I don't feel like it."

The misery on her face made his chest clench. "What is it then? You can talk to me."

"I can't...oh, dash it. It's that time. Of month."

Understanding flooded him. So *that* was what had ruffled his little termagant. With his knowledge of female biology, he ought to have guessed, but the truth was the topic had never come up with past lovers. His partners had all been experienced; he'd assumed that they kept track of such things and simply didn't schedule rendezvous during those times. Whatever the case, they'd never discussed such intimate feminine matters with him.

That Beatrice was doing so filled him with tender amusement.

Lips twitching, he said, "You have an inconvenient visitor, do you?"

"I discovered it as I was changing for bed," she said in a small voice. "It doesn't last long. Usually three days or so."

He hugged her close, kissing the top of her head. "Then we'll do something else instead."

"You're staying?" She angled her head to look at him.

He raised his brows. "Unless you're kicking me out."

"No, I'd like for you to stay." Her smile was shy, unbearably sweet. "I like being with you, like this."

Christ, he liked it too. He'd spent a fair amount of time in bed with lovers, but never time spent not fucking. There hadn't been a woman whom he'd wanted to just talk to and cuddle with...until Beatrice.

"I like it too," he said honestly.

"Even though we're just talking?"

"Especially because we're talking," he told her. "I want to know you, angel, and not just in the biblical sense."

Cheeks rosy, she asked, "What would you like to know?"

"You haven't said much about your family."

Once again, she stiffened, and he wasn't surprised. He suspected that all was not well in the familial realm. Why else would her kin allow her, a vibrant woman, to live like a hermit? When she'd briefly spoken of her father, her expression had grown distant...as if she were barricading herself off from pain. It was the same expression she'd worn when Knighton had brought up her brother's name.

"There isn't much to say." A wall of remoteness rose in her eyes. "My papa died about a year after my accident, my mama soon thereafter."

"What about your brother?"

"He and I are...not close."

Feeling her retreat farther, he switched to a different strategy.

"Are you far apart in age?" he asked conversationally. "My brother Richard is older than I am by seven years, and I think that age difference caused a rift between us for a time."

"Benedict is a year younger." Her brows drew together. "What kind of a rift?"

He hesitated because he wasn't used to talking about his past. One of the primary principles of negotiation was *quid pro quo*, however. She'd shared about her scar; it was only fair that he should divulge some of his own unpleasant history. The difference was, of course, that she'd done nothing to deserve what had happened to her whereas he'd been the architect of his own downfall.

"Truthfully? One caused by my stupidity," he said baldly. "In my younger days, I was an arrogant, reckless fool. You couldn't tell me anything because I knew it all. I got myself into debt with a moneylender and even more serious trouble. When Richard tried to help me, I took out my anger and frustration on him."

"Why did you do that?" Her tone held no judgement, only curiosity. "Didn't you know that he was trying to help you?"

"I knew." Even after a decade, that time in his life—who he'd been—shamed him. "I was just too proud to admit that I was a failure. I'd always looked up to Richard, you see. He was the dutiful son, the one that our father was proud of and rightly so. When I ended up discharging my debt to Garrity, the money-lender, by working for him, Richard did not condemn my choice. Instead, he told me that an honorable man always pays his debts, and he has stood by me, through thick and thin. He even manages to be civil to Garrity—who, by the by, founded GLNR and invited me and our other partner, Harry Kent, to join the company."

When she remained silent, he felt a stab of concern. Had he revealed too much? He hadn't shared the worst of his sins...not by a long shot. A wise negotiator always began by testing the waters. Working for a usurer wasn't exactly a noble pastime, yet he'd never regretted his sojourn in the underclass. It had cured him of his pride and arrogance and given him the skills to make his own way in the world.

But Beatrice, with her distinguished pedigree, might not see it that way. Although his own bloodline and money allowed him to move within the *ton*, there were the sticklers who looked down their noses at him because of his past profession—or for having any profession at all. He'd learned not to give a damn what they thought, but what Beatrice thought mattered.

"Your brother sounds like a wise and decent chap," she said with a wistful smile. "Are you close to him now?"

Her matter-of-fact acceptance humbled him. Gave him hope that she might be able to accept his greater trespasses when it came time to share them with her.

"Very close. In fact, he, my sister-in-law Violet, and their three hellions are staying with me in London for the summer. They're due to arrive at any moment."

"Shouldn't you be there to host them?" She looked adorably concerned.

"I sent word that I would be delayed. They'll get on fine without me." He stroked her cheek, enjoying the privilege of touching her. "After we deal with the problems at hand, I'd like for you to meet them. I think you and Violet, in particular, would rub along famously."

"You don't think..."

"What is it, sweetheart?"

"Will your family find me...odd?" she asked anxiously.

He burst out laughing.

"I'm serious," she protested. "I'm not exactly a conventional lady."

"I'm not laughing at you. I'm laughing at the notion of Vi finding anyone unconventional." He grinned at her. "Compared to her, you're as proper as the queen."

"How can you think I'm proper given the way we met?"

"You should ask Violet about her first meeting with Richard. It made a splash in the papers."

She raised her brows. "Then I think I shall enjoy meeting her and your family."

The idea of introducing Beatrice to his kin filled him with pride. Then he wondered if she'd feel the same way about him. Although descended from aristocratic stock, he was the younger son of a minor Scottish viscount whereas her brother was a duke.

He'd never been introduced to the Duke of Hadleigh, although he knew the man by reputation. Hadleigh was said to be an arrogant hothead, possessed of a vindictive streak. During Wick's tenure as a moneylender, one of his clients had apparently offended the Duchess of Hadleigh with some off-handed comment. His Grace had avenged his wife by calling the man out and putting a hole in the other's arm.

Wick cleared his throat. "What about your brother? Do you think he and I will get along?"

Her smile faded.

"I'm not that bad of a catch, am I?" he said lightly.

"It's not you." She exhaled. "Benedict is not an easy man to get along with. He wasn't always that way. I mean, he was quick-tempered even when we were growing up, but he had a kinder, gentler side."

"What made him change?" *Second rule of negotiating: ask the right questions.*

"It's a long story."

"We've got a long night of not making love ahead of us."

His quip had its intended effect of relaxing her. Particularly her eyeballs, which rolled in their sockets before she continued with her story.

"Before my accident, my family was a happy one. Papa and Mama were devoted to one another. Benedict and I grew up at our country seat, and our days were filled with riding, swimming, and playing with other children. It was a carefree time." Her expression darkened. "My first visit to London was for my debut at age seventeen. Mama never liked the city, so Papa would go on his own while we stayed at the estate. Benedict and I were both overwhelmed, I think, by our first taste of city life. I was swept into the ballrooms of the *ton*, and he fell in with a crowd of neck-or-nothings, lordlings who would bet a thousand pounds on whose carriage would win a race."

Wick understood because the same thing had happened to him. "London is a dangerous place for a young man of means who thinks he's more experienced than he is."

"You've described Benedict to a tee. Those initial months in London fed his recklessness and his temper. Then my accident occurred..." She swallowed before continuing. "It was like a lightning rod for his rage. He insisted my honor had to be avenged, even when I begged him to let the matter drop."

Wick recalled the details she'd shared. "The man in the park, the one you stopped from abusing the urchin. Your brother wanted him to answer for what happened?"

"Yes. The man's name was T. Edgar Grigg."

The name rang a bell. "Was Grigg a coal merchant?"

"You know of him?"

"My partner, Harry Kent, who oversees the technological aspects of GLNR was quite interested in one of Grigg's innovations. Grigg designed a prototype for a coal drop...essentially a warehouse with a railway running over it so that the train can dump the coal directly into the building. Quite clever, really; there's a model operating now near Regent's Canal, although Grigg died before he could see his plan come into fruition..."

Wick trailed off, recalling the rest of Grigg's story. The man had been a rising star of industry, a middle class businessman poised for great success. Then his fortunes radically turned.

"After Papa's death, Benedict came into the title." Beatrice continued her tale in a hollow voice. "He was barely eighteen at the time, immature yet full of pride. He used his influence to ruin Grigg's business. As it turned out, those lordling friends of Benedict were well connected. All it took was the right whispers in the right ears in the right clubs. Grigg's investors fled, banks called in his loans, even some of his patents were overturned. It got so bad that..." Her throat worked. "Grigg hung himself."

"Bloody hell."

"I couldn't be around Benedict any longer, so I purchased Camden Manor. Shortly after he came into the title, he got married...to Arabella, the girl who I'd thought was a friend but who I'd overheard calling me Lady Beastly. She has brought out the worst in him. Five years ago, Benedict and I got into an argument, and I told him what I'd heard her say about me to my ex-fiancé, and he accused me of making it up. Said I was jealous of her. And he called me..."

He stroked her hair. "What did he say, angel?"

"He called me..." Her voice cracked. "The destroyer of happiness."

Seeing anguish darken her beautiful eyes, Wick wanted to punch her idiotic brother. It took all his willpower to keep his voice gentle. "You didn't destroy anyone's happiness—*he* did, the foolish bastard. You bear no fault in any of this."

She looked as if she might say something more. But she only bit her lip.

Knowing her tender heart, he asked, "Do you miss him, angel?"

"He's my brother, the only kin I have left." She heaved out a breath. "At the same time, I want to wring his neck. That sounds absurd, doesn't it?"

"That sounds like family. But he's not your only kin."

Her brow puckered. "He isn't?"

"There's the family you're born with, and the family you choose. And you, angel, have created your own clan here at Camden Manor. The Sheridans, the Ellerbys, the rest of your tenants—they understand how special you are and, because of that, they deserve a place in your life. Hadleigh, it seems to me, has yet to earn that privilege."

She stared at him as if he'd hung the moon in the sky for her. And, devil and damn, he'd give her the sun and stars as well just to have that look from her. A look that filled that empty well inside him, replaced loneliness with something beautiful and rare.

"How did you become so wise, Wick?" she said softly.

He gave her the truth. "By making mistakes and earning my privileges."

## 16

BEATRICE OPENED HER EYES. SHE WAS LYING IN BED FACING Wick. They must have fallen asleep this way, curled together like a pair of quotation marks or two children sharing secrets deep into the night. The watery light that slipped in through the curtains suggested it was early yet, and she wanted to let Wick sleep on.

Quietly, she eased from the bed and went to use the necessary.

When she rejoined her dozing lover, she curled on her side to face him. He was absurdly attractive, even in slumber. A wave of hair lay over his brow, his lashes thick against his cheeks. A night beard shaded his jaw and drew attention to the sensual shape of his lips. Through the vee of his sleep shirt, she saw the taut, hair-dusted planes of his chest.

He was a beautiful man and not just on the outside. Last night, she'd told him things she'd never shared with anyone. Goodness, she'd even told him about her *flux*. Yet he made it easy to let down her guard. He listened and understood, sometimes questioned or teased. What he never did was judge.

With Wick, her secrets felt safe. *She* felt safe.

The currents of trust flowed in both directions. For he carried his own hurts from the past and was unpacking them with her bit by bit. It seemed impossible that a man with his looks and accomplishments could have any insecurities at all, but when he'd talked about his younger self and his older brother, she'd heard his self-doubts. Knowing that he, too, was subject to human frailties made her feel even closer to him.

A tender spasm hit her heart. *I care about him. So very much.*

The realization was thrilling and terrifying at once. In a week and a half, Wick had slipped through defenses she'd spent years building as easily as he'd scaled her garden wall. And what she felt was not the *tendre* of a girl—that first blush attraction she'd had for Croydon—but something far deeper. Something that the woman she was now hadn't thought she would ever feel.

Wick had convinced her that he was attracted to her, that his courtship wasn't just based on honor. But did his feelings go beyond sexual desire? Might he someday come to...care for her?

Yearning made her reach out and curve her palm around his jaw. The abrasion of his virile scruff made her skin tingle. She explored gently so as not to awaken him. She feathered a fingertip over the firm seam of his lips, the strong line of his chin. He murmured sleepily, and she grew bolder, sliding her hand into the opening of his shirt.

His chest was hard and warm, his vitality thrumming beneath her palm. She enjoyed the contrasting textures of his chest hair and taut skin. With her index finger, she traced the flat disk of his nipple until it pebbled. She wondered if that part of him was as sensitive as the corresponding part of her. Indeed, her breasts were extra sensitive during her menstrual cycle, the tips budded and throbbing against her nightgown. Her gaze drifted downward, and her breath caught at the jutting bulge of his manhood. His cock was a huge, thick bar pressing against the fine linen.

*He can get aroused in his sleep?* she thought wonderingly.

Fascinated, she couldn't resist touching him, running a finger along the distended ridge. At his sharp exhale, she jerked her hand away, her gaze darting to his face. He was awake, just barely, his eyes a slumberous gold-green.

Her cheeks hot, she said, "I'm sorry to wake you."

"As you can see, I'll get up for you anytime, sweetheart." His husky double entendre ruffled her senses. "Would you like me to disrobe so that you can see what you're touching?"

Feeling very bold, she nodded.

His slow smile made her shiver. That shiver turned into a full body tremor as he got out of bed and, in a languid motion, pulled his sleep shirt over his head. The display of rippling muscle and hollowing grooves slackened her jaw. She hadn't seen him fully naked before and, heavens, he was a visual feast.

She scooted closer, kneeling by the edge of the mattress to get a better look. From his wide shoulders to his sectioned abdomen, he was sleek and muscled everywhere. His hips were lean, girded with a striking vee of sinew. He had the long legs of an athlete, his bulging calves sprinkled with hair. And between his corded thighs...

Goodness, his cock was huge. The heavy lance was aimed in her direction, a pearly bead dripping from the tip. At the base of that enormous weapon, his dusky stones hung in a nest of male hair.

Her palms twitched, a molten feeling spreading from her core to her pussy.

"Feel free to touch," he murmured. "And to do whatever else you wish to."

Images bombarded her brain. Of things he'd done to her...of things she might like to do to him. His permission fanned the wicked flame inside her. She placed her hands on his abdomen, felt the leap of the washboard-like ridges. She slid her palms upward, circling his nipples with her thumbs.

"You've kissed me here before." She looked up into his heated gaze. "Would it feel good if I did the same thing to you?"

"Why don't you try and find out?"

His question was both a challenge and a tease. It gave her the nerve to rise on her knees and put her lips to his flat nipple. She kissed him, and his half-smile suggested that he liked what she was doing...and perhaps would like something more. Recalling how he'd tended to her breasts, how good that had made her feel, she kissed him again, this time using her tongue.

His shiver told her she was on the right path. She continued to lick him, his flesh budding beneath her soft flicks. She experimented with suction, and that appeared to be a success, if the low purr in his throat was any indication. She moved to his other nipple, licking, sucking, winnowing out pleasured grunts from him.

The scent and textures of him made her feverish with want. She felt like an acolyte worshiping at his altar. She couldn't get enough of him, using her hands and lips to learn his sensual contours.

Arriving at his jutting manhood, she looked up at him.

"Show me how to touch you," she said in a throaty whisper. "How you like to be touched."

The look in his eyes made her throb between her legs. It was strange to realize how hotly her fires burned this time of month. If it wasn't for her "visitor" as Wick had put it, she would want him to touch her pussy, do all those wicked things he did to make her spend.

That would have to wait for later. For now, she would have the pleasure of pleasuring him.

"Wrap your fingers around my cock," he said.

Shivering with excitement, she followed his command. His member was so big that her fingers didn't fully circle the veiny girth. She moved her fist experimentally, surprised to discover how the soft skin moved over the turgid core, and he hissed out a breath.

"Christ, your touch is heaven. But you can frig me harder— like this."

Her nipples pulsed at the naughty new word. He folded his hand over hers, teaching her a pumping motion, the grip tighter than what she would have dared to try. The flush on his high cheekbones conveyed that he was enjoying her touch, her *frigging*. He must have judged her competent for his hand left hers, going to stroke her hair from her cheek. More moisture leaked from the tip of his cock, making her grasp slippery, and he grunted, seeming to like that even more.

"Use your other hand on my stones," he instructed. "Rub them...ah, like that. Just like that, sweet lass."

Her breath puffed from her lips as she fondled his heavy sac whilst frigging him with her other hand. It excited her to obey her lover's intimate instructions and witness her effect on him. Cords stood out on his neck, his shoulders and biceps bunching. She pumped him harder, squeezing his balls, and he let out a pleasured growl. She squeezed her thighs together, trying to still the throbbing in her pussy.

"I'm going to shoot my seed into your pretty hands," he rasped. "Feel me, angel..."

His shaft turned harder than steel, and he groaned, shoving himself roughly into her clasp. He exploded, shooting pulse after hot pulse into her hands. She panted as his abundant essence dripped between her fingers, splattering on her nightgown.

With a swiftness that made her gasp, he hauled her off the mattress, planting her back against the wall by her bed. He was naked, his muscular thigh insinuated between her legs. He pressed in, applying friction where she craved it: exquisite, breath-stealing friction that she could feel through her nightgown and the discreet padding she wore.

"Ride me," he ordered.

Her cheeks flamed. "But I can't. You know...it's that time..."

"It doesn't matter what time it is." His hot eyes seared through her inhibitions. "We decide what's right for us. Now kiss me."

With a shameless moan, she did. His kiss fanned the fire inside her and soon she was rubbing herself wantonly against him, riding his leg toward her own finish line. She cried out, her hands clutching his bulging biceps as ecstasy crashed over her.

Floating and boneless, she slumped against the wall, would have fallen if he hadn't held her.

He nuzzled her ear. "I like waking up with you, sweetheart."

"I like waking up with you, too," she whispered.

## 17

"LET ME DO THE TALKING," BEA SAID.

Wick handed her down from the carriage in front of the parish church. "As you wish."

She squinted at him through her dark veil, which she'd worn for the trip into the village. His expression was as suspiciously bland as his reply had been.

"You're just going to agree to let me take charge?" she asked.

"I'm learning how to negotiate with you, angel. When I let you take the initiative, the results are outstanding. Take this morning, for instance."

The lazy smolder in his eyes caused an answering flare in her belly. She glanced around, worried that someone might have overheard. Luckily, the only one within earshot was her chaperone, who she'd brought along for appearance's sake. Curled up in a corner of the carriage, Tottie couldn't be seen through the open door, her light snores the only reminder of her presence.

"You oughtn't speak of such things in public," Bea whispered.

"No one knows what we're talking about. Unless your whispering is making them suspicious."

Rolling her eyes, she said, "Let's stick to the plan at hand.

We'll question Reverend Wright about his whereabouts the night of the fire. I'll show him the pocket watch, see if there's any reaction. 'H. C.' doesn't match his initials, although his given name *is* Henry. Maybe he has another name that begins with C."

"Where you lead, I will follow," Wick said gallantly.

She placed her gloved hand on his offered arm. They entered the front gate, heading toward the stone church with mullioned windows and a square tower at the far end. She pinned up her veil before passing through the arched entrance into the nave, which was small and plain, with white walls and rows of dark pews.

She saw Frank Varnum, the curate, arranging something on the altar.

Mr. Varnum had been assigned to the church a few months before Reverend Wright. With sandy brown hair and spectacles, the curate was in his twenties and had a slightly bumbling but kind manner. In the times they'd met, before Bea had stopped attending the reverend's services, Mr. Varnum had always been nice to her. And to her tenants as well, who spoke well of him.

He didn't seem to register their presence as they approached the chancel.

Bea made a clearing sound in her throat. "Good morning, Mr. Varnum..."

Despite her effort not to startle him, the curate spun around, knocking a candelabrum off the altar and sending candles rolling in all directions.

"Oh, pardon! It's you, Miss Brown." He flushed to the roots of his sandy hair. "Please excuse me for a moment..."

He scrambled to get the candles that had disappeared beneath a table. Seeing his panic, Bea was about to help him but Wick said, "Allow me" and went to collect the other dispersed sticks. He returned, handing them over to the grateful young man.

Bea made the introductions.

"Pleased to meet you, Mr. Murray." Mr. Varnum bent at the waist before turning his bespectacled gaze to Bea. "I was sorry to hear about the fire, Miss Brown. And thankful that the heavenly Father watched over you and your tenants, ensuring no one was harmed."

"Thank you. I was wondering if Mr. Murray and I might speak to the reverend?"

"Oh, do you have an appointment?" The curate blinked owlishly. "I'm in charge of Reverend Wright's scheduling, and I'm ever so sorry if I forgot..."

"We don't have an appointment, Mr. Varnum." Bea gave the flustered fellow a reassuring smile. "Would the reverend be available to see us?"

"Unfortunately, he's left for London. His mama has not been in the best of health, and she's apparently taken a turn."

"I'm sorry to hear it," Bea murmured.

Inwardly, she was disappointed that the outing had been for naught. She looked at Wick and noticed the direction of his gaze. He was looking beyond Mr. Varnum, to an open door off the chancel which led to the vestry. She recalled that Reverend Wright used it as his office, a memory corroborated by the desk and bookshelves visible through the doorway.

The idea took hold of her. If they searched the reverend's personal domain, would they find any clues? Wick lifted his chin slightly, as if to indicate that he'd had similar thoughts.

"It's a pity to miss the reverend," he said in a genial manner, "but I was wondering if I might have a tour, Mr. Varnum? I confess I have a great interest in churches."

"I'd be delighted." Mr. Varnum beamed. "Shall we start in the church yard?"

"Please excuse me, sirs, I'm afraid I've developed a bit of a megrim," Bea said. "I shall have a rest with my chaperone in the carriage. Please do go on without me."

Wick led the way through the nave toward the exit, keeping the curate occupied with questions. Bea dawdled behind. Once the men left the building, she quickly turned around and returned to the vestry. She gave a furtive scan of the environs before ducking inside the reverend's office.

She started her search at the sturdy oak desk. A copy of the Bible, a leather-bound appointment book, and a tray of writing utensils lay on its tidy surface. She opened the appointment book, her pulse accelerating at the owner's name inscribed on the very first page:

*The Reverend Mr. Henry Cartwell Wright.*

Henry Cartwell—H. C.

Could the pocket watch belong to Wright?

She continued leafing through the pages. The multiple appointments with Squire Crombie caught her eye. Were the two discussing village business, as Crombie had claimed? Or was the reason for their meetings more infamous?

The second thing she noticed confirmed what the curate had said about Wright's visits to London. In the past few months, it appeared that Wright had taken three trips to the city, all lasting a week or more.

Knowing that Wick could not keep the curate occupied indefinitely, she took her search to the cupboards that lined one wall. Opening and closing the doors, she found ceremonial equipment, folded robes, and...her heart shot into her throat.

On a shelf sat three cans marked "Linseed Oil."

"...the roof of the nave was reconstructed in the early eighteenth century," Mr. Varnum's distant voice drifted into the office.

Closing the cupboard, she flattened herself against the wall next to the open door, a position that put her out of view of anyone walking by. Her heart skipped as the footsteps got closer, Mr. Varnum droning on about the architecture of the chancel. Her mind raced through possible excuses—she'd been looking for the necessary and got lost?—when Wick's deep voice cut in.

"I say, could we have a closer look at the stone tracery in the transept?"

The footsteps receded. Peering out the doorway, seeing that

the coast was clear, Bea exited the vestry and the chancel as stealthily as she could. She spotted Wick and Mr. Varnum at the far end of the transept. The curate had his back to her and was pointing out some detail in the window, but Wick caught her glance, and she gave him an excited nod.

She couldn't wait to tell him what she'd discovered.

## 18

Two days later, Wick exited the inn at Stoke-Upon-Trent where he'd stayed the night and instructed his driver to take him to Thomas McGillivray's office. Through the carriage window, he had a view of the town, with its pleasant square lined by shops and dining establishments. In the backdrop were rolling rural hills and sprawling earthenware factories which had sprouted up here and in the nearby towns. Despite the clear summer day, the sky was dark from the coal smoke billowing from the large bottle kilns.

As Wick mulled upon the best strategy to take with McGillivray and the other factory owners, he found his mind wandering to Beatrice. Leaving her yesterday hadn't been easy. The discoveries she'd made in Wright's office had been concerning but insufficient to prove the reverend's guilt. Linseed oil was, after all, a common substance. It was used for everyday projects such as varnishing wood, of which there was plenty in the church. And the fact that Wright had the initials "H. C." in his name was suggestive but hardly proof positive that he was the owner of the pocket watch.

Thus, both Squire Crombie and Wright remained on the list

of suspects. Leaving Bea alone with those two nearby had tight-ened the knot in Wick's gut, even though he knew that his trip to Stoke was necessary to protect her. His concern had prompted him to have a private word with Knighton after supper last night. He and the other might be rivals, but they were also men from the same world. If Beatrice's life was threatened, he knew Knighton would have the wherewithal to protect her.

He hadn't told Knighton all the details, just that Beatrice had dangerous enemies. Knighton had understood and given Wick his word to keep an eye on her. Of course, the bastard probably intended to put more than just an eye on her, and Wick was fully prepared to have to kill Knighton upon his return. In the interim, however, Bea's safety was paramount.

Moreover, he trusted his lass. She was not a woman to play games, and she'd told him that she had no interest in Knighton. To strengthen his claim, Wick had visited her chamber the night before he left. She'd still had her flux, but he'd coaxed her out of her nightgown, petting and kissing her lovely breasts, rubbing at the seam of her drawers until she'd sweetly cried out her release.

He would have been content to leave things at that. Beatrice being Beatrice, however, had insisted on returning the favor. Kneeling between his legs on the mattress, she'd frigged him, her soft yet firm pumping bringing him close to the brink. Then she'd shyly asked if she could kiss him there the way he'd kissed her pussy. Wick knew for certain then that he was the luckiest bastard alive.

The image of her rosy lips stretched around his prick, the smoky desire in her eyes as he'd instructed her in the art of fellatio was enough to make his balls swell and heart pound with the possessiveness to which he'd become accustomed. He no longer questioned whether marrying Beatrice was what he wanted; he *knew* it was. Not just because she happened to have a natural talent for oral pleasures (thank you, God) but because she was right for him in every conceivable way.

He admired her spirit and tenacity. He enjoyed working with her, playing with her, just being with her. With her, he felt able to let down his guard for she neither judged nor coddled. Instead, she listened, asked questions, and gave her honest opinion. She tamed his restlessness and made him want to be a man who was deserving of her.

He looked down at the signet ring gleaming on his right hand, the symbol of his past mistakes, and realized that Beatrice was different from any other woman he'd known.

Especially Monique.

*Don't leave me, Wickham. I swear I'll die without you.*

His jaw tautened as he thought of Monique's suffocating passion, the quicksand of their relationship. Since her death a decade ago, he'd been wary of emotional dealings with women. From then on, he'd made it crystal clear that all he had to offer was a good time between the bedsheets. If a woman showed signs of expecting or wanting more, he ended things.

Yet with Beatrice, *he* was the one with expectations. He wanted a future with her and would do everything in his power to make her happy. At the same time, he knew her sense of self did not depend upon him; his failure would not destroy her. That knowledge came as a relief and freed him to examine the deeper yearnings he'd long ignored.

After years of wondering if he would find that special connection—if, indeed, he had the capacity for it—he now had the answer. In the words of his brother Richard, he "just knew it." He had found his lass, the one he wanted to spend the rest of his life with. He thought he had a fairly decent chance of convincing her to take a risk on him.

But first he would have to protect her and prove himself worthy of being her mate.

The carriage rolled to a stop in front of McGillivray's red-brick office, and Wick wasn't surprised to see the factory owner waiting at the entrance to greet him. Of medium height,

McGillivray was a stocky, balding man whose bold brass buttons matched his forceful personality. He radiated impatience, from his tapping foot to his twitching moustache.

Behind him stood five other factory owners, dark-suited replicas of him. They were like a pack of wolves led by their most aggressive member. As united as they appeared, one had the sense that they would turn on one another at the first show of weakness.

Wick alighted, and McGillivray stepped forward, clearing his throat importantly.

"We've been waiting for you, Mr. Murray." He extended his hand.

Wick took it. The handshake was more akin to a bone-crunching contest than a greeting, but he gave as good as he got.

"Thank you for seeing me on short notice," he said.

"On the contrary, the Coalition and I were honored to receive your missive." McGillivray's hard gaze glinted with ambition...enough to drive him to try to scare Bea off her land? "We hope you bring good news."

Determined to keep his lass safe, Wick said evenly, "We'll discuss it inside."

## 19

"IT WASN'T NECESSARY FOR YOU TO BE PRESENT, YOUR GRACE," Beatrice said. "Nothing is going to happen to me in my own home."

She and the Duke of Knighton were standing in her drawing room, which had been recently vacated by her tenants. She'd called an informal gathering to address a number of concerns.

First, she'd thanked the farmers for their bravery in fighting the barn fire. Rumors were swirling about arson, and she'd confirmed that the fire might have been caused intentionally, although the motive was unclear. She'd urged everyone to keep an eye out for any suspicious characters or activities on the estate and to report them to her immediately. Above all, they were to put their personal safety first.

She'd also told her tenants that she would bear all the costs for the new barn as well as for the supply of hay she would purchase to see their livestock through the winter.

Then, taking a breath, she'd informed them of Wick's true identity.

Pandemonium had broken loose.

If it hadn't been for the years of trust she'd cultivated with her farmers, Bea was certain the reaction would have been much worse. As it was, she'd had to confront Mr. Ellerby's anger and his wife's fear. Sweet Sarah Haller's blue eyes had brimmed over, tears spilling down her porcelain cheeks. Bea had let everyone have their say, and when the room had quieted at last, she'd delivered words from her heart.

*Camden Manor has been a refuge not only for you but me. I value this estate and your good will more than you can know,* she'd said with steadfast sincerity. *You have my word that, as long as I draw breath, no railway will be built unless your homes and mine can be preserved.*

"You handled that situation with finesse, my lady," Knighton said. "I don't know many females who could have managed a mob so adroitly."

"They aren't a mob. They're my tenants and friends," she replied.

Yet she knew that her speech wouldn't mollify them for long. She wished Wick could have been present: he had a way of smoothing things over and winning people to his cause. She knew he'd written his principle surveyor and engineer, Mr. Norton, and was awaiting the reply. For the sake of her people's morale—not to mention her relationship with Wick—Bea prayed that Mr. Norton would be able to provide a solution.

"When money and survival are at stake, friendship may become a luxury that few can afford," Knighton said.

She lifted her brows. "That is rather cold of you, Your Grace."

The duke's broad shoulders moved up and down without disturbing the crisp lines of his charcoal jacket. "Where I come from, that is merely a fact of life."

His words stirred her curiosity for she'd never met a duke raised in the underbelly of London. She had other questions for him as well. Heading to the tea cart, she poured them both a cup.

"How do you take it, Your Grace?" she inquired.

"Cream, please."

Handing him his cup, she led the way to the settee by the fire. Knighton sat beside her.

"I apologize that we haven't had the opportunity to finish our last chat," she said.

"You've had a full plate." Knighton sampled his tea. "Please know that I would be honored to assist you in whatever way I can."

"I would not dream of involving a guest in such unpleasant business."

Nor would she ever want to be indebted to a man like Severin Knight. While she liked him, she did not trust him. Especially since she did not fully understand his connection to her brother.

"Murray has a different take on the situation," Knighton said.

She frowned. "I beg your pardon?"

"He asked me to look out for you in his absence. Given that he and I do not see eye to eye on certain issues," the duke said dryly, "he must indeed be concerned about the danger you're facing."

Knowing that Wick had enlisted his rival to protect her warmed her insides like a drink of hot chocolate. She was touched by his care for her, by the fact that he'd set aside jealousy and competition for the sake of her well-being. At the same time, she was a bit exasperated at his highhandedness: as she'd told him countless times before he'd left for Stoke, she could take care of her own affairs. She'd had plenty of practice at it, being an independent woman of five-and-twenty and not some miss fresh out of the schoolroom.

"On that topic, I am curious to know the exact nature of your differences," she said.

"Murray didn't tell you?" Knighton gave her an impassive look.

The truth was that Wick had been rather evasive about his dealings with Knighton. He'd said that the two had faced off over various negotiations, resulting in bad blood when he'd repeatedly trounced the other. In essence, he'd painted Knighton as a sore loser.

"I'd like to hear your perspective," she said.

"We've found ourselves in competition on numerous occasions." Knighton smiled thinly. "Murray does not enjoy losing."

"The way he told it, he wasn't the one who lost."

"Murray was always prone to delusions." Knighton raised his brows. "Are you certain you wish to keep company with a man like him?"

"I am." As she was not a woman to play games, she wanted to make that point clear. She set her cup down on the coffee table. "Mr. Murray and I have an understanding, Your Grace."

Knighton's gaze flicked pointedly to her bare ring finger. "How firm is this understanding?"

"You will have to find yourself another duchess."

"That is a pity because you happen to be the one I want."

His intensity gave her an odd, shivery feeling. She attributed it to the strangeness of having not one, but two men after her hand when she'd believed that no one would want her after her scar.

"The more I know of you," he went on, "the more convinced I am that you possess the rare wherewithal to manage my unique situation."

"As delightful as shepherding your illegitimate half-siblings through Society sounds, I'm not the lady for the task. I have no interest in making a reappearance in the *ton* or London for that matter."

"What do you want from marriage then?"

The question took her aback. But it was easy to answer: all the things that she didn't think she'd find and that she was finding... with Wick.

"Honesty, respect, and a passionate connection." She met Knighton's gaze with a hint of defiance because while he might want to use her as a mother hen, Wick desired her for who she was.

"And you think you will find all of that with Murray?"

She didn't like his bland tone. "What are you implying?"

Knighton placed his cup down next to hers. "There are things you might not know about your suitor. Murray is well-known for his ability to achieve his ends, particularly with the gentler sex. I wish for you to be in full possession of the facts before making any final decision."

"He has been honest with me," she said stiffly.

"Has he? He's told you he wants your land—nay, needs it to build his railway? His company has invested a great deal of money in this project, and shareholders will not wait forever."

"We have discussed the issue of his railway at length, and he and I have reached an agreement. As you see, I am in possession of the facts."

"Did he tell you what happened to his mistress?"

She felt the first shiver of uncertainty. "Are you saying Mr. Murray has a mistress?"

"Not currently, that I know of," Knighton said calmly. "The mistress I'm referring to was a famous French acrobat with Astley's Amphitheatre and the business occurred some years ago. However, the woman's death does give one pause."

"She's dead?" Bea stared at him. "What happened?"

"According to rumor, she and Murray had been engaged in a torrid affair for months. She, like so many women, fell madly in love with him, even though he was known to leave a trail of broken hearts in his wake. He soon ended their affair, leaving her in such a state of despair that she threatened to kill herself. They ended up at a house party together, where she was found dead."

"Did Wick...have anything to do with her death?" Bea asked over her thudding heart.

"He didn't kill her, as far as I know. But as to whether he held any responsibility for her demise...that is a question best posed to Murray himself."

She would most *definitely* talk to Wick when he returned

tomorrow. Knowing him the way she did, she couldn't imagine that he was responsible for his mistress's death. There had to be a reason why he hadn't told her about this woman...just as Knighton had a reason for imparting this sordid piece of history.

"Why have you told me this?" She studied the duke's inscrutable features. "To further your own cause?"

"I want you to understand your options, my lady. All of them."

She rose, and he followed suit.

"I thank you for the information, Your Grace," she said, "but it will not change my mind about your offer."

Knighton's eyes darkened...with disappointment?

"Then I see no reason to intrude upon your hospitality any longer." He inclined his head. "I will take my leave tomorrow morning."

## 20

AFTER THE MEETING WITH MCGILLIVRAY AND THE OTHERS,
Wick decided to make the journey back to Camden Manor rather
than staying another night in Stoke as planned. He travelled all
day, arriving after dark. After a quick bathe to rid himself of the
travel dust, he changed into his dressing gown and went to find
Beatrice.

Although they'd only been apart for one night, it felt longer to
him. Strange, because he wasn't a sentimental man, yet here he
was rushing to her like an overeager bridegroom. It wasn't just
about lust, either. He'd missed everything about her: her conversation, wit, the scent of her hair. In her presence, he felt settled
and...right.

He knocked before entering. Zeus greeted him with a happy
wag, and he scratched the brindle bull terrier behind the ears
before letting him out. Seated at her dressing table, Bea had been
combing her hair; she swiveled, her gaze meeting his as she set
down her brush. He strode over, took her chin between thumb
and forefinger, turning her head this way and that.

"Can it be possible," he murmured, "that you've become even
more beautiful in my absence?"

A smile lurked in her peerless eyes. "Or that you've become more silver-tongued?"

She was like a glass of lemonade, perfectly tart-sweet. He bent to kiss her, her lips soft and plush beneath his, yielding in a way that made his heart and cock pound with desire. Holding her delicate jaw between his palms, he feasted on the sweetness of her surrender...the surrender that only a woman with her strength and spirit could give.

He ended the kiss. Her lips were swollen, her eyes glazed with need, and a primitive part of him wanted to scoop her up, carry her to bed, and have his wicked way with her. But he wasn't a troglodyte...or not only that, anyway. He was experienced enough to know that talking was foreplay for them. And he simply enjoyed keeping her on her toes.

He reached for her brush. "Turn around, angel. I'll finish up for you."

He saw the surprised flash in her eyes; obviously she'd expected him to commence their lovemaking. Hiding a smile at the reluctant way she obeyed his command, he stood behind her and ran the bristles through her hair. He felt her intimate shiver in his balls, which were already pulled taut against his erection. It aroused him to do this intimate duty for her, to know that no other man would see her with her hair down thus. Possessiveness surged through him, his hands curling in those pale silken streamers.

"How did you get back so early?" she asked him.

"After the meeting, I headed straight back. I missed my lass."

Her cheeks pinkened. "How did the meeting go?"

"Part of it went as I expected. I asked McGillivray and the Coalition if they were responsible for the barn fire, and they denied it. I believe them," he said frankly. "They're aggressive, cutthroat businessmen: they favor direct attacks and want their adversaries to know they're responsible. Setting fire to a barn without claiming responsibility is not their modus operandi." He paused. "In fact, McGillivray had an interesting piece of information to share."

Beatrice tilted her head.

"A few days before the fire, he had a visit from a man claiming to be your former tenant. The man said his name was Randall Perkins. McGillivray described the fellow as brutish looking, with a prominent brow and red birthmark on the left side of his face."

"That description matches Perkins." Her eyes widened. "What did the bounder want?"

"According to McGillivray, Perkins offered to help 'persuade' you to sell your land in exchange for payment."

"The *cad*. When I think of how I took him in...*grr*." Her indignant little growl was so adorable that Wick's lips twitched. "How did McGillivray respond to Perkins's odious offer?"

"He told Perkins he wouldn't give him a cent and booted the wastrel out of his office."

"Does he know where Perkins went?"

"When McGillivray turned down the 'partnership,' Perkins tried to beg a few quid off him. Claimed he needed money to get back to London where he could stay with family."

"When Perkins first came to the estate looking for work, he said he'd come from London. He claimed that his parents lived in some cramped tenement in the Seven Dials, and he needed to get away," she mused. "If he was the arsonist, I wonder if he went into hiding there. No one seems to have seen him since the fire."

"It's a possible lead to pursue," Wick agreed.

"What else happened at the meeting?" Beatrice studied him. "You mentioned that only a part went as you expected. What happened during the other part?"

That was his clever lass, never missing a beat.

"When I told them in no uncertain terms that GLNR would not tolerate them harassing you about the railway, they issued a threat of their own." He turned her back around so that he could continue brushing her hair. The soothing strokes helped to keep his anger at bay. "They said they would sell their shares of GLNR stock and tell the public they lost confidence in our company."

"How would that impact your business?" she asked in a troubled voice.

"The factory owners are significant investors, but we have others and could manage the fiscal side of things without them. The larger problem is their threat to go public," he said starkly. "If the Coalition begins to cast doubt on our project, then the other investors might start to panic and start selling. Then, like dominoes, the entire venture might fall."

"Wick, if you can't find a way to build the railway while preserving the farms..." She turned in her chair again, her throat working above the frilly collar of her nightgown. "It will be my fault if your company fails."

"No, angel. It would be my fault for not finding a solution, but that won't happen."

A furrow formed between her brows. "How can you be sure?"

"Because this is the most important deal of my life." He set down the brush, placed his hands on her slim shoulders. "I've received a reply from Mr. Norton. He's dealing with a problem with a viaduct in Sussex but promises to be here in a week or so. He will come up with a viable alternative. Trust me, sweetheart."

He refused to give into doubt. He would find a way to make things work. He wouldn't fail her, his future bride, and he needed to know that she believed in him.

"Wick...there's something I have to ask you."

At her uncharacteristic hesitancy, his nape prickled. "What is it, love?"

"It's about your mistress. The one...who died."

His insides turned to ice. Of all the things he'd been expecting, it had not been this. How had she found out about Monique? The answer slammed into him like an opponent's right hook—which this was, in a manner of speaking.

*Bloody Severin Knight. I'm going to beat him to a pulp.*

"Knighton told you about her, I presume?" he bit out. "What did he say?"

"That she was an acrobat, and she was in love with you. When you ended things, she said she wanted to...hurt herself. And then you were together at some house party, and she died. He said you didn't kill her, but you were involved?"

Her gaze was searching. Many women would have taken such revelations and turned them into accusations. Or hidden them, not speaking of them at all, letting them fester in suspicion and secrecy. But not his Beatrice. Her forthright nature would not allow anything but the truth between them, and her honor deepened his shame.

He exhaled. "All of that is true."

"But there is more to the story, isn't there? I want to hear it."

He gave a terse nod. "Shall we sit by the fire?"

They headed to the hearth beyond the bed, sharing the settee there. Taking a breath, he began the story that he had told twice before. Once to his brother and sister-in-law. A second time to the magistrates when he'd been taken into custody.

"The affair took place a decade ago. Her name was Monique, and she was the star acrobat at Astley's. We met after one of her shows, and she became my mistress." Remembering the terrible pride he'd felt securing such a celebrated lover, he felt his gut knot. "It was a purely physical relationship, at least on my end. I thought I had made the expectations clear, but apparently I was wrong. A few months into the affair, I had to break things off; I believe I've told you about the debt I incurred with Garrity. My only means of paying it off was to marry an heiress, and thus I couldn't keep things going with Monique."

"She didn't like that," Bea said.

He smiled grimly at the understatement. "I'd never seen her like that, simultaneously weeping and enraged. She said she'd...kill herself if I left her."

The memory of that sliced through him: her agitated threats

and frenzied tears, his own helplessness and panic. He hadn't known how to calm her; when she'd sobbingly asked for his signet ring as a keepsake, he'd gladly given it to her. The ring had later been recovered...from her dead body.

"Eventually, she seemed to accept that our affair was over," he said, his throat dry. "But soon thereafter we were at a house party together; I'd had no idea she would be there. She engaged in some mischief—I won't get into the whole sordid tale—and was killed because of it. At one point, because of our past, I was taken into custody as a suspect for her murder."

He swallowed, recalling being dragged from his horse by constables, the weight of irons clamped around his wrists. His dishonor had been witnessed by a houseful of party guests and now, dredging it all up again, in front of the woman he hoped to make his wife, he felt like the veriest scoundrel.

"Oh, Wick," was all Bea said. What *could* she say after all?

He'd gone too far to stop now. Best to purge it all. "The situation was one of my own making. And even though I didn't kill Monique, I acted dishonorably and failed her."

"How did you fail her?"

He speared his fingers through his hair. "I was careless with her feelings and acted selfishly. If I hadn't broken things off with her, maybe she wouldn't have lost her mind. Maybe she wouldn't have sought out trouble at the house party and ended up dead. If I hadn't started the affair, maybe she would be alive today."

"That is utter claptrap."

Beatrice's sharp reply cut through his self-condemnation.

Blinking, he said, "Pardon?"

"Your reasoning lacks logic. What does your affair with Monique have to do with her murder?"

Since this was a painful subject he avoided talking about, he'd never had to justify his belief before. "It...just does. She was my lover, and I failed to protect her."

"First of all, she was not your lover at the time of her murder.

Second, your affair, no matter how acrimoniously it ended, had nothing to do with her death. Did you know that she intended to cause trouble at the house party?"

"No."

"Or that someone intended to murder her?"

"Of course not," he said slowly.

"Then how on earth would you have prevented it?"

Stunned, he realized he couldn't answer the question. Yet he *had* to bear some responsibility.

"Even if I couldn't have stopped her murder, I should have been better to her," he said heavily. "I ought to have shown more care for her feelings—perhaps then she wouldn't have become overwrought. Perhaps she would have thought more clearly and decided against engaging in the business that got her killed."

"You cannot take responsibility for someone else's actions," Beatrice said softly. "Perhaps you could have done better. Maybe you would choose to act in a different manner if given the chance. Yet the fact remains that you would still have no control over the choices Monique made."

He frowned, trying to absorb her words.

"Was Grigg's death my fault?" she went on. "If I hadn't interfered with his beating of that boy, and he hadn't whipped my horse, would my brother have left him alone? Would Grigg then still be alive today?" She shook her head. "I've asked myself these sorts of questions countless times—enough to make myself mad. In the end, I have no answer except that Benedict did what Benedict decided to do...just as Monique acted in accordance to her judgement."

Beatrice's insight permeated his consciousness. It illuminated his darkest corners, pushing back the shadows of his shame. It seemed so simple, the way she said it.

"Even if her death was not my fault, I wish I had acted more honorably," he said gruffly.

"You made mistakes." She looked him in the eyes, not letting him off the hook. "But you were a young man back then, and the important thing is that you've changed, grown up. Knowing you as you are now, I can vouch for the fact that you are a true gentleman, one with a keen sense of honor."

"You think I'm honorable?"

After baring his ugliness to her, he didn't believe it possible.

"I *know* that you are." She brushed her fingers against his jaw, her touch like a benediction. "Wick, you're the first to give aid when someone is in need. You intervened when that man assaulted me at the masquerade, and you stormed a burning barn. You're doing your damnedest to protect me and my property even though it is against your company's interests."

"I would never let anything happen to you," he said fiercely.

"I know because that is the kind of man you are. A man who not only protects others but who shows kindness to people who are different—who, indeed, need compassion the most."

He was stunned by her assessment of him. Her words resonated like a church bell, expanding his chest with wonder. With the knowledge that somehow, despite his failures, she still saw the best of him.

"And let's not forget that your honor prompted you to propose to me, and you've been hounding me about marriage ever since."

Her smile told him that she was teasing.

"Would you mind if I hounded you right now?" he murmured.

With his thumb, he traced the path of her scar, felt her tremble as he followed that heart-shaped curve. Reaching the bottom, he continued upward, creating his own invisible line until the heart was complete.

Whole...the way she made him feel.

"I want to marry you, Beatrice," he said, his voice roughened with emotion. "Not just because of honor but because...I care for you."

*I CARE FOR YOU.*

His words and touch penetrated her like warm rain, seeping through years of disappointment and pain, landing on the parched surface of her heart. He didn't profess his undying love, and she was glad because she didn't know if she would have believed him. But the wonder in his voice, the way he turned her scar into something beautiful and whole caused hope to bloom within her.

"Beatrice?" He dropped his hand, his brows edging together. "How do you feel...about me?"

Now that she knew about his past, she understood his uncertainties. Wick's problem, as she saw it, wasn't a lack of honor but an *excess* of it. He'd made mistakes in his youth, and his noble nature made it difficult for him to forgive himself, even when he'd clearly spent years making amends and turning a new leaf.

*He's such a good man*, she thought achingly.

"I care about you," she whispered. "So very much, Wick."

He let out a breath, one that she hadn't realized he'd been holding. "You do?"

She nodded, her eyes dampening.

"Enough to marry me, lass?" He didn't miss a beat in pressing his advantage, but then she liked that about him. Liked that his will and determination were a match for her own. "You know my faults, the mistakes I've made. But know this too: if you take me on, I will do my best to be a man who is worthy of you."

He was offering more than she'd hoped to have, the promise of something lasting and true. Even though she recognized the risk—the danger of trusting in happiness—how could she resist this magnificent male?

"Yes, I will," she said. "I will marry you."

No sooner had she said the words then he was kissing her. She kissed him back, joy and desire combusting inside her. Then he was carrying her to the bed, her arms looping around his neck as he claimed her mouth with masterful thoroughness.

He tossed her onto the mattress, the primal light in his eyes making her giggle. He reached for the belt of his robe: apparently now that they'd laid themselves bare, it was time to bare other parts of themselves as well. In a flash of insight, she understood that it hadn't been easy for Wick to expose his emotions to her—and now he meant to re-assert his manhood in other ways.

She was gleaning that beneath her husband-to-be's civilized exterior lay the dominant instincts of his ancient Scottish ancestors. As Wick stripped, bearing all those hard, lean edges and sleek muscular bulges, she could well imagine him as a Highland warrior and she a product of his midnight raid. The fantasy shivered through her as he stood before her, proud and strong, so fiercely virile.

He clasped his huge erection, and watching the casual motion of his fist made her pussy clench with need. His mouth took on a feral, hungry slant.

"You're getting an eyeful of what you'll be getting soon," he said in a deep voice. "Now give me the same. Undress for me, angel."

Inflamed by his command, she knelt up on the bed, unfastening the pearl buttons at her throat. Just enough so that she could pull the voluminous nightgown over her head. She wore nothing beneath, her core melting as he raked a hot, proprietary gaze over her nakedness. She felt the same possessive hunger watching the slow glide of his fist along his fleshy sword.

"The monthly visitor's gone, I take?" he inquired silkily.

The hard glint in his eyes told her it mattered naught to him one way or another, and that depraved thought stirred her even further.

"Yes," she said.

"Good. Then show me how wet your little pussy is for this big, hard cock of mine."

*Goodness.* Inflamed by his naughty words and her own throbbing need, she slid her hand between her trembling thighs. As she encountered her own wanton slickness, a whimper left her lips.

"That's a pretty sound, love. Do you like touching yourself?" At her blush, his lips curled in a wicked grin. "You needn't be shy with me, the man who's to be your husband. I want you to enjoy your beautiful body. Lay back, and give me the pleasure of watching you play with that pretty cunny."

Her cheeks hot, she wasn't sure she could do something that depraved. He came to stand by the side of the bed, looking into her face, his looming maleness kindling her most brazen impulses. He continued to frig himself, and with each controlled stroke of his fist, he made her hotter and hotter, burning away her inhibitions. She found herself reclining against the pillows, her fingers moving to her intimate cove.

"That's it, love. Rub that nice pink slit," he said. "Don't forget to pet your little pearl."

She gave herself up to his sensual command. To the delicious sin of what she was doing.

"Did you miss me when I was away, Beatrice?" His voice wrapped around her like dark velvet, blocking out everything but him. "Did I distract you the way you distracted me?"

"Yes," she breathed. "I thought of you often, Wick."

"What about at night, when you were alone in this big bed? Did you think of me then?"

Dew gushed along with embarrassment. "Yes."

"Did you touch yourself?"

Fire blazed in her cheeks and her sex. Lord, she was hot and needy...

"Answer me, angel. Did you masturbate thinking of me? The way I did thinking of you?"

"Yes," she gasped.

"Did you play with your tits and your pussy, make yourself come?"

With a wild nod, she took his suggestion. She squeezed the aching tips of her breasts with her free hand as with the other she made wet swirls over the center of her sensation. She was so close...

"My naughty angel." His heated approval took her to the brink, her toes curling into the coverlet. "Are you going to come for me now?"

His gaze swept over her, his biceps flexing as he jerked steadily on his erection.

"*Yes.*" Her climax broke free, and she soared into bliss.

She'd barely caught her breath when his hand slid into her hair, bringing her to the edge of the mattress. With his other hand, he guided his erection to her lips, the fat scarlet head glossy with his desire.

"Make it wet," he coaxed. "All over, lass, so it will fit into that tight cunny of yours."

With a moan, she parted her lips, and he thrust inside. This was the second time that they'd done this. The first time, he'd instructed her, at her request, on how to suck his cock. She'd thought she'd done quite well, yet now she realized how much he'd been holding back. Before, he'd let her explore at her leisure: she'd lapped at the flaring dome, trailed her tongue along the intriguing ridges of the shaft, kissed the velvety weight of his balls.

*This* time, he was fully in control. He dictated the depth and speed, his hand holding her head still as his hips set the rhythm. Rough noises scraped from his throat as he took her mouth the way he did her pussy...and she loved it.

When he drove too deep, her throat clenched reflexively around his hardness. With a savage groan, he pulled out of her mouth. He mounted the bed, his hard, hairy chest teasing her nipples, making her squirm with anticipation. The head of his cock prodded her cleft.

He looked into her eyes. "I want to be inside you with nothing between us, love. I won't come in your cunny; I'll pull out before that happens."

In answer, she arched her hips, painting her wetness over his thick crown.

His pupils dilated, he bent down to kiss her. At the same time, he notched his cock to her opening and pushed in. They both moaned at the perfection of the fit. He stretched her, filled her, taking away the empty ache. He seated himself so fully that she felt his stones pressed up against her.

He nuzzled her ear. "Good, love?"

"So very good," she sighed. "Don't stop."

He began to move. Deep, soulful plunges that made her gasp with delight, that made her realize the vast difference between self-pleasuring and this shared ecstasy. She ran her hands down the undulating musculature of his back to the taut, flexing hills of his buttocks. She dug her fingers into his hard arse, and he growled.

"Want it harder, angel? Want to take my cock deeper into your tight little hole?"

Staring into his beautiful, hungry face, she said, "I want everything you have to give, Wick."

"Such a good, greedy lass you are."

He pounded into her. He slammed his hips, drilling his shaft into her core, his stones slapping wetly against her swollen folds. She came, her pussy rippling along his steely length, gasping as liquid pleasure burst inside her.

"You squeeze my prick so nicely when you come." He didn't stop thrusting, his hazel eyes fierce. "I want to feel you do it again."

His thumb found her pearl, circling and pressing it against his pistoning cock. She felt herself responding, her hips lifting to meet his thrusts, the heat inside her building once again. Then he bent to capture her nipple between his lips. The suction blazed to the part of her crammed full of him, setting off new convulsions of delight.

"Now I'm going to spend for you," he rasped.

He pulled out, and despite her sated state, she tingled at the sight of him: kneeling between her spread legs, his thighs ridged with muscle, his fist jerking on his thick, glistening stalk. She saw the instant the pleasure overtook him, the bulging sinew on his neck and upper arms, the gritting of his teeth against a shout. He exploded, directing the sensual geyser at her breasts and belly. His seed rained upon her, and she dipped her fingers into his essence, rubbing it into her skin. He watched, his chest heaving and nostrils flaring.

Afterward, he cleaned her up with a towel. Gathering her close in bed, he kissed the top of her head. With her cheek pressed against his chest, sated and warm, she fell asleep.

She woke to darkness and the sound of knocking.

Beneath her, Wick stirred sleepily. "Is that someone at the door? What time is it?"

She fumbled to light the lamp. "I'll go see what's going on."

Slipping from the warm cocoon, she quickly tugged on her

nightgown. She went to the door, opened it. At the sight of Lisette's distraught features, a cold droplet slid down her spine.

Dread gripping her throat, Bea said, "What is going on?"

"Mr. Sheridan's here, my lady," the maid blurted. "He's looking for Miss Sheridan. She was working in the village last night and didn't make it home."

NEARING MIDDAY, THERE WAS STILL NO TRACE OF FANCY Sheridan.

As Wick headed back to the manor house, his mood was grim. He'd organized search parties to look for Fancy, and his own team had gone through the village from top to bottom. All he'd discovered was that Fancy had left the inn where she'd been hired to help in the kitchen around eight o'clock. Her brother Godfrey, who'd also been working at the inn, was supposed to walk home with her, but he'd ended up dallying with a barmaid.

Rather than waiting, Fancy had headed home alone.

From there, Wick had the reports of several people who saw her walking down the main road back toward Camden Manor. She hadn't made it to her family's cottage at the edge of the estate. In his gut, Wick knew that something sinister had happened to Beatrice's friend.

Wick's hope that someone else had located the missing girl vanished when he entered the manor's drawing room and saw Beatrice. She'd just returned from searching some nearby fields with her team, which consisted of her tenants, George and Sarah Haller, and the curate, Frank Varnum. All four had bleak, pinched expressions. Mr. Haller was comforting his blonde wife, whose reddened eyes betrayed the fact that she'd been crying.

When Wick went up to Bea, the others wordlessly gave them space.

"No news?" he asked quietly.

"Everyone's back except for Mr. Sheridan's group and Knighton's," she said tremulously.

Knighton had delayed his departure to help look for Fancy, and Wick was grateful. They needed all the help they could get. With each passing moment, the chances of Fancy's survival grew dimmer.

"I don't know what to do, where else to look." Bea swallowed. "I can't bear to think of Fancy alone and afraid somewhere or even worse..."

Her voice broke, and he put an arm around her waist, drawing her close.

"Keep your chin up, for Fancy's sake," he said.

"I'm trying, but I'm scared, Wick," she whispered. "What if her disappearance is related to the fire, that threatening note? She could be in terrible danger...and it's my fault."

"Even if Fancy's disappearance is related to those other threats, there's nothing you could have done." He headed her off at the pass. "You are not responsible for whoever is carrying out these heinous acts."

"I *am* responsible for the welfare of all who live at Camden Manor. And if someone is trying to hurt me by harming those I care about, then this *is* my fault. Fancy is my best friend. I should have made sure that she understood the danger, that she had an escort, but instead I was distracted by..."

She bit her lip, but he knew.

"By me. Is that what you were going to say?" he asked.

"I didn't mean it that way," she said, her voice quivering.

He tipped up her chin. "It's all right if you did. But you're wrong, you know. Your happiness has nothing to do with Fancy's disappearance."

"I...I know. You're right. But the thought of something happening to her..." Her gaze went past him to the window. At her widening eyes, he turned to see what she was looking at.

Knighton's carriage had pulled up to the house. He was getting out.

With Fancy Sheridan in his arms.

"Fancy," Beatrice breathed. "Oh, thank God!"

An instant later, she was running for the door, Wick following behind her.

"I'm fine, Bea," Fancy murmured sleepily. "Stop fretting. I just need me rest..."

The laudanum that the physician had given Fancy took effect, and she drifted off. Gently, Bea brushed a strand of hair off her bosom chum's cheek. As her fingers trailed over the angry purple swelling at Fancy's temple, her chest burned.

*Who did this to Fancy and why?* she thought with helpless rage.

Tucking the coverlet around her sleeping friend, she left the guest bedchamber and went to the family parlor where Wick, the Duke of Knighton, and Mr. Sheridan were waiting. Wick and the duke were in the wingchairs by the fire, while Fancy's papa had the divan. They all rose when Bea came in.

"Fancy's asleep now," Bea told them.

She joined Mr. Sheridan on the divan. Seeing the anxious furrows on the tinker's brow and his ashen cheeks above his beard, she took his hand and gave it a squeeze.

"The physician said that rest is good for her," she assured him. "He did a thorough examination, and the bruise on the temple and chafing at her wrists were the only injuries he found. He said no permanent damage was done and that she ought to be right as rain after a few days."

She felt the swell of relief in the room, a collective breath releasing. No one said anything, but it was in all their minds. Despite the trauma Fancy had suffered, she had been lucky: what happened to her could have been far, far worse.

"Who would do such a thing to me Fancy?" Mr. Sheridan asked, his blue eyes bewildered. "She's a good girl, never done 'arm to a fly."

"Fancy didn't do anything to deserve this," Bea said tersely. "It's my fault."

Earlier, Knighton had given a brief account of how he'd found Fancy. He and his team had been scouring the woods that straddled Bea and Squire Crombie's properties when he'd heard muffled sounds. He'd followed them to Fancy, who'd been gagged and bound to a tree.

Terrified, the girl didn't know how long she'd been there, only that she'd been on her way home last night when she'd heard a noise behind her. She'd reacted too late: something had hit her on the side of her head, and everything had gone dark. When she'd awakened, she'd been in the forest, tied to the tree.

Cold and confused, she'd had no idea how she'd got there. Nor did she have any memory of the person who'd done this to her. But a note had been pinned to her skirts:

*Friends of the Bitch beware.*

It didn't take a genius to surmise who the "Bitch" was. And if the note wasn't enough of a clue, then what Knighton told Bea was: when he'd found Fancy, she'd had a red line painted on her right cheek—a crude replica of Bea's scar. Afraid of increasing Fancy's distress, Knighton had wiped it off her cheek on the pretense of removing dirt.

The message was clear: whoever had hurt and terrorized Fancy had done so to get to Bea.

*Why? Who would do such a heinous thing…just to punish me?*

"The fault is not yours."

Wick and Knighton had both spoken at the same time. Now they were staring at each other, eyes narrowed.

"O' course this ain't your fault, Miss Bea," Mr. Sheridan said. "You've always been a friend to us Sheridans and Fancy especially. If I know me daughter—and I do, seeing as I raised 'er since she was a babe—she would not be wanting you to feel responsible for the actions o' the bastard who did this, pardon my plain speaking. She'd be telling you to concentrate on 'ow to keep yourself safe from this sneaky coward."

"Mr. Sheridan is correct." The Duke of Knighton leaned forward in his chair. "We must plan for your safety, Lady Beatrice, and the safety of Miss Sheridan."

When he'd returned with Fancy in his arms, he'd been disheveled, his dark hair ruffled, a rip in his jacket, his boots covered in mud. Now he was back to his usual elegant self, although a dangerous glint lingered in his grey eyes. Beatrice was grateful beyond words that he'd stayed to aid in the search for her friend.

"Knighton and I have a plan," Wick said curtly.

"What sort of a plan?" She canted her head.

Wick rose, stalking before the fire. "It's not safe for you or Miss Sheridan here at Camden Manor. In London, I have the resources and men to ensure your proper protection. Let me finish," he said, when she opened her mouth to argue.

His stern tone startled her into remaining silent, and he continued on.

"If you stay here, you compromise your safety and the safety of those around you. Whoever is trying to hurt you will continue to strike—and next time the results could be far worse than the barn fire and Miss Sheridan's kidnapping." He held up a hand when she again tried to speak. "It's time to stop this dastardly villain. The clues we've found thus far all lead to London. We know the pocket watch was made there; we can have it looked at by watchmakers, try to track down its origins and owner. We can also investigate Randall Perkins, see what we can find out about his past. He may even be in the city, along with another suspect, Reverend Wright. Going to London is the logical course of action."

His lecture apparently coming to an end, Wick faced her with his shoulders drawn back and his jaw set. He had the look of a warrior ready to fight for what he believed was right. She realized he was ready for her to dispute his plan. That *had* been her initial impulse. To say that she couldn't leave her estate or the people under her care. That she wouldn't run from some cowardly attacker.

Yet she had to admit that Wick's logic was sound. She was, at this moment, a liability. If her foe's aim was to terrorize her, then her very presence threatened the welfare of her tenants, who could get caught in the crossfire, the way Fancy had. The sooner Bea identified the villain and saw to his capture, the sooner everyone around her would be safe. And her instincts told her Wick was right: the answers lay in London.

London, where Wick had the resources to keep Fancy and her safe.

London, where she'd have to face the ghosts of her past.

"What do you think of the plan?" Wick asked.

His jaw had a stubborn line, and his posture was braced, prepared for a battle.

She lifted her brows. "When do we leave?"

## ❦ 23 ❦

It took Beatrice two days to get ready for the trip to London. Since Wick had expected much more resistance to his plan, he was happy to let her take her time. Her decision to trust him was a gift, and he wanted her to feel good about it. Where he could, he helped her cross tasks off her lengthy checklist of preparations.

Her main concern was the welfare of her tenants in her absence; accordingly, he went into the village to hire men to guard her estate. He also briefed the farmers on the situation, setting up a patrol system whereby the tenants themselves took turns keeping watch. Although his former harvesting comrades had been less friendly since discovering he represented Great London National Railway, their concern for Beatrice, Fancy, and the immediate threat to the estate made them amenable to his suggestions.

Wick also had his own arrangements to make. He'd sent a discreet letter to his colleagues, Garrity and Kent, informing them of his imminent return and promising to fill them in on the situation in Staffordshire. He'd also written to Richard and Violet, who by this time had arrived at his house in London, and told them he'd be bringing back house guests. Knowing his angel's anxieties about being accepted by his family, he'd spent several paragraphs extolling Bea's virtues.

Finally, he'd sent a rush order to his preferred jeweler, Rundell, Bridge & Co.

The day before they were set to depart, Mr. Sheridan paid a visit to Beatrice. Wick and Knighton were in the drawing room as well.

"We won't be going to London with you, Miss Bea," the grey-bearded tinker announced.

"Why not?" Beatrice asked with clear surprise.

"Sheridans ain't city folk," he said. "We do be'er in open fields, with the sky above our 'eads."

"But it's not safe here. After what happened to Fancy—"

"It's precisely what 'appened to my girl that has me mind made up. We be moving on, Miss Beatrice. The road's our true 'ome and where we be the safest. We travelling folk know places that others don't and, what's more, we be looking out for one another."

Beatrice bit her lip. "But Fancy's not fully recovered. She needs to be looked after."

"Allow me to offer my escort," Knighton said.

Everyone stared at him.

"You?" Bea blinked.

"My carriage will offer Miss Sheridan the comfort she needs during her recovery. I will stay with her and her family until they are safely out of harm's reach. You have my word."

The tinker eyed the duke dubiously. "The travelling life ain't suited for toffs."

"I'll manage," Knighton said dismissively. "Miss Sheridan's safety must come first."

That had been that.

Thus, on the third day, two groups were ready to head their separate ways. As they made their farewells, Beatrice enfolded Fancy in a tight hug, her worry for her friend evident. Wick understood her concern. She'd stayed with Fancy every night since the kidnapping for the girl had been having night terrors, waking up screaming. Although the swelling on Fancy's temple was improving, fear lingered in her brown eyes. She startled easily, like a frightened doe.

"Take care, my dear," Bea said fretfully. "I shall miss you."

"You be careful, too." Her friend managed a brave smile. "Until we meet again."

They departed, the Sheridans and Knighton headed for destinations unknown and Wick and Beatrice for London.

Given the chaos and demands of the week, Wick hadn't had much time alone with Beatrice. The trip to London lacked privacy, for she'd brought along her lady's maid and Wick had his valet Barton. He could have had Barton travel back on a coach, but the man had been with him since his underworld days and was as handy with a gun as he was with a cravat or shaving implement. Wick didn't fool himself that they were out of danger; throughout the journey, he and Barton took turns keeping an eye out for any sign of ambush.

Luckily, the time passed uneventfully. On their last leg to London, Wick even found himself alone with Beatrice, Lisette and Barton opting to ride outside with the driver. As soon as the carriage rolled off, Wick closed the curtains and hauled Bea onto his lap. He proceeded to kiss her until she was panting and squirming deliciously.

"What was that for?" she asked breathlessly.

"For being you and being irresistible," he told her. "I missed you, angel."

She flushed, looking adorable in her primrose carriage dress and little straw hat.

"It has been a busy week, hasn't it?" She fiddled with his cravat pin. "I'm sorry we haven't had time together."

"Not sorrier than I am," he said with feeling.

Unfortunately, he couldn't keep the curtains closed; the others might notice, and he didn't want to damage her reputation. He kissed her on the nose, then returned her to the opposite seat and parted the drapes once more. As he settled back on his own side, he saw Bea's pretty lavender gaze linger on the distinct bulge at his groin. She wetted her lips, the little minx.

"Talk to me, sweeting. If you don't distract me," he said ruefully, "I'll ravage you here and now, your reputation be damned."

"I wouldn't mind."

"Beatrice," he said in a warning tone.

She laughed. "All right. Tell me more about your family then, since I'm to meet them soon."

"What do you want to know?"

"Well..." She worried her bottom lip with her teeth. "How will your brother and his lady react to meeting me?"

In her hesitation, he read her genuine concern that Richard and Violet might not welcome her into the fold. Given the ostracism she'd endured in her past, he understood the risk she was taking. She'd left the safety of the haven she'd created in order to return to London, the place where she'd suffered much pain. The fact that she was doing it because she trusted him— trusted in his plan and ability to keep her safe—swelled his chest with tenderness.

He was determined not to fail her.

"Richard and Violet will adore you as I do," he said. "Richard will admire the fact that you run your own estate, and he'll bore us all to tears pestering you with questions about land management. Violet, on the other hand, is a hoyden despite being a viscountess and mama. She will undoubtedly involve you in countless scrapes, and Richard and

I will have our hands full keeping the two of you out of trouble."

"That sounds lovely." Wistfulness edged her tone. "But won't they wonder...about our relationship?"

When Beatrice had conceded to his plan to go to London, she'd had one contingency: she did not yet want to make their engagement public. She'd wanted to direct their energies toward stopping her enemy before planning for their future happiness. When he'd argued that there was no reason they couldn't do both, she'd said in tremulous tones, *The bastard targeted Fancy because she's my friend. I won't endanger you, Wick, by making our relationship public. I couldn't live with myself if anything happened to you.*

He'd told her he wasn't afraid of anyone, least of all the sort of bloody coward who terrorized innocent young women. But Beatrice wouldn't be moved; while he didn't agree, he understood her resolve. Her sense of honor was as great as any man's, and she'd do anything to protect those she cared about. For that reason, he'd agreed to keep their engagement a secret...for now.

"I agreed to keep our engagement under wraps, but I'm not going to hide my interest in you, lass," he said bluntly. "Even if I could, Richard knows me too well. I've never brought a lady to meet him before."

"Never?" She looked adorably pleased.

"Never," he confirmed. "The women in my past weren't the sort I'd introduce to my family. You're the only woman I've ever wanted to marry."

Her nose wrinkled when he mentioned those other women, but he wanted to be honest with her. He hadn't been a saint. He was discovering, however, that he was perfectly capable of devotion and fidelity: he'd just needed to find the right woman. Since Beatrice had come into his life, his past lovers had faded into insignificance. He had no desire to be with anyone else. She filled that emptiness inside him that others hadn't even touched.

"What about your mama? Will she approve of me?" Bea

tipped her head to one side. "You've mentioned your papa's passing, but you haven't said much about her."

There was a reason for it. The mention of his mother, the dowager viscountess, stirred up a mix of love, affection...and embarrassment. It had taken him years to come to terms with the fact that while his mama adored him, she was not always kind to others. It shamed him to admit that she might be the one person in his family to find Beatrice lacking.

"Mama prefers the family seat in Scotland, which is for the better. She is...not an easy person."

"She won't like me?" Bea asked instantly.

He sighed. "She isn't overly fond of most people—including Richard and my departed papa."

Her brow pleated. "Why?"

"My mama tends to notice only the superficial." It hurt to admit the truth about his mother, whom he loved despite her faults. "In her day, she was a celebrated beauty, and appearances mean a lot to her. Her parents arranged her marriage to my father, a Scotsman who adored her but who wasn't the most refined gentleman. Richard takes after him, and I take after Mama, and Mama...well, she always favored me. Spoiled me rotten, truthfully. She taught me to believe that my looks and charm would guarantee my success in the world—lessons I took too much to heart. My arrogance and conceit led to my disgrace."

"And your honor saved you," Bea reminded him. "You made mistakes, but you worked diligently to get yourself out of debt, to earn your current success. I hope your mama understands that?"

"On the contrary, she refuses to see that I was at fault in any way," he said wryly. "In her eyes, I can do no wrong, and I was a mere victim of bad circumstances. Richard, the poor chap, has done everything right, including working his arse off to salvage the family seat and refill the coffers. She has never once thanked him for his efforts."

Bea frowned. "That hardly seems fair."

"It isn't. *She* isn't," he said bluntly. "She is my mama, and I love her, but I wouldn't put much stock in her opinion, if that makes any sense."

"It does. I could say the same about my brother. I care about Benedict, but I don't trust in his judgement either."

"Will you contact him when we're in London?"

"I don't think I will," she said hollowly. "Five years is a long time, and I don't want to dredge up the past. Perhaps it's best to let sleeping dogs lie."

Knowing the nature of the estrangement, Wick understood her ambivalence. She had a loyal nature and cared deeply about her only surviving kin. At the same time, Hadleigh was like a hurricane: since one couldn't stop his path of destruction, the wisest thing to do was to stay out of the way.

"Whatever you decide, I'll support your decision," he said. "You're not alone now, angel."

Her smile was so sweet that his heart ached. "What would I do without you, Wick?"

"You'll never have to find out."

Unable to resist, he reached over and snatched her onto his lap again. She giggled, straddling him, her skirts covering them in frothy yellow waves.

"We're in this together, lass." He brushed his lips over hers. "Through thick and thin."

She peered at him through her lashes. "I'd say this is an instance of *thick*...wouldn't you?"

She moved her hips, rubbing herself against the wide ridge of his erection.

He yanked the curtains closed, started working on the fasteners of his trousers.

"What about my reputation?" she asked demurely.

Searching out the slit in her drawers, he found her ripe and juicy with desire. He gripped his cock, running his bulging crown along her slick folds. She jerked in surprise; this was a new position for them. One that he thought his little termagant would take to like a duck to water. Notching himself to her opening, he pulled her down on him, impaling her in a swift stroke.

She moaned, her pussy fitting him like a wet, tight glove.

"We'll make this quick. Ride me, angel," he ordered.

As predicted, she was more than up for the task.

## 24

WICK'S RESIDENCE TURNED OUT TO BE A GRACEFUL HOUSE
situated on a leafy street close to Russell Square. The arched
windows sparkled, the porticoed entryway adding to the place's
grandeur. As Bea entered, she saw that the interior was equally
refined. The antechamber featured a tiered chandelier and
polished mahogany staircase, veined Italian marble gleaming
beneath her shoes. A landscape painting graced one wall, and a
rosewood console held an immaculate arrangement of hothouse
blooms.

Wick was looking at her, gauging her reaction. The furrow
between his brows revealed that her opinion of his home
mattered to him. She let her approval show in her admiring smile,
and his handsome features relaxed. He took her hand, kissing the
gloved knuckles briefly. His heat penetrated the soft kid, causing
a pleasant swirl in her blood, a quiver of the well-used muscles
between her thighs.

Goodness, the man was potent. He'd brought her to climax
twice in the carriage, yet a simple kiss on the hand brought her
lust up to a simmer again. As if he gleaned the direction of her

thoughts, his eyes got that languid, heavy-lidded look that made her want to have her way with him here and now, on the gleaming marble tiles.

She summoned up a polite smile as Wick introduced the members of his household staff, who were lined up to greet them. A sudden stampede of footsteps overhead interrupted him. Shouts and whoops of joy erupted as three boys appeared at the top of the stairwell, racing down and shoving at each other in their eagerness to get to Wick first.

"Uncle Wick, you're back!"

"Oof—get out of my way. I want to say hello to Uncle Wick."

"You get out of the way, numskull. I was here first!"

Bea couldn't tell who had said what for the dark-haired trio was as tangled as a tumbleweed, a collection of arms, jabbing elbows, and kicking feet. They were all jabbering at once, trying to outshout one another in an attempt to be heard.

"Now, lads, mind your manners," Wick began.

His admonition only served to raise the volume as the boys tried to talk to him while simultaneously arguing with each other.

"Enough, lads."

The boys quieted at the sound of the booming male voice that came from the top of the stairs. A brawny dark-haired man was descending, a slender brunette dressed in a buttercup yellow gown by his side. Bea knew that the man must be Wick's brother, although there was little in the way of family resemblance. As Richard Murray approached, she saw that his features were more rugged than refined, his dark eyes rather somber. Unlike Wick, who exuded a natural charisma that drew people to him wherever he went, the older Murray had the look of a man who would be more comfortable sporting outdoors than doing the pretty in drawing rooms.

Indeed, his lady bore more of a resemblance to Wick with her pretty caramel-colored eyes and vivacious features. She moved with a natural energy and grace that would serve her well on a ballroom floor. Her air of lively mischief made for an appealing contrast to her husband's stoic gravity.

Despite Wick's reassurances, Bea knew she had to be prepared for any reaction to her scar. Her last foray into polite society had taught her just how much the *ton* judged by appearances. Her pulse beat a rapid tattoo as she realized that she ought to have freshened up before meeting his family. In addition to her damaged cheek, she'd engaged in vigorous lovemaking in the carriage; what if it showed?

*Stop panicking. It's too late. Take a breath...*

She braced for the lady's greeting.

"You must be Lady Beatrice," Wick's sister-in-law exclaimed. "It's jolly good to meet you! Wick never brings anyone around to meet us, and you're every bit as dashing as he described in his letter. He also mentioned that you're an ace shot; is that true? I've been taking archery lessons, and you're welcome to practice with me, although fair warning...I've been accounted an excellent shot myself," she ended with a raffish little grin.

Bea blinked, not sure how to respond.

"Before Lady Beatrice decides whether she'd like to participate in your games, lass, perhaps she'd like to know who 'we' are."

Although Wick's brother's tone was chiding, amusement warmed his earth-brown eyes as he regarded his lady. Turning to Bea, he inclined his head. In the unaffected elegance of that gesture, she began to see the similarity between the brothers.

"Richard Murray, Viscount Carlisle, at your service," he said. "This modest, demure lady is my wife Violet, and these are our boys: Ewan, Duncan, and Wickham."

At the mention of their names, the lads hastily bowed. Their gentlemanly manners bore the stamp of their father. Catching one of them—Duncan—surreptitiously stick his tongue out at his youngest brother, Bea felt her lips quiver; their mama obviously had an influence as well.

Bea's tension drained away. Curtsying, she said, "A pleasure to meet you all. And I should very much like to practice archery with you, Lady Carlisle."

"Only if you call me Violet," the lady said cheerfully. "I shan't answer to anything else."

"Sometimes she doesn't even answer to that," her husband said.

Violet wrinkled her nose at him; he chucked her under the chin in a gesture of casual affection.

"Before you shove a bow and arrow at my guest, Vi," Wick said, "it has been a long journey. I'm sure Beatrice would like to get settled in first."

"Of course. In fact, I'll take her to her rooms. That way,"—Violet gave a Bea a conspiratorial wink—"we can gossip about you men."

Smiling, Bea followed the lady up the stairs.

"I suppose this means we men must fend for ourselves." Carlisle's comment to Wick drifted up toward them. "Don't know how we'll manage without Violet telling us what's what."

His lady paused on the landing, wearing a look of mischief as she turned around.

"Boys?" she called.

"Yes, Mama?" her sons chorused.

"While you're with Papa and Uncle Wick, might I remind you that there's only one rule you must abide by?"

"What is the rule, Mama?" Ewan, the eldest, asked gravely.

"Don't do anything that *I* wouldn't do," she said.

The boys looked at each other...their eyes rounding with delight.

The Murray brothers groaned.

Bea found herself chuckling as the viscountess continued up the stairs.

~

As Beatrice was fatigued from the journey, Wick instructed Cook to have a tray sent up to her while he dined with Richard, Violet, and their brood. While the children of the *ton* typically took supper in the nursery, Violet's middle class background made her a more involved mama than most, and Wick could tell his brother thrived in the familial closeness fostered by his viscountess.

God knew it was a far cry from their own upbringing.

With the boys present, Wick couldn't get into the details of Beatrice's enemy and the purpose of their return to London, but he liked catching up and hearing news of Violet's family, the Kents, with whom she was very close. Since her brother Harry was one of Wick's business partners, they were all family, in a way. After supper, Violet rounded up the boys and left the brothers to enjoy their cigars and spirits.

Wick led the way to his study. He'd spared no expense in having the masculine retreat done up to his exact preferences. Mahogany wood, rich tobacco leather, and burgundy rugs gave the room an inviting feel. As Richard settled into one of the deep tufted wing chairs by the fire, propping his booted feet on the footstool with a sigh of satisfaction, Wick felt a sense of pride that he could offer this hospitality to his brother.

For years, he'd taken from Richard; it was nice to give back, even in this small way.

Going to the spirits cabinet, he asked innocently, "Port or brandy?"

Richard shot him a look. "Whisky. And it had better be the Tobermary."

It was, of course. Wick knew his brother's lips would never touch anything but the best Scotch whisky. But just because he'd matured in some ways didn't mean he couldn't enjoy pulling Richard's leg now and again. It was the right of the younger brother, after all.

He poured the amber liquid into two cut-crystal glasses. He

brought one to his brother, then took the adjacent wing chair. He enjoyed the companionable moment, listening to the crackle of the hearth and appreciating the smooth burn of the spirits.

"I like your Lady Beatrice," Richard said. "Violet does as well."

Social niceties and chit chat had never been his brother's forte. Richard took after their papa in that way: a stoic, serious man who never saw the point in taking any route but the most direct.

"I'm glad she has your stamp of approval," Wick said.

Richard's brow furrowed. "I didn't mean to imply that she needed it, lad. You're your own man and have been for some time."

"I'm in earnest," Wick said hastily, realizing that Richard had misconstrued his comment for sarcasm. "It matters to me that you and Violet get along with her. It means a lot to Beatrice, too, because she hasn't always had that welcome after her accident. That was partly why she left London five years ago."

"Bloody *ton*," Richard said with disgust. "Well, I hope you've convinced her not to pay any mind to that pettiness. Your lass is fair and kind, capable to boot. I should like to learn more about her land management techniques since I'm thinking about expanding my own holdings."

Wick's lips quirked. "I'm certain Beatrice would be happy to discuss crop rotation with you."

"It's good to see you settling down and with a sensible female. Have you asked her to marry you yet?"

That was Richard: straight to the point.

"I have, but we're waiting before we make our engagement public."

"Why wait?"

"If I had my way, I'd have the bans read tomorrow. But Beatrice...she's not yet ready."

Richard frowned. "Why not?"

Wick gave an account of the dangers Bea faced and their purpose in London.

"So you intend to track down the owner of the pocket watch and delve into the past of this Randall Perkins character. And perhaps locate this Reverend Wright as well." Richard took a meditative sip of whisky. "You'll need help, and I'd be glad to lend a hand. I'll also try to keep a rein on Violet, but you know how she is."

As Wick had been friends with Violet even before she met Richard, he was well aware that his sister-in-law would not countenance being left out of an adventure. Richard indulged his viscountess quite shamelessly, although Wick knew he would draw the line at her putting herself at risk. Nor would Wick be willing to endanger the lady he loved like a sister.

"Since you and Violet solved the mystery of Monique's murder all those years ago," he said, "I would welcome your assistance."

At the mention of his dead mistress, his brother's brows lifted. Wick knew why. He rarely mentioned Monique or that shameful time in his life. Yet his talks with Beatrice had quieted the rattling of skeletons so that they now felt to be what they were: memories that would always be with him but no longer felt like a cross to bear.

"Have you told your lass about what happened?" Richard asked quietly.

"Yes. And she thinks that I'm honorable, even with the mistakes that I've made."

"A sensible woman, as I said." His brother gave an approving nod. "Your problem never was a lack of honor, Wickham, but an excess of it."

"I don't follow."

Richard set down his glass, leaning his forearms on his thighs. "Since you were a wee boy, you've cared about doing the right thing, but when you failed to meet your own high standards or made a mistake, you were always hard on yourself. Excessively so.

To the point where no one could tell you anything without you lashing out in anger. But the true anger, lad, was at yourself, no? You've been this way your entire life."

Stunned, Wick stared at his brother. "When did you become this insightful?"

"Since I got myself a wife who informs me my problem isn't a lack of emotion but an excess of it." Richard rubbed the back of his neck, his expression rueful. "According to Violet, the quieter I get, the more 'feelings' I'm having. That's when she pesters me until I talk to her."

"I wonder how our tendencies came about," Wick said, bemused.

"Need you ask? Papa and Mama each had a favorite, and you knew when you weren't it." Richard's tone was wry. "In Mama's eyes, I'm the dull, staid son who lacks your charm, good looks, and ease with people. Which is fine by me, since Violet values my other qualities." His chest puffed out a little, his expression that of a man who's found exactly what he needed in his marriage. "As for Papa, he was stricter and harsher with you, expressing his disappointment at the slightest thing."

"He compared me to you, the dutiful heir, and I always came up short."

"We're different, Wick. Like apples and oranges, neither is better or worse." Richard paused. "I'm learning this with my own lads: Ewan has the brains, Duncan is the mischief-maker, and Wickham...well, he takes after his namesake. The lad's got all the servants wrapped around his finger, and even his grandmama can't resist his smile. As different as the boys are, however, I love them equally."

"Something our parents never managed to do." Wick paused. "By the by, how is Mama?"

"Spitting mad that you didn't manage your usual visit in the spring. She blames me and Violet for keeping her from you, although we've told her more than once that she's welcome to leave the dowager house and join you in London." Richard's expression was sardonic. "I'm sorry to say she hasn't taken us up on that offer."

"I'm not sorry," Wick said with feeling.

His brother's look turned sympathetic. "You should know she's been making noises about visiting her 'handsome lad,' and clearly she didn't mean me."

Wick grimaced. The *last* thing he needed right now was for his mama to show up.

"Then I'd better solve the mystery behind the attacks and wed Beatrice before that happens," he muttered. "If she meets Mama before she has my ring on her finger, she might change her mind about taking me on."

"How do you plan to proceed with your inquiries?"

"First thing tomorrow, I'm hiring guards for Beatrice." His tenure in the underworld had made him some useful connections in that regard. "I know a fellow named Wilcox who specializes in that line of work. Then I'll be meeting with Garrity and Kent to apprise them of the situation. And, hopefully, to gain their assistance in stopping Beatrice's enemy."

Richard grunted. Being the protective older brother, he'd never liked Adam Garrity, the former moneylender who'd once held Wick's vowels. Wick could never persuade his brother that while Garrity was undoubtedly ruthless, a true product of the London underclass, he was also a fair man, one who was true to his word. Not only had he allowed Wick to work off the debt, he'd recognized and encouraged Wick's potential.

For years, Wick had been Garrity's right-hand man in the moneylending business, his specialty being loans to the *ton*. When Garrity had gained controlling interest in a failing railway company a few years ago, he'd invited Wick to become a partner. Between the two of them and Harry Kent, they'd turned GLNR into the success it was today.

In short, Wick owed a lot to Garrity. He considered the older man a mentor and a friend.

Insofar as Adam Garrity had friends.

"And you're certain that Garrity will be keen on helping the woman who's standing in the way of his railway?" Richard asked, brows raised.

"It's my railway as well. And Garrity isn't as bad as you think. He has his good points."

"You mean his wife," his brother muttered. "That woman is a saint."

If Garrity had any soft spot, it was for his wife Gabriella. Gabriella Garrity, in turn, had a soft spot for everyone. She was great friends with Violet and the rest of the Kent family, who'd befriended her during her wallflower days. Years ago, she'd also been the one who'd pleaded on Wick's behalf, convincing Garrity to give him a chance to work off his debt. If Mrs. Garrity took a liking to Beatrice—and she would, since she liked everyone—she could undoubtedly persuade her husband to offer his assistance.

Wick didn't think it would come to that. He knew his partner: as hard a man as Garrity was, he, too, had a code of honor. He wanted the land, but he wouldn't stand for a woman to be terrorized because of it.

"At least you can count on Harry," Richard said. "He's an obliging chap. And you'd get Tessa's assistance as well, which could come in handy."

Harry's wife, Tessa, came from one of the ruling families of the London underclass. Her grandfather, Bartholomew Black, was known as the King of the Underworld because of his power and ability to mete justice in places beyond the reach of Peelers and magistrates. In recent years, Tessa had taken over some of his duties, and she had connections in the darkest parts of London.

"Let us reconvene after I speak to Garrity and Kent tomorrow," Wick said decisively.

"Whatever you need, let me know." Richard rose, rolling his

shoulders. "I'd better head up. Violet will be chomping at the bit to know what we just discussed."

"Are you going to tell her?"

"Aye, lad." The wolfish gleam in Richard's eyes suggested that perhaps he wasn't the proper, staid brother in all ways. "But I might make her work for it."

## 25

"You're the one who insisted on coming," Wick muttered as the carriage rolled to a stop. "Stop fidgeting, things will be fine."

"I'm not fidgeting," Beatrice informed him. "I'm merely gathering my things."

All right, she *had* been fidgeting with her gloves and reticule, but Wick didn't have to know that. Earlier, they'd had a disagreement at the breakfast table when he'd told her that he would be asking his partners to assist in finding her foe. She'd told her that she would accompany him since she didn't want anyone speaking on her behalf. He'd countered that he also had other business to discuss with his colleagues, which was best done in privacy. She'd asked him if he had secrets he was hiding from her...

And on it had went. Until Carlisle had put down his fork with a sigh.

"You two are squabbling worse than the boys. For God's sake, Wickham, you're a negotiator, aren't you?" The viscount had sounded exasperated. "Find a compromise with the lady before you give us all indigestion."

Which had led to the present plan. Beatrice, Violet, and

Carlisle had accompanied Wick to his offices located in the City. Wick was going to introduce Beatrice to his partners, and she planned to make her views very clear to them. Even if they chose to help her, she would not part with her land, not unless some solution could be found that would spare the farms. She trusted Wick, but she did not know the men he worked with and didn't want them to harbor any misunderstandings.

It was best to begin as she meant to go on, even if it meant sacrificing popularity with Wick's colleagues. Coming to London had been a huge step for her, and she had her misgivings. For even as her feelings for Wick deepened, she couldn't shake an accompanying sense of...fear.

Fear that her happiness was transient. Fear that she was opening herself up to pain again. Fear that losing Wick would make all her past losses pale in comparison.

She tried to tell herself the fear was irrational. After all, Wick cared for her and was doing everything in his power to help her, even to the detriment of his own cause. He wasn't anything like Croydon. Yet in her bones she knew that things, no matter how perfect they seemed in the moment, had a way of falling apart.

Thus, as seductive as it was to find a haven in Wick's arms and to be welcomed into the fold of his family, she couldn't lose herself in the relationship. Her independence had saved her the last time; when her world as she knew it had disintegrated, she'd had only herself to count on. And she couldn't forget that.

The door opened, and Wick alighted, handing her down. On the pavement, she turned to speak to the Carlisles, who remained in the carriage.

"I shan't be long," she said.

"Take your time, dear," Violet said blithely. "We'll wait for you here."

The "compromise" Bea had reached with Wick involved meeting his partners and saying what she needed to say. Then she would leave him to convene privately with his associates; in the interim, she and the Carlisles would pay visits to watchmakers, to see if they could trace the origins of the pocket watch.

As Bea followed Wick toward his offices, she noticed a small boy standing across the street. She didn't know why he'd caught her eye: he wore the drab brown garb that was the uniform of street urchins, a battered cap atop his mop of brown hair, streaks of dirt on his cherubic face. Perhaps it was his stillness that snagged her attention, the way he stood unmoving by the lamp post amidst the hustle and bustle of the street.

An unbidden thought popped into her head. *Is he...watching me?*

A hackney stopped in the thoroughfare, cutting him from her view. When it drove off, the boy was gone.

Telling herself she was imagining things, Beatrice followed Wick into a handsome, sprawling brick building. Located in London's financial center near the Bank of England, the offices of Great London National Railway were characterized by restrained elegance. The lobby was a masterpiece of dark wood paneling, richly upholstered furnishings, and brass fixtures. Everything from the spotless grey marble underfoot to the sweeping velvet framing the tall windows whispered, rather than shouted, that this was a prosperous business.

The clerk behind an imposing front desk of carved mahogany jumped to his feet at the sight of them.

"Welcome back, Mr. Murray. It's good to see you." He bowed to Beatrice. "Welcome, miss."

"It's good to be back, Mr. Lyall," Wick replied. "Where are Mr. Garrity and Mr. Kent?"

"They're awaiting you in the main meeting room."

"Thank you." Wick steered Beatrice toward the staircase.

As they ascended the steps, she said, "Your offices are impressive."

"We expanded them last year. Garrity owned the original

building, and we purchased the one next door as well, merging them both. We also acquired a separate warehouse for Kent."

As Wick had explained the roles of his partners previously, she knew that Harry Kent was the scientist of the group. According to his proud sister Violet, he was a bona fide genius, whose latest innovations with the steam engine were set to revolutionize the industry.

"Mr. Kent needs the space for his experiments?" Bea asked curiously.

"*We* need the space away from Kent and his experiments," Wick said ruefully. "There's no denying the man's a genius, but he also has a propensity to blast things to smithereens."

On that comforting thought, they arrived on the next floor. Wick led the way down a corridor flanked by offices, stopping to acknowledge greetings from a veritable army of employees. At the end of the hallway, they entered through a set of double doors, two men rising from a long table to greet them.

From what Wick had told her about his partners, Bea had no problem identifying who was who. The man at the head of the table had to be Adam Garrity. He appeared to be in his forties, his coal-black hair slicked back, his gaze the same fathomless shade. Although his sharp features were handsome, they had a cold, ruthless quality. His somber clothes were immaculately fitted to his lean form. Framed by the windows behind him, which gave an expansive view of the city's financial center, he radiated an aura of power.

"Good morning, Murray." His tone was cool. "You didn't mention you would be bringing company."

"There was a last-minute change to the plans." Wick gave her a wry look before making the introductions. "May I introduce my partners, Mr. Adam Garrity and Mr. Harry Kent? This is Lady Beatrice Wodehouse, who we also knew as Miss Beatrice Brown."

"Pleasure to meet you, my lady," Harry Kent said with a bow.

Even without the introductions, Bea had guessed his identity from his resemblance to Violet. Tall and athletically built, he had clean-cut, handsome features, his intelligent brown gaze taking in the world from behind a pair of wire-rimmed spectacles. His unruly dark cowlick added to his professorial appeal, as did the stains on his waistcoat.

Catching the direction of her gaze, he smiled ruefully and took out a handkerchief—one that, she noticed, already bore traces of dirt—and started rubbing at the splotches.

"My trial with an ignition device didn't go as planned," he said.

Bea's gaze shot to Wick, who shrugged as if to say, *At least the building's still standing.*

"I'm gratified to make your acquaintance at last, my lady." This came from Garrity, who'd been quietly assessing her. "Would you care to sit?"

"Thank you, no. What I have to say will only take a few moments."

"This concerns our bid on your land, I assume."

She nodded, and Mr. Garrity's dark gaze flicked to Wick, who seemed unbothered by the reptilian stare. "As Murray's recent missives have been rather scant on details, may I presume from your presence today that negotiations have gone well?"

Wick cleared his throat to speak, but Beatrice beat him to it.

"I hope what I have to say will not detract from the pleasure of our acquaintance." Seeing no reason to beat around the bush, she said crisply, "Mr. Murray and I have not yet reached an agreement concerning the building of your railway upon my land. I have my farms to consider, and while Mr. Murray is exploring a potential solution to preserve said farms whilst laying track, the welfare of my farmers must take precedence for me. I will not agree to any scenario that would jeopardize their livelihoods."

Mr. Garrity's expression was unreadable. "You came to London to inform us of this?"

"No." She drew a breath. "I came to London because it appears someone is trying to scare me off my land. I've received a threatening letter, and in the past fortnight my property was subjected to arson and my best friend was kidnapped and terrorized."

"Bloody hell." This came from Mr. Kent, whose gaze had shot to Wick. "That is what you were referring to in your letters as 'unexpected complications'?"

Wick gave a grim nod. "I thought it best to be discreet."

"Do you have any idea who is behind these crimes?" Mr. Kent asked.

"We have several suspects," Wick replied, "and clues that have led us to London. I've offered Lady Beatrice my protection and assistance in tracking down the villain."

"What needs to be done?" Mr. Kent's brown eyes were keen. "Unfortunate timing, but Ambrose—my older brother, who's an investigator," he clarified, "is travelling abroad, and he and his partners decided to close the agency for the summer. I believe his partner Mr. Lugo may still be in Town and available for consultation. And I'd be glad to lend a hand, of course. All of us Kents are rather well acquainted with murder and mayhem."

Bea couldn't help liking Harry Kent, who was clearly a decent chap.

"Lady Carlisle said the same thing," she said, smiling at him.

"Violet isn't just acquainted with mayhem, she *is* the mayhem," he countered.

Bea's smile deepened into a grin. "Speaking of which, she's waiting for me in the carriage, and I'd best take my leave. I'll leave Mr. Murray to explain the rest of the details." She curtsied. "Thank you for your time and assistance, gentlemen."

"Before you go, my lady." The imperious tones matched the expression of the speaker. Mr. Garrity's pitch-dark gaze had a glint that she could only describe as calculating. "It would be our honor, of course, to assist you. Once we apprehend the villain, may I assume that our negotiations will continue in a favorable manner?"

"Garrity." Wick's tone had a warning edge, his shoulders bunching beneath his jacket.

She couldn't let him fight her battles for her. This was the reason, she told herself, that she'd insisted on coming today. Because no matter what perils she faced, she wouldn't sacrifice her independence—wouldn't be beholden to anyone, including Wick's partners.

"Let me be clear, Mr. Garrity: my land is not *quid pro quo*." She matched her tone to his. "If you assist me, you will have my gratitude...and a monetary reward, if that is your wish."

At the mention of a reward, she saw insult flash in his eyes, but making her point was more important than preserving his pride. If she'd learned anything from managing her own estate, it was that, as a woman, she couldn't back down. To do so was tantamount to an invitation for men to walk all over her—and some men would try to do so regardless.

She returned Mr. Garrity's unflinching gaze, aware of Wick's bridling presence beside her.

It was Mr. Kent who broke the tense silence.

"You don't owe us anything," he said firmly. "It would be our privilege to assist you. Any friend of Murray's is a friend of GLNR. Isn't that so, Garrity?"

After a pause, Mr. Garrity inclined his dark head. "Indeed."

"I'll see Lady Beatrice out. When I return,"—Wick aimed a hard stare at Garrity—"we'll discuss the specifics of our plan."

"By all means." His partner appeared unperturbed. "It was a pleasure meeting you, my lady."

After loading Beatrice into the carriage with his relations, Wick stalked back up the stairs to the meeting room. Garrity was seated at the head of the table again, Kent standing by the window.

Slamming the door shut, Wick demanded, "What the bloody hell was that about, Garrity?"

"What are you referring to?" Garrity's tone was mild.

"You know perfectly well what I'm talking about. How dare you treat her that way?" Wick gritted out. "She's a defenseless female under attack by some infamous villain. And you try to leverage her troubles to your advantage?"

"She is a female, but is she defenseless?" Garrity steepled his hands, his black brows winging. "She's the one obstruction to our railway, and she's managed to wrap our negotiator around her little finger. I'd say Lady Beatrice Wodehouse is the one holding all the cards."

Wick gripped the back of a chair, trying to rein in his temper. "You don't know what she's suffered. The danger that faces her now. She has no one—"

"But you, is that it? What exactly is the nature of your relationship with her?"

"That's none of your bloody business."

"It is if I'm to commit resources to her aid...and, I might add, to our company's detriment."

"Fine, then don't help her. I'll do it myself."

"I'm sure that's not what Garrity means." Kent had one shoulder propped up against the glass, his bespectacled gaze watchful. "He's just on edge from our meeting earlier this week."

"What meeting was this?" Wick asked.

"The one in which several key shareholders questioned our ability to deliver on the railway," Garrity said succinctly. "The one in which Kent and I gave them our personal reassurances that you had the matter well in hand."

*Devil take it.* Guilt joined the fray of Wick's roiling emotions. Engrossed by the problems Beatrice faced, he hadn't been paying enough attention to his work. To the company and stockholders that were depending upon him.

Frustrated, he shoved a hand through his hair. "I'm working on it."

"I am, of course, relieved to hear your perspective. Because from the outside, it appears as if you've spent the time in Staffordshire courting the lady instead of convincing her to sell her land."

"Damnation, the situation is complicated."

"And will only become more so if anyone gets wind that you're romantically involved with the woman who's put our project—nay, our company—in jeopardy," Garrity snapped. "Ask yourself this, Murray: is a female worth it?"

Wick was about to retort a reply when there was a tapping on the door. A few seconds later, it opened slightly, and guileless blue eyes peered in through the crack. The eyes were set in a pretty rounded face framed by fiery curls.

"Am I interrupting a meeting?" Gabriella Garrity whispered the question to Wick, who was nearest the door. "I was looking for Mr. Garrity and thought I heard his voice."

She looked so sweetly worried that, in spite of his frustration, Wick felt his lips quiver.

"You've found him, madam," he said.

Garrity was already at the door, pulling it open for his wife. "There's no need to skulk about, my dear. Come in."

"Are you certain? Because if you're engaged in something important..."

"Nothing is more important than you, Gabriella," Garrity said.

Anyone who knew Garrity knew that he was being sincere; he was as single-minded in his devotion to his wife as he was in closing a business deal. Which was why he, of all people, ought to understand the complexity of Wick's situation with Beatrice. Garrity knew, first-hand, that some women were worth making sacrifices for.

Some women were worth everything.

Ignoring Wick's pointed look, Garrity ushered his lady into

the room. Straightening her bonnet, which had gone askew on her red curls, he murmured, "What brings you here, love?"

Before answering him, Mrs. Garrity first waved at Harry, who gave her a friendly grin in return. Then she turned back to her husband. "Originally, I was going to see if you'd care to go to lunch. But now I have the most exciting news. You will never guess who I just ran into outside."

"Actually, I think I can guess." Garrity's tone was drier than sand.

"It was Violet and Carlisle! And they had the loveliest lady with them, a Lady Beatrice Wodehouse. They said she was a friend of yours, Mr. Murray?"

Faced with her ingenuous blue gaze, Wick could only say, "Indeed, ma'am."

"She seemed ever so nice." Mrs. Garrity exuded concern. "And I was dreadfully sorry when Violet mentioned that she is in London because of some trouble."

*And the point goes to Violet.* Wick made a mental note to thank his sister-in-law for her clever gambit.

"I thought we could host a small supper to welcome Lady Beatrice and get better acquainted. I should like to catch up with Violet as well. And Tessa, of course—I didn't mean to forget her." Charmingly flustered, Mrs. Garrity said in a confiding tone to Kent, "It's just that your wife and I visit all the time, so there's less to catch up on, although I'm sure we could chat for hours anyway. Or at least *I* could. Tessa is such a dear for listening to me prattle on."

"My wife enjoys each and every visit with you, ma'am," Kent said.

Mrs. Garrity flushed with pleasure. "That's ever so kind of you to say, sir."

"When is this supper?" This came from her husband, who now looked resigned.

"Oh, didn't I mention it? This evening, eight o'clock," she said brightly. "The Carlisles said they were free, and strike while the iron's hot, as they say. I hope you and Tessa can make it, Mr. Kent?"

Kent looked like he was trying not to laugh. "Tessa and I will be there."

"Splendid." Beaming, she tipped her head at Wick. "Mr. Murray?"

He was enjoying the turn of events almost as much as Garrity's annoyed stare.

Taking Mrs. Garrity's hand, Wick kissed her knuckles gallantly. "I wouldn't miss it for the world."

## 26

IT HAD BEEN AN ALTOGETHER BIZARRE DAY, BEA THOUGHT OVER supper that evening.

After the confrontation with Garrity, Wick had escorted her downstairs to the carriage where the Carlisles awaited her. No sooner had Wick left then another carriage pulled up behind them, a pretty redhead descending. Violet had shrieked, "Gabby!" out the window and bounded out, she and the newcomer greeting each other with unabashed delight.

Carlisle had met Bea's startled gaze.

"Mrs. Garrity," he'd said by way of explanation. "She and Violet are old friends."

Violet had tugged her friend over to make the introductions, and Beatrice had been more than a little surprised that this lovely lady—who positively radiated kindness—was the wife of the calculating businessman she'd met upstairs. Before she knew it, Mrs. Garrity had invited her and the Carlisles over to her home that evening, with a merry, "I shan't take no for an answer!"

Thus, Bea presently found herself in the Garritys' home, a mansion of understated opulence. The dining room was paneled in dark wood, gilt-framed portraits on the walls. The table had been immaculately set: against the backdrop of snowy linen, silver gleamed and crystal sparkled, elegant floral arrangements adding color and fragrance to the ambiance.

Bea had been seated next to her hostess, in the place of honor. Wick was on the other side of Gabby...which was what Mrs. Garrity insisted Bea should call her. Mr. Garrity presided over the other end of the table, flanked by the Carlisles, and the Kents took up the middle.

Tessa Kent, Harry's wife, was another surprise. Since Wick had given Beatrice a primer on the party guests, Bea knew that Kent's wife wielded significant clout in London's underworld and held the honorary title of "Duchess of Covent Garden" for the territory she oversaw. That was unusual, to say the least. In her head, Bea had pictured Mrs. Kent as an Amazon, a fierce female warrior with a larger-than-life presence.

In reality, Tessa Kent was an elfin beauty with large jade eyes and curly raven hair fashionably coiffed. Her grass-green silk gown showed off her petite figure, her waist accentuated by a diamond-studded ceinture. She was possessed of a lively, roguish temperament that was an amusing foil to her husband's scholarly earnestness.

Supper was being served *à la russe*, and as the liveried footmen put the oyster course in front of each guest, Gabby leaned over and said, "May I ask what jeweler you use, Beatrice? Your brooch is ever so divine."

Bea brushed her fingers over the jewelry pinned to the neckline of her azure satin gown. Wick had presented it to her before they'd left for supper, saying it was a belated birthday gift. Fashioned of gold, the brooch took the form of a butterfly, its body made up of large, sparkling diamonds, its wings glittering with sapphires ranging in hue from deep blue to rare lavender.

Emotion had welled in Bea. It was the finest gift anyone had given her. Yet for some reason, she'd felt obliged to protest that it was too much, that she couldn't accept such an extravagant present. Her refusal had almost turned into an argument until Wick had shushed her with a kiss. The kiss had raged out of control, which was why they'd nearly been late for supper. Glancing at him now, she saw from the lazy glow in his eyes that he, too, was recalling those steamy moments.

To her hostess, she replied softly, "Thank you, it was a gift. And I was admiring your ensemble. Your bracelets, in particular, are stunning."

Gabby looked ravishing in a crimson taffeta gown which bared her shoulders and clung to her lush curves. She had on a pair of unusual bracelets, one at each wrist, bands of delicate gold filigree studded with diamonds and rubies.

"Mr. Garrity commissioned them from a goldsmith in Florence," Gabby said as she lovingly touched the cuffs.

From the opposite end of the table, Mr. Garrity was watching his lady with a dark, slightly predatory gaze, and the charged look that passed between the two made Bea's heart skip a beat. As different as man and wife were, the strength of their bond was palpable. Indeed, the same could be said of all the couples present. It seemed that everyone at the table had found passionate love matches.

Bea looked at Wick and felt a hard tug on her own bonds of attraction. The way the man filled out his evening clothes ought to be a sin. He was conversing with Kent, who was expounding upon techniques to increase the efficiency of locomotive steam engines. Other men might have glazed over as Kent went on about his experiments with various fuel sources, but Wick listened intently, asking keen questions that had Kent taking out a notebook and jotting down notes.

"Most men wax poetic about horses and the hunt." The remark came from Tessa Kent, who sat to the right of Bea. "My husband is fascinated with coal."

Since Wick had alluded to his partner's interest, Bea smiled. "Having an interest is healthy, is it not?"

"Trust me, it's more than an interest," Mrs. Kent said. "It's his obsession."

Kent glanced over, his intense gaze shifting to his wife. "Not my only obsession, sprite."

Mrs. Kent pinkened but gave her husband an impish look. "In fact, Harry loves coal so much he's even made up his own saying about it. Go on, darling, tell them."

Kent sighed. "Must I?"

"Oh ho, I know this one." Wick grinned at his colleague's beleaguered look. "Kent has it written on the chalkboard in his office. *As constant as coal*—isn't that it?"

"It's meant to be inspirational," Kent said with great dignity. "Coal transport has driven the reliability and innovation of the railways. If we can get our passenger trains running with that same degree of consistency and accuracy, then we will have accomplished something."

"A worthy goal." Garrity raised his glass. "I'll drink to that."

"Speaking of worthy goals," Mrs. Kent said briskly, "Harry has informed me about your situation, Lady Beatrice. I think there's nothing more cowardly than a villain who hides behind anonymity and preys upon women. We would like to help you in any way we can."

Bea hesitated, glancing at Wick who gave her a subtle nod.

Earlier, he'd told her that Tessa Kent would be an invaluable ally, and gaining her assistance would be key to their efforts to find the foe. When Bea had argued that she didn't want to be beholden to a stranger, he'd replied, *What is more important, angel, your pride...or protecting your estate and people from danger?*

There was a reason the man was a top-notch negotiator.

Wick had also told her that he would trust the people at the table with his life, and being in their company showed Bea why. Wick's friends were a far cry from the group she had associated with before her accident. Back then, her supposed friends—even her fiancé—had cut ties with her after she'd been scarred. A superficial mark on her cheek had been enough to send them scattering to the winds.

Now she was facing true danger, with an enemy who could strike at any moment and make collateral damage of those around her. Yet in the eyes of Mrs. Kent—a woman whom she'd just met—Bea saw concern and empathy, as if the lady had known her own travails. Mrs. Kent's willingness to help was genuine...and that decided things for Bea.

In her life, she'd had few enough offers of true friendship; she wasn't about to turn one down.

"You're very generous, ma'am," she said. "I don't know how I shall repay you."

"You can start by calling me Tessa. Now would you mind giving a summary of the essential details?"

Bea obliged, going through the timeline of attacks and leads they had to follow.

"In sum, you're in London to chase down clues about a disgruntled ex-tenant, a mysterious pocket watch, and perhaps a shady priest." Tessa tilted her head. "What is your plan?"

"I've secured guards for Lady Beatrice's protection," Wick said. "And sent several of my men to locate the Perkins family, who we believe live somewhere in the Seven Dials."

"And the pocket watch?" Tessa asked.

"The Carlisles and I spent the day visiting watchmakers in hopes that someone might recognize the workmanship or identify the initials 'H. C.' Our efforts were in vain," Bea admitted. "The lack of any hallmark or maker's stamp makes identifying the watch nearly impossible."

"Butter and jam, we must have questioned every watchmaker in Clerkenwell and Soho." Violet gestured to her empty plate. "No wonder I'm famished."

"When are you not?" Carlisle asked mildly.

Her reply was a shrug and a good-natured grin.

"Do you have the item with you?" Tessa asked.

Wick removed the watch from an inner pocket and passed it around. As Tessa took the timepiece, she studied it with keen concentration. She opened and closed the case, scrutinizing the dial face and cover, front and back.

"This *is* mysterious, isn't it?" she concluded. "The watch is clearly of high quality, and I'd wager my pet ferret that this gold is no less than eighteen karat. Why would anyone omit to have it hallmarked, when that would substantiate the value?"

"Because the monetary value of the watch means less to them than its symbolic value." This came from Garrity, who sampled the lobster consommé newly placed in front of him, his lips curving faintly. "The soup is exceptional, Mrs. Garrity."

"Well, it is your favorite. I'll be sure to convey your compliments to Cook." Brow pleating, his wife asked, "Could you explain your theory of the watch? I don't quite follow."

"If the owner never planned to sell the watch, instead intending to keep it as a personal memento, then he wouldn't care whether the piece was stamped by the Goldsmith's Hall."

"Yes, but why *not* have it stamped anyway?" Gabby persisted.

The answer struck Bea.

"Perhaps it is the kind of memento that the owner wouldn't want anyone to know about," she reasoned slowly. "He wouldn't want it to be traceable to him."

"My thoughts precisely." For the first time, a hint of approval appeared in Garrity's eyes as he regarded her. "The watch could be from a paramour, for instance. Perhaps he is married, and the discovery of that connection could cause a scandal."

"A secret lover's token—that would make sense. Or perhaps..." Tessa drummed her fingers on the table, her opal ring flashing in the candlelight. "Perhaps the watch has another secret meaning. The papers are always speculating about those secret societies infiltrating London. You know, those groups that are supposedly plotting the overthrow of Christianity or engaged in the occult?

Apparently, the members speak in secret code and use objects to verify their membership. Maybe the watch is such an object."

"You've been reading sensation novels again, haven't you?" Kent's bespectacled gaze held a scientist's skepticism. "Those groups are a figment of the popular imagination, sprite."

"I wouldn't be so sure," his wife countered. "From what I've seen of the world, anything is possible. Can you prove that there aren't ghosts of the past...and that they can't be summoned into the present?"

A chill whispered over Beatrice's nape.

"It wasn't a ghost that set fire to Beatrice's barn." Wick took up the voice of reason. "H. C. is no specter but a flesh-and-blood man with a human agenda."

"I concur," Garrity said. "The problem remains how we identify this H. C. We could question more watchmakers, although that strategy hasn't proven effective thus far."

"I've got it," Tessa said suddenly.

Kent cocked his head. "You have a better idea, love?"

"I know someone with more knowledge of pocket watches than any watchmaker in the world," she declared. "If anyone could help us identify it, it's him."

"Clever girl." Kent's eyes lit with appreciation. "Why didn't I think of Alfred?"

"Is Alfred a horological expert?" Bea asked.

"In a manner of speaking. He owns a shop that deals with many pocket watches." Tessa picked up her fork, looking pleased with herself as she dug into the next dish of pheasant braised with bacon and chestnuts. "We'll go see him first thing tomorrow."

## 27

AT A QUARTER PAST MIDNIGHT, AS WICK WAS CHANGING IN HIS dressing room, he heard the door open in his adjoining bedchamber. Since he'd told Barton not to wait up for him, he had a fair guess who his visitor was. With a private smile, he didn't bother with his nightshirt and shrugged into his dressing gown. He headed into the next room to see Beatrice wandering about, an angelic contrast to the dark masculine furnishings. Clad in a white satin robe embroidered with peonies, her hair a shining curtain that reached her waist, she greeted him with a blush and a smile.

"I was hoping you wouldn't mind company," she said.

"Since I was about to come find you, you saved me a trip." He kissed her thoroughly. "Lucky thing too, since I'm feeling rather lazy at the moment."

"Not all of you is in a torpid state." Her gaze dropped pointedly to the growing bulge of his erection, her smile both sweet and a bit smug. "Thank heavens for that."

"Come to take advantage of me, have you?" He took her hand, leading her toward his bed. "Ah, well, I suppose I'll have to suffer."

"You *are* a martyr, aren't you?"

"The things I do for you," he agreed as he untied her robe.

Pushing the garment off her shoulders, he felt heat swirl in his blood. She wore only a thin, sleeveless chemise beneath. In the lamplight, the material was translucent, showing the curves of her breasts, their pouting tips pressing against the fabric.

"You are making things easy for me this eve," he murmured. "No masks or corsets. No endless column of buttons."

"I'm trying to be accommodating." She was smiling, but the expression in her eyes grew serious. "If I've been difficult, Wick, I do apologize. I don't mean to be ungrateful for all you've done—that you're doing—for me."

"You have no need to apologize." If she had been a bit prickly since their arrival in London, he understood. She was under significant duress, and being back in the city couldn't be easy for her.

"Even if I was less than friendly to Mr. Garrity this morning?"

"He deserved it for being a right arse to you." Wick slid a finger under the strap of her chemise, savoring her smoother-than-satin skin. "After you left, I let him know in no uncertain terms that I wouldn't stand for him turning your misfortune into his advantage. I think he got the message. If not from me, then definitely from his wife."

"Gabby is lovely, isn't she? And the Kents and Carlisles are as well." Bea sounded wistful. "You have wonderful family and friends, Wick."

"I'm glad you like them because they're your friends now as well." Drawing her close, he looked down into her incomparable eyes. "You can trust them, Garrity included. His bark is worse than his bite, and having known him for years, I can attest that he is a man of honor, albeit in his own fashion."

"I can't believe how generous everyone has been. How willing to help," Bea mused. "The people you know...they are very different from the ones in my past."

Seeing the shadows in her gaze, he tipped her chin up. "You're safe, angel. I won't let anyone hurt you."

"Sometimes it scares me how easily I've let down my guard

with you," she said tremulously. "Being back here in London reminds me that I haven't depended on anyone for a long time. Not since my accident."

In her admission, he heard heartbreak and hope. He knew, then and there, that he would happily spend the rest of his life proving to her that he was worthy of her trust. That he was worthy of *her*.

"Trusting someone and becoming dependent upon them are two different things." He traced the slant of her cheekbone with his thumb, feeling her shiver when he grazed over her scar. "You can lean on someone without losing your independence. You can count on me and still be the strong, fearless lady of Camden Manor."

As he spoke, he felt a tightening in his chest, a mounting unease about the difficulty of his quest. He was determined to protect Beatrice and her land; at the same time, he had his obligation to GLNR and his partners. Garrity could be a cutthroat bastard, but he was never a liar. Privately, Kent had filled Wick in on how rife with tension the meeting with the shareholders had been, increasing Wick's concern...and guilt.

People had invested their life savings in GLNR. His partners had trusted him to negotiate the most important deal in their company's history. Garrity, in particular, had taken a risk bringing Wick on as a partner, and Wick could not—*would* not—repay the other's faith and years of mentorship with failure.

"Your surveyor will be arriving at the estate soon, will he not?" Beatrice asked.

As usual, she showed an uncanny ability to read his thoughts.

"Norton's latest missive said that he and his team should arrive by tomorrow." Not wanting to add to her worries, he said, "Norton is an expert in the field; he'll figure out a solution. We should direct our energies toward what we can accomplish here in London."

"We do have a full day ahead of us," she agreed. "Let's enjoy ourselves for the rest of the evening."

"What did you have in mind?"

She fiddled with the lapel of his dressing gown. "I wouldn't mind a repeat of what you showed me in the carriage the other day."

"I knew you'd like that position. And it's even better with the absence of clothing."

He casually removed his only garment, showing her the impact she had on him. His erection bobbed beneath its own weight, his stones taut and heavy with seed. He cocked a brow at her. Blushing but obviously game, she followed his lead, pulling the chemise over her head. Her femininity never failed to affect him. His cock surged even higher, aiming at her tender blonde furrow.

He fitted his hands to her narrow waist, lifting her onto his bed. Standing between her splayed thighs, he cupped her jaw with both hands and kissed her. He took his time, dipping his tongue into her sweetness, swirling inside. She answered him with dainty parries, the soft, silky strokes making his prick jerk with envy for that decadent caress.

"Last time when you rode me, I didn't get to watch these pretty tits bounce." He thumbed her budded nipples. "I'm looking forward to it this time."

Her eyes turned smoky. "Shall we get on with it, then?"

"Greedy lass," he said with appreciation. "All right, time for your next riding lesson."

He climbed into bed, lying on his back with his head propped up on the pillows.

He crooked a finger at her. "Climb on."

She did, with such eagerness that he had to smother a grin. He adored her honest, generous passion...as much as he adored showing her the many variations of desire.

He clamped his hands on her hips, and she almost seduced

him from his purpose when she rubbed her cunny against his turgid shaft. At the kiss of her dewy cleft, he nearly abandoned his plan in favor of sheathing himself inside her ready little passage. Instead, he tightened his hold on her hips and dragged her upward along his body until he had her where he wanted her: with her knees clasping his head, her sex hovering over his mouth.

"What are you...*oh heavens*," she gasped.

He finished running his tongue along her plump, pink seam. Christ, she was delicious.

"Hold onto the headboard," he instructed. "Ride my mouth, angel."

He steered her hips, moving her over his lips as he delved into her honeypot. Her sweetness coated his tongue. As was characteristic of his lass, once she lost her initial hesitation over a new activity, she threw herself in fully. Soon she was riding him like a contestant in the Derby, rocking herself over his lips, rubbing her bold little nub against his tongue. He ate her pussy until she came, her nectar pouring into his mouth, making him starved for more.

He pulled her off his face and over his cock. He fitted himself to her hole, watching her expression as he thrust his hips up while pulling hers down. He groaned at the decadent constriction.

"Oh, Wick, you're so...big." Since her gaze was sultry and her sheath clutching him with demanding insistence, he didn't think she was complaining.

"Your little pussy can take it. In fact, I think it wants to be fed some of my cream."

Her cheeks turned rosy. "That's naughty."

"It is, and the delightful squeeze of your cunny tells me you don't mind." He tucked a silken strand behind her ear. "Now I'd like to stuff you as full of cream as a profiterole, but we must think of the consequences. You'd better take your ride like a good lass before I have to pull out. This ride may not last long."

She took him at his word. Bracing her hands on his shoulders, her knees framing his hips, she began to ride. She rose and fell, impaling herself on his prick. She grew bolder, circling her hips, grinding on the way down, finding the motions that made her moan and his breath hiss through his lips.

Watching her, he was entranced. By the firm jiggle of her tits as she speared herself on his weapon. By the way she pouted on an upstroke and bit her lip in pleasure on the downstroke. Her gaze grew unfocused as she reached the finish line again, her back arching and fingers tangling in his chest hair, her dew anointing his staff.

Grasping her hips, he took over. Guided her back down on his cock, at an angle that brought her pearl against his hard shaft. With each pass, he grazed the most sensitive part of her body. He held onto her sweet bottom, spreading and massaging those firm cheeks as he thrust his hips up.

She whimpered as he pounded into her. Moving a hand to her breast, he rolled the tip between finger and thumb, tugging gently. The answering clench of her passage was almost his undoing. But he didn't want to go over the edge without taking her there once more. He leaned his head up, capturing her nipple between his lips and sucked.

She moaned his name as spasms rocked her slender body.

With a growl, he rolled her off him. He gripped his cock, jerking it rapidly. To his everlasting delight, she fondled his balls as he frigged himself and kissed him passionately. The heat boiled over, climbing his shaft, exploding like a geyser into their shared touch as he buried his shouts in her mouth.

Afterward, they lay in a sweaty tangle of limbs. He had sufficient energy to pull a coverlet over them, tucking her head against his shoulder.

As his heartbeat slowed, he heard her say, "Wick?"

"Hmm?"

"Thank you for the brooch. I'm sorry I was ungracious about it earlier. It's the most beautiful gift anyone has given me."

At her whispered admission, his chest warmed with pride. He kissed her hair.

"My pleasure, angel," he murmured.

"And thank you for the riding lesson as well. I think my seat is improving, don't you?" she mused. "That's two different mounts I've tried."

"You're a natural. Now go to sleep. And if you're a good lass, I'll give you another ride in the morning."

He felt her lips curve against his shoulder, and he fell asleep smiling.

## 28

THE NEXT DAY, THE KENTS PICKED UP BEATRICE AND WICK IN a glossy carriage. They were going to visit Tessa's friend, whose shop was located in a dodgy area of London. As both Tessa and Wick had brought along armed guards, Bea wasn't too worried about safety.

They arrived at a busy thoroughfare in Whitechapel. From the carriage window, Bea saw people milling everywhere and shops jammed shoulder to shoulder. Their destination stood out due to its sign: "Doolittle's Emporium of Wonders" was painted in large gilt letters above the storefront window. Through the glass, Bea saw a puzzling plethora of merchandise, with no apparent rhyme or reason to the variety of the goods.

"I thought your friend was a horological expert?" she asked Tessa, who sat across from her.

"He is," Tessa assured her.

Bea peered at the storefront. "I don't see any watches or clocks in the window."

"Alfred keeps the valuable goods behind the counter. Come along," Tessa said as she alighted with the help of her husband. "We want to catch him before his nap."

"Nap? It's only ten o'clock in the morning," Bea whispered to Wick. "Who is this Alfred?"

"I'm certain Mrs. Kent knows what she's doing," he whispered back before handing her down.

As her feet touched the ground, Bea caught sight of a small figure at the end of the street, and her hand tightened around Wick's.

"What's the matter, sweeting?" he asked.

"There's a boy at the end of the street," she blurted. "I saw him yesterday, outside your office."

Wick looked over. "I don't see a boy."

She darted her glance back that way. Sure enough, no one was there.

"No time for dawdling, you two," Tessa called from the doorway of the shop.

Wick cocked a brow at Bea.

"I...must have imagined it." She forced a smile. "Let's go on in."

Inside, Doolittle's Emporium was a labyrinth of shelves overflowing with merchandise. Mayhem seemed to be the main method of organization. Teapots sat next to inkwells, handkerchiefs were piled onto a silver platter. Rounding a corner, Bea jerked back in surprise: she'd come face-to-face with a stuffed chimpanzee lounging on a shelf, his bored eyes disturbingly lifelike. Atop his head was an elaborate grey periwig, the attached tag reading, "Antique, last century. 35 shillings."

Whether the tag referred to the monkey or the wig was ambiguous.

To Wick, she said in a hushed undertone, "What kind of a shop *is* this?"

"It appears our expert is the owner of a pawn shop." He sounded amused. "You have to hand it to Mrs. Kent: who deals in more pocket watches than a fence, after all?"

Beatrice had to contain her surprise for they'd arrived at a long, battered counter at the back of the shop, behind which stood a buxom blonde in her forties. She wore her hair in sausage curls, her rather hard features lacquered in paint.

She and Tessa greeted each other with air kisses.

"Lady Beatrice Wodehouse and Mr. Murray," Tessa said, "I'd like you to meet my dear friend Sally Doolittle. She's the proprietress of this fine establishment."

"Call me Sal." The blonde's wink was aimed at Wick. "Everyone does."

"Charmed," Wick said easily. "Lady Beatrice and I were hoping you could help us."

"What kind o' 'elp are you looking for, 'andsome?" Sal cooed.

She leaned her elbows on the counter, causing her abundant bosom to nearly spill from its scanty neckline, Bea saw with growing annoyance.

"We wish to identify a pocket watch, Mrs. Doolittle," she intervened crisply.

Sal's penciled brows lifted. "Well, you've come to the right place, dove. No one knows more 'bout kettle and hobs than my Alfred."

Bea's confusion must have shown because Wick clarified, "*A kettle and hob* is Cockney slang for a watch."

"Is Alfred available?" Tessa asked.

"I'll check," Sal said. Turning, she shouted toward the curtained entryway behind her, "*Alfredkins!* Are you awake?"

"If I were catching some shut-eye, I ain't anymore," a male voice called back.

"Then get your lovely arse out 'ere. Tessa's 'ere...and she brung friends wif 'er."

A few moments later, a man passed through the curtain. He was slight, his freckles and mop of brown hair lending him a perpetually youthful countenance even though, as he came to stand by Sal, Bea saw that he must be in his thirties. His large, wide-spaced eyes and gap-toothed smile gave him an innocent, sugar-wouldn't-melt-in-his-mouth quality.

A quality that probably served him well in his career as a dealer of stolen goods.

"Ain't seen the pair o' you for a dog's age," he greeted the Kents. "'Ow's the tot?"

"Little Bart is a holy terror," Tessa replied. "It doesn't help that Grandpapa indulges him shamelessly."

"Your fault, ain't it, for not only giving the old codger 'is only great-grandchild but a namesake as well. Told you to fink twice 'bout naming your brat after the King o' the Underworld."

"I suggested Newton," Kent muttered.

"*That* name would 'ave guaranteed your son a black eye for 'is first two decades or so." Doolittle shook his head. "What about my suggestion, eh?"

"I already have an Alfred in my life, thank you very much," Tessa said.

"One can ne'er 'ave enough o' Alfred...ain't that true, Sal?"

"I always come back for a second 'elping," his wife replied with a giggle.

"Greedy wench." He gave her a good-natured swat on the behind.

Obviously used to the bawdy by-play, Tessa rolled her eyes. "If we might get to business? My friends here have a pocket watch that they need identified. It's a matter of life or death. They've gone to watchmakers and shops from Clerkenwell to Soho, to no avail. I told them they needed to consult a real expert: you."

Doolittle peered over at Bea and Wick. "Life or death, you say?"

Despite Doolittle's boyish exterior, Bea saw the shrewdness in the man's eyes.

"I'd be happy to compensate you for your time, sir," she said steadily. "And yes—it is a matter of life or death. Whoever owns this watch committed arson to my property. He may also be responsible for kidnapping and terrorizing my bosom chum."

"Crikey." Doolittle tilted his head. "Got the ticker wif you?"

"Yes." Wick removed it from his jacket pocket and placed it on the counter, the gold disk gleaming against the scratched wood. "The watch has no maker's mark or stamp from the Goldsmith's Hall. Other than the initials on the cover and the inscription on the dial face that says it was made in London, there are no other clues to its origin or owner."

"To find clues, you 'ave to know where to look." Doolittle picked up the watch, tossing and catching it expertly several times. He rubbed the initials with his thumb, once, twice, three times. Without opening the cover, he pronounced, "Eighteen karat gold, good English parts and not those foreign knock-offs... and hmm." His fingers closed around the watch, his features furrowed in concentration as if he could somehow sense what was within. "There's a symbol—like a horseshoe, next to the word *London?*"

"How could you know all that?" Bea asked, stupefied.

Even Tessa looked impressed. "I knew you were an expert, Alfie, but that was spot on. How did you get all that just from holding the watch?"

"I didn't. Some cull brought in a watch just like this a few months ago." Doolittle flashed a puckish grin. "Wanted to use it as collateral. Same initials on the cover, same everyfing."

"Do you still have the watch?" Wick asked alertly.

"Nah, the cove failed to make good on 'is loan by the agreed upon date, so I put it up for sale. Fine ticker like that flew out the door." Doolittle paused. "But I keep a record o' all customers who pawn their goods wif me. Sal can look 'im up in the ledger for you."

❧

While at Doolittle's, the Kents received an urgent missive. Apparently, their son had gotten into the pantry, consuming an entire pudding, and said pudding was now making a second appearance. The pair rushed home, and Wick declined their kind offer to drop them back at his residence. Instead, he hailed a hackney for himself, Beatrice, and their pair of guards, setting off for the address that Sally Doolittle had looked up.

They arrived at a street of terraced houses in Cheapside. The homes were modest and dilapidated, and the one they were looking for was situated in the middle of the block. With the guards keeping vigilant watch, Wick escorted Beatrice up the steps and rang the bell.

A slovenly maid answered. She looked none too pleased to be disturbed from whatever she had been doing—tippling on the job, probably, if the sherry stains on her apron were any indication. When Wick told her he was looking for Stuart Yard, the name Sal had given him, the maid's countenance shuttered.

"'E ain't home," she said. "You wif the cent-per-cents?"

Her question revealed a lot about her master. Stuart Yard was in debt, to the extent that he'd instructed his servants to lie about his whereabouts.

"We're not here about Mr. Yard's finances." Wick handed her his calling card. "A mutual friend recommended that we consult with Mr. Yard on a business matter. We would compensate him, of course, for his time."

At the mention of compensation, the maid widened the gap in the door and ushered them inside. "Rest your 'eels in the parlor then. I'll inform the master that you're 'ere."

Minutes later, Bea and Wick were joined by their host in the cramped, dingy parlor. Stuart Yard was a scrawny fellow, with shifty eyes and a nervous manner. According to Doolittle, Yard had once been a well-to-do banker before he lost his fortune investing in some ill-advised scheme. The shabby state of Yard's home and clothes verified that he was a man who'd come down in the world.

"Good afternoon." His boisterous tones had a ragged lining of desperation. "I understand you are looking to consult on a business matter? May I ask which of my fine friends I can thank for providing the introduction?"

"Alfred Doolittle," Wick said.

Yard's eagerness vanished.

"I'm afraid I am not acquainted with any Doolittle," he said unconvincingly.

Wick took out the watch, letting it dangle from his fingers. There was no mistaking the flash of recognition in Yard's eyes.

"How did you...I thought he sold it...?" he stammered.

"This isn't your watch, sir, but you have confirmed that you owned one like it," Beatrice said in crisp tones. "There's no reason for further prevarication. We wish to know the origin of the watch, and we will pay you for the information."

Yard wetted his lips. "How much?"

Wick withdrew a twenty-pound banknote. When Yard reached for it, he held it back, saying, "This is yours—if your information proves useful."

"If I tell you, you have to swear you'll tell no one you heard it from me." Yard's eyes darted toward the door. "Mrs. Yard is out shopping at the moment, but if she finds out about this, my life will be worth even less than it is now."

"We will not reveal the source of the information," Wick said. "You may speak freely."

"Back in the day, I was part of a club," Yard said after a moment. "A secret club open only to men and women with money and power. The membership was quite exclusive."

"A secret society," Beatrice breathed.

Wick lifted his brows. "What do the initials H. C. stand for?"

"Hellfire Club," Yard replied. "Although it wasn't like what they describe in the papers: we had no satanic rituals, nor did we summon ghostly apparitions. The purpose of our club was the pursuit of earthly pleasures."

He paused, sliding a glance at Beatrice, whose eyes were as big as dinnerplates.

"If you want your blunt, continue," Wick said.

"The founders railed against the puritanical constraints of society. Why should we be barred from the enjoyments that our natures demanded? As long as we hurt no one and were willing to pay for the entertainment." Yard's gaze had a faraway quality, as if he were allowing himself to sink into the memories of his better days. "I was a member for two years, until my fortunes changed. Then I could no longer afford the membership. The founders did have a scholarship program of sorts, for select men and women who added to the club's prestige but could not afford the fees. Alas, I did not qualify."

"We'll need to know the names of the founders and members," Wick said.

"That I cannot tell you. For the one inviolable tenet of the club was anonymity: the members wore masks and took pains to conceal their identity. When I applied for admission, I had my interview with a secretary and was told that any indiscretion concerning the club and its members would lead to disbarment.

"The only thing members knew about one another was that we were titans of industry, aristocrats, and leaders of communities. Given the, ahem, nature of the activities conducted within the club," Yard said, "I'm sure you'll understand why these people would not tolerate being exposed."

"What was the nature of the activities, precisely?" This came from Beatrice.

Yard had the grace to redden. "With a few exceptions, whatever the member desired was usually available. Bacchanals, for instance, were a popular offering."

"Where is the club located?" Wick asked.

"In a private house in Mayfair," Yard replied. "The secretary conducts all Hellfire Club business from that address. The club events are held on the first Saturday evening of every month."

"That's tonight," Beatrice said in an undertone.

Wick's thoughts were headed in the same direction. Going to the club might be the only way of finding the watch's owner. But how would he get inside?

"How does one apply for admission to the Hellfire Club?" he asked Yard.

"Typically, through the referral of an existing member. In this instance, however, you may not need it."

Wick angled his head. "Why not?"

"You're holding the admission ticket. The watch," Yard explained, "permits entry for you and a guest. As long as it has not been deactivated."

Bea pursed her lips. "What do you mean by 'deactivated'?"

"When my membership was withdrawn, they took the watch from me. I raised a fuss since I'd paid for the blasted thing; as I'd lost my bank and my fortune, I needed every quid I could get." The ex-banker huffed. "The watch was finally returned to me, with a note saying that it would no longer provide valid entry into the club. When I examined the watch, I saw that the face of the dial had indeed been subtly altered. Here, let me take a look at the one you have."

Wick handed over the watch, and Yard flipped open the cover.

"Ah, yes. This watch appears to be still active," he said.

"How do you know?" Beatrice crowded in to see.

"See this symbol?"

"The horseshoes, you mean?" she asked.

"Those aren't horseshoes. The two lines are meant to be a flame, the symbol of the Hellfire Club. When my watch was made inactive, they removed the inner line. I, ahem, made the mistake of trying to get in one time after my membership had been withdrawn; the guards at the door turned me away after examining the dial."

Wick thought back to Doolittle's description of Yard's pawned watch. "Come to think of it, Doolittle did say there was a symbol like a horseshoe...not *horseshoes*, plural."

"You're right." Beatrice nodded. "I was so amazed by his presentation that I didn't even notice that small discrepancy between the watch he described and ours."

"If my guess is correct, then this watch is a valid admission ticket." As Yard spoke, his grasp tightened on the timepiece, a covetous look sharpening his features.

"I'll take that back," Wick said.

Reluctantly, Yard released the watch into Wick's palm.

"Will they ask for any other identification?" Beatrice asked.

"There was a password." Yard snuck another glance at the watch as Wick tucked it away. "When I was a member, it changed regularly. The last one I recall was *Altar of Pan*, but I'm sure it's changed since then."

A bridge Wick would cross when he got there.

He held out the banknote. "We'll need the club's address."

## 29

"WE'RE NOT TO BE SEPARATED, UNDERSTOOD? YOU STAY BY MY side, and you do not stray. Not for any reason," Wick said with emphasis. In the dim light of the carriage, his features were set in stern lines. "And for Christ's sake, do *not* take off your mask or wig."

"I'm not an idiot, you know."

Bea's wig was perfectly secured; she'd asked Lisette to use extra pins to keep the brunette curls in place. She did, however, adjust her white satin mask to appease him.

She figured the placating gesture wouldn't hurt since they'd had yet another row earlier, and she knew Wick was less than pleased with the outcome. He'd been adamant about going alone to the Hellfire Club; she'd been equally adamant that she should go with him. It was *her* adversary, *her* land, *her* people at stake— she would not stay at home and wring her hands.

Their battle had waged on back at Wick's house. When they arrived, the Carlisle family had been in the drawing room, the boys crowded around their parents who were involved in some life-or-death card game.

Glancing at his brother's face, Carlisle had folded his cards. "Let's give them some privacy."

"But I was about to beat you..." Violet had trailed off when she saw Bea's expression. "All right, boys. Who wants to have an archery competition?"

At her sons' cheers, she'd herded them to the door, Carlisle shutting it behind them.

"I will not have you risking your neck," Wick had bit out.

"Why should you risk yours?" Bea countered. "The problem is mine, after all."

"Goddamnit, I thought we were beyond this. You are mine, Beatrice." He glowered at her. "Being mine means your problems are mine."

Although her tummy had fluttered at his possessiveness, she could not yield, not on this point.

"I'm not yours yet." She persisted even as his nostrils flared, his hazel eyes blazing. "I care for you, Wick—trust you more than I've trusted anyone. But if this relationship of ours is to work, you will need to return the favor. Trust me to handle my own affairs— or, at the very least, to participate in the resolution of my own problems."

"It's not a matter of trust but common sense. You're a *lass*, and this Hellfire Club is naught more than a bloody orgy—"

"We met at an orgy. You didn't question my presence then."

"That was different." He dragged a hand through his hair. "You weren't mine then."

"The fact that we *are* together makes my argument even more compelling. I will only marry a man who treats me like a true partner: not just a warm body in bed, a conversationalist at the supper table, or a mama for his children." She drew a breath and drove in the stakes, establishing the boundaries in their relationship. The fences she would not allow him to cross. "I believe in beginning as one intends to carry on. If you won't include me in your present plans, then I will have to reconsider our future."

"You're issuing me an *ultimatum?*" The muscle bulged in his jaw.

"I'm being honest. If we can't come to a compromise now, how will we deal with other problems in our marriage? I don't want a relationship that works only during the good times."

*I don't want to end up like Mama.* Her throat constricted. *I won't entrust my happiness and future to someone, only to have him smash it to smithereens.*

Wick had contemplated her in brooding silence. He'd remained quiet for so long that wings of anxiety had beat in her breast. What if he decided that she wasn't worth the trouble? What if he simply called everything off?

*It's better in the long run to know now,* her inner voice said. *The pain will be easier to bear.*

Only she didn't think the pain *would* be easy to bear. Not now, not later, not ever. Because she knew there wouldn't be another man for her.

*Then why are you being so dashed difficult?* Since arriving in London, she'd been digging her heels in more frequently. Insisting on talking to his partners, clashing with Garrity—arguing over a gift, for heaven's sake. There'd been other tiffs as well, and she knew full well she'd been at fault. To top things off, now she'd given him an ultimatum.

She couldn't seem to stop herself. It was a compulsion, this need to preserve her independence...

Wick had turned on his heel with an abruptness that lodged her heart in her throat. With clawing panic, she'd wondered if she'd finally pushed him too far.

As his hand closed on the door handle, she managed, "Where are you going?"

"To make arrangements for this evening," he snarled. "I have to figure out the security—and our damned disguises."

Before she could fully digest that he'd included her in his plans, he'd stalked out.

Which brought them to the present moment and her desire to smooth things over with her lover, who she knew was acting against his own better judgement. In fact, she was amazed that he'd capitulated to her wishes...and was determined to prove to him that working together was the key to success.

The carriage came to a stop. She parted the curtain, peering out. The street was jammed with businesses, taverns, and houses of ill-repute.

"We're in Covent Garden, not Mayfair," she said with a frown.

"I have a stop to make first." He put on his hat, not bothering with his mask or cloak. "I'll be a few minutes so stay put here—and don't argue for once, all right?"

Deciding to pick her battles, she nodded. He alighted, giving instructions to the guards riding up top to keep a sharp lookout. Then she watched him enter a shady-looking tavern called "The Golden Buck."

A half-hour passed before he returned. He tapped the ceiling with his walking stick, and the carriage once again rolled off. Beatrice thought she smelled something on his breath...ale?

"Have you been *drinking?*" She didn't hide her disapproval.

"I can hold my spirits," he said curtly.

"Yes, but why would you imbibe at this critical juncture?"

"Because if you want a fellow to talk, you share a tankard with him." Before she could ask who he'd talked to and why, he said, "Staff of Dionysus."

"What in heavens does that mean?"

"On a literal level, it refers to the walking stick that the God of Wine used to turn grapes into wine. On a symbolic level, I'm guessing it alludes to a man's cock," Wick said sardonically. "On the level that we're most interested in, it is the password for getting into the Hellfire Club."

Her jaw slackened. "But how..."

"I told you I was making arrangements this afternoon. The most critical one being ascertaining the password for entry. One of my contacts runs The Golden Buck, and he overheard two of his regular patrons—young rakehells—celebrating gaining entrée into the "H. C.," which he gathered from their drunken toasts was some sort of a club. He said the rakehells' habit was to stop at his tavern the first Saturday evening of the month on their way to the club."

"How did you manage to get the password from them?" Bea asked, amazed.

He shrugged. "After a few rounds on me, they were foxed. They would have told me the combination to the safe holding the Crown Jewels if they knew it. Hopefully the information they provided will get us into the club tonight."

"How extraordinarily clever of you," she said with admiration.

He gave her a disgruntled look. "I told you that you could trust me."

"I do," she said earnestly. "And I want you to trust me too."

"For God's sake, this isn't about trust. This is about keeping you safe."

"Don't worry, I came prepared." Reaching into her skirts, she pulled out her trusty pearl-handled pistol. "You know I won't hesitate to use this if necessary."

"You're going to be the death of me." He sounded aggrieved.

She tried her hand at flirtation to patch things up. "I promise to make up for it when we get home tonight."

Despite his obvious frustration, his gaze heated. "Are you trying to sweeten me up?"

"I'm trying to show my appreciation."

"That you'll be doing when we get home this eve. In a manner of my choosing."

The dominance in his tone caused her to shiver. When it came to sexual matters, she enjoyed surrendering to him. It was the one area of their relationship where she would gladly let him take charge.

"Whatever you want, Wick," she said demurely.

His nostrils flared, but he said no more. Instead, he donned his mask and domino as the carriage came to its second stop that evening. He helped her down, nodding to the pair of guards perched on the carriage. Dressed in footmen's livery, they were to keep watch outside, on the alert for any suspicious activity.

As Bea ascended the steps to the large, elegant mansion at the end of a leafy cul-de-sac, the pedimented windows discreetly shaded, she was reminded of the first time she and Wick met. Then, as now, they were both wearing costumes and masks to conceal their identity.

This time, it wasn't pleasure they were after but a deadly villain.

Wick rang the bell, and the painted black door opened.

"Good evening. May I help you?" the butler asked courteously.

Nothing in the servant's tone or demeanor betrayed that this was anything but a regular residence. Bea heard only faint sounds from within, muffled and indistinct, nowhere near the volume of what one would expect of a masquerade. Had Stuart Yard given them the wrong address?

Wick took out the watch. "I was hoping you could tell me if my watch had the correct time."

"Gladly, sir." Taking the proffered timepiece, the butler opened the cover and examined the face. "Everything appears to be in order. Would you and your guest care to step inside?"

Following Wick into the antechamber, Bea saw that it was walled off from the rest of the house, a pair of burly guards standing by yet another door. With growing excitement, she saw that this one was made of thick metal, like the door to a bank vault.

"Password, sir?" one of the guards said.

"Staff of Dionysus," Wick replied easily.

The guards exchanged a glance, then one of them removed a golden key on a chain, inserting it into the door. A sharp click followed, and the partition opened to reveal a flickering corridor.

"Enjoy your evening." The guard waved them through and shut the door, sealing them inside.

Her eyes adjusting to the dimness, Beatrice saw that the corridor sloped downward, in a spiral that prevented one from seeing beyond the next corner. Wall-mounted sconces cast eerie shadows.

"Shall we?" Wick's eyebrows lifted above his demi-mask.

The passageway was narrow, requiring that they walk single file. Wick led the way, and she shivered at the crypt-like feeling of the place, the low ceiling and barren stone walls seeming to close in with each descending step. They soon arrived at another guarded door.

The watchman bowed. "Have an enjoyable evening."

As he opened the door, sounds blasted through. Voices, laughter...and animalistic noises. A mélange of scents assailed Bea's nose: perfume, spirits, and the musky scent of sex. She felt a quivery sensation low in her belly.

Wick took her gloved hand, her black skirts whispering as she crossed the threshold. She was glad for her mask then for it hid not only her face but her expression of shock. After attending that other masquerade, she thought that she'd seen the full spectrum of debauchery and that nothing could astonish her.

She was wrong.

The huge room was set up like an arena, with a large stage in the middle and some dozen alcoves lining the perimeter. Mimicking boxes at the theatre, the nooks were sumptuously decorated in scarlet velvet fringed with gold. Their furnishings included chairs, settees, one even had an enormous bed. And what was occurring in those boxes...Bea gulped.

While some of the alcoves had curtains drawn for privacy, others were fully revealed to the rest of the room. Within those boxes, masked occupants were engaged in a variety of sexual acts. To Bea's right, a naked woman sat on a man's lap, her back to his chest...a position that, frankly, had never entered Bea's imagination. The woman rode her partner enthusiastically as he fondled her bouncing breasts.

Cheeks warm, Bea slid a glance at Wick.

"That's a rather advanced riding technique, which I'll teach you, if you wish." Framed by his mask, his eyes held amusement along with a spark of male heat. "Now concentrate, angel. Let's make the rounds and see if we recognize anyone."

They walked along the alcoves, Bea's embarrassment growing along with an undeniable feeling of arousal. She couldn't help but be affected by the openly fornicating couples—and several groupings that included three or more. In the next box, there was a woman with a red wig, her lips and nipples painted to match. She was kneeling on a settee, her hands gripping its carved back, as a dark-haired man inserted his shaft into her glistening slit from behind.

A blond man stood on the other side of the settee, his fist in her brassy curls as he thrust his member betwixt her cherry lips. As one man filled her from behind, the other plunged deep into her mouth. Caught between light and dark, the woman let out a moan—muffled by her mouthful of flesh—that sent a shiver down Bea's spine.

"Don't get any ideas." Wick's breath warmed her ear. "I'm not a man to share."

"I wouldn't want to be shared," she whispered back.

It was the truth: the thought of any man but Wick touching her left her cold. With a flash, she realized that what aroused her wasn't the acts themselves, but the utter lack of inhibition in the room. Of the way these people were surrendering to their darkest impulses. Letting go so completely that one wouldn't care about the judgements of others: that one would exhibit oneself like that woman riding the man in reverse or the one with two cocks moving inside her...

*That* was the notion that stiffened Bea's nipples and caused her pussy to flutter.

A sudden stillness came over the room, the participants seeming to freeze in their libidinous acts, their gazes all directed to the center stage.

"You're blocking my view, wot," a male voice called from an alcove. "The show's about to begin, so find a seat. Or you're welcome to join us."

Bea saw his eyes leering at her through his mask. Two women knelt between his legs, their mouths working on his cock and bollocks. Wick put a proprietary arm around Bea's waist, guiding her to an unoccupied chaise longue in the next alcove.

Then he stiffened, muttering, "Hell and damnation."

She followed the direction of his gaze: a woman dressed in a diaphanous Roman toga had entered the arena. She was leading a man...by a leash connected to his collar. *Dear God.* The man was tall and thin and wore no garments save for the leather harness strapped around his hips, his erect member protruding through a hole. His black leather mask molded to his sharp features, his hair —a notably unnatural black—falling over his brow. Bea could see the feverish excitement glittering in his ice-blue eyes.

"Dear heavens." Shock percolated through her. "Is that... Reverend Wright?"

## 30

ONCE SEEN, THERE WERE THINGS THAT COULDN'T BE UNSEEN, and if some benevolent God offered to wipe Wick's memory of the last quarter hour, he would have gladly taken the deal. The reason wasn't because he was a prude. Nor did he judge the sexual preferences of others any more than he wanted to be judged for his.

But, Christ, he'd rather have his eyeballs poked out than to watch another minute of the Reverend Mr. Henry Wright being flogged over a whipping block. As the mistress plied her leather whip on his backside, she scolded him for being a "naughty boy" while he writhed and moaned. When she donned a harness fitted with a giant ivory dildo, Wick couldn't help but wince.

He slid a glance over at Beatrice. She was watching with wide eyes that could have indicated fascination or horror. He sincerely hoped it wasn't the former.

"Don't be getting any ideas," he said in her ear. "Of the two of us, the only one bending over is you."

"This is all rather eye-opening." She let out a shocked giggle. "Do you think he enjoys being flogged?"

"That's not as unusual as you may think. There are bawdy

houses specializing in flagellation: for patrons who like to whip or be whipped."

"Really?" Her lashes fluttered in the eyeholes of her mask. "Have you been to one before?"

"It's not my particular cup of tea." He curled a finger under her chin. "I don't need a whip to be in control."

Her response—swiping her plump lips with her little pink tongue—aroused him more than all the debauchery taking place before them.

"Save that thought," he murmured. "Wright's bound to finish soon, no pun intended, so we best get ready to corner him."

"While his hypocrisy is beyond galling, do you think he's the one behind the attacks?" she asked with a frown. "According to his calendar, he was in London when Fancy was kidnapped."

"Calendars can lie. Either way, we'll get our answers," Wick said grimly.

The reverend's crescendo of pleas continued until he reached his finale. Then his mistress released him from the whipping block, leashing him and leading him out of the ring to the applause of the crowd. Wick took Beatrice's hand, the two of them following at a discreet distance.

The passageway from the arena had chambers sprouting off both sides. Wright entered a room two doors down while his mistress continued on to the end of the hall, disappearing up some stairs.

Wick led Beatrice to Wright's door and knocked.

A few seconds later, the door opened. The reverend still wore his mask although, thankfully, he'd donned a robe. "The room is presently occupied—"

Whatever words he'd intended to say next vanished as Wick shoved him backward into the room, Beatrice closing the door behind them.

"What in God's name?" Shocked recognition flashed in Wright's gaze. "Miss Brown...is that you?"

"Indeed, Reverend Wright," she said coolly.

His jaw slackened. "I d-don't understand. How did you find me here...?"

"We have your pocket watch," Wick growled. "The one you dropped when you set her barn on fire."

"Wh-what? I didn't start the fire," Wright sputtered.

Either the man was an excellent actor, or his innocence was real.

"Why should I believe you? You've been sowing discord against me and my tenants since you arrived in the village." Beatrice folded her arms beneath her bosom. "You've been working to get rid of me from the start."

"No. That is, *yes*," Wright said quickly when Wick gave him a menacing look. "I know that I've caused trouble for you. But it wasn't my idea—it was Squire Crombie's."

"What is the nature of your association with Crombie?" Wick demanded.

"He's been...paying me to spread rumors about Miss Brown and her tenants," the reverend admitted. "To tarnish her reputation in the community. He wants her estate, you see, and he thought that making her feel, ahem, unwelcome might persuade her to sell. To pack up and leave."

"Was it Crombie's idea for you to persecute Mrs. Haller?" Beatrice said scathingly.

"No." Wright drew himself up with a righteousness that Wick could only marvel at. "Sarah Haller was a prostitute and has a bastard to boot. For the sake of my congregation's spiritual and moral well-being, I had to make an example of her—"

"While you, yourself, cavort in the most lascivious manner," Beatrice said with disgust. "How *dare* you judge her? You, sir, are the worst sort of hypocrite."

"You won't tell anyone...about what you saw tonight?" Apparently, Wright finally registered that he was in a glass house and paused in his slinging of stones. "It would ruin my career, my standing in the community, devastate all who depend upon me."

Wick's fists curled. Christ, he wanted to plant a facer on the sniveling, duplicitous bastard. It was obvious that the reverend felt no remorse for the pain he'd caused Mrs. Haller or for accepting a bribe to defame Beatrice. Nor did he give a damn about his congregation.

He was only sorry for himself...that he got caught.

Yet punching Wright, while satisfying, wouldn't advance the cause.

"Why was your watch at the barn then?" Wick demanded.

"It wasn't. I can prove it to you." Wright went to fumble through a pile of clothes on a nearby chair. He returned, holding out...a pocket watch.

"See?" he said eagerly. "I have mine here."

Wick examined the watch. It was identical to the one that currently sat in his pocket.

Which posed the question: whose watch had he found in the barn?

Beatrice's brow pleated. "The watch we have belongs to someone else?"

"We need a list of the club's members," Wick said.

"I don't have it. No one does," Wright said quickly. "The founders—whoever they are—have been very hush-hush about its membership. That is why I joined. A man of my standing couldn't risk, ahem, indulging otherwise."

Resisting the urge to plow his fist into the other's smug face, Wick said tersely, "There's a secretary. How does one contact him?"

"He has an office upstairs." Wright licked his lips nervously. "Take the stairs at the end of the hallway to the uppermost floor. But he might not be here tonight."

*Even better.* Wick would search that damned office until he found what he was looking for.

"I've told you everything I know," Wright whined. "Do I have your word that my secret is safe with you?"

"We will keep no secrets for you," Wick said with loathing. "In the future, if you don't want to be caught, don't bloody do the deed. Now begone."

With a frightened look, Wright gathered his clothes and scurried out of the room.

"What a *weasel*," Beatrice burst out.

"Undoubtedly. But I believe he's telling the truth. And there's no denying he had his watch."

Chewing on her lip, she said, "Do you think Crombie is behind the fire and kidnapping?"

"There's a way to find out. If Crombie's on the membership list, we'll have proof."

"Let's go search the secretary's office," Beatrice said.

"Will you consider waiting in the carriage?" He knew the answer, but he had to try.

"The searching will go faster with the two of us," she said decisively.

For the sake of expediency, Wick refrained from arguing and led the way out. The hallway was empty, the boisterous roars of the crowd conveying that the current performance was a hit...and hence the perfect distraction. Now was the time to act.

He motioned for Beatrice to follow him to the stairs that Wright had said would lead them to the office. They ascended the carpeted steps, arriving on the next floor. Here a large chamber was decorated to resemble a sultan's palace. Round mattresses covered in jewel-toned silks were tossed over the floor, men and women groaning as they fucked in various permutations upon them. Heavy velvet curtains covered the walls, presumably to muffle the noise.

"Next floor," Wick muttered.

As they started up the next flight, their path was blocked by a pair of prostitutes wearing masks, feathers in their wigs, and nothing else.

"O'erdressed for the occasion, ain't you?" The auburn harlot winked at him. "Do you need 'elp getting comfortable—or getting your tart in line? I've a steady 'and with a birch."

Seeing Beatrice's scowl, Wick said quickly, "No, thank you."

"If you change your minds, come find us," the other trollop cooed. "We'll be in the sultan's seraglio, where the show's 'bout to begin."

"I wonder which brave souls will be performing in the glass cage tonight?" her friend said with a giggle.

The tarts sauntered off, and Wick and Bea continued their trek to the uppermost floor. Seeing a guard posted outside a door at the end of the hallway, Wick pulled Beatrice against the wall, out of the guard's field of vision.

"That must be the secretary's office," Beatrice whispered. "How will we get past the guard?"

Wick thought quickly. "I have a plan. Wait here."

When Wick returned a few minutes later, he was accompanied by the two naked whores they'd encountered on the stairs. The redheaded harlot—who'd offered to *birch* Bea—flashed her a saucy smile before continuing down the hall with her blonde friend, arm in arm, their dimpled bottoms swaying.

"What are they doing?" Bea whispered to Wick.

"What they're good at. Stay out of sight."

Peering carefully around the wall, Bea saw the women flirting with the guard who was doing his best to resist. He soon gave in, and the pair dragged him into one of the other rooms off the corridor. The blonde poked her head out, sending a thumbs-up signal.

"They'll keep him occupied for as long as they can," Wick said. "But we'd better hurry."

They rushed stealthily toward the office. Wick tried the knob —locked, of course.

"Hair pins," he said in a low voice.

Plucking a pair from her wig, Bea handed them over, watching in fascination as he inserted the pins, working them adroitly in the lock. A slight click...and the knob turned.

"Is lock picking a required skill in the underworld?"

"No, but it is at Eton." He scanned the environs with an alert gaze. "Let's get inside."

The fire in the hearth bathed the office in a shadowy, orange glow. A large desk and floor-to-ceiling cabinets dominated one end of the room, with a seating area and another door off to the right. They headed to the desk, where Wick again applied his boarding school tricks to unlock the drawers. In the top drawer, they found assorted writing implements, papers, and a ledger with the club's accounts...but no list of members.

"Keep searching. I'll check the cabinets," Wick told her.

She rifled through the remaining compartments, grimacing at the pair of smelly stockings and a toupee that resembled a dead rodent. While Wick systematically opened and closed the doors of the cabinets, she stepped back, looking around the room.

*If I wanted to hide something important, where would I put it?*

She wandered over to the seating area, where a bookcase stood against the wall. The shelves were crammed with books. Even knowing where to begin the search was daunting, and they probably only had minutes left before the guard returned.

She chose a book at random from the middle shelf, opening it, rifling through, finding nothing.

Staring at the rows of volumes, she tried to think like a member of a secret society. She skimmed the spines. The secretary had an eclectic collection: treatises on property management, a handful of Shakespeare, some history books, and hold up... Dante's *Inferno*?

A book about the journey through Hell.

With prickling intuition, she reached for the battered volume on the next-to-highest shelf. She had to stand on tiptoe, her gloved fingertips curling around the spine. As she pulled it down, she felt a slight shifting in the weight of the book, as if something had moved...inside? Examining the book, she saw that it wasn't a book at all: it was a wooden box with a leather cover, the edges carved to resemble pages.

She shook it, heard a faint movement from within. But there was no way to open it.

"Wick," she whispered excitedly. "I found something."

He was over in an instant. "*Inferno*—ah, clever thinking. May I?" Taking the box, he set it on the desk and methodically ran his fingers over the seams. "The leather cover isn't attached here by the spine. There's probably a switch..."

Bea heard a faint click, and the cover popped open like a lid.

Inside, nestled in a piece of silk, was a black leather book.

Wick lifted the small volume, flipping through it.

Names. Pages of them. With the date of acceptance and membership status listed.

"The list," Bea breathed. "We found it—"

She froze as footsteps and voices approached.

Wick moved quickly. Shoving the book into his jacket pocket, he replaced *Inferno* on the shelf, and pulled her to the door by the seating area. He made short work of the lock: on the other side was a set of stairs leading downward. He pushed her inside, shutting the door behind them just as the other door to the office opened. As they raced down the steps, Bea's heartbeat thumped in her ears, mimicking the sounds of footsteps.

Had the guard realized that they'd been in the office? Was he giving chase?

The stairs led to a small corridor lined with more doors, all of them unmarked. No indication of which way was out. Wick grabbed the nearest door knob; when it turned, he went in first, his posture braced. Bea followed closely, the door swinging shut behind her.

It was another chamber, smaller than the office they'd vacated. A desk and chair were curiously placed in the center of the room. The walls were made up of large floor-to-ceiling windows...the curtains strangely positioned on the other side of the glass.

Bea's nape tingled. "Something doesn't feel right."

"Let's get out of here," Wick said grimly.

He went to the door, tried to open it. "Bloody hell, someone's locked it from the outside."

"Ladies and gentlemen, it appears we have performers in the glass cage tonight!" a voice boomed.

A cheer exploded from the other side of the glass, and the curtains began to part.

"What the devil?" Wick ground out.

He pushed her behind him, standing protectively between her and the exposed windows, but she peered over his shoulder in shock. The large panes of glass gave an unimpeded view into the sultan's seraglio that they'd passed by earlier. Men and women lounged upon bright silk pillows, sipping flutes of champagne. Their masked faces were turned to Wick and Beatrice, as if they were expecting...a performance?

"Christ," Wick said softly.

"Don't just stand there," someone yelled. "Get on with it and fuck!"

## 31

Damnation...they were trapped.

As the crowd began to chant "Fuck! Fuck!," Wick's mind worked furiously, trying to find a way out. He was acutely aware of the book in the inner pocket of his jacket—the key that would lead them to Beatrice's enemy. They were *this* close to solving the mystery; all he had to do was get them out of there without revealing their purpose.

But how? The longer he and Beatrice remained paralyzed in the "glass cage," the greater the chances were that someone would realize that they were not Hellfire Club members. Their charade would be exposed. Throughout the evening, he'd seen guards posted throughout the rooms and knew he couldn't fight an army of burly brutes and protect Beatrice at the same time.

*Think, man. Don't fail now. Don't fail Beatrice...*

Beatrice moved from behind him, and he turned, intending to keep her back. To shield her from the leering crowd. Yet she evaded him, lowering herself gracefully to her knees in front of him. Startled, he stared at her upturned face, hidden by her white mask, which left only her shimmering eyes and lush mouth bared.

"Angel...?"

"Trust me," she whispered.

While his brain couldn't seem to keep up as she placed a palm on the placket of his trousers, his body responded as ever to her touch. He grew hard in an instant. As she slipped her fingers into his waistband, working on the fasteners, a hush fell over the crowd, their chanting replaced by humming lust. Hot, pulsing energy swirled around and inside the glass room.

Wick couldn't believe that Beatrice was doing this. Perhaps the anonymity offered by their disguises emboldened her. Whatever the cause, her brazen stratagem set fire to his blood and, rationally, he couldn't deny that it might be the one way out of their predicament.

She managed to free him, his stiff cock falling into her gloved hands.

She gently caressed his rigid length, her silk-covered fingers stroking him as a roomful of strangers watched. The hunger in her eyes told him that she wanted to do this, that it aroused her to serve him in this public way...and, bloody hell, that made him turn to steel beneath her touch. He didn't mind putting on a show as long as *she* remained dressed and protected from the rapacious gazes.

Having his lover kneeling so sweetly before him brought out his dominant instincts. Since their arrival in London, he'd sensed her building walls between them. She'd dug in her heels at the slightest provocation, sometimes for no reason at all. At times, it had felt like she was deliberately goading him and testing the limits of his patience. His annoyance had been tempered by his understanding of her and her need for independence.

In life, Beatrice was his equal. He respected that fact. He also had the desire to assert his own will. And what better way, he thought with dark hunger, than to push the boundaries of her sexual surrender? In bed, he enjoyed taking the reins as much as she enjoyed relinquishing them. She might have initiated this scene, but he knew how to draw the utmost pleasure from it for them both.

He curled a finger under her chin, deliberately deepening his voice to avoid recognition.

"Keep your eyes on mine. At all times."

Her consent was in her shiver of excitement, the yielding softness in her eyes.

"Now frig my cock with both hands. Firmly, if you please."

She obeyed, using both fists to pump his rod, her gaze connected to his. He imagined what it must look like to their audience: the beautiful masked woman, kneeling before a man, frigging his veined stalk with such sweet alacrity. The thought aroused him almost as much as her soft touch...and also ignited his darker desires.

"I'd like to sample your mouth next," he said. "Tongue out, pet."

"Pet" wasn't his usual endearment for her, but it suited the occasion.

He took her hands from his cock, placing them on his thighs. "Keep them there."

"Yes, sir."

Her use of "sir" had a cheeky edge that was pure Beatrice. As much as she liked surrendering to him, she was also used to being in control. Used to doing as she pleased. He knew she wanted to suck his cock, and he would give her what she wanted...but he'd do it in his own fashion.

Taking his erection in hand, he placed just the head of it on the pink shelf of her tongue. He rested it there, not moving, relishing the velvety softness. Savoring her obedience which was all the sweeter for its rarity. He heard murmurs from the crowd as she continued to look up at him, with an adoring lust that could not be missed. Knowing the strength of the woman who so prettily cradled his prick betwixt her lips for all to see gave the act a special meaning that warmed his heart and brought a raging fire to his loins.

"Very nice," he allowed. "Now keep this pretty mouth open for me while I fuck it."

He slid a hand into the brunette curls of her wig, holding her head still, and entered her mouth in a deep thrust. He grunted as slick, wet heat enveloped his cock. Since he'd introduced her to the art of fellatio, she'd come a long way, and he knew exactly how much she could take. Knew how to bring forth her moans with the demanding drives of his shaft, knew that his rough use of her mouth was making her pussy wetter and wetter.

He plunged all the way in, butting the back of her throat, groaning as he felt its exquisite clench. The small gurgling sound she made inflamed his lewdest impulses. He withdrew, letting her draw a breath through her nose, then he did it again and again, deeper with each pass. Until, finally, his balls rested upon her delicate chin.

He traced the stretched, quivering outline of her lips.

"Do you like having me buried in your throat, pet?" he inquired silkily.

Her eyes were lambent with desire even as diamonds glimmered on her lashes. She nodded, and he eased his prick from her, giving her a moment to recover before he skewered her throat again. He was close: the silken submission of her mouth and the lustful sounds of the crowd were bringing him rapidly to the edge. A dark, animalistic edge that, in all his sexual adventures prior to Beatrice, he'd never reached before.

It was one thing to fuck with abandon. Another entirely to fuck the woman you cared about in such a fashion. To know that you could share your ugliest failures, your darkest lusts, your tenderest dreams...and she could take it all.

Because she was that strong.

Because you trusted her...loved her.

The recognition blazed through him. His chest heaving, he pulled out.

"Keep your mouth open, pet," he gritted out. "Hold it nice and wide for me."

She parted her lips, red and swollen from the pleasure he'd taken between them. Fisting his cock, he aimed, jerking rapidly. His orgasm blew through him like a storm, jolts of sizzling bliss that forced his seed from his cock and into her keeping. Shuddering, he watched as she held his pleasure, proudly displaying what she'd drawn from him, her eyes radiant with emotion.

Applause exploded from their audience...the audience that had faded from his consciousness in the heat of his coupling with his lass. He saw her start, as if she, too, had lost herself in the bond between them, forgetting the world beyond. A droplet of his seed clung to her chin, and he thumbed it away, feeling her erotic shiver. He saw the need in her gorgeous eyes—and damn if it didn't send a fresh wave of heat to his loins.

"I'll take care of you soon, angel," he murmured as he helped her to her feet. "For now, take your bow, and let's get out of here."

In the carriage, Wick tucked Beatrice into his side. She trembled with unassuaged desire, her hand stroking his thigh in a delightfully needy manner, but there were guards riding atop the carriage. He would wait until he got her home, then he would make love to her until dawn.

In the meantime, he took out the black book. In the wavering lamplight, they began reading through the names. The members were listed in alphabetical order by surname, with columns showing date of acceptance and membership status in the Hellfire Club.

Many names were familiar to Wick: aristocrats, industrialists, more than a few politicians.

As he turned the page to the surnames starting with "G," he heard Beatrice's sharp intake of breath. Her face drained of color.

"What is it, angel?" he asked. "Recognize someone?"

"T. Edgar Grigg." Her hand fluttered to her marked cheek. "The man who caused my scar...he was a founding member."

## 32

"BEATRICE, LOVE, WAKE UP."

She opened her eyes to a feeling of disorientation. She saw Wick drawing open the curtains, recognized that she was in his room. After they returned from the Hellfire Club, he'd made love to her until the early hours. It was as if their time in the glass cage had unlocked a new level of intimacy, nothing forbidden between them. He'd shown incredible stamina and virtuosity, taking her in positions that made her blush to think of them now.

At one point, he'd arranged her on her hands and knees, her cheek pressed against the mattress and her bottom raised. Gripping her hips, he'd hammered into her from behind, the heavy siege of his bollocks against her tender entrance a jarring bliss. He'd breached another place too, his thumb pressing deep into territory so shocking and wicked that she'd climaxed on the spot. He'd wrung countless releases from her, her throat raw from her sobs of pleasure.

After that, she'd fallen asleep. But her slumber had not been restful. It had been plagued by images and memories that not even Wick's lovemaking could keep at bay.

Grigg, the man who'd played such a pivotal role in her past, had made his way into her present. In her dreams, he'd been a looming ghost, a specter out for blood...something she could never escape. She'd run and run, at times believing she'd finally left heartbreak behind, but it always caught up with her in the end.

Her temples throbbed. She knew she wasn't thinking clearly, knew it was the lack of sleep and traumatic revelations of just hours ago that had sent her into this strange spiral. She tried to tell herself that everything would be all right: she and Wick had a plan.

Today, they would seek out Mr. Lugo, the investigator Harry Kent had recommended. They would ask Mr. Lugo to look into the family Grigg had left behind, to see who might have inherited the watch...and who might wish to gain revenge against Beatrice for the death of their kin.

Bea had briefly considered going to her brother—who, given his vendetta against Grigg, probably had some information—yet she decided against it. What if Benedict decided to take matters into his own hands? Knowing him, he might try to destroy this new villain, without even recognizing that this present situation was the result of his need for vengeance.

She quaked, thinking of the havoc her brother could wreak. She couldn't risk it. Better to wait a few days for a professional investigator to find the answers.

*If only Benedict had left Grigg alone*, she thought with despair. *If only I hadn't interfered with Grigg's beating of that boy...yet how could I see such cruelty happening and do nothing?*

She rubbed the heels of her hands over her eyes. Lord, she needed more sleep. Why had Wick awakened her so early? From the light he was letting stream into the room, the day was in its infancy. And it wasn't as if they had to worry about the servants: his valet was as discreet as Lisette and wouldn't blink to find Beatrice in his master's bed.

Wick must have read her expression correctly for he sat on

the mattress beside her, stroking a tendril from her cheek. "Sorry to wake you, love, when I'm responsible for depriving you of sleep."

She felt her cheeks grow hot. Under the cover of night, it had been easy to abandon herself to the eroticism of their lovemaking. Now, with everything else stirred up inside her, she felt intensely self-conscious. As if a layer of skin had been ripped off, leaving her raw and exposed.

She smiled to cover her discomfiture. "Is there a reason for being up at this ungodly hour?"

"I'm afraid there is."

Wick wasn't the sort to dissemble. He usually delivered news, good or bad, in a straightforward manner. Therefore, his hesitation heightened her feeling of unease.

"What's happened?" Scenarios flooded her brain. "Did someone discover we were at the club? Dear God, did something happen at my estate—"

"No, angel. Nothing like that. It's not bad news..."

"What is it then?" she said in a rush.

"It's my mama." Wary lines carved into his handsome face. "I received word that she'll be arriving here today."

"My *darling* Wickham. Since you haven't come to see me in ages, my naughty boy, I had to come to you!"

As Wick dutifully accepted his mama's embrace in the drawing room later that morning, Beatrice stayed back with Violet, quietly observing. The Dowager Viscountess Carlisle was a striking woman. She was probably in her sixties, but her carefully maintained complexion and figure took decades off her appearance. She'd blessed Wick with her coloring and bone structure and perhaps his innate elegance also came from her: she looked effortlessly chic in an emerald carriage dress with a Chinoiserie border, her golden-brown hair a shining chignon beneath the sweeping brim of her hat.

After giving Wick a thorough inspection—peppered with comments that he looked "tired" and "ought to try that new eye cream" she'd brought with her—she turned to her eldest son.

"Carlisle," she said with a brittle smile. "I didn't see you standing there."

Since Carlisle had been standing next to Wick the entire time, his brawny figure rather hard to miss, Beatrice couldn't help but wonder at the dowager's comment.

"Don't mind her," Violet muttered under her breath. "I never do. But poor Richard—he's always been subject to her blasted games. She plays favorites, even with our boys. If she had her way, she'd spoil Wickham—ours and yours—rotten."

While not dutiful, Violet's comment seemed at least accurate.

"Mama, I'd like to introduce you to my friend," Wick was saying.

"Is that her, standing by...Violet, my dear." The dowager glided over. "I was momentarily blinded by the brightness of your gown and didn't realize it was you."

Bea thought that Violet's sunflower yellow morning dress set off the other's brunette coloring beautifully. Vi had no outward response to her mama-in-law's barbed comment, leaning in to exchange air kisses with the lady.

"Good morning, Mama," she said brightly. "Perhaps you ought to have your eyes checked while you're in Town? Overlooking Carlisle, being blinded by my dress...those could be symptoms of weakening vision in your dotage, you know."

Carlisle cleared his throat, obviously trying to smother a laugh.

"There is nothing wrong with my vision," the dowager hissed.

"Spectacles are quite fashionable nowadays," Vi said with an innocent expression. "Many of the older set carry them as accessories."

The dowager drew up her shoulders, pointedly walking past her daughter-in-law to pause in front of Beatrice. "Wickham, dearest, introduce me to your...friend."

As Wick made the introductions, Bea felt his mother's gaze sweep over her. Since she had been observing the dowager since her arrival, she knew that the other had been observing her in return. This meant that Wick's mama had had plenty of time to see Bea's scar. Plenty of time to school her reaction.

Yet the dowager made a show of her surprise nonetheless, her hazel gaze widening and lingering on the ridge that now seemed to throb and burn on Bea's cheek. In the eyes of the beautiful lady, Bea saw the reflection of a beast.

As pain knifed her in the chest, she told herself that it shouldn't matter what Wick's mama thought of her...but it did. In the other's expression, she saw what had led her to flee London all those years ago: disgust hidden behind feigned sympathy.

"My dear Lady Beatrice," the dowager said with a solicitous smile. "How I admire your courage. It cannot be easy to make an appearance in London."

"Mama," Wick said in a tone of warning.

Bea wasn't about to let him fight her battles for her. Pretending to misunderstand the dowager's comment, she replied, "Thank you, my lady. Coming from the country, I confess it does take courage to confront the commotion of Town. I am unused to the crowds and the noise."

The dowager's smile did not waver. "Now I know of several Wodehouses. Are you any relation to the Duke of Hadleigh?"

"He is my brother, but we have not been in contact for some time. It is my preference that things stay that way."

The lady's fine brows rose, but Bea felt she had to be blunt. The last thing she needed was for the other to alert Benedict to her presence in Town.

Wick must have shared her concern for he said, "I trust you will be discreet, Mama. I am assisting Lady Beatrice with a matter which must be handled with the greatest care and caution. Her life could be at risk if her personal details are bandied about."

"Goodness, how dramatic." The dowager's hands fluttered to her breast. "Not to worry, my dears—you know I am the soul of discretion. I shan't breathe a word to anyone of Lady Beatrice's presence."

## 33

THE DAY AFTER HIS MAMA'S ARRIVAL, WICK RECEIVED WORD from his men that they'd located Randall Perkins's family. They'd spoken with a couple by the name of Palmer living in the Seven Dials. Although the Palmers didn't know a Randall Perkins, they said they did have a nephew named Ralph—a troublemaker, apparently—whose age and physical description, down to the port-wine stain, matched that of Perkins.

Leaving Richard and Violet to deal with settling Mama in— the latter being none too pleased that Beatrice occupied her favorite suite—Wick wasted no time in making the journey over to the address his men had given him. Since he was accompanied by Beatrice, who refused to be left out, he took along guards for good measure.

They arrived at a tenement at the heart of the Seven Dials. At night, the neighborhood was the playground of thieves and cutthroats, and anyone heading into the narrow, winding streets and dead-end alleyways was taking their life into their own hands. By day, the thickly populated area appeared less menacing, but pickpockets were everywhere, on the lookout for pigeons to pluck.

As Wick handed Bea down from the carriage, her hand gripped his.

"What is it?" Wick asked.

"I swear it's that same boy again," she whispered. "The urchin I saw outside your office three days ago and again outside Doolittle's Emporium. He's hiding in the alley across the street."

Wick casually glanced in the direction she indicated. Sure enough, he saw a movement, the flash of brown hair, a ragged sleeve disappearing into the shadows.

"I'll send Wilcox after him," he said, gesturing to the guard atop the carriage.

"No, don't." She stayed his hand. "He's just a lad. I'm sure he means no harm."

"You're too soft-hearted love. That 'lad' had the look of a mudlark."

"A what?" Bea tilted her head.

"A mudlark. A band of street urchins who scavenge the Thames and pickpocket for a living. They may look innocent but try taking on a flock of them. Mudlarks are notoriously enigmatic of purpose and loyal to their own." Wick took a hard look into the alleyway. "If you see the boy again, let me know. I'll have a talk with their leader."

"You know their leader?"

"I've hired The Prince of Larks in the past to gather information." At her puzzled look, he explained, "The mudlarks are known as scavengers and pickpockets, but their main trade is the acquisition and sale of knowledge. They have eyes and ears everywhere...which is extremely useful when, for example, you want to know a competitor's bid on a project or how a Member of Parliament plans to vote. And while the Prince doesn't mind his larks engaging in petty theft now and again, he doesn't countenance them harassing females."

"You have rather colorful acquaintances, don't you?" she said after a moment.

"Welcome to the London underworld." He led her toward the tenements, a ramshackle building with a sagging roof that resembled a collapsed soufflé. "Now stay close and keep your wits about you."

The number his man had given him was on the fourth floor, which necessitated climbing a set of exposed, creaking stairs that felt as if they might collapse at any moment. They passed flats with peeling doors and some without doors at all, a ratty curtain serving as the only means of privacy. They stepped over men passed out in the hallway, too drunk or uncaring to take the final steps home. Women in dirty aprons dealt with squalling children, some of the younger females still wearing the face paint of their profession. The air was ripe with greasy, pungent smells.

Wick found their destination, a corner flat that had a door painted a cheerful blue. He knocked, wincing when that set off the screaming of a babe within. Those cries were joined by more cries and still more cries, the effect like auditory dominoes: within seconds, the rising cacophony could be heard down the hall.

The door swung open, a stout matron wearing a cap glaring out at him.

Toting a crying babe in each arm, a third one strapped to her back, she demanded, "Wot you want, eh? Spent an 'our, I did, getting the sprats down and there you go, knocking loud eno' to wake the dead."

"My sincere apologies, madam." Wick bowed. "I'm Wickham Murray, and this is Lady Beatrice Wodehouse. My man was here earlier, and he said you had information regarding Randall Perkins...whom I believe you know as Ralph Palmer?"

"Why are you after Ralph?" she asked bluntly.

Wick decided honesty was the best policy. "We suspect he may be involved in a plot against Lady Beatrice. One that has thus far involved arson and kidnapping."

"That ne'er-do-well. Wouldn't surprise me one bit." Snorting, the woman stepped aside. "Come on in, then. I'm Mabel Palmer. You can speak to my 'usband David 'bout 'is scoundrel o' a nephew."

"Thank you, Mrs. Palmer. May I?" Wick extended his arms, intending to relieve her of one of her squalling burdens. He owed her that much for waking the babes.

Her eyebrows shot up. "Lardy-dardy, ain't you a gent? Don't mind if I do."

Before Wick knew it, he had a babe in each arm and another strapped to his back. He amicably took on the task, bouncing the babes as he walked into the flat. Within a minute, the two in the crooks of his arms were cooing up at him, the third one dozing against his shoulder.

"How the bloody 'ell did 'e do that?" Mrs. Palmer muttered to Bea.

Bea's mouth quivered. "I have no idea, ma'am."

They were in the main living area, which contained the kitchen, a table and chairs, and a tangle of children playing on the floor. A curtain hung across a doorway to the right, through which a man passed. He was barrel-chested and balding, his bushy whiskers in sore need of a trim.

"David, this 'ere's Mr. Murray," his wife said. "The toff who wants to know 'bout that no-good nephew o' yours. Ralph done 'em wrong, just like 'e done us."

David Palmer gave Wick a once-over. "Why's the cove got the triplets?"

"Do *you* want 'em?" Mrs. Palmer retorted.

In answer, Palmer sat in one of the chairs, putting his feet up on an old crate. "Pull up a seat, Mr. Murray. You keep the babes, and I'll tell you what you be wantin' to know."

≁

Wick's ability to engage with people never failed to amaze Bea. From farmers to underworld denizens to his own upper-class family, he found a way to connect. His charm was more than skin-deep; his true beauty lay in the way he treated everyone as his equal.

As a result, three strange babes were snuggled happily against him as their father, an out-of-work carpenter, related his story of woe concerning his nephew Ralph Palmer...who did indeed match the description of Randall Perkins, from his belligerent attitude down to the birthmark on the left side of his face.

"Now Ralph, 'e didn't 'ave an easy start to life. 'E was teased by the bullies on account o 'is birthmark and then 'is ma and pa, my older brother, cocked up their toes when he was twelve. Me and Mabel took 'im in, tried to do our best by 'im—"

"But a bad seed will grow into poisonous fruit," Mrs. Palmer declared from the cooking area where she was peeling potatoes. "Ralph was trouble from the start."

"How so?" Bea asked.

"'E ne'er took to schooling, always involved in fisticuffs and the like." Mr. Palmer sighed. "By the time the lad was sixteen, 'e 'ad more than a few brushes wif the authorities. 'E ran wif a bad crowd, see, and they led 'im to do stupid things. The females, especially. Weren't nothin' the lad wouldn't do to impress a pretty face. One time, 'e lit Roman candles in an abandoned warehouse and set it on fire—"

"He committed arson?" Wick said alertly.

"Not on purpose. Like I said, 'e was trying to impress some fancy piece—"

"'E's a liar, thief, and criminal, and I'm tired o' you making excuses for 'im." His wife tossed a peeled potato into a wooden bucket. "'Ave you forgotten Ralph got you sacked from your job and left you to pay the damages?"

"Damages?" Wick asked.

Mr. Palmer huffed a breath. "For years, I was the principal workman for a builder—"

"Good-paying job, that was." His wife plunked another potato into the bucket. "'Til that bounder Ralph ruined it all."

"Do you want to tell the story, or do you want me to do it?" Mr. Palmer asked.

"Go ahead and tell it," she grumbled. "But don't go making light o' 'is misdeeds. You always were too kind-'earted, David Palmer, and look where that's got us. Living in this cesspool, that's wot."

"As I was saying," Mr. Palmer went on, "I worked for a builder, and 'e trusted me wif the keys to 'is workshop. A workshop that 'ad tools and materials, all o' it worth a pretty penny. About a year ago, I woke up to find my keys and Ralph gone. 'E used my keys to get into the workshop and cleared it out."

"And left us 'olding the bag." Wielding a knife, Mrs. Palmer took her rage out on a carrot. "All our savings and our 'ome went toward paying for 'is crime."

Bea had a great deal of empathy for the Palmers, who seemed like decent folk. She knew intimately what it was like to have the actions of kin affect your future, whether you liked it or not.

"We 'ad to pay the debt," Mr. Palmer said stiffly. "It were a matter o' honor. Ralph may not care 'bout the family name, but I do."

"And where did that get us?" Mrs. Palmer demanded of the room at large. "After that incident, Mr. Palmer couldn't get steady work, despite being the best carpenter this side o' the Thames."

"The lady and gent don't need to 'ear all our troubles, Mabel." Clearing his throat, Mr. Palmer said, "Ralph was responsible for our misfortune, but 'e weren't the only one. I blame that female 'e was stepping out wif as well. 'E was always short o' the ready trying to keep 'er 'appy."

"That one was always be'er than she ought to be," Mrs. Palmer agreed. "Didn't 'ave the common courtesy to pay us a visit. Only met 'er once, in the street wif Ralph, and Miss Hoity-Toity all but ran away rather than be seen wif us."

"What was her name?" Bea asked curiously. "What did she look like?"

"Mary Smith...don't know much else 'bout 'er. She did 'ave looks and knew 'ow to do 'erself up like a lady," Mrs. Palmer said reluctantly. "Blonde, blue-eyed, and pretty, like one o' em porcelain shepherdesses."

"When was the last time you saw Ralph or this Mary Smith?" Wick asked.

"Since 'e ransacked the workshop, Ralph knows be'er than to show 'is face 'round 'ere." The carpenter slid a significant look at his wife, who went on chopping as if she wished it were Ralph on the block instead of the vegetables. Lowering his voice, he added, "But a few days ago, I 'eard talk about 'im being in town."

Bea's pulse sped up, her gaze meeting Wick's. Randall Perkins —Ralph Palmer, that was—might be in London this very moment?

"Where was he seen?" Wick asked.

"Someone said they spotted 'im at The Baited Bear, but I talked to the barkeep—a friend o' mine—and 'e couldn't confirm seeing my nephew. I'm sorry I ain't got more to tell you and even sorrier for whate'er trouble Ralph's caused you both," Mr. Palmer said gruffly.

"It's not your fault, sir," Bea said. "You've been most helpful."

She rose, the men following suit.

The carpenter took back his sleeping babes. "Least I can do."

"My company is always in need of good men." Wick took out his card, leaving it on the crate. "If you're looking for work, tell the manager I sent you."

Surprised emotion tautened the carpenter's face. "Sir...I don't know what to say..."

"*Thank you* will do," his wife declared. "Or *Hallelujah!*"

## 🌺 34 🌺

UNABLE TO SLEEP, BEA CAME DOWN TO BREAKFAST EARLY THE next morning. She was glad to see Wick already in the dining room, a freshly filled plate in front of him. He rose to greet her courteously and asked the room's other occupant—a footman—for some of Cook's currant jam. As soon as the servant departed, Wick took her into his arms and kissed her thoroughly.

"God, I missed you," he murmured.

She ran her fingertips along his smooth-shaven jaw, inhaling his spicy-crisp cologne.

"I didn't sleep nearly as well without you beside me," she admitted.

Due to the dowager's presence, they'd mutually decided to forgo their bedtime activities for the time being. Wick didn't want to do damage to Bea's reputation, and Bea didn't want her future mama-in-law to have additional reasons to dislike her. For despite Wick's assurances to the contrary, she knew that the dowager did not think she was a suitable match for her son.

While she could learn to live with the Dowager Viscountess Carlisle's ill opinion of her, she didn't need to add to it. It was clear that Wick loved his mama, and the dowager doted upon her younger son. The idea of causing strife in the relationship churned Bea's stomach.

"We'll figure out better arrangements soon." Wick kissed her knuckles. "You could, of course, let me make our engagement public. If you don't mind a small wedding, I could get a special license. Then you'd be mine, and this nonsense of sneaking into bedchambers would be done with."

"Let's not worry about that just yet." She forced a smile. "With the discoveries we made yesterday about Randall Perkins—or Ralph Palmer, I should say—I know we're getting close to unmasking the villain. We can't afford distractions, and there's no harm in waiting a while longer to make things official."

*And to make sure our happiness will last.*

She trusted Wick, trusted that he cared for her. And she couldn't deny that her feelings for him were deepening day by day. He was everything she'd ever hoped to find in a lover, a partner, a husband. Yet so many things remained unsettled. Not only was there a secret adversary to stop, but Wick's surveyor, Mr. Norton, had yet to deliver his report. In her experience, the journey to happiness never went as planned...

"As you wish, angel." Wick released her hand. "Why don't you fill a plate, then, and we'll plan our next steps."

Bea was returning from the sideboard with coddled eggs, juicy sausages, and sliced tomatoes just as Carlisle arrived. He made up his own plate and joined them at the table.

"Do you think this Ralph Palmer character is in London?" he asked, forking up a bite of kippers.

"Possibly," Wick said. "But after meeting with the Palmers, Beatrice and I went to the Baited Bear and the barkeep confirmed what Mr. Palmer told us: he didn't know anyone who saw Ralph Palmer personally. So the sighting could just be a rumor." He took a drink of his coffee. "I could dedicate men to finding Palmer, but that's looking for the proverbial needle in the haystack."

"My intuition tells me Grigg is the more important lead," Bea agreed as she buttered a crisp slice of toast. "Thankfully, we have Mr. Lugo assisting us in that regard."

"Lugo knows what he's about," Carlisle said. "He and my brother-in-law Ambrose have solved some of the most difficult cases in London. You'll have your answers soon enough."

The butler arrived with the paper, setting it next to Wick.

"*Bloody hell.*"

At Wick's vehement oath, both she and Carlisle stared at him.

Heart thudding, she asked, "What's the matter?"

"I'm going to *throttle* McGillivray. He and the Potteries Coalition are behind this," Wick ground out. "They threatened to go public if I didn't go along with them, and now they have."

"What's happened, brother?" Carlisle said quietly.

"This." Rising, Wick threw the paper down on the table.

Even from her angle, Bea couldn't miss the headline printed in bold capitals:

INVESTORS FLEE GLNR AS MURRAY FAILS TO DELIVER ON PROMISES.

Her chest clenched as she saw the white lines of anger carved on Wick's face.

"What...what will you do?" she stammered.

"I don't know." His hazel eyes were hard, remote. "The investors were already getting agitated; once they see this they could start jumping ship. And others will follow like lemmings. The whole project—our company—could go under."

"Whatever I can do, Wickham..." Carlisle began.

"Stay here and look after Beatrice," Wick said tersely. "I've got to get to the office."

Before Bea could think of what to say, he strode from the room.

～

Wick had expected mayhem at the offices of Great London National Railway.

What he found there exceeded his worst expectations.

An angry mob had gathered in front, and it took the escort of six guards to get Wick through the front door. Even so, he didn't escape unscathed. He was wiping raw egg and rotted produce from his sleeve as he entered Garrity's office.

Garrity was seated at his desk, Kent on the other side. Both wore grave expressions.

"It was McGillivray," Wick bit out, stalking over to face his colleagues. "He and the Potteries Coalition threatened to take us under and support the competition if we didn't start laying track."

"One cannot blame them," Garrity said coldly. "We have failed to keep our end of the bargain to them. To all the investors who entrusted us with their money."

Guilt speared Wick. He knew that the other was right. They had failed...no, *he* had.

*Devil take it, why didn't I do better? How could I let down my partners and investors, who were counting on me? What the bloody hell is wrong with me?*

His frustration and anger at himself felt brutally familiar.

"Perhaps there is salvaging the situation yet. If we were to issue a counter-statement with a plan and timeline, we might be able to staunch the bleeding." Kent's bespectacled gaze was not unsympathetic. "Any word from the surveyors?"

"Norton's verdict should be arriving today or tomorrow." Wick's gut tautened as he let himself consider the worst-case scenario.

*What if Norton can't come up with an alternative plan? What then?*

In his head, he hadn't allowed for the possibility—or rather, he'd believed that, whatever Norton's findings, he could find a way to make things work. That, with time, he would sort out a solution, the way he always did, even with the most difficult of negotiations. In his arrogance, he'd believed that he could manage anything.

Failure had never been an option. Until now...when it was staring him in the face.

"Norton's verdict is no guarantee of a solution," Garrity said flatly. "The only immediate action that will prevent certain disaster is gaining Lady Beatrice's support of our plan. For God's sake, Murray, it's clear you're going to marry the woman. What's hers will be yours anyway, so she might as well get used to the idea now."

"That strategy worked well for you, didn't it?" Wick retorted.

He knew his point hit home when Garrity said nothing, his eyes narrowing into dark slits.

Two years ago, Garrity had undergone a crisis in his marriage when he'd tried to force his wife's hand in a matter regarding her inheritance. He'd nearly lost Gabriella as a result, and in the end he'd discovered that nothing mattered more than his wife's love. Since Wick had witnessed first-hand his mentor's painful soul-searching and ultimate redemption, he knew Garrity had learned his lesson.

"Fine. We'll buy Lady Beatrice and her goddamned tenants a new refuge." Garrity's jaw muscle ticked. "In Staffordshire—on the bloody moon, for all I care. Make her an offer she can't refuse."

"I started with that tactic. It's not about the money. Camden Manor isn't just a piece of land to Beatrice." Hell, he didn't know how to make his partners understand. "It's not...replaceable. Trust me, I've tried—"

"Try. Bloody. *Harder*," Garrity said.

"In the interim, we should assemble the investors," Kent cut in. "I could give a demonstration of the new engine. Perhaps the technological advances we've developed will reignite some confidence. It will buy us more time to get the rest of our plan in order."

"Good thinking," Garrity said curtly. "I'll personally contact our largest stakeholders and assure them that while plans have been delayed, they will proceed. I'll tell the clerks to toe the company line. All right, gentlemen, we have our tasks: let's each do our part."

Wick left the office, his chest tight. He knew what his part was: to get the railway built. Which meant he either had to renege on his vow to Beatrice and ask her once again to sell her land—or fail the company and people who'd trusted him.

Either way, failure and dishonor were closing in.

When Wick arrived home, the conversation he dreaded having with Beatrice was delayed by the appearance of Mr. Lugo. The three of them met in the drawing room, Beatrice perched on the settee, Wick standing behind her, the investigator facing them both. A strapping fellow, Mr. Lugo had mahogany skin and penetrating eyes, his deep voice bearing the accent of his native Africa. He declined the offer of tea and got straight to the point.

"I have started making inquiries into Thomas Edgar Grigg," he said. "While the case is in its early stages, I believe I have some information that may be of interest."

"Since we spoke to you only two days ago, I'm amazed you have any information to share," Bea said with clear admiration. "Your reputation is obviously well earned, sir."

Mr. Lugo inclined his close-cropped head in acknowledgement. "To begin, Grigg was an only child born in Manchester. Both his parents died when he was in his adolescence, and he worked as a coal miner as a young man. He managed to catch the eye of a coal merchant's daughter visiting from London, a woman by the name of Madeline Johnson. He married her and got into the family business.

"After his father-in-law died, he took over and expanded operations, amassing significant wealth. He and his wife had one child, a son named Thomas Franklin Grigg, born in 1816."

Wick made the mental calculation. "That would make Grigg's son four-and-twenty today. Do you know what happened to him after his father's death?"

"The specifics of that will take longer to trace, but I was able to ascertain a few facts. After Grigg's business was ruined and he took his own life, his wife and child were left destitute. They lived with her relatives, moving from home to home. Eventually, when the boy was old enough, he pursued a career in the Church."

Bea's gaze collided with Wick's: the shock in her eyes told him that she'd come to the same conclusion that he had. Male, early twenties, position in the Church—that described one person in her immediate circle.

"You don't think Grigg's son is...Frank Varnum?" she said to Wick.

"Varnum, you say?" Lugo cocked his head, his brown eyes alert.

"Yes, he's the curate of the village church." She hesitated. "He's very nice."

"Nice has nothing to do with it," Wick said grimly. "He was around when all the attacks happened. If he is indeed Grigg's son, then he has motive as well: revenge for his father."

"In my inquiries, I encountered the name Varnum." Lugo had removed a small notebook from his burgundy frock coat and was flipping through the pages. "Ah, yes. Varnum was the married surname of Mrs. Grigg's sister, with whom she and her son stayed for some time after her husband's death."

"That can't be a coincidence." Certainty filled Wick. "Frank Varnum and Thomas Franklin Grigg must be one and the same, which makes Varnum our most likely suspect."

Bea gnawed on her lip. "You're right, even though I wish you weren't."

"You've a tender heart, angel." Wick placed a hand on her shoulder, squeezing gently. "But you mustn't forget what this villain has done and what he's capable of."

"I'll need another few days to follow the trail of Thomas Franklin Grigg," Lugo said. "I should then be able to confirm whether or not he is indeed this Frank Varnum of which you speak. In the meantime, I urge you to alert those on your estate of the possible connection. Better safe than sorry."

"Thank you, sir." Beatrice nodded. "That is excellent advice."

"We have one suspect, a very likely one, but I will continue to pursue other leads as well. There may be other persons with intimate connections to Grigg who have reason to do you harm. I will return in a few days' time."

"You have my gratitude, for not only taking on my case, but doing it so expeditiously."

"It is my pleasure, my lady. Any friend of the Kent family is a friend of mine. And I have more reason than one to close this case quickly." Mr. Lugo flashed a smile, dazzling in its brevity. "Mrs. Lugo tells me she will proceed on vacation without me if I do not complete the investigation in a timely manner."

"Please express my sincere gratitude to her as well," Bea said warmly.

The investigator bowed and left.

Wick joined Bea on the settee. "At least we're making progress."

"I still cannot believe Mr. Varnum is behind these attacks, but I must write Gentleman Henderson immediately." Her brow lined with worry, her hands clasping in her lap. "Now that we know who the villain is, I need to return to Camden Manor. I don't feel right being here while Mr. Varnum could launch another attack at any time."

Wick's jaw tautened, her words reminding him of the conversation they had to have. The one that Mr. Lugo's revelations had delayed and, at the same time, made even more necessary.

"I don't want you to travel without me," he said firmly. "It's too dangerous. And while Varnum is the most likely suspect, Lugo still needs time to confirm that he is, indeed, Grigg's son and to investigate any other leads. Waiting a few more days for Lugo's findings seems prudent."

Her chin rose to a mutinous angle. "All the same, I feel like I should go home."

He didn't have time for another argument. He had to take the bull by the horns.

"I cannot escort you at the moment. Not with what is going on here," he said bluntly.

Remorse filled her lavender eyes. "I'm being dreadfully selfish. Of course, you cannot leave. How...how bad was it at the office?"

"It wasn't pretty." He met her gaze squarely. "Some investors are panicking and trying to sell their shares, which means prices are starting to dip. We need to issue a statement that we will start building the railway as planned—or the panic will turn into wide-spread pandemonium. Then shares will go down...and perhaps our company with them."

"But how can you make that statement without Mr. Norton's verdict?"

He hated himself for what he had to ask of her.

"I need to ask you to sell your estate to GLNR," he said.

Silence tautened between them.

"You said that you would not ask that of me." She looked bewildered. "That the choice would be mine."

"I know I said that. But circumstances...have changed." He forced himself to go on, even as hurt spread like ink through her clear eyes. "The company is depending upon me, and I have to do the right thing. We can offer you money, Beatrice, enough to buy another estate anywhere you want—"

"I don't want another estate. You know what Camden Manor means to me," she whispered. "How can you ask this of me when you promised you would not?"

He had no answer for her. She was right. He was breaking his word to her, violating his code of honor, proving himself to be the failure he'd always been.

"I..." He felt walls closing around him. "Just forget I asked."

"Of course I can't forget it. Wick, I *want* to help you—but just as you have people depending on you, I have people depending upon me."

At the anguish in her voice, self-loathing rose like bile in his throat. Damn him for putting her through this—especially when she had other worries to contend with. It was his job to protect her, and he was doing a shoddy job on all fronts.

"I understand," he said gruffly.

"Do you?" Now anger threaded her words, and he was glad because he deserved it. "This isn't the first time I failed to meet expectations, you know. After my accident, I was no longer the beautiful debutante Croydon wanted or the daughter my father was proud to call his own. My own brother couldn't even look at me without being consumed by rage and the lust for revenge."

His chest knotted. "I'm not like them. Beatrice...I love you."

It wasn't the way he meant to tell her of his feelings, but he felt the urgency to speak the truth, as if they were suddenly on borrowed time. He knew she cared for him, but did she love him in return? If she did, then surely they would find a way...

"Is love enough?" Her scar seemed to flinch against her pale skin.

Although it wasn't the response he'd hoped for, he saw her despair and couldn't stand to see her hurting. He reached for her hands, which were startlingly cold.

"Of course it is," he said.

"My parents were in love," she said in a remote voice. "They were utterly devoted to one another...until my accident. Then my papa couldn't stand to be near me, stayed away from the family more and more. When he died, it was in the arms of his mistress.

He broke my mama's heart, and she passed away not long after. Happiness never lasts."

Her story chilled him. Nonetheless, he rubbed her hands between his own.

"Our happiness will last," he said firmly.

"How? If I do not yield, then your company will fail. How could you forgive me for destroying your success? And your partners and friends will surely see me as a pariah, as they would have every right to do."

"That won't happen—"

"And if I do yield,"—she let out a ragged breath—"then I could not forgive myself."

He fought the growing tide of powerlessness. There had to be a solution.

"Mr. Norton's report isn't back yet," he said doggedly. "There's still hope that we can find an alternative solution. Listen to me, Beatrice: love will find a way."

"The difference between you and me," she whispered, "is that you actually believe that."

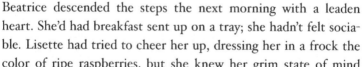

Beatrice descended the steps the next morning with a leaden heart. She'd had breakfast sent up on a tray; she hadn't felt sociable. Lisette had tried to cheer her up, dressing her in a frock the color of ripe raspberries, but she knew her grim state of mind showed. Although Wick had wanted to come to her last night, she'd refused him.

She'd needed to be alone, to have time to think...and prepare.

How she wished Fancy were here right now. Her bosom chum had been there after her life had disintegrated the first time, and Fancy's presence would be a great comfort. For as much as Beatrice had grown to like Wick's family and friends, she didn't think she could rely on their kindness once she destroyed his company and career.

She wouldn't even like herself.

*I should have never left Camden Manor. I belong there—not here.*

The impulse to return home was stronger than ever. Although she'd sent a note to her butler, telling him to be on the alert for Mr. Varnum, she felt like she was being derelict in her duties. The relief of identifying her secret enemy was dimmed by the knowledge that she wasn't where she ought to be...and by her growing certainty that her time with Wick was coming to an end.

She didn't blame him for asking her to reconsider yielding her land. Because of her, he was in a terrible bind. If only she could do as he asked, but she couldn't.

*I'm not like them. Beatrice...I love you.*

His profession should have brought her joy, but all she could think about was the pain. The pain of losing him, a pain that would make all her other losses pale in comparison. A pain she would never recover from...because she loved him.

With every fiber of her being, even though she ought to have known better.

She reached the ground floor and went to see if Wick had left for the office. She heard his voice as she neared his study; she halted, hearing another voice. The door was cracked open, Wick and his mama's conversation coming through.

"It's not that I don't like her, Wickham, but you could do so much *better*."

The dowager's words pricked like needles upon Bea's heart.

"Mama, we've been through this." Wick's reply was firm. "I'm going to marry Beatrice, and it would give me the greatest happiness if you did not interfere."

"Your happiness is precisely why we must have this conversation. Is it because she is a duke's sister that you consider her a worthy bride? While her family's blood may be blue, Hadleigh has more than a touch of madness, they say. From what my friends tell me, he—and his duchess, who reeks of trade—are no longer considered good *ton* due to their scandalous behavior."

Bea ground her teeth together. She did not like the woman spreading gossip about her brother. Whether or not the gossip might have validity was irrelevant.

"I'm marrying Beatrice, not Hadleigh. And, as she told you, she is estranged from him."

"Blood always tells, Wickham, you know that."

"God, I hope not." This last was muttered.

"What did you say, dearest?"

"Nothing, Mama. Now I hate to be rude but..."

"That is your problem, Wickham. I suppose it is my fault: I raised you to be a gentleman and, as a result, you are far too chivalrous for your own good. Given Lady Beatrice's defect, I understand why you feel pity for her—"

"Pity is not what I feel for her, and I will not tolerate you speaking of defects she does not have." The steel that entered Wick's voice made Bea cling to her ever-dwindling hope. "I love her, Mama."

"Oh, my dear boy, when did you become so bourgeois? I blame Carlisle. He and Violet practically live in each other's pockets. The result of her upbringing, no doubt."

"Richard is happy, thanks to Violet. Surely you can find no fault in that?"

The dowager sniffed. "Carlisle has always lacked refinement; he takes after your papa. But you, my boy, take after me, which means I understand your sensitive nature."

"Is that where I inherited my sensitivity from?"

"Wickham, do not make light of the situation." Frustration entered his mother's voice. "The papers this morning say that a mob has congregated in front of your offices—a *mob*. After *your* blood for failing to negotiate the purchase of the land from some Beatrice Brown, who I presume is Beatrice Wodehouse. What sort of a disreputable creature has an alias?"

"She has a reason for wanting her privacy, Mama. None of this is her fault. If you must blame someone, blame me."

"I most certainly will not blame you," the dowager said hotly. "This morning's papers are saying that she seduced you, that she's using her feminine wiles to make a fool out of you—all so that she can get more money for her land."

*The papers are saying that...about me?* Bea thought, stunned.

She didn't know why she was surprised. In truth, she ought to have been prepared for the worst. But to be again brought into the public eye, to be again cast in a shameful light hurt more than she would have imagined.

"This beastly chit is about to ruin you. To destroy all that you've worked for and render you a spectacle of public failure. And still you will stand by her side?"

Agony splintered through Bea. While the dowager's earlier comments had angered and humiliated her, she could disregard them for what they were: the petty concerns of a petty woman. She could not, however, ignore the veracity of the last statement, spoken with the desperation of a mother's love.

Bea would end up ruining Wick. And he would still stand by her side.

*But how will I live with myself?*

As the dowager continued to rant, Bea's temples throbbed. She wished she had a solution, a way out of this mess. She wished she could just abandon Camden Manor. At the same time, the very notion brought about visceral panic: her throat clenched, her palms dampened, every part of her bracing in denial.

Her estate was the one true refuge she'd ever had. The only thing that had kept her and those depending upon her safe. How could she knowingly give that up? She'd been in London for just a week, and already she was experiencing the hostility of the real world. Already she was feeling the intense urge to go home, where she belonged.

"Beg pardon, my lady."

The butler's voice startled her from her reverie. She stumbled back guiltily from the door.

"I was, um, just passing by..." Her cheeks burned. She was a terrible liar, and she wished she hadn't felt compelled to fib, which only made her seem guiltier.

Being well trained, Wick's butler did not blink an eye. "It is fortunate you are here, my lady. The letter you and Mr. Murray were expecting just arrived."

*The surveyor's report.* Her heart raced.

"I thought I heard a commotion out here." Wick emerged, his hazel gaze honing in on her face. "Is everything all right?"

"The note from Mr. Norton arrived," she managed.

Wick's handsome features tautened as he took the letter from the butler. He ushered Beatrice into the study, where his mother waited. "Mama, I need to speak with Lady Beatrice in private."

"Is that quite seemly?" the dowager began.

Something in Wick's expression made her relent, and she departed in an offended swish. Wick went to his desk, sliding a letter opener under the seal. He paused, exhaling.

"Just read it," Bea pleaded, clutching her hands.

He unfolded the page and scanned it.

"Norton says there is no other way through the property." He looked up at her, his expression one of stunned defeat. "It's either the farms...or the railway."

## ❧ 36 ❧

BEA SAT IN THE WINDOW SEAT OF HER ROOM, STARING OUT THE clear pane. An hour had passed since the arrival of Norton's unambiguous report, the nail in the coffin of her future with Wick. If she didn't give up her land, she killed his railway project. Any option she chose would end in pain...and she knew she'd already made her choice.

Wick's reaction had told her he knew it too. He'd grown distant and cold; for once, he'd been bereft of words. What could he say, really? That he wouldn't mind marrying the woman who'd destroyed his career, made him a public laughingstock? That he could still love such a woman?

It was over. He was just too honorable to admit it.

After he left to deliver the unwelcome news to his partners, she'd come up here. She didn't want to be subjected to the dowager's accusing looks. Nor did she feel up to the company of the Carlisles, whose kindness and compassion only made her feel worse.

A knock sounded, and Lisette entered. "I'm sorry to disturb you, my lady, but a letter came."

Premonition slithered over Bea's nape when she saw the note

was addressed from her estate. She quickly broke the seal. Air rushed from her lungs as she read the brief sentences, written in her butler's untidy hand.

"What is it, my lady?" Lisette asked with concern.

"There's been another fire," Bea said numbly. "The Ellerbys' cottage burned down...and Mrs. Ellerby has been badly hurt."

"*Mon dieu*," the maid gasped.

*This is my fault.* Bea's chest constricted, heat welling behind her eyes as she thought of the hurt she'd caused. *Mrs. Ellerby was injured because of me. I should have been protecting her. I should have stayed at Camden Manor where I belong.*

Instead, she'd allowed herself to be seduced by an impossible dream. She'd abandoned safety and good sense to go after happiness when she *knew* it could not last.

She shot up from the window seat. "I must get back."

"But my lady, is it safe? Surely Mr. Murray would not allow it."

The maid was right: Wick wouldn't permit her to go alone. But hadn't she caused him enough trouble? He had his failing company, a mob of angry investors to deal with...and Bea realized what she had to do. What she should have done from the very start.

*I am responsible for my own affairs. The only one who controls my future is me.*

Her mistake had been forgetting that. When things fell apart, she had to count on herself to pick up the pieces. Determination filled her, momentarily blocking out the pain.

"We'll leave without his knowledge." She paced as she plotted. "Who is in the house presently?"

"The pair of guards at the front of the house. And the servants," Lisette said uncertainly. "Lord and Lady Carlisle took the dowager out shopping."

Knowing Violet and Richard, they'd removed the dowager from the premises for Bea's benefit as much as their mama's. She was grateful for their consideration...for more reasons than one.

"I'll need to hire a private travelling coach. It needs to be done quickly, before the others get home. Can you see to that, Lisette?"

The maid nodded.

"Have the driver wait in the back lane. Once the servants sit down for their luncheon, we'll slip out the back to avoid being seen by the guards. Go now, hurry."

As the maid rushed off to do her bidding, Beatrice sat to compose a letter.

*Dear Wickham,*

*By the time you read this, I will be on my way home. There has been another attack, and Mrs. Ellerby has been hurt. I must attend to her—to the responsibilities I should not have left behind.*

As pain seeped through her numbness, she forced herself to continue.

*This parting comes at a natural time. You must deal with your world as I must deal with mine. I am sorrier than I can express to be the barrier to your success and happiness. Being the honorable man that you are, I know that you would try to forgive me...but I could not forgive myself.*

Her hand shook, a drop of ink splattering on the paper. A tear joined it, and she dashed away the others that threatened to follow. She couldn't be weak. Couldn't let her stupid heart cause more grief than it already had.

She reminded herself that it wasn't the first time she'd broken off an engagement. Back then, hadn't releasing Croydon felt like the end of the world? Eventually, she would get over losing Wick too.

*No, you won't,* her heart cried. *Because Wick isn't just an infatuation: you love him. And you always will.*

Taking several hitched breaths to regain control, she wrote on.

*I will always cherish the time we had together. Please accept what I know to be true: happiness such as ours was not meant to last. It is best that we part ways now, to preserve the sweetness of the memories we have and forgo the bitterness that would surely taint our future.*

*Yours,*
   *Beatrice*

*P. S. Please do not worry about my safety. Now that I know Mr. Varnum is my enemy, I will take the necessary precautions.*

Walling off her emotions, she addressed the letter to Wick and left it on the escritoire. Then she went to the wardrobe, pulling out a wooden box. She removed the pearl-handled pistol from its bed of velvet and loaded it.

The roar of the mob outside the office grew.

That morning, someone had tossed a brick through the front window, terrifying the clerks. Garrity had had to bring in a fleet of guards, who were at present doing their best to control the chaos. Wick and his partners had congregated in Kent's office since it was situated at the back of the building, farthest from the rioting. They'd had to carve out a space to meet as Kent's private domain was a cross between the study of an absent-minded scholar and the laboratory of a mad scientist.

They sat around a table cluttered with books, gears, and unidentified odds and ends used in Kent's experiments. Jaw tight, Wick informed his colleagues of Norton's findings. He felt numb with the knowledge that his failure had caused all of this: the frothing fury outside, the public humiliation of the woman he loved...and the tension of the men in this room, whose trust he'd betrayed.

"We'll wait a few days to announce the project is dead," Garrity said flatly. "We'll close the offices so the clerks won't be subject to harassment. And I suggest you gentlemen have a plan in place for your safety and that of your family. A vacation might be in order."

"Tessa has already refused to leave Town." Kent was idly spinning a coin-sized gear on the table. On the wall behind him was his "thinking board," the black slate surface covered in diagrams and scribbles that only he could decipher. His motto—*As constant as coal*—was emblazoned at the top.

"She's not worried about the rioters?" Garrity asked.

"She says that any mob that harasses her or her family will regret it." Kent's mouth curved. "She's probably right."

"I suppose that's one perquisite of being married to the Duchess of Covent Garden."

"One of many." Kent's smile was smug.

"Spare us the details," Garrity said, shaking his head.

This sort of banter was normal amongst Wick's partners. But it didn't feel normal now, when the sky was crashing on their heads...because of him. He wished the two would just berate him, yell at him—or better yet, take a swing at him. God knew he deserved it.

"Well, Murray?"

Lost in his brooding thoughts, Wick had missed whatever Kent had said. "Beg pardon?"

"I said Tessa has guards available if you want extra security for your lady. The claims put forth by the papers this morning were not only slanderous but damned reckless," Kent said with clear disgust. "You and Lady Beatrice could be at risk because of those lies."

The papers were characterizing Bea as a conniving seductress and Wick as her willing dupe. It was preposterous, but the public didn't know that. Once they got wind of her living in Wick's house, they would figure out she was the mysterious Miss Brown, placing her in greater peril than she was already in.

*Bloody perfect. We've just solved the mystery of her attacker, and now I've given her a whole city full of people out for her blood. What kind of an incompetent bastard am I?*

"I appreciate the offer," he said tersely.

Kent looked at Garrity and subtly lifted his chin.

The latter cleared his throat. "My hunting lodge in Hertfordshire is only a half-day's travel from London and quite pleasant this time of year. You and Lady Beatrice are welcome to use it until things blow over."

Garrity's generosity was the straw that broke Wick's self-control. The emotions he'd been holding at bay broke free. He shoved away from the table, rising to his feet.

"You can both stop pussyfooting around me," he bit out. "Why don't you come out and say it?"

Kent blinked. "Say...what?"

"What you're thinking—that this situation is all my bloody fault! I've failed you, the company, and our investors." Wick shoved a hand through his hair. "Because of my inability to negotiate the most important deal of our lives, GLNR will go under."

"When did you become a mind-reader?" Garrity asked mildly.

Wick glowered at him. "You regret offering me a partnership. Why don't you just admit it? I'd rather have you yell at me than be so goddamned,"—he threw up his hands—"*nice* about things."

Garrity raised his brows at Kent. "You told me I should be more agreeable."

Kent shrugged. "How was I supposed to know he liked your surliness?"

"Just be honest," Wick said starkly. "Tell me how angry you are, how I've failed you. I can handle it—hell, I *deserve* it."

"Of the three of us in this room, only one is angry," Garrity said. "And it's not me or Kent."

"That cannot be true." Wick curled his hands. "I ruined *everything*."

"Don't give yourself too much credit, Murray," his former mentor said. "You weren't able to see a venture through. That is hardly the same as ruining everything."

"How can you say that? The money I've cost this company, the investors—"

"Money can be replaced." Coming from Garrity, this was a remarkable statement. "Kent and I can both take the loss, and investors got into this knowing there was a risk. We never lied about that. You cannot take responsibility for the decisions of others: that was the first thing I taught you when you worked for me in the moneylending business. Have you forgotten?"

Wick's chest constricted. "You're being too easy on me."

"I personally wouldn't mind pummeling you, but you've beat me to it." Humor and understanding laced Kent's words. "Look, we've all made mistakes."

"Remember when Kent blew up the warehouse last year?" Garrity said. "We're still paying for that one."

He dodged the gear that Kent threw at him.

"The point being, we've all been where you are, Murray," Kent said. "Speaking from personal experience, I'll say the hardest part is not earning the forgiveness of others: it's forgiving oneself."

Kent's words resonated through Wick. He *was* angry at himself. But wasn't it justifiably so? He'd failed GLNR...and Beatrice. God, he'd subjected her to public scrutiny and humiliation when she'd already suffered more than her fair share. And he'd gone back on his word, putting her in the untenable position of choosing him or her estate.

He wouldn't blame her if she never wanted to see him again.

"I don't know how I managed to bungle things so completely," he said hoarsely.

"It's part of the human condition." Garrity steepled his hands. "You were trying to do the right thing, but it didn't turn out the way you planned. Trust me, I've been there," Kent said with feeling. "You can't blame yourself for trying to find a way to balance your lady's interests with that of the company."

Was that true?

Wick looked at Garrity. "You're being strangely blasé about this. Yesterday you wanted me to force Beatrice into selling her land."

"And yesterday you reminded me that there are more important things than money." Garrity flicked a speck off the sleeve of his dark frock coat. "When I got home, Mrs. Garrity reminded me of that as well. She said that we owed you for you helped to rescue her two years ago, and she's right. You protected that which I treasure most. As a man of honor, I must return the favor."

Wick frowned. "It was my privilege to assist Mrs. Garrity. There is no debt."

"I say there is, which is why I offer this piece of advice." Garrity's black gaze was penetrating. "Do not allow your past to interfere with your present happiness. Let it go. Be the man you are today—the man your lady deserves."

The words triggered the memory of what Beatrice had said to him when he'd told her about Monique. *The important thing is that you've changed, grown up... Knowing you as you are now, I can vouch for the fact that you are a true gentleman, one with a keen sense of honor.*

He *had* changed. He was no longer the wayward spare to the heir who'd never gained his father's approval, nor the young rake who'd lived a reckless life. He had earned his right to be called a gentleman—and a failed project couldn't change that.

"You're right," he said slowly.

Garrity lifted an eyebrow. "When am I not?"

A knock sounded. Wick went to open the door; the guard he'd assigned to Beatrice stood there.

"Wilcox?" he said tersely. "Why aren't you with Lady Beatrice?"

The guard's throat bobbed. "She's gone, sir. She and her maid left without saying a word."

"Leaving was easier than I thought it would be," Bea said as the coach wound through Pall Mall. "I don't think anyone saw us go."

"It was most lucky, my lady," Lisette agreed from the opposite bench.

They'd found the right moment when the servants had been distracted by luncheon. Slipping out the back, they'd dashed into the waiting conveyance. The resourceful maid had thought of everything for the carriage had taken off immediately, without Bea having to give orders to the driver whom she'd barely glimpsed.

The delay now was getting out of London; the coach was creeping along at a snail's pace.

Bea drew back the drapes and peered out. The thoroughfare was congested with carts, carriages, and throngs of people on foot and horseback. She saw two men arguing, gesticulating wildly, an upended crate of eggs between them. One of the men lurched toward the other, and Bea's heart skipped a beat when she saw who was standing behind him.

The cherub-faced boy with the cap. The mudlark...it couldn't be a coincidence.

Certainty pierced her. *He's watching me.*

Heart pounding, she released the curtain. "Lisette, across the street, behind the men arguing over the eggs—do you see a brown-haired boy?"

The maid looked out her window. "I see the men, my lady, but no boy."

Bea peered out again. The maid was right. The boy had vanished.

"He was there," Bea insisted. "A street urchin with a cap."

"London is full of such boys, my lady." With a puzzled smile, the maid reached into a basket by her feet. "I had the driver pick up provisions since it's to be a long journey. Shall I pour you a cup of tea to soothe the nerves?"

"You think of everything, Lisette." Bea took the cup, sipping as she stared out the window.

*Who is that boy...and what does he want?*

## 37

"WHY WOULD SHE LEAVE?" WICK PACED THE LENGTH OF HIS drawing room in an agitated stride. "Christ, doesn't she know the danger she could be in wandering off alone?"

His questions were met with silence from his audience. Garrity and Kent had accompanied him back from the office and sat stony-faced in wingchairs. Richard, Violet, and Mama had returned home minutes earlier and shared the settee. Wick's brother and sister-in-law looked worried; his mama calmly sipped a cup of tea.

"You're certain she didn't leave a note telling you where she'd gone?" Violet asked.

Wick shook his head in frustration. "There's no note, no message, nothing. And I questioned the staff. No one saw her leave; their best guess is that she departed around luncheon. The guards discovered her missing an hour later."

*Why would you do this, angel? Why would you leave me?*

Cold emptiness spread inside him as he faced the inevitable answer. She'd left because he'd failed her. Because he'd broken his promise to her and brought public scandal down on her head. Because he'd failed to protect the only woman he'd ever loved.

"Why is everyone surprised at Lady Beatrice's behavior?" Mama set her cup into the saucer with a delicate click. "You've all read the papers, I assume. Given what they're saying about her, would it be a surprise if she decided to leave Town? She has been utterly disgraced. If it were me, I'd never want to show my face again in London."

At his mama's conjecture, Wick balled his hands. *This is my fault. I did this to Beatrice, subjected her to pain.*

"Have a care, Mama," Richard said in a cautioning tone.

"I am only speaking the truth." With a sniff, Mama put her cup on the table. "If you ask me, Lady Beatrice has done the right thing. Better to end things cleanly. You must respect her wishes, Wickham, and let her go."

Wick felt as if he'd been punched in the gut. Had Beatrice ended things with him? Was her departure a permanent goodbye?

*To hell with that.* He pinned his mama with a burning stare.

"I love Beatrice. I will *never* let her go," he grated out. "Not without a fight."

"She's not worth the trouble, dearest. Indeed, my friend Lady Osmond was mentioning that her lovely niece just arrived from France—"

"All right, Mama. Let's go join the boys for tea." This came from Vi, who unceremoniously tugged the dowager up from the settee and toward the door.

"But I am not finished," Mama protested.

"You will be if you don't leave Wick alone," Violet said under her breath.

Obviously, his sister-in-law read him well.

With the ladies gone, Richard said briskly, "What is the plan?"

"I have guards out." Wick tried to organize his chaotic thoughts. "They, along with Garrity and Kent's men, are canvassing the area to see if anyone saw Beatrice leave and what direction she might have gone."

"Could she have gone back to her estate?" his brother asked.

He expelled a breath. "I've sent riders to check the coaching inns on the route to Staffordshire. If they find her, they'll send word. But my gut tells me something's off. While it's true she wanted to return home when she learned about Frank Varnum and the stories about her in the papers likely enhanced that desire, I know her...know that she wouldn't want me to worry. She'd leave a note, something, to tell me where she'd gone."

As he spoke, he felt a growing certainty. He *knew* his lass. Knew that she was responsible and caring, not the sort of woman who'd leave him or end their engagement without an explanation, no matter what he'd done. Then what could explain her abrupt flight with her maid?

The ringing of the doorbell spurred a sudden wild hope in his heart. Devil and damn, maybe Bea had just stepped out for a moment. Maybe this was some stupid misunderstanding...

He ran from the drawing room. Halted in the antechamber.

The newcomer his butler had ushered in was a man he knew by sight and reputation. Even without a formal introduction, he could guess who this tall, aristocratic stranger was by his physical resemblance to Beatrice. The Duke of Hadleigh had a darker, masculine version of the Wodehouse looks—and a haughty manner to go with it.

"Where is my sister?" Hadleigh said without preamble. "I wish to speak with her this instant."

"She's not here." Aware of the pain Hadleigh had inflicted on Beatrice, it took all of Wick's willpower to bridle his temper and extend a hand to his beloved's kin. "I am Wickham Murray."

"I know who you are." The duke's midnight blue gaze slid contemptuously over him. "The papers have detailed your relationship with my sister quite clearly, and I will deal with you later—after I've spoken with Beatrice."

"As I've said, she is not here," Wick said curtly.

"Where the devil is she then?"

"That's what I'm trying to bloody figure out."

"You *lost* my sister?"

The accusation was not only galling, it was damned ironic: *Hadleigh*, of all people, was accusing Wick of not looking after Beatrice's welfare? When it had been Hadleigh's actions, his lust for revenge, that was at the root of her troubles?

Wick didn't blame Beatrice for wanting nothing to do with her brother. He knew she feared that Hadleigh would wreak even more havoc were he to get involved. Wick was not afraid of the bastard, however.

"Your sister left, and yes, I accept some responsibility for that," he clipped out. "The papers are full of lies, and I should have protected her better against them. But you, Your Grace, bear your share of blame as well for her situation. I think you and I both know what I'm referring to."

Hadleigh stared at Wick, his gloved hand tightening on his walking stick. Although the duke was still a young man, his life of dissipation had left its mark. Deep lines were carved around his mouth, and his eyes were bloodshot from lack of sleep, drink, or drugs—probably all three. Hollows stood out beneath his cheeks, and his well-tailored clothes did not hide the gauntness of his tall frame.

"That is between my sister and me," he said with lethal softness. "You had best not interfere."

Wick couldn't be bothered to mince words with the pompous ass. "Your sister has been subjected to countless attacks because of Grigg," he said flatly.

The mask of loftiness slipped. A stricken look came into Hadleigh's red-rimmed eyes.

"H-how is that possible?" he stammered. "Grigg's dead."

"I don't have time to get into the details," Wick said with disgust. "Suffice it to say, Beatrice was not safe at her estate. I brought her to London to protect her—and to track down clues to her enemy."

"Why didn't she come to me? I would have helped. I would have done anything to make up for..."

Hearing the pain in the duke's voice, the remorse of a man who knows he's done wrong even if he can't admit it, Wick would have felt compassion, under ordinary circumstances. But now he was impatient: he didn't have time for the bastard's soul-searching...he needed to find Beatrice.

"Those clues led us to Grigg's only child: his son, Thomas Franklin Grigg, who we believe is using the alias of Frank Varnum. Varnum is the curate of the church close to Beatrice's estate, and she may have gone back to protect her people from him. I have men out looking for her, but if they don't find her, I'm going straight to Staffordshire so I would appreciate it if you didn't delay me any further."

Hadleigh stared at him. "Varnum isn't Grigg's only child."

"Pardon?" An icy hand gripped Wick's nape, premonition prickling through him. "Our investigator said that he had only the one heir."

"One legitimate child, yes. But he had a by-blow with his French mistress...a daughter. Her name was Marie, I believe."

The frost spread to Wick's gut. "What do you know about Marie?"

"Not much. After what...happened with Grigg, I sent money, anonymously, to the wife. I tried to find the mistress, but she'd disappeared, taking the girl with her." Hadleigh swallowed. "I know that Grigg's son eventually went into the Church, and a couple of years ago, my man briefly picked up the daughter's scent. She disappeared before he could approach her, but I suppose it was too late for that. At any rate, she'd found herself a respectable trade."

"Doing what?" Wick asked...but he already knew.

"She was in service. A lady's maid, I believe."

## 38

BEA OPENED HER EYES. HER VISION WAS FUZZY, HER MIND TOO.

All she registered was dimness, the overwhelming acridity of coal.

*Where am I?* she thought groggily.

She tried to remember where she'd last been...the coach heading for Camden Manor. Was she in a carriage now? She attempted to move, realizing with a jolt of panic that she couldn't. She was *bound*...to a column, rope winding around her chest, arms, and legs. A handkerchief was tied around her mouth, muffling the fearful cry that rose in her throat.

*What is happening? Who did this to me?*

She gazed wildly around, her skull rocking against the pole as she scanned her environs. There was just enough light to make out the long rectangular room with blackened brick walls and windows covered with soot. She made out vague shapes through the glass; it seemed like she was above the level of the street. The ceiling was high, some sixteen feet above her...and for some reason it had a large rectangular hole cut into it, framing a patch of dusky sky.

She squinted upward: were those...railway tracks running along the edges of the opening?

Closing her eyes, she listened, trying to gain additional clues to her whereabouts. She heard...waves? Ambient sloshing against the banks, distant cries—human or gulls, it was difficult to tell. But it seemed that she was near water, the Thames or a canal perhaps.

How had she arrived here without knowing? The light suggested that it was dusk, so she'd been unconscious for some time. Had she been drugged? The last thing she remembered was being in the carriage with Lisette...drinking tea.

Sweet heavens, had her tea been poisoned?

Panic thrummed as the shadows deepened with startling swiftness. In the darkness that spread through the room like pitch, frantic theories raced through Bea's head. Was Frank Varnum in London? Had he somehow managed to drug her—oh, Dear God, what had happened to Lisette? The notion of yet another innocent being hurt because of her made her renew her frantic struggles.

The rope only dug deeper. She was trapped.

In those dark moments, her thoughts went from escape to Wick.

By now, he'd probably read her letter and, knowing him, he'd gone after her. He was likely on his way to Staffordshire by now, with no idea that she was here, trussed up in some dark warehouse, awaiting an even darker end.

Moisture sprung to her eyes as she realized that she would die in the same solitary state in which she'd lived. With sudden clarity, she saw how stupid she'd been to leave Wick, how she'd been lying to herself. She'd convinced herself that she had to go back to Camden Manor for his sake, for the sake of her tenants...when she'd really done it for herself.

Because she was scared. Terrified of the depth of her love for him, the man who'd scaled not only the wall of her estate but the one she'd built around her heart. She was so afraid of losing him—of losing the greatest happiness of her life—that she'd caused it to happen through her own foolish actions.

*I love you, Wickham Murray.*

Desperate resolve filled her to say those words to him in person. She'd waited her entire life for him, and she wasn't giving up on her dreams. Not when he'd shown her they could be real.

Voices came from outside. Footsteps up a stairwell. The sound of a lock clicking, squealing hinges. Bea tensed as a figure walked toward her, his bulky form limned by the lantern he was holding. When he was close enough, she recognized him—the port-wine stain on his jaw, the protruding brow and leering features.

Ralph Palmer reached out and yanked off her gag.

She let out a scream—the sound abruptly cut off when he backhanded her. The metallic taste of pain flooded her mouth, her vision blurring.

"Try that again, and I'll won't go easy on you the next time," Palmer said. "Ain't no point in screaming. No one's 'ere to 'elp."

"Why are you doing this?" She took a serrated breath, raised her head to look at him. "Because I threw you off my property?"

His laugh was nasty. "You're a domineering bitch, but that ain't the reason."

"Then what is?"

The door opened again, a blonde woman with a lantern advancing, the dimness obscuring her features. Palmer went to meet her halfway, the two of them kissing with blatant sexuality before the woman broke away and came to stand in front of Bea.

It took Bea a moment to get past her shock. "*Lisette?*"

"*Oui*, you stupid whore, it is me."

"I...I don't understand," Bea stammered. "Why are you doing this?"

"Because you killed my father, you hideous bitch."

"Your father? Who..." Understanding slammed into Bea. "You're Grigg's *daughter*?"

"The one and only. Born to the woman he loved, not the ugly hag he had to marry."

Lisette abandoned her French accent, sounding like a different woman entirely. She looked and acted like one too. It was as if she'd shed her skin, showing her true reptilian side.

Catching Bea's gaze on her hair, she said with a wide smile, "Like my *coiffure*? This is a wig for now, but once I dispense with you, I look forward to returning to my natural roots. Ralph prefers me as a blonde, don't you, lover?"

"I'll take you anyway I can 'ave you, dove," Ralph said with a slavish smile.

"And you'll have me soon," Lisette cooed. "Right after I deal with the murderess."

"I didn't kill your father," Bea said desperately.

"Oh, but you did." Her former maid gave a little shake of the head. "You poked your haughty nose where it did not belong, and that led to my father's disgrace and death. But that's the aristocracy for you, as Papa liked to say. Always lording it over the hardworking middle class."

"I wasn't lording it over your father. He was beating a boy—"

"Shut your gob, or I'll have my Ralph shut it for you."

Ralph cracked his knuckles in readiness, and Bea swallowed.

"As I was saying, your outburst seven years ago cost my papa everything. Your damned brother ruined Papa's reputation and his living until finally Papa had only one honorable way out." Tears glimmered in Lisette's eyes...but they were tears of rage bordering on madness. "He was going to marry my *maman*, you know. She was so beautiful—he told us he was saving up for the day when he didn't need his witch of a wife's connections. Then he would divorce her and take us, his true family, to France and start anew. But *you* ruined all that. Instead of that beautiful dream, I lived a nightmare." Lisette shoved her face in Bea's. "Do you know what happened to me after Papa died—*do you?*"

Trembling at the other's hostility, Bea shook her head.

"*Maman* grew afraid that your brother the duke would come after us, so she fled with me. We had no money, no friends, and she had to sell her only possession—her beautiful body—to survive. *Maman* was delicate, could never survive such a disgraceful life. She died not long after, leaving me, a sixteen-year-old girl, to fend for herself. Do you know what a sixteen-year-old does to survive, *my lady*?"

"I'm sorry," Bea whispered. "So sorry for what you suffered. But it was not my doing."

"It was all your doing, bitch!" Lisette slapped her, so hard that she saw stars. "I whored because of you. I, a gentleman's daughter, had to fight to survive in the worst slums of the worst cities. Until finally I got myself a regular patron, a valet in a gentleman's house who convinced the lady's maid to train me. I wrote myself a few letters of recommendation, and thus my new career began. I saved enough money to return to London...where I met my dear Ralph."

She stroked Ralph's chin, and he purred. "I knew then and there I had the partner I needed to carry through my life's work."

"Anyfin' for you, my little cabbage," he said.

"After gathering some funds—revenge doesn't pay for itself, you know," Lisette said, chuckling at her own joke, "we headed off together to Staffordshire where a little bird had told me you'd gone. And by little bird, I mean the investigator I hired to find your whereabouts."

*And by "gathering some funds" she means stealing from David Palmer's workshop...and God knows what else she and Ralph Palmer have done.*

Bea was beginning to see the depth of Lisette's lunacy, the *folie à deux* between her and her lover. Both Lisette and Ralph believed that Lisette could do no wrong, that her actions were entirely justified, no matter who she hurt. The pair was mad, living in a shared, twisted universe... and Bea needed to find a way to escape.

Perhaps Wick would figure out that she wasn't on the way

back to Staffordshire. Knowing him, he'd do a thorough check of
the coaching inns on the route. He'd find it suspicious that she
hadn't checked in. Hope and determination filled her.

*Keep Lisette talking. Buy time. Find out their plans.*

"So you pretended you'd been beaten to get my sympathy," Bea
said.

"It worked like a charm, didn't it? You hired me on the spot."
Lisette smirked. "Poor Ralph. Giving me that shiner hurt him
more than it hurt me."

"I ne'er want to 'urt my dove again," Ralph said with a
shudder.

More pieces fell together for Bea. "When Gentleman
Henderson caught the two of you in the barn, Ralph wasn't
assaulting you, was he?"

"No, but I had to claim that he was in order to avoid suspicion
about our relationship." Lisette wagged her finger at her lover as
if he were a disobedient dog. "I told you that it wasn't the proper
time for a tickle."

Ralph gave her a pleading look. "But I missed you, my
princess. I couldn't resist."

"You cannot resist a great many things, it seems. Including
trying to get money from those factory owners," Lisette said
sharply. "That little ploy left a trail leading straight to us."

"I thought it was a good idea," he whined.

"Don't think, Ralph. It's not your strong suit."

"Whate'er you say, my treasure," he said in conciliatory tones.

Lisette returned her attention to Bea. "You weren't the worst
employer I ever worked for, I'll grant you that. You were always so
grateful for anything I could do to make you less beastly."

Bea wouldn't let herself be baited. "Why didn't you just
murder me and get your revenge? You had ample opportunity."

"Did you think I would let you get off that easily?" Lisette's
smile was sly. "Oh no, Lady Beatrice Wodehouse, you deserved to
suffer. To know fear like I did. To feel pain like I did."

"You sent the note, set the barn on fire. The pocket watch we found...it was yours."

"That was an unfortunate loss. My one memento of my dear papa. He met my *maman* at the Hellfire Club, you know. At the end, he didn't have much to bequeath, but he left the watch to her...a symbol of their love. She never sold it, even when we were in dire straits. When she died, she left it to me. And I kept it close to my heart, a reminder of the vengeance owed to me."

"And Fancy? What did she do to earn your vengeance?"

Lisette gave her a reproving look. "She chose to be your friend."

Anger built in Bea, edging out fear. On principle alone, she couldn't let this lunatic win.

"What about the fire at the Ellerbys?" she pressed. "They're good people, just trying to make a livelihood—"

"Get off your high horse, you bitch. There was no fire. I forged that note from your butler to get you to leave with me."

Bea allowed herself a moment's relief that Mrs. Ellerby had not been harmed.

"What about Frank Varnum?" she asked. "He's your half-brother, isn't he? Was he involved?"

"You think that pious twit could have come up with this plan?" Lisette scoffed. "Varnum has nothing to do with this. He doesn't know about me, although I know plenty about him. Papa always said his son was a useless milksop, and Varnum proved it by shedding Papa's name and legacy, as if it were something to be ashamed of."

Bea sent silent apologies to Mr. Varnum for doubting him.

"Wick will be looking for me," she said aloud. "I left him a note, and he knows I left with you—"

"This note, you mean?"

Lisette removed Bea's letter from the hidden pocket of her skirts. She tore it in two, letting the halves plummet...Bea's hopes along with them.

"I'm afraid Mr. Murray will think you quite rude for leaving without saying goodbye," the maid said. "But given the brouhaha about the two of you in the papers, he'll probably assume that your departure is your way of ending your affair."

"He knows I wouldn't do that to him." Bea's throat clenched. She couldn't bear for Wick to think that she could be so callous with his feelings, not when he meant everything to her.

*Why, oh why, didn't I tell him I loved him?*

"If I were him, I wouldn't bother looking for a scarred lover who just ran off—and who destroyed my company before doing so," Lisette said with a sneer. "I might just have a drink, lick my wounds, and seek solace in other ways. London has so many lovely diversions."

Bea pushed back despair. *Don't let her poison your thoughts. Concentrate.*

"What do you plan to do with me?" she demanded. "Why am I here?"

"Alas, my game, as enjoyable as it has been, cannot last forever. It's time to end it." Lisette's smile was sweet and deranged. "To end you."

Wick received news from the men canvassing the area. A pedestrian had seen a travelling coach drive into the lane behind the house around the time Bea had gone missing.

The witness said he'd seen a maid descend, stopping to exchange a rather lurid embrace with the driver, who had a distinct red mark on his face like a burn, which he then covered with a scarf. The maid had disappeared into the house, returning a few minutes later with a young lady, the two of them dashing into the coach. The witness added indignantly that he'd nearly been run over by the vehicle as it barreled out of the lane.

The account solidified Wick's suspicions. Lisette was the key to his beloved's disappearance, and she was apparently in cahoots with that bastard Ralph Palmer. Indeed, she fit the description that Mrs. Palmer had given of Ralph's sweetheart, Mary Smith—with the exception of her hair color, which could be altered.

Wick conveyed the new description of the coach to the group helping in the search.

Then he went to the maid's room.

The quarters were furnished simply with a bed, wardrobe, and small table. Given Lisette's hurried departure, she hadn't had much time to pack, leaving behind most of her belongings. In the dresser, he found a spare set of clothing and grooming products, his gut clenching when he saw the bottle of black hair dye.

On the table was a folded, day-old newspaper and a stub of a pencil.

"I know you're behind this, Lisette-Marie-whoever you are," he said under his breath. "Where did you take Beatrice, what are you planning?"

Part of being a successful negotiator was the ability to step into another's shoes. He tried to think like the maid. If Lisette's motive was revenge, then she could have killed Beatrice long ago. She had access; a few drops of poison would have done the trick. Instead of murdering her mistress, however, she'd engaged in nefarious activities designed to inspire fear and uncertainty.

The woman was like a cat toying with a mouse. She enjoyed the game, the suffering she was causing. Perhaps she saw Beatrice's torment as her true retribution. And there was no doubt Lisette was a show-off: using the surname *Collier,* indeed. It was as if she needed to flaunt her cleverness, to rub their noses in the fact that she, the coal miner's daughter, had outwitted them.

Which meant she probably had some grand finale in mind. A reckoning that would have some specific significance in her twisted mind—poetic justice, perhaps, for the father she'd lost. Something that she'd taken the time to plan, something that she'd been dreaming about, perhaps obsessing over...

He picked up the newspaper, unfolding it. The front page had the story about his failure to close the deal for GLNR. It mentioned Miss Beatrice Brown of Staffordshire, and his pulse leapt when he saw the circling of her name in pencil.

Had Lisette put that mark there?

At the bargaining table, it was what he'd call a "tell": an unconscious betrayal of one's private thoughts. Here, by circling Beatrice's name, emphasizing it, Lisette was communicating something.

*This woman is my target*, perhaps. Or *she's getting what she deserves.*

He continued turning the pages, scanning each one thoroughly. He saw no other marks until the last page. In the margin, next to an advertisement for a colic remedy, were numbers printed in pencil:

*6:00*

*2:00*

*10:00*

Heart thudding, he snatched the paper, bringing it downstairs. His partners were in his study, pouring over a map of London, marking out areas to search next. Richard, he knew, had gone to join the foot search for Beatrice. Surprisingly, Hadleigh was still there. The duke sat with a glass of Wick's whisky, his expression brooding, his walking stick tapping to some agitated internal rhythm.

"I found something." Wick slapped the paper down on the desk next to the map, the men gathering around to see. "I think Lisette wrote these numbers. They're times, possibly."

"A schedule, perhaps? For train, coach, or ship?" Kent mused. "Do you think she plans to make an escape with Lady Beatrice through one of those means?"

"Bringing a kidnapped woman on public transport doesn't seem like the cleverest of plans," Garrity said. "How would she escape unnoticed?"

"My gut tells me that she doesn't intend to leave London with Beatrice." Starkly, Wick shared his hypothesis. "Lisette's been toying with us, but she knew we were getting too close to discovering her identity. She's going to end the game—it's a matter of where and how she's going to do it. These times...they mean something."

"Six o'clock, two o'clock, ten o'clock." Kent drummed his fingers against the blotter. "The times are spaced eight hours apart. What operates that regularly and at nighttime?"

The moment he said it, his bespectacled gaze widened, colliding with Wick's.

"*As constant as coal,*" they said in unison.

Wick's heart thundered. "It makes sense that Lisette would want to take her revenge there. At the site of her father's greatest innovation." He looked at the clock on his desk. "Devil take it, it's eight. We have no time to spare."

He took off running, Kent and Garrity behind him.

"Where are we going?" Hadleigh asked, scrambling to catch up.

"To the coal drop by Regent's Canal," Wick shouted.

## 39

BEA WAS EXHAUSTED FROM TRYING TO ESCAPE HER BONDS. EACH time she heard a rumble, she trembled, wondering if her end was approaching. Lisette had delighted in telling her just how she would die.

"Because of you, dear Papa didn't live to see his idea for a coal drop brought to fruition. This warehouse should have been his—and my—legacy. But, never fear, I will leave my mark on this place. An hour from now, the next train will come. Do you know how a coal drop works?"

Bea had stared at her numbly.

"You're in the part of the warehouse known as the hopper. When the train passes above, the bottoms of the wagons will open, dropping its cargo directly into the hole over your head. Rather efficient, don't you think? The coal is going to bury you alive...that is, if it doesn't crush you to smithereens first. You might not even be recognizable when the coal sorters open the hopper in the morning and find you beneath the pile."

Bea fought back the clawing panic. Lisette and Palmer had left maybe ten minutes ago, to prepare for their imminent departure.

They planned to watch Bea get crushed by coal before heading to Gretna Green.

Apparently, she was to be the starting point of their unhinged wedding trip.

She stared at the flickering shadows cast by the lamp on the ground. Lisette had left it there, wanting Bea to see the moment of her death, the avalanche of coal as it fell upon her...

"Psst."

Bea stilled like a bird hearing the wings of a predator. Where had that sound come from?

"Psst, up here. Don't worry, milady. I'm coming down to get you."

She looked up—and saw a small, shadowy figure coming through the hole in the ceiling. The boy had a rope tied around his waist and was being lowered smoothly and swiftly until his boots hit the floor. He untied the rope and ran over to Bea, cutting her free.

She shook off her bonds. Stared at the familiar round-cheeked face, mop of brown hair, and tattered cap.

"You're the boy," she said in wonder. "The one who's been watching me—why?"

"Long Mikey's the name. But we 'aven't time to palaver. We 'ave to make ourselves scarce afore that stinkin' bitch returns."

He had a point.

"Tie this around your waist, milady."

He handed her the rope; she quickly did as he instructed.

"Now 'old on tight."

As soon as her fingers closed around the rough twine, the boy gave a whistle. A distinctive sound like a bird call, one note high, two notes low. She felt tension on the rope and then she was pulled from above, her feet lifting off the ground. She clung on as she soared through the darkness toward the opening in the roof, her rescuer becoming smaller and smaller below.

When she reached the top, hands helped her through the hole. More children, dressed in the same tattered uniform as Long Mikey. As soon as she rolled onto the roof, next to the tracks where the train would soon pass, she gasped, "Long Mikey..."

"Don't worry, milady. 'E's coming next," a pretty amber-skinned girl said.

They tossed the rope down again. The children—six of them—hauled Long Mikey up to safety, their small hands pulling the rope with coordinated efficiency, Bea helping as best as she could.

"I can't thank you all enough," she began.

She froze as she heard voices, the door to the hopper opening below.

"You can thank us later," Long Mikey whispered. "For now, we'd better run!"

Wick and his group arrived at the coal drop yard at a little after nine.

The moon streamed through the fog, bathing the yard in an eerie silver glow. The compound was situated next to Regent's Canal, a viaduct soaring over the walled yard and the warehouse where the coal would be dropped from the train. At this time of night, the workers would be gone, but guards would remain on the premises.

Wick ran toward the entrance, the others following him.

The iron gate was ajar. He entered cautiously. A guard stall took up the entryway, necessitating that workers and visitors past through the lanes on either side of it. He passed to the right of the stall...and froze when he saw the bodies.

The guards, two of them, lay on the gravel just beyond. They had dark blooms on their shirts, their sightless eyes telling him they were beyond help. The warehouse, a long, three-story brick building with the track running over the uppermost floor, sat fifty yards behind them.

Wick took out his pistol; Garrity and Kent did the same. Hadleigh gripped his walking stick.

"We'll split up, surround the warehouse," Wick said in a low voice. "Garrity, you and your men take the north side, Kent the east. Hadleigh you go south, and I'll take the west. Any questions?"

"Who're *they?*" Kent whispered.

Following the direction of Kent's finger, Wick saw a line of shadows descending the side of the brick building. They moved with ant-like precision. One by one, the figures dropped to the ground and began scurrying toward the gate. Wick's hand tightened on his weapon as they neared. The first one spotted him, letting out a whistle that brought the rest to a halt.

Christ, *mudlarks*...what were they doing here?

"Wick? Oh, Wick, is that you?"

Relief slammed into him as Beatrice emerged from the group, running toward him. He got to her first, drawing her to him fiercely. For an instant, he just held her to his pounding heart.

"I was so afraid I'd never see you again," she said in a muffled voice.

"I'm here, love." He pulled back to look at her. "Are you all right?"

"I'm fine, thanks to Long Mikey and his friends. They got me out of the warehouse," she said breathlessly. "Lisette is back there with Ralph Palmer. She's—"

"Grigg's daughter, I know." Wick cupped his beloved's cheek. "Go and wait in the carriage. Garrity, would you and your men keep watch over her and the mudlarks?"

"Of course," Garrity said.

A clearing of the throat. "Hello, Beatrice."

Bea looked beyond Wick. "*Hadleigh?* What are you doing here?"

The duke, Wick noticed, didn't quite meet her eyes.

"You're my sister," Hadleigh said, his voice strained. "Did you think I would not help?"

Footsteps neared—Lisette and Palmer. Wick had an instant to see the shocked rage on Lisette's face when she registered that Beatrice was no longer alone.

"Shoot 'em, Ralph!" she cried.

Palmer raised his pistol.

"Everyone, down," Wick shouted, tackling Beatrice to the ground.

The shot went wide, the bullet blasting bits off the entry stall.

Wick jumped to his feet, returned fire. Kent did the same.

Lisette and Palmer turned tail and ran back into the yard.

"Garrity, take Beatrice," Wick said as he reloaded.

"Come, my lady." Garrity offered Beatrice his arm, his men forming a protective circle around her and the mudlarks.

"Be careful, Wick," she called.

He jerked his chin in acknowledgement. Then he, Kent, and five men headed back into the yard. To his surprise, Hadleigh followed.

Wick spotted the dark figures entering the warehouse. "They're headed back inside. You four,"—he gestured to three guards and Hadleigh—"cover the exits. The rest, follow me."

He entered the ground level of the warehouse. Wall sconces illuminated the empty bays where wagons could be parked, coal dropped into them from the floor above. He heard a scuffling to the left of him—saw Palmer racing up the steps.

"Lisette went to the other end of the building," Kent said. "I'll take her. You go after him."

Each accompanied by a guard, he and Wick raced in opposite directions.

Wick pounded up the steps, Wilcox behind him. Reaching the next floor, he motioned for the guard to go clockwise around the room, while he went the other way. The smell of coal was suffocating in the hopper. The hole in the ceiling let in patches of moonlight, shadows dancing over the walls, causing Wick to aim his pistol this way and that. The columns were disorienting, easily mistakable for a man in the dimness. Wick crept along the room's perimeter, his weapon at the ready, when a movement caught his eye.

Palmer—coming out from behind a column, his pistol pointed at Wilcox.

"Look out!" Wick yelled as he took aim.

The shots went off simultaneously, two bodies hitting the ground.

Wick headed to Palmer, even as he called out, "Wilcox?"

"Fine, sir," came the guard's panted voice. "Bullet just grazed my arm."

Wick stood over Palmer; the brute was sputtering, his hands clutching the gushing wound in his chest. Even as Wick knelt to see what could be done, Palmer's hands slid lifelessly to his sides.

Gunfire exploded above them.

"Get away from me, you bastard!" Lisette's screech came from overhead.

Wick raced for the steps. They took him to the uppermost floor: this third story was fully exposed to the night, the yard below dizzily distant through the drifting fog. Moonlight glinted off the tracks spanning the opening where the coal would be dropped. Spotting a figure doubled over on the platform next to the tracks, Wick ran over, pistol drawn.

It was Kent.

"Are you hurt?" Wick crouched.

"Not...permanently," the other gritted out. "She kicked me."

Comprehending where Lisette's kick had landed, Wick winced in sympathy.

"Hadleigh went after her," Kent said between pants. "They're up ahead."

At that instant, the ground rumbled.

"*Christ*, the train," Wick bit out. "Stay here. I'll get them."

He straightened, squinting in the darkness. He saw them twenty yards ahead: two figures struggling dangerously close to the edge of the opening to the floor below. Locked in their struggle, they seemed oblivious to the locomotive heading toward them, the widening disk of its headlamp as it crossed the viaduct, barreling toward the warehouse. The ground vibrating beneath his feet, Wick was sprinting over, shouting out a warning, when he saw Lisette stumble backward, her feet slipping on the edge. She lost her balance, falling through the hole—but Hadleigh lunged forward, somehow grabbing her by the hand.

Lisette hung, suspended by that perilous connection.

The duke was trying to pull her up, calling to her, ignoring the blasting horn of the oncoming train. As Wick reached them, Lisette turned her head and looked at him. Her lips curved in a triumphant smile...and she let go.

"*No.*" Hadleigh's shout could be heard above the roar of the train.

Wick dragged the duke to the safety of the platform. An instant later, the train whipped by. The pounding thumps of coal filling the warehouse echoed through the night.

## 40

SEEING WICK EMERGE ALONG WITH THE OTHERS, BEA PUSHED through the ring of guards and ran to him. Wick caught her, crushing her against him, surrounding her with his reassuring strength.

"I was so worried," she said, her voice hitching. "What happened in there?"

"Lisette and Palmer are both dead. I shot Palmer."

At his statement, she tilted her head back to look at him. His expression was stark, but she saw no conflict on his handsome face. He'd done what had to be done, and he accepted it.

"And...Lisette?" she asked.

Wick drew her close, murmuring in her ear, "She fell to her death. Hadleigh tried to save her—risked his own life to do so."

Bea's eyes widened at the news. She pulled away, her gaze searching for her brother. He hung away from the group, his shoulders hunched, his eyes fixed on some distant point. Drawing a breath, she went over to him.

"Hadleigh?"

Although she spoke softly, he flinched, as if he hadn't noticed her approach.

"Beatrice." His voice was gruff. "You are well?"

It was absurd, exchanging niceties at a time like this. Equally absurd was the fact that he was her brother, her only surviving kin, and they'd not spoken for years. The chasm caused by pain, betrayal, and pride had once seemed impassable. It was still vast, and she didn't know if they could ever heal that breach...but she took the first step.

"I'm fine. And you?"

Surprise flickered in his eyes. "I'm fine as well. Thank you...for asking."

God, this really was ridiculous.

"Hadleigh, you just tried to save a woman's life. A woman who fell to her death. How are you *feeling*?"

"I failed you." His words, wholly unexpected, made her jerk in shock. As did the volcanic emotion in his eyes. "I should never have gone after Grigg. I was angry—at so many things. I blamed him, targeted him...but I never meant for him to die." His throat worked above his cravat. "It doesn't absolve me of anything, but I want you to know that, Beatrice. *I never meant to kill him.*"

Hearing her brother's gut-wrenching remorse, seeing the torment in his eyes, she took a step closer. Touched his quivering arm. "I believe you."

A sheen appeared in his eyes, and he quickly looked away. She gave him the space to gather himself and, in truth, she needed it too. The emotion roiling inside her—the amalgamation of past and present—was overwhelming. She felt Wick behind her. His arms closed around her waist, and she let herself lean into his solid warmth.

After a few moments, Hadleigh cleared his throat. "Am I to congratulate the two of you?"

"Yes," Wick said, the firmness of his tone giving her a thrill.

"I don't expect I shall be invited to the wedding, but perhaps, in the future, at your convenience...I might call upon you, Beatrice?"

Was she ready to have her brother back in her life? She wasn't sure. But she wasn't ready to close the door either.

"I would like that, Ben," she said.

At her use of his familiar name, the lines eased on his weary features, making him look more like the younger brother she'd known.

"Thank you." He gave a gruff nod. "I'll bid my adieu. I believe your attention is wanted elsewhere."

As her brother left, she turned to see the mudlarks had lined up behind her.

"We'll be on our way, milady," Long Mikey said.

"How will I ever repay you? I still don't understand why—"

"A wrong against me you'll regret, but a favor to me I'll ne'er forget."

The words stroked her memory like a match against a tinderbox, recognition flaring.

"That boy in the park with Grigg..." she said in wonder. "He said those exact words."

"It's the motto o' the mudlarks. The boy you saved, 'is name is Long Joe, and e's my brother. 'E gives his regards, by the way."

"Long Joe is here?" she asked, surprised.

"Yes, milady. O'er there."

She followed the direction of Mikey's pointed finger. A strapping brown-haired lad well over six feet tall was heading toward them. When he saw her, he grinned—showing the familiar gap between his teeth.

"We larks 'ave long owed you a favor," Mikey went on. "When we 'eard you arrived in London and were in a spot o' trouble, we knew it was time to pay the debt. Been keeping an eye out for you for days."

"That's why you were following me...to protect me?"

Mikey nodded. "Now the ledger is clean."

A whistle pierced the night. It came from the canal, where a lighter was floating by the banks. A figure stepped from the boat's cabin; from the distance, Bea couldn't see much of him. He whistled again, and the children filed into line, Mikey leading and Joe shepherding. They scampered to the boat and boarded, the vessel gliding off into the darkness.

Bea looked at Wick. "I can't believe the mudlarks were looking out for me all this time."

He brushed his knuckles against her jaw, his eyes warm. "Your good deeds did not go unnoticed."

"But yours have." She drew a breath. "I've been so selfish, Wick. So stubborn and blind."

"That's untrue," he said, frowning.

"Let me finish. It was stupid of me to leave with Lisette. She forged a letter from my butler, saying that there'd been another attack at Camden Manor. I panicked and decided I needed to go back straight away."

"That's understandable. You're a strong woman, love, used to looking after your estate and those who depend upon you."

"But that wasn't really why I fled." She took one of his hands, so big and strong, knowing that that strength would always protect her. "I fled because I was afraid of how much I loved you."

*"Angel."* His eyes flared, his hand gripping hers.

"I should have told you earlier...but I'm so in love with you Wick, I can hardly think straight. And it terrifies me. How much I need you, how I'd do anything for you...how you are everything to me."

"You are everything to me, Beatrice. I love you," he said fervently.

"I know you do. That is the miracle of it." Her breath hitched at the power of all she was feeling, but there was more she needed to say. "For so long, I believed that I would never find a man who could love me as I am, and then to find you, to find such happiness—I kept waiting for it to end. The way my former life did when I got scarred. And when things with the railway came to a head, I told myself that that was it: that was the end to our joy, which I'd always known would come."

"Nothing is ending," he declared. "You're mine, and nothing can change that. The railway venture won't go as planned, but that doesn't make me a failure. You've given that to me, angel. Shown me that the redemption I sought was already mine. What I truly need is *you*: your love fills me with joy and purpose and makes life worth living."

She knew that she would treasure his words forever.

"You'll have my love for as long as I live," she vowed. "And you'll have my estate as well."

He frowned. "No, Beatrice. I won't take it."

"You will because Camden Manor is to be my wedding gift to you. Well, not gift exactly—I'll expect a fair price for the land, and I'll use that money to make sure my tenants are well settled wherever they wish to go."

He shook his head—stubborn man.

"I won't let you make such a sacrifice. I know what your estate means to you. It's the refuge you built for yourself and others, the one place where you feel safe, and I will never take that away from you."

She knew he meant it, which made her choice even easier.

"Do you know what I was thinking when I was trapped in the warehouse, thinking I was going to die?"

His features hardened, his hands closing convulsively around her waist. "What, love?"

"I was thinking how foolish I was for leaving you. *You* make me feel safe, Wick, not some piece of land. I put up walls to protect my heart, but what I truly needed was for you to tear them down. You taught me to trust again, to see that true beauty —beauty not of the skin but of the heart and soul—does exist. Your love is the greatest security I'll ever know, and your arms are the only haven I need."

The love in his eyes warmed her to the depths of her being.

"In that case," he said, "I believe a negotiation is in order."

She gave him a quizzical smile. "What sort of negotiation?"

"If you want me to buy your land, then you'll have to do something for me in return."

She had to laugh. "Isn't that rather a winning proposition for you?"

"I'm not London's best negotiator for nothing." He winked at her, then went down on one knee. "Lady Beatrice Wodehouse, would you do me the honor of marrying me by special license because I cannot wait another damned minute to make you my wife?"

What could she say to that, except "Yes, yes, *yes!*"

To the cheers of their friends, he rose, spinning her in a circle that made her dizzy with joy. Then he claimed her with a kiss that proved that, in this deal of a lifetime, there would always be two winners.

# EPILOGUE

"Wɪᴄᴋ, ᴡᴇ ᴄᴀɴɴᴏᴛ ᴀʙᴀɴᴅᴏɴ ᴏᴜʀ ᴏᴡɴ ɢᴜᴇsᴛs," ʜɪs ᴡɪꜰᴇ said breathlessly.

He pulled her into their shared study and closed the door, muffling the sounds of the masquerade.

"The Ellerbys are showing off their reel," he replied. "No one will notice that we're gone."

They were hosting the party to celebrate their new home—or rather, the renovation of Beatrice's former manor. After she'd sold her property to GLNR, Wick had been determined to help her find the perfect new situation. As it turned out, they didn't have to look very far.

Squire Crombie had cocked up his toes, leaving his unentailed property to a distant and indifferent heir who promptly auctioned it off. Bea snatched up the land at a bargain of a price. With the help of the surveyors, Wick was able to redraw the lines of Bea's new estate to include her old manor house.

Thus, Wick had his railway, and she kept her home. Her tenants had been delighted at the short distance of their move. And the grass was truly greener on the other side: according to

Ellerby and the other satisfied farmers, the new land was fertile pickings indeed.

"*I'll* notice," Beatrice said now. "It's bad form, darling."

"I'll show you bad form." He tossed off his domino, revealing the urgent state of matters down south. "If I get any harder, I may burst a seam and then we'll have a true scandal on our hands."

She gave a breathless laugh. "You haven't been like that all evening, have you?"

"From the instant I saw you come down the stairs," he said solemnly.

Beatrice had kept her costume a secret from him until the last minute. Just before the arrival of their guests, she'd come down the stairs, and his breath had lodged in his throat: she'd dressed up as a Common Blue butterfly. Not that there was anything common about her. Her shot-silk gown of periwinkle blue clung to her flawless figure, filmy wings of silver-blue at her back. She wore the jewels he'd given her: the butterfly brooch glittered on her bodice and her engagement ring, a lavender sapphire surrounded by diamonds, winked on her finger.

She hadn't bothered with a mask.

Instead, she'd applied face paint, exotic swirls of blue, purple, pink, and silver framing her luminous gaze. She'd integrated her scar into the pattern, highlighting her unique beauty. As she'd descended to him, like a goddess to a mere mortal, he'd never been prouder.

Or randier.

He pulled his lass in close. "You're the most beautiful sight I've ever seen, and I want to screw you senseless."

"Likewise." Her eyes sparkled up at him. "Your desk or mine?"

"Mine. It's closer."

Her laugh washed over him as he swept her off her feet and onto his desk. This wasn't the first time they'd christened the furnishings—the benefit of sharing a study with one's spouse. He placed her in one of his favorite positions: on her back on his blotter while he sat in his chair. Tossing up her skirts, he feasted on her pussy, loving the way her fingers clutched his hair, her slippered heels digging against his shoulders as she reached her crisis.

Rising, he flipped her onto her belly. He ran a possessive hand over the smooth hills of her bottom while he freed himself with the other. His nostrils flared as he brought the dripping tip of his rod to her pretty pink cleft. He pushed in slowly, enjoying the sight of her hole stretching to receive him, the wickedly lewd delight of sinking his shaft inside his wife.

"Don't stop," she moaned when he held inside her, balls-deep.

"You're right, angel. It isn't polite to make our guests wait, is it?"

He lunged inside her. Her tight cunny massaged his prick as he slammed his hips, his stones slapping her dewy lips. She writhed against him, leaving a wet stain on the leather blotter that he knew would make him hard every time he saw it.

Feeling the precursory sizzle at the base of his spine, he panted, "Frig yourself, love. Make yourself come and take me with you."

With a whimper, she obeyed, sliding a hand beneath her. The sight of her slim fingers rubbing her pussy brought him to the edge. Luckily, she was already there: she soared over with a cry, her silver-blue wings fluttering, her rippling sheath drawing his fire. He bit back a shout as he found his fulfillment inside his beloved, the hot waves of bliss rocking him to the core.

When he caught his breath, he tended to her with his handkerchief and helped set her to rights. Reluctant to let her go just yet, he wrapped his arms around her waist. Enjoyed the simple, profound pleasure of holding his wife close.

"Wick?"

"Hmm?"

"There's something I have to tell you."

The thread of uncertainty in Beatrice's voice was uncharacteristic. He tipped his head back to look into her face. Sure enough, a hint of anxiety shadowed her eyes. Since they talked frequently, he could take a stab at the cause of her concern.

"Are you worried about Fancy and Knighton?" he asked.

Shortly before he and Beatrice had wed by special license, Fancy and Knighton had showed up in London. Knighton had read the papers blaming Beatrice for the demise of GLNR's plans, and Fancy had insisted on rushing to aid her friend. Luckily, all had been well by then...and that was when Fancy had shared her own shocking news.

She and Knighton had wed; the tinker's daughter was now the Duchess of Knighton. From what Beatrice had gleaned from her friend, the marriage had been one of necessity and was off to a rocky start.

Bea chewed on her lip. "I *am* worried about Fancy, and I plan to corner her once she and Knighton arrive. But that's not what I was referring to."

"What is it, then?"

"Wick, how would you feel about expanding the manor?"

"But we just renovated..."

He trailed off, his eyes widening as her meaning struck him like a hammer to the skull. For once, he was speechless. He tried to summon words, but they got stuck somewhere between his brain and mouth.

Beatrice peered at him. "Are you quite all right?"

And he, London's top negotiator, stammered, "Are you...are we...*baby*?"

"Yes." She gave him a shy smile. "I hope you're as pleased about it as I am."

"Angel." He cupped her jaw with hands that shook. "I'm more than *pleased*. You've already given me so much—and now a babe too..."

"Come to think of it," she said, a playful curve on her lips, "I will be doing most of the work, won't I? I should definitely be asking for some concessions in return."

"Whatever your heart desires," he said reverently.

"That's not fair. You've already given me that."

"Whatever *else* your heart desires, then."

She mulled that over, then rose on tiptoe to whisper something in his ear. At her naughty request, he choked back a laugh. Then he kissed his wife, overflowing with the love and joy of their happily ever after.

## AUTHOR'S NOTE

The role played by coal in Victorian England cannot be over-stated. Coal fueled the everyday lives of the Victorians and also powered the era's technological advances, from the steam-driven locomotives and ships to sprawling manufactories. Indeed, Britain was the world's largest supplier of coal in the nineteenth century, with yearly production reaching over 60 million tons by 1854[1].

In *The Duke Redemption,* I make use of a prototype "coal drop," a warehouse over which a train runs and unloads its cargo by opening the bottom of its wagons. I modeled my coal drop from one that exists in London to this day (although it has now been repurposed into a shopping area). I must confess to some artistic license: the coal drop in London wasn't built until 1850, a decade after Wick and Bea's story, but I figured the idea for a prototype could have existed before then...and the fictional symbolism was simply too delicious to resist.

---

1. *Special Report of the Commissioner of Labor, Volume 12: Coal Mine Labor in Europe.* (1905). Washington: United States, Bureau of Labor.

# ABOUT THE AUTHOR

*USA Today* & International Bestselling Author Grace Callaway writes hot and heart-melting historical romance filled with mystery and adventure. Her debut novel was a Romance Writers of America® Golden Heart® Finalist and a #1 National Regency Bestseller, and her subsequent novels have topped national and international bestselling lists. She is the winner of the Daphne du Maurier Award for Excellence in Mystery and Suspense, the Maggie Award for Excellence in Historical Romance, the Golden Leaf, and the Passionate Plume Award. She holds a doctorate in clinical psychology from the University of Michigan and lives with her family in a valley close to the sea. When she's not writing, she enjoys dancing, exploring the great outdoors with her rescue pup, and cheering on her favorite basketball team.

Keep up with my latest news!
Newsletter: gracecallaway.com/newsletter

facebook.com/GraceCallawayBooks
bookbub.com/authors/grace-callaway
instagram.com/gracecallawaybooks
amazon.com/author/gracecallaway

# ACKNOWLEDGMENTS

*The Duke Redemption* was written during power shutdowns, wild-fires, and storms. It was written during writers' retreats, weekly sessions at the coffeeshop with my besties, and the wee hours of the morning in my she-shed. It was written despite sickness, early school dismissals, and other life surprises. In other words, this book was written because I needed to tell the story.

Writing is my passion—even when it makes me want to tear my hair out—and I consider it the greatest privilege to be able to share that joy with you, my dear reader. Thank you for joining me on this journey. Your support means everything.

To my writing pals: this journey would not be half as fun without you. Thank you for the friendship, inspiration, advice, and laughter. I am in awe of your brilliance and generosity.

Thank you to my editor for loving my characters as much as I do and helping me to show them off in their best light.

And to my family...we made it through another book! Thank you for your patience, support, and love.

Made in the USA
Las Vegas, NV
18 April 2024

88828672R00208